Postmarked Castle Cove

An MC McCall Novel of Suspense
Book Three

By

Judy M. Kerr

LAUNCHPOINT PRESS

Portland, Oregon

A Launch Point Press Trade Paperback Original

Postmarked Castle Cove is a work of fiction. Names, characters, places, and incidents are either the product of the author's imagination or are used in a fictitious manner. Any resemblance to actual persons living or dead, business establishments, events, or locales is entirely coincidental. Internet references contained in this work are current at the time of publication, but Launch Point Press cannot guarantee that a specific reference will continue or be maintained in any respect.

All other rights are reserved. Launch Point Press supports copyright which enables creativity, free speech, and fairness. Thank you for buying the authorized version of this book and for following copyright laws by not using or reproducing any part of this book in any manner whatsoever, including Internet usage, without written permission from Launch Point Press, except in the form of brief quotations embodied in critical reviews and articles. Your cooperation and respect support authors and allow Launch Point Press to continue to publish the books you want to read.

Copyright © 2025 by Judy M. Kerr

ISBN: 978-1-63304-075-5
E-Book: 978-1-63304-076-2

FIRST EDITION: First Printing: 2025

Editing: Terri Bischoff
Formatting: Anne Battis
Cover: Lorelei

www.LaunchPointPress.com

Praise for *Silent Service*
An MC McCall Novel of Suspense Book Two

"With skill and purpose, author Judy Kerr provides a truly satisfying read in *Silent Service*, the second installment of her MC McCall series. The novel is filled with creative language that dances off the page, storytelling that draws you into the lives and environs of its characters and shares an immensely empathetic understanding of the ravages of loss and heartbreak." **~Cheryl A. Head, award-winning author of the Charlie Mack Motown Mystery Series**

"In Judy Kerr's stellar sophomore release, *Silent Service*, Kerr thrusts her beautifully flawed, all-too-human protagonist, US Postal Inspector MC McCall, into the middle of a dangerous narcotics investigation stretching from the gritty streets of St. Paul to Minnesota's snowy, windswept North Shore. MC—reeling after the murder of her beloved partner Barb just months prior—must balance her desperate obsession to find Barb's killer with maintaining a decorated, successful career she's on the cusp of losing as she attempts to bust wide open an opioid distribution ring. In turns suspense-filled, heartbreaking, and hopeful, Kerr takes the reader on a journey they'll never forget. I absolutely loved it!" **~Jessie Chandler, award-winning author of the Shay O'Hanlon Caper Series**

Praise for *Black Friday*
An MC McCall Novel of Suspense Book One

"In her debut, Kerr has penned a satisfying, suspenseful multi-agency police procedural with a protagonist touched by tragedy who has to battle her own demons while she fights for justice." **~Greg Dahlager, Writer's Digest award winner and contributing author of *Dark Side of the Loon: Where History Meets Mystery***

"Judy Kerr may be the new mystery kid on the block, but *Black Friday* is a crime novel you won't want to miss. This engaging debut will not only have you guessing as you move deeper into the story but perfectly sets up the next in the series. Highly recommended!"
~MWA Grandmaster Ellen Hart, author of the award-winning Jane Lawless series

An MC McCall
Novel of Suspense Series

Black Friday
Silent Service
Postmarked Castle Cove

Author's Note

Dear Reader: Please keep in mind when reading the story that I've taken liberties with investigative techniques and protocols of the law enforcement agencies mentioned in this book (US Postal Inspection Service, Lake County Sheriff's Office, and US Attorney's Office.) The agencies are real, but the circumstances and characters are not. The town of Castle Cove is fictitious. I've placed this little hamlet between Two Harbors, Minnesota, and Split Rock Lighthouse. While I did research, please know that any mistakes are my own.

The US Postal Inspection Service (USPIS) protects the postal service and postal employees and enforces two hundred federal statutes related to crimes that involve the postal system, employees, and customers. Postal Inspectors investigate crimes from mail fraud and identity theft to cybercrimes and child exploitation. Much of their behind-the-scenes processes must remain confidential, but people should know and appreciate the great work the USPIS does worldwide every day.

Fiction writers make things up and at the same time work to make the story believable for you all—it's what we do in the name of entertainment. I hope you find the escape into MC's world entertaining and worth your time.

For Mom, in loving memory.

Chapter One

May Day was International Workers' Day. In MC McCall's life, Mayday, Mayday, Mayday was more fitting because she was in a continual underlying state of distress.

Sobriety should have given her clarity. Instead, on the morning of what might rank in the top five worst days of her life, Postal Inspector MC McCall sat in her car, in a parking lot. The clinic in front of her, near the Minneapolis-St. Paul International airport, was a two-story tan smudge against the backdrop of the spring morning. The building set MC's nerves on edge. Was she about to face the death knell of a storied career? Should she shut off the engine and go inside?

Stay?

Go?

Great, now she'd have an ear worm of the Clash's hit song. Snap out of it, McCall.

What if the US Postal Inspection Service designated doctor didn't clear her for return to duty? Did she want to chance hearing negative news? Face a possible death sentence? She drummed her fingers on the steering wheel of the Subaru her murdered life-partner Barb had driven, contemplating the nondescript tan-brick structure bathed in deceptively happy May sunshine.

The interior of the car came to life, closing in around her. The air, thick and pulsating with strands of sunshine, pinned her in the driver's seat, as if holding her hostage. She closed her eyes, counted to ten, and opened them. No pulsation. The air thinned. Warm bright rays enveloped her. She felt like an extra from a *Twilight Zone* episode.

Sun sparked off the windshield, revealing a film of road grime. Time to wash the car. MC could leave now and reschedule the doctor's appointment. Evasion was not the better part of valor, she reasoned. Did she care? No? Yes? Maybe.

She swiveled the rearview mirror so she could see herself. One of the first things she'd done after finishing rehab to prep for returning to the job was get a haircut. Her spiky do showed more salt than pepper. Age, stress, maybe both. More wrinkles lined her forehead and around her eyes. And those eyes, the vibrant blue Barb had always said were a beacon of light, were now as washed out as a hot August sky. A reflection of her life. Lackluster. Dull.

She had become the opposite of pre-sober MC. She considered

whether the weekly AA meetings were beneficial. The LGBTQ+-specific group made her feel only slightly less ambivalent. The proclamation of one of the attendees at her first meeting stuck with her. "Cover your ass and don't worry about saving face." She couldn't pinpoint why that sentiment had embedded in her brain.

Well, you aren't into the Serenity Prayer, so at least you had one takeaway.

Perhaps illogically, Barb's voice tethered MC to the here and now in times of turmoil and indecision. More than six months had passed since Barb had been murdered, and MC still heard her.

But right now, she needed to decide. Where was a Magic 8-Ball when she needed one? Easier to leave decision-making to chance.

Chances were strong she'd pass the exam with flying colors. Then she could hit up the 5-8 Club for a celebratory burger and beer. A beer, nothing harder. Totally doable. Not like she'd be hitting the hard stuff. The Goose had taken flight out of her life. Hadn't it? But she'd deserve a little pick-me-up to get her through the day and ready to face returning to the job on whatever date the good doc prescribed.

More than six weeks earlier, during one of the worst blizzards in years, MC had cast aside every vestige of defense and drunkenly shown up at her co-worker Cam White's door in the middle of the night.

She'd awoken the next morning on his couch, feeling like a wrecking ball had bashed her life into a smoldering pile of rubble. With nary a scintilla of memory of the previous night, she attempted to piece together how she'd landed on his doorstep and what had transpired after her arrival. She staggered to the kitchen. Her stomach heaved at the mere thought of coffee, so Cam's wife, Jane, prepared some tea. Cam proceeded to explain the previous evening's events in technicolor detail.

"I showed up without any boots? Or shoes?" MC twirled a tea bag in the steaming mug of water.

"No shoes. No gloves. MC, you were beyond sloshed. I was freaked out thinking you had alcohol poisoning. I was on the verge of calling 911," Cam said.

"I don't remember anything after my second drink at home." MC massaged her temples. "I didn't wake up the kids, did I?" The last thing she wanted to do was scare Jameson and Hailey.

"No. The kids slept through it all. I don't doubt for a minute you don't remember anything. You had us both worried. But the important thing to remember is you asked me to drive you to a rehab place. Today." Cam gazed at her over the rim of his cup. "I hope you haven't changed your mind in the bright light of day."

"Yes. I mean, no. I don't remember, guys." She peered at Jane, who now sat across the table next to Cam. "I did? I said that?"

Jane reached for MC's hand. "Yes. You did. I think you're brave and chose the best path for your survival. And I speak not only from the heart, but from experience." Cam rested his arm across Jane's shoulders.

Right. Jane had gone through rehab. Recovering pothead after going down a dark and twisty path in college. Meeting Cam had changed her life—in the nick of time. She'd gotten clean because getting married and having a family was important to them. No way would Cam commit unless Jane made the hard choice to get clean.

Had MC's subconscious mind or the guiding spirit of Barb brought her to them at her lowest point last night? But it wasn't like Jane was the only person in her life who could understand MC's issues. Dara, one of her best friends, was a recovering alcoholic. Dara had been nagging MC for months to go to an AA meeting—had even offered to attend with her. Every time, MC had shut her down faster than a computer crashing during a power surge.

Maybe because you knew deep down Dara was right, but she was too close. You know Jane, but there's six degrees of separation there. Enough anyway, to cause you less angst in appealing for help. Barb's reasoning centered MC.

"But I wonder if I can't do this on my own?" She tried to stifle the voice of logic narrating in her head. "Find local AA meetings. Go that route."

Why was she backpedaling?

MC ran a hand through her hair and realized she probably looked like death warmed over. "That could work, right?" Even to her own ears the words sounded feeble. Pathetic.

"MC, I think we all know the answer." Cam's voice was gentle but firm.

"Yeah." She took a tentative sip of the Earl Grey, a wisp of steam causing her eyes to water. Or was it something else? God please, don't let me break down.

Cam's right. No denying that. Barb's words swirled as tears tracked down her cheeks.

"Yes. We do know the answer." MC swiped her hands across her face.

Cam drove her home on that winter morning. He'd offered to stay while she placed the call to a rehab facility. MC declined, told him she wouldn't back out.

"MC, I'm married to an addict. If I leave you to your own devices, all bets are off. Trust me. You go take a shower and I'll make coffee. Then we'll make the call together."

After a shower and with a pot of coffee in her system MC, with Cam by her side, called Renewal Ridge Recovery, located in a bucolic suburb south of the Cities. The website claimed the facility was LGBTQ-friendly, which caught her attention. Once they determined her insurance would cover a good portion of the cost, MC was transferred to an Intake Coordinator. The person dug uncomfortably deep into MC's history and then informed her he'd send the information to the facility's clinical program team where they'd determine the appropriate level of care she'd need.

"Hang in there, and someone will contact you later today," he'd said.

The chain of events led to Cam driving her to Renewal Ridge Recovery, where she entered the inpatient alcohol recovery program on of all days, Friday, March 13, 2015.

She'd done the thirty days. Many times, she'd been close to walking out, especially during the hellish five-day detox. Every fiber of her being fought the drying out, almost to the point of having to be restrained.

And she continued to fight every day.

Every molecule screamed for booze.

But she'd stuck with it. Did her time inside, so to speak, though not always a model prisoner, or rather, patient.

She took an additional three weeks to get herself re-acclimated to the outside world. Set up appointments on Mondays with her therapist, Dr. Zaulk.

Perhaps most surprising, MC reluctantly allowed Dara to drag her to an AA meeting. Dara had nagged her for almost two weeks until MC finally relented. She consented to attend a meeting, one strictly billed as for gay men, lesbians, and trans folks, the last Sunday in April.

The Sunday evening meetings were held in a dank church basement with a broken-down piano in one dark corner and a sagging, folding table weighed down with store-bought cookies, a silver metal coffee maker, and stacks of disposable cups and napkins. The epitome of AA tropes.

A circle of twenty clay-colored metal folding chairs beckoned. Gals, some of whom reeked of cigarettes, slunk in to take a seat along with sprightly dressed gay men. She hated every moment of the experience. After listening, with a dizzying number of mental eyerolls, to several women complain about what a shitty week they'd had, and a number of the men intermittently whine and sob through their hard luck stories, she was ready to hop in the car and drive to the nearest dive bar to chug a gallon of whatever they had on the shelf. She'd have settled for the nasty star anise-laden Jagermeister at that point. Anything to numb the pain, dull her senses. At the end of the meeting, she accepted a copy of *The Big Book*, the AA bible, from the meeting leader. Dara urged her to take the book as encouragement to stick with the program. MC then fast-walked to the parking lot while promising Dara she'd continue to attend the weekly gathering. And no, Dara didn't need to act as her sponsor. Hopefully, she'd done so in a convincing tone of voice.

MC began to repair her relationship with Dara and Meg, her two best friends. Her family of choice. She really didn't want to jeopardize their bond again.

Now here she was, a month post-rehab, about to go into this clinic and sit with some doctor she didn't know while they evaluated her ability to return to her job. More than likely, they had no clue what her job entailed.

The job she loved. The work she craved. Almost as much as she still jonesed for alcohol.

She should say screw it all and drive the couple miles down the road to the 5-8 Club and drink the day—and her life—away in a dark and dreary corner of the bar.

Really? And throw away all the hard work you did in rehab? The day is wasting away. Time to face the truth.

Those words soothed some of the emotional whitecaps breaking inside her. MC sucked in a deep breath, exited her car, and marched toward the entrance. If the doctor didn't tell her what she wanted to hear, there was always the 5-8 Club.

Note to self: buy a Magic 8-Ball at the next opportunity. Leave future decisions to a toy. What could possibly go wrong?

MC walked into Flannel, her favorite coffee shop in St. Paul. She was surprised to see her best friends and shop owners, Dara and Meg, seated at one of the tables near the front. Her favorite young barista, Zane, stood behind the counter, an added bonus. His sandy brown skin and perfectly groomed dark stubble accented by Buddy Holly-esque glasses were a sight for sore eyes. Suddenly she was glad she'd foregone the visit to the 5-8 Club and the pull of a burger and beer combo.

Well, almost glad.

"Hi, Zane." She waved and continued to the table where her friends sat. "Hey, you two. I didn't expect to see you here." She'd stopped expressly to get a cup of good java and take a breather. She gave Meg a hug. "How was radiation?" Meg was being treated for Stage 1 breast cancer.

Meg said, "Tell us what you found out. Today was the big day, right?"

How Meg had the bandwidth to worry about anyone else amazed MC. Her friend was the most selfless person she knew. "One of the big days, I guess. There have been so many lately it's difficult to keep track of them all."

"Jesus Christ on a bike. Would you tell us already?" Dara's voice bounced off the brick walls.

Zane and a smattering of customers around the cafe focused their attention on the trio.

MC said, "Cool your jets, Dara. The whole world doesn't need to hear about my business."

Easy now. She's only got your best interests in mind.

Dara rolled her hand. "Cough it up."

"Okay. Okay. I've been cleared to return to duty effective Monday."

Meg clapped her hands, and her eyes lit up. "Yay, you. I completed my first of five weeks of radiation therapy. I don't even glow in the dark. Double win."

"Always the comedian," Dara said. "I wanted to take her home so she could rest, but she's stubborn in her old age."

"Who are you calling old?" Meg pinned Dara with her ice-blue gaze. "My parents are old. I'm only fifty-one."

Dara cleared her throat and gazed at Meg as if memorizing every feature. "We're all getting old. As I was saying, Meg insisted on stopping by to see how things were going."

MC knew full well the throat clearing was supposed to cover the catch in Dara's voice. The toughie hated anyone to think of her as being soft.

"Yeah, but you love me anyway." Meg tweaked Dara's cheek. "Besides, I'm fine. For now. You worry too much."

MC absorbed the scene unfolding before her. Her best friends. Her family. The two people who'd been by her side through thick and thin. Through drunk and now sober. How had she got so lucky?

Dara waved a hand in front of MC's face. "Yo, MC. You with us?" Typical Dara. Some things never changed.

"Just appreciating you both, and yes, we all worry." MC slid into a chair across from Dara. "How about you, tough gal? How're you holding up?"

"Fine. Got paperwork. Orders for beans and a million other things. We should probably double the bean order with you back." Dara laughed.

"Now who's the comedian? But now that you mention it..."

Meg pushed away from the table. "I'll have Zane pour you a cup, MC."

"You stay put." Dara jumped up and papers flew across the table. "I'll get MC some coffee." She trudged toward the counter, muttering to herself.

MC leaned toward Meg. "Are you really okay? Did something happen at today's treatment? Dara seems a bit frazzled, more so than usual."

"Oh, pfft." Meg waved a hand in the air. "Dara worries too much. Today's appointment was the same as the previous four. I'm as well as can be expected. More tired than usual. But no pain. At least not so far. One week of radiation down. Four weeks to go. A fifth of the way through. Something to cheer about."

"Yes, of course. But what about the area they're radiating? Any skin issues? Really, you're not having any pain?" MC scanned Meg's face, searching for any telltale signs of side effects.

Meg tended to downplay her pain, putting everyone ahead of herself. MC's internet research filled her head with the unusual symptoms Meg could develop. If she showed signs of coughing, sweating, fever, or unusual pain, they'd need to contact her doctor immediately. On the face of it, Meg appeared mostly upbeat, if a tad weary.

"None. Truly, MC. I wouldn't hide anything from you or Dara. Not about this. Besides, there's enough on your plate. I can't help but say again how proud we are you followed through with rehab. We were scared."

Dara plunked a giant mug in front of MC. "Here ya go. With creamer and sweetener." Dara twisted a towel in her hands. "Scared? What? Who?"

"Thanks," MC said.

Meg pulled Dara down onto a chair. "Settle yourself. I was telling MC how proud we are of her for accomplishing the month in rehab."

Dara said, "We are. And for going to AA. I was happy to hook you up for your first meeting. I wish you would've listened to me sooner."

MC took a deep breath, held it for a four-count, and released it. "You were right, Dara." The words were true but so difficult to utter. Shame still bubbled beneath the surface. "I apologize for shutting you down. I was so mortified by the end. I didn't know what I was doing. I'd spiraled so far down I couldn't see a way up."

Meg said, "We completely understand. Don't we, hon?" The look she gave Dara left no doubt about what Dara's response should be.

"Yes. But—"

"No. No but." Meg crossed her arms.

"Yes, dear. Hand me those pages, would ya?" She pointed at the sheets on MC's side of the table.

MC slid the pages across to Dara. "I love you both. I'm so sorry for putting you through so much, especially when you're dealing with a lot yourselves." She swallowed hard. "I'm lucky to have you guys. And I promise I'm going to do everything I can to make it up to you."

"How about helping out here this weekend?" Dara asked.

"Sure. Whatever you need."

"Only if you have the time," Meg said. "You have work on Monday. Maybe it'd be better if you took the weekend. Get in the right mindset. It's a huge step."

"It's better for MC if she stays busy." Dara glanced up from the forms in front of her. "The more distraction the less she'll think about booze."

Fat chance.

All she thought about was Grey Goose. She could still taste the smooth French vodka. Feel the slick burn. Little did her friends know how close she'd come to bailing on her appointment. Even had herself convinced beer didn't count. Why did it have to be so damn difficult?

MC finished her beverage and thought about her life choices. God, she needed to be on the job. Anything to keep her mind off everything.

She stood. "I do have some errands I need to run."

"No, stay," Dara said. "Don't run. I promise I'll lay off."

"It's okay. It's nothing you said." MC smiled. "Well, maybe it was a little bit what you said. But you're right. You were right then. And now. I'll be better going forward. I promise."

MC, uncross your fingers. Don't make promises you might not be able to keep. Be realistic. No one expects you to be perfect.

"I'll be by in the morning. You can boss me around all day. I'm sure you'll be delighted."

Dara grinned. "Nothing would give me greater satisfaction, pal. Zane will be in later in the day to close out, so you'll have two of us telling you what to do for a while."

"Excellent. Can't wait. Thanks for the brew." She hugged Meg one more time. "You take care of yourself and let me know if there's anything you need." Louder she said, "See you tomorrow, Zane."

Zane tossed a quick wave as a customer approached the counter.

"Later, gator," Dara said.

Chapter Two

"Pass." MC shifted on the metal folding chair and refused to make eye contact with the expanding circle of addicts. No way was she going to talk about anything to do with what landed her at this meeting on this Sunday evening in May. Not in front of God and everyone. She didn't even want to get started on *The Big Book*, a misnomer in her opinion. Stephen King's *The Stand*, now *that* qualified as a big book. Despite Dara's incessant reminders that the book was an imperative tool, she'd left her copy on the back seat of her car. Wasn't the idea of being at a meeting to pay attention to the meeting, not read a book?

Fluorescent Fashionista guy was quick to pick up the slack. What was his name? Maybe she should pay closer attention. But then again, his whiny, nasally voice wore on her last nerve, so probably best she didn't remember his name. She balled her hands into fists, ready to launch from her seat. The beast within roared.

Take a breath. Open yourself to hearing what these brave people are sharing.

Barb's words flowed over and through her. She sucked in a ragged breath. At least if her butt was in a chair in this dingy church basement then she wasn't at home or anywhere else pouring Grey Goose down her gullet.

She executed a mental head shake and tried to tune in for the remainder of this, her second meeting. Dara had challenged her to attend at least six before she made any decisions about quitting. "What's six Sunday evenings out of your life?" Dara had asked.

Six hours I'll never get back, MC thought. But here she was, making good on her word.

The Trusted Servant asked if anyone else had anything to share. What's up with that title anyway, Trusted Servant? Jesus, were they living in the Victorian ages? Why not call them Meeting Leader? Big Kahuna. Senior Recovering Addict sounded even better. But, no, Trusted Servant it was.

When no one else spoke up to share, the Trusted Servant moved on to the next order of business. She named a couple people who volunteered to be a sponsor if anyone was interested.

Thanks, but no thanks. The last thing she needed was yet another person in her life keeping tabs on her, trying to keep her on the straight and narrow.

Pastor Curtis Thackeray entered the lower level of the meeting hall, passed by his office, and climbed the stairs to the main floor. He used a towel around his neck to wipe sweat from his head. No better way to unwind after a long Sunday than a full-blown workout in his home gym. The last item on his agenda was to lock up for the night.

The Whispering Aspen Ministries compound in Castle Cove, Minnesota, had originally been a kid's summer camp. In the mid-70s another pastor had purchased the camp buildings and the land they sat on via a sweetheart financial deal made with an old, wealthy logger who owned the property. The former pastor had transitioned the old camp into the home of the Evangelical ministry now under the guidance of Pastor Thackeray.

He walked into the front lobby as the last stragglers from the AA meeting were exiting the building. He wiped down his arms and flexed his tree-trunk-sized biceps. What he lacked in height he made up for in muscle. People found it hard to believe he was nearly fifty. His brown hair showed no hint of gray and though his hairline was receding, he compensated for the annoyance by wearing it long. "Have a great evening. God bless," he called out.

A mishmash of mumbled responses was tossed his way and then the door slapped shut behind them. He figured they were going directly to the Dirty Minnow or one of the other watering holes in surrounding towns.

Thackeray heard the clatter of someone stacking chairs in the large main room, which had been the camp's dining hall. The lights flicked out and Ned Hargreve, the local postmaster and leader of the Sunday evening AA meeting, walked out.

"Evening, Ned." Thackeray craned his head back as Ned towered a good four inches over him.

"Pastor. Nice to see you. Been working out, I see."

"The Lord demands I keep my vessel in good condition." He tugged the moisture wicking T-shirt away from his barrel chest to allow some air to circulate. "You should join me sometime for a workout."

"Aw, heck, an old guy like me is lucky to be able to heave bags of mail around. I'll stick with walking and fishing. All the exercise I need."

"Ned, you aren't much older than me."

"I'm sixty-four. Old enough to know when not to push my aging bones too far."

"I hear you. God bless you for overseeing another meeting." He rested his hand on Ned's forearm. "I pray you all keep the faith and have continued strength in your recovery journeys."

Now hit the bricks so I can get home and take a shower.

The front door to the meeting hall creaked open and two kids from the Spring Fun and Frolic youth event at the church entered and immediately halted.

The girl scuffed a foot on the wood floor. "We didn't see Mom and Dad's car. Are they here?"

She wore a wrinkled flowery cotton dress. The boy, a year or two younger, had his Skechers on the wrong feet and the Velcro straps were twisted.

Thackeray dropped his hand from Hargreve's arm. "Gracie. Cole. Didn't I tell you to wait in the turnaround?" He checked his watch. "It's past eight. Your parents not here yet?"

Ned scrunched up his wiry gray eyebrows and bent toward the kids. "You two all right?"

Cole slid closer to his sister. Gracie grabbed his hand. Neither would look at the men.

Thackeray said, "They're fine. Maybe tired, been a long day with service this morning and Fun and Frolic this evening. Plus, there's been a flu bug going around the youth groups." He clapped his hands once. Both children flinched. "Or maybe they've got the Holy Spirit. What do you think, kids?"

Cole drifted behind his sister. Gracie stood taller. "I'm not sick. And I don't have the Holy Spirit."

Ned said, "She sounds quite adamant about the Holy Spirit, Pastor."

Thackeray's pulse notched up a few beats at the hint of defiance coloring Gracie's words and Ned's apparent amusement. "You kids should go back to the turnaround so your parents can see you when they arrive." He put a hand on the shoulder of each kid and ushered them out the door.

Ned frowned. "I suppose I'll head out myself. Good evening, Pastor." He eased past the man and stopped. "I almost forgot. Would it be possible to change the Sunday AA meetings to Wednesday evenings? With summer coming people want to have their weekends free."

"Yeah, sure. I'll make a note of it on the calendar. Starting next week?"

"Well, probably this week. Don't want folks to have to go more than a week between meetings. Lord knows what shenanigans they could get up to."

"Fine. Wednesdays starting this coming week."

"Appreciate it, Pastor."

The gravel turnaround was between the meeting hall and the

church. Thackeray watched Ned stop on his way to the parking lot and say something to the kids. Gracie shook her head and peeked over her shoulder at the hall. A car came around the bend and stopped. Gracie and Cole's parents, finally. The kids hopped into the back seat.

Ned waited until the car pulled away to continue toward the parking lot in front of the church.

Ned's attentiveness toward the kids gave Thackeray pause. The guy reminded him of an aged Shaggy from *Scooby-Doo*. Note to self, talk to Bradford Symons, the town supervisor, and get the lowdown on Ned. He wasn't a parishioner. Thackeray only knew him through the AA meetings and running into him at the post office.

He shut off the lights and locked the door before making his way across the wide yard to the old farmhouse he called home. Something told him the postmaster might be the type to stick his nose where it didn't belong. The last thing he needed was to have to deal with a Nosy Ned.

Chapter Three

Travel mug full of high-octane brew in hand and messenger bag slung across her body like a suit of armor, MC entered the portal of no return. Well, the portal of return was more accurate. No Monday morning blues for her, this first day back in the saddle. She was grateful the first person to greet her was Chelsea Gray, the best administrative assistant the Inspection Service, Twin Cities Domicile, had ever seen. She was organized, responsible, and protective of the inspectors. Even though she was only about thirty, she was a Mama Bear when it came to watching out for the teams. No one got past her if she didn't want them to.

"Good morning, Chelsea."

"MC, welcome back. I'm so happy to see you." She leaned over the counter and waved MC closer. "Did anyone share the good news with you while you were out?" Chelsea's brown eyes sparkled.

"Which good news?" MC figured Chelsea was referring to the long overdue retirement of MC's nemesis, Roland Chrapkowski, aka Crapper, the supervisor who almost broke her before she broke herself a couple months ago. But she wanted to give the young woman the chance to say it out loud.

"Roland retired," Chelsea pseudo-whispered the news as a giant grin spread across her face. She swiped a strand of reddish-brown hair behind one ear and a giggle escaped her lips. She clapped both hands over her mouth.

"Try and contain your sorrow. I'm positive you'll miss Roland as much as the rest of us."

"Yeah, but not nearly as much as you, MC."

They both burst out laughing.

God, it felt good to laugh out loud.

"You have so little respect for your superiors," MC teased. "But I'm with you. I've been here two minutes, and I swear the atmosphere feels lighter. Positivity is a good thing."

"You're so right. Anyway, I took the liberty of emptying your mail slot and stacked everything on your desk. Let me know if there's anything else I can do. Seriously, it's so great to see you."

"You're the best, Chelsea. I swear they don't pay you enough for all you do around here. Guess I better get to it." MC continued down the hall to her office.

Roland's old office was at the end of the hall next to MC's. Jamie

Sanchez, her supervisor now, had informed MC that Cam occupied the office while he was temporarily detailed to fill Crapper's job as the other supervisor in the Twin Cities Domicile. The Twin Cities office fell under the purview of the Denver Division. The inspectors locally reported to the two supervisors, Jamie and Cam, and they in turn answered to the Assistant-Inspector-In-Charge. MC was sure the AIC in Denver would make the right decision and award Cam the promotion, but the wheels of progress ground slowly in the US Postal Inspection Service, as in many government agencies.

In order to give everyone a fresh start, Jamie had moved MC to his team from Cam's.

She unlocked her office and flipped the light switch. The air was slightly stale, but the office was neat as a pin. A tiny succulent plant in a terra cotta pot sat on a corner of her desk, a pop of bright green in the otherwise, beige-tinged office. MC grabbed the note card from beneath the plant. A welcome back message and care instructions for her new officemate. God bless Chelsea. Then her breath caught. Barb had been the green thumb, MC not so much. What if she failed to keep this little fledgling alive like she'd failed Barb? She rotated the four-inch pot in circles on its saucer and the white-spotted green leaves reached out like tiny arms. Her apprehension morphed into determination. This was a challenge, and she chose to accept it. "It's you and me buddy. But you need a name. Pearl feels right. All those bright white dots you're wearing remind me of pearls." She slid the card back under Pearl and rounded her desk.

Spring was in the air. Fresh and clean. She wondered how long the clean part would hold up. Her hand shook slightly as she set her cup on the desk. If she'd had a slug of Grey Goose, the tremor wouldn't be an issue.

No. Stop. You've got this.

MC set her bag on the floor next to her chair and for the first time in months booted up her desktop computer. She drank and scanned the mail and memos and whatever other detritus Chelsea had piled on her desk.

Her computer screen lit up and awaited her logon information. She typed in the information and swallowed hard at the hundreds of emails in her inbox. The entire day would be eaten up wading through the physical mail and email backlog.

MC sagged in her chair and wondered if she had the wherewithal to conquer the mountain of communications before her. Life would be so much easier if she could bust out of here and find the nearest watering hole.

You can do this. Take a breath. Drink your coffee and remember progress happens one step at a time.

Barb always knew what to say to reel her in, even though she was gone from this world.

She glanced at the time on her computer screen. Already 7:30. Soon other inspectors would start rolling in. The whole office would be abuzz. Life moved along with or without her. She may as well hop on the rollercoaster. She'd gone through several emails and was merrily deleting spam messages when someone knocked on her door.

"Come in." MC's hands hovered over the keyboard.

The door opened and Jamie stuck his head in. "Got time to talk?"

"Sure." She sounded surprisingly spry even to herself.

Jamie hadn't changed in the past eight weeks. His blond crew cut was razor sharp. Brown eyes behind black plastic-framed glasses studied her. She was dazzled by his bright white button-down dress shirt and maroon and navy striped tie. He could pass for a Ray-Ban model. Dark blue trousers were pressed to within an inch of their life. Jamie was the epitome of professional in dress and attitude. But he was also accessible.

"Welcome back." He sat in one of the two chairs in front of her desk. "The plant is a nice touch."

"Thanks. That's all Chelsea."

"I believe that. So it looks like you've got some catching up to do."

"Paperwork and email." MC waited, heart hammering. Why was she so nervous? Hopefully, he wouldn't notice and think she'd been hitting the bottle again. Good grief. Would she ever stop thinking about booze?

Jamie frowned. "MC? You okay?"

"I'm fine. First day jitters. After more caffeine I should be firing on all cylinders. But I'm good. I swear."

"I'm not doubting you. But I don't want you to push too hard too soon. I'm happy to have you on my team. The crew is buried with work, so they're eager to have you back."

Yeah, everyone, now that Roland was gone. She wondered about Cam. Was he excited to have her back on duty? A conversation for another time.

"Good to hear. I appreciate the positivity. So are team meetings still on Tuesdays? When can I expect to get cases?"

"Yes, team meetings are on Tuesdays. As far as cases, my plan is to give you a few days to get a handle on the mundane stuff. Then we'll see what's on the docket. Oh, and..."

Here it comes. He's going to give me some type of "you're

walking on thin ice" talk. Crapper's voice echoed in her head. She stiffened.

"And what?"

He put his hands up. "Easy. Nothing bad. You're not in trouble. I'm not Roland, MC. Let's clear the air right now."

"Whew. It's a relief to have you say it out loud. Because I was preparing myself to take a lashing. To be told I had one last chance, and I better not blow it, that you'd be watching me like a hawk." She lifted her head like a flower reaching for sunlight.

Jamie said, "Not how I operate. What I was about to say is, I want you to mentor Jim Bob. You remember him, right? The newbie?"

Hope drained right back out. Remember him? How could she forget. Jim Bob O'Malley, the six-foot-five red-haired dork whose best asset was his emerald green eyes. He was built like a football linebacker and had the sense of humor of a middle schooler. And now Jamie was telling her one of her duties was to mentor the goofball. Great. That in itself would be enough to drive her to drink.

"I don't know if I'm ready to be responsible for another person besides myself quite yet. Gotta get my sea legs under me." Maybe if she acted pathetic enough Jamie would reconsider.

"Nah. MC, I know better. You are the best of the best. You took a detour for a while. But I can still see it in you. You're champing at the bit to get to work. Investigating is in your blood."

MC opened her mouth to protest.

Jamie held up a hand. "Let me finish. This isn't a form of punishment. Newbies spend time being mentored by all the inspectors on the different teams. It's your turn at the wheel." He leaned forward conspiratorially. "The kid admires you. He thinks you're the best inspector we have and wants to learn from you. Give him a chance, eh? He's rough around the edges, but I think he'll make a good inspector once he gets his head screwed on straight. If anyone can get him up to speed, it's you."

MC was stunned that Jim Bob thought she was the best inspector. She wasn't sure the guy who made a vibrator joke when they'd been on scene investigating a suspicious package was a good judge of what made a "best" inspector. She sighed. "Got it. I'm mentoring Jim Bob. God save me from going crazy from his stupid jokes. If you walk in and I'm banging my head against the wall, you'll know why."

Jamie laughed. "Thanks for the warning. I'll let Jim Bob know we spoke, and he can fill you in on what he's working on. I'll let you get back to your coffee and addressing your correspondence."

"Thanks, Jamie. I'm glad to be back. Hey, before you go, will Cam be in today?"

"Actually, he's out. He'll be in tomorrow though. I know he's glad to have you back at it."

"Thanks." Well, at least she had one more day before having to face Cam. She hadn't seen him since he'd dropped her off at Renewal Ridge Recovery. She'd been too embarrassed and ashamed to even contact him. But tomorrow that would change. They had to work together, and hopefully their friendship would remain intact. She had so many amends to make to so many people.

The prospect of addressing amends and working with Jim Bob ramped up her anxiety. She added these concerns to the list to hash out with Dr. Zaulk at her next therapy appointment. The list seemed to be growing instead of shrinking—no pun intended.

Chapter Four

Three days in, MC felt like she'd never left. She appreciated the grind and even looked forward to her meeting in an hour with Jim Bob. Jamie had assigned him a case involving mail theft at several apartment complexes in the Twin Cities. She hoped Jim Bob had been able to get a start on it.

The previous day she and Cam had met for about an hour in his office, clearing the air and alleviating her stress level considerably. At first MC sensed Cam's reticence to trust her, which triggered her usual reaction of wanting to flee to the nearest bar. Instead, she swallowed her pride and remained positive. Her less-addled self stepped up. They'd been close co-workers and friends for too many years to let it all slip away on an alcoholic's wave of self-justification.

In that vein, they had a great discourse on rehab and the sobriety journey. He shared stories about the kids and Jane, and how he felt about his new position as a team leader.

"A supervisor. Congrats."

Cam's face flushed pink. "It's only temporary."

"Aw, c'mon. I'm happy for you. The head honchos would be fools not to give you the promotion. You deserve it. You'll be a great supervisor." All true. Her goal was to re-earn his trust after the shitshow of the previous six months, those horrendous months following Barb's murder. Time for a new chapter, for them both.

With the Cam monkey off her back, she focused on Jim Bob. She wondered if Jamie had her mentoring the kid as a means to keep an eye on her. She reminded herself that Jamie wasn't Crapper. No hidden agenda.

A knock rattled her door in its hinges. She cringed. "Come in."

Her office door was flung open, and it banged against the wall. Jim Bob, the giant farm-grown Iowan, filled the doorway. "Hey, McCall we have a meeting." He stuck out a hand to catch the door as it bounced back. "Don't make doors the way they used to, huh?" He grinned.

MC could picture him on a football field, surrounded by cornfields, mowing down opponents and lifting his teammates off the ground in celebration. He was massive. He was annoying. He was massively annoying. But he was also kind of engaging. Jim Bob was complex.

"Yep, we do have a meeting. Come in, Red. Park yourself in a chair." She pointed at the two chairs in front of her desk.

He tossed a mess of papers and manila folders on the desk, and one slid off and hit the floor. Jim Bob bent to pick up the rogue folder and then slammed his body onto a chair. "I'm stoked we get to work together on these apartment mailbox robberies. We'll be a great team—postal inspector's version of Benson and Stabler. Do you watch *Law and Order: SVU*? Amazing show."

"Stop. Please. You're giving me a headache. Try and keep in mind this is our job, not a made-for-TV drama." She ached for a couple of shots to smooth the rough edges.

"Speaking of TV dramas, do you know who my all-time favorite TV detective is?" Jim Bob shuffled papers. "Columbo. He was sublime. I've got the entire series on DVD, watch them all the time. But hey, let's dig in. More thefts have been reported. A couple places in St. Paul, the East Side. One farther east, outside Woodbury. The latest report was from a small apartment building in Bloomington. Nowhere near the others. Then—"

"Whoa, Red. Slow your roll. Take a breath." Yes, she'd spouted a Barb phrase at Jim Bob. Take a breath. How many times had she heard those words over their almost twenty years together?

"You okay, McCall?" Jim Bob leaned forward, hands on the edge of her desk, and peered at her.

Jesus, if he leaned any harder, he might flip the whole desk over. The kid was a tank. "I'm fine. Let's view the big picture from the earliest to the latest. Take things one step at a time. Tell me what you've done so far." She flipped open a fresh Moleskine reporter-style notebook, her go-to brand and something Cam had always teased her about when they'd worked together. The world tilted back on its axis and MC felt solid. Ready for the challenge in front of her.

"Um, sure." Pages flittered off the edge of the desk and seesawed to the floor.

MC held her breath for a ten-count, every neuron inside her screaming for a drink. Lord, this was going to be a long day. Jim Bob gathered the errant pages, and MC came around the desk to sit beside him. She slid Pearl across the desk, out of the line of fire. "First, we organize. Each apartment complex gets its own folder. Then we sort the documents into the applicable folders. You know this. It's basic stuff. But I think you'll find the process easier if you're organized from the outset."

They spent the next thirty minutes compiling and filing documents in order, with one quick pause for Jim Bob to retrieve more folders from the supply room. He labeled the folders with surprisingly neat printing. A plus in MC's estimation. One positive trait.

"Okay, done with that. What's next?" She wanted him to take the reins instead of her leading him.

"I should visit each site again and interview residents, even if their mail hadn't been stolen. Waiting on fingerprints results from the lab," he said.

"All good. What else? Was there evidence the mailboxes had been tampered with?"

"No pry marks. I should talk to the carriers who deliver the affected routes." He brightened. "Yeah. For sure. And…"

"We should inquire if any carriers have reported lost or stolen Arrow Keys. Especially in light of no forced entry on the boxes. If someone obtained one of those keys, they'd have the ability to open any mailboxes in the area, as well as collection boxes. Are there security cameras in the areas of the mailboxes? Or anywhere outside or inside the complexes?"

"Arrow Keys. How'd I miss something so obvious?" He knocked his fist against his head.

"Easy. Don't want to rattle anything loose in there."

Jim Bob dug a steno notebook from beneath the mess of files and began a list. "Arrow Keys. Security cameras. Resident interviews."

"Excellent. We can visit the sites and scope out the camera situation. Do knock-and-talks with residents. And you can research Arrow Keys after."

"All right." He jumped up. "When do you want to leave?" Jim Bob shuffled his stuff into a pile and tidied it.

"Sign out a car for us and I'll meet you up front in fifteen minutes. I have some email I need to attend to first."

"You got it, chief."

"No." MC wagged a finger at him. "We aren't doing 'chief.'"

"Too high up the chain of command for you?" He snorted.

MC stared at him.

"Right. No 'chief.' I'll go with McCall."

"Good choice. Now go get the car, Red."

He hesitated, and she wondered if he wanted to argue about her giving him a nickname when he couldn't assign one to her. "Just one more thing…" He waited in the open doorway.

"What?"

He didn't respond.

She looked up from her computer screen and noticed the lopsided grin on his face. "What?" Did he have trouble hearing?

"Don't you get it? Columbo's signature exit line. He says it and then goes on to ask the bad guy some question that makes it clear they did the crime. Brilliant. Such a great detective." He exited the office, closing the door behind him.

He's going to drive me to drink. No. Stop thinking about booze.

She quickly dispatched the emails and stuffed her notebook, pen, and credentials in her blazer pocket.

"Lord, give me strength." She wasn't the praying type, but an afternoon out in the field with Jim Bob warranted an exception.

After a long afternoon, MC called it quits. Time to decompress. Either she'd belly-up to a bar and drown her sorrows or she'd spend some time with her friends at Flannel and order takeout.

Bar or coffee shop. Coffee shop or bar.

"Dammit." She set sail for Flannel.

MC arrived at the front door at the same time as Zane, and he pulled the door open for her. "Thanks, Zane."

"No problem." They entered Flannel to find Dara behind the counter and Meg seated at their usual table at the far end of the counter.

"Hey, ho, y'all." Dara slapped a towel over her shoulder. "Zane, it's been a slow afternoon."

Zane dumped his backpack in the kitchen area and said, "I'll wash my hands, then take over."

"Sounds dandy," Dara said. "MC do you want coffee?"

"Is the sky blue? Yes, please." She gave Meg a quick squeeze and then slid into a chair across the table. "How're you, Meg?" She reached over and covered Meg's hand with hers. "How was radiation?"

"It was okay. I'm a little wiped out, but not too bad. I hoped to see you. How're you? How's work?"

"Well, third day done, and I haven't killed Jim Bob yet."

"He the kid with the red hair? The one you call Red?" Dara slid a mug across the table to MC and sat next to Meg.

"Yup. We're working a series of mail thefts. Apartment building mailboxes. Several different buildings around the Twin Cities."

Meg cradled her warm mug of tea. "How's it going? Different from working with Cam?"

A couple entered the cafe and Dara stood to help them.

Zane emerged from the kitchen. "I've got 'em."

"Thanks, Zane." Dara returned to the table. "Okay, MC, continue."

MC took a drink. "So smooth and rich." She closed her eyes and savored the brew, almost having vanquished the dastardly demon inside her demanding booze.

"You falling asleep?" Dara boomed.

MC opened her eyes. "No, just soaking in the ambience."

"Wishing it was something a bit stronger, I bet," Dara said.

Meg smacked Dara on the arm. "Stop."

"Sorry, MC." Dara rubbed her arm. "Anyway, you were saying something about working with Red."

"Right. We were out doing field interviews this afternoon. He spent I don't know how much time telling me his favorite detective is Columbo. A damn idiot TV detective."

Meg's blue eyes twinkled. "Does he aspire to be like Columbo?"

Dara guffawed. "Why not Monk? Or...wait. Better yet, Sherlock Holmes."

"Stop already," MC said. "I don't know. But right now he's more like Daffy Duck as Duck Drake, the trench coat-clad detective in *The Super Snooper*. Remember the animated short? I think it originally came out in the 1950s."

"I totally remember Duck Drake," Dara said.

"To add insult to injury, he dubbed us the Inspection Service version of Benson and Stabler." This time MC did a massive eyeroll.

"Hot chick!" Dara's voice squeaked.

Meg said, "Good grief, Dara, you're making a spectacle of yourself."

"I've never heard you squeal. Careful, you might lose your butch card." MC pulled out her phone and redirected everyone's attention before Dara could cause more of a scene. "Anyone hungry for pizza? Or Thai?"

"I think pizza," Meg said, "but plain cheese for me. You two order whatever you want."

MC scrutinized Meg between taps on her phone. She was chipper, but MC saw more lines around her eyes and her mouth. Her complexion was pale. "Cheese pizza for Meg. You okay with pepperoni, Dara?"

"Yup." Dara scooted her chair closer to Meg and slid an arm around her shoulders. "You sure you're up to sticking around? Not too tired?"

"I'm fine, dear. Tired, yes. But I'm also hungry, and I enjoy being here with you and MC. It's cozy, like being home."

Dara frowned. "I'm not totally convinced you're feeling up to staying." She held up a hand to ward off Meg's retort. "I'll make you a deal...we'll order food, eat, and visit with MC. But at seven-thirty we make like trees and leave. Gives us plenty of time. Deal?"

"Fair enough. But I may want some dessert too." Meg huffed

and finished her tea.

At 7:30 on the dot MC walked Dara and Meg out to the Jeep parked behind the cafe. In her absence, a line of customers formed. "Need help, Zane?"

"No, thanks. I can handle it."

MC cleaned up the detritus from dinner and wiped down the table, then stored the leftover pizza in the fridge. She hung around the kitchen until Zane finished filling all the orders, then she ventured out. "Thought I'd hang and help you close. What can I get started on?"

"Hey, I appreciate it. We've got an hour and fifteen minutes, so if you don't mind, maybe, you could wash the dishes?"

"Dishes it is. If you get too bogged down, holler."

The final hour flew by. The mild spring weather brought folks out in droves, and Zane was barista-ing iced and warmed beverages like mad. Once dishes were done, MC did what little she could, dumping and cleaning the giant silver coffeemakers and restocking the sweetener packets.

At nine, MC locked the front door and shut off the OPEN sign in the window. Zane got busy closing out the cash register.

MC asked, "Would you like me to mop the floors?"

"Yes, please. Thanks."

MC filled a mop bucket with hot water and cleaning solution and rolled it out front. "Hey, Zane, how's school going? Remind me what you're going for."

"I'm at the University of Minnesota in their Psychology graduate program. I see myself working as, like, a school counselor specializing in LGBTQIA, especially trans, advocacy. My vision is to help kids navigate through the tough times and get them to a healthy place. I feel my own lived experience plus getting sober will help me help them. Speaking of..." He glanced at MC.

She stopped mopping. "I'm guessing you're delicately broaching the question of my sobriety and how it's going?" She plunged the mop into the bucket of water. "I truly despise the word sobriety. I find it cringy. I really don't want to talk about it."

Zane moved out from behind the counter and pulled the bag from the trash can near the condiment station. "It's how you feel. Everyone's journey is different."

Had he not heard she didn't want to talk about this?

He's being supportive and open. What would it hurt for you to open up and be honest?

"All I can think about is booze…how much I want it…how close I come daily to taking that first drink. Then I get pissed and have to consciously redirect my energy to something positive. Which brings me right back to booze because booze equals positive. Until it isn't. The vicious circle spins like an out-of-control merry-go-round. How's that for a journey?" Zane didn't deserve her sarcasm, but it spewed forth like a geyser from a wide-open fire hydrant.

"I hear you. Personally, I found it lifesaving, sobriety. In fact, I still hit up meetings when I feel the need."

"Why would you go to meetings any longer than you have to?" She was confounded by the idea of participating in AA years after she'd been off booze. Not her. No way. Her goal was to do the six meetings she promised and call it good.

"In my case," Zane said, "I find it extremely helpful. For instance, when I experience harassment for being trans or racism because I'm Black, going to a meeting helps me process the incidents instead of running to the nearest liquor store or bar. Expressing my feelings…releasing my anger and fear in a safe and supportive environment…is a much healthier way to handle those situations."

"Have you been harassed lately? I don't mean to pry."

Zane twisted the top of the trash bag and knotted it. He set it at the end of the counter. "I'm going to get the garbage from the restroom."

Well, that was a non-answer if she'd ever heard one. MC finished mopping the floor. Zane came out of the restroom holding a white plastic bag. He scooted around the bucket but then came to a standstill. "Yes."

One single word.

At first MC wasn't sure what he meant. Then it hit her like a lightning bolt. "Yes, you've been harassed lately? When? Where? By whom?" The investigator in her kicked into gear.

"Walking to my car off campus. A couple nights ago. Two guys…white guys. Typical crap. Asked me if I was a guy or what. Started following me and yelling transphobic crap at me." He filled her in on the ugly details. "But then a massive Black man, I bet he was six eight, walking in the opposite direction stopped. He got between the two white men and me. Threatened to call up some of his friends to come help 'take care of' the twosome. That's all it took. They backed off and left. I got lucky that night."

"Lucky? Jesus, Zane. Did you notify the cops or campus police?"

"No. Cops wouldn't do anything."

"If anything like that happens again, call 911. Or at the very least, call me."

"Past experience has taught me that cops won't do anything about a couple assholes harassing a trans person."

MC felt anger bubble. Not everyone in law enforcement was uncaring. Most, in fact, were good public servants. "Call me, then. Immediately. Helping here at Flannel keeps me in check. Even after a challenging day with a new inspector I was able to fend off the devil screaming for fire water simply by coming here. Being present for my friends. I consider you a friend. I know we're not contemporaries, but we are friends. A lesson I'm still learning is I need to recognize when to shift focus from me to what my friends need. This is one of those times. So like I said, you call me if they show their faces again."

"Okay. Thanks, MC. I do appreciate you." He hefted the garbage bags. "I'm going to get these out to the dumpster. Only thing left to do is restock beans." He headed for the back door.

MC wanted an investigation to sink her teeth into and to take her mind off living life without Barb and steering clear of booze. Protecting Zane from racist transphobes hadn't been on her bingo card. *But hey, when life throws hate your way, or your friend's way, then you kick those haters' asses.*

Chapter Five

Jim Bob bounded into the break room where MC was filling her coffee cup. "Hey, are you free this morning? I'd like to roll on the Winsome Garden Apartments in St. Paul. I thought we could talk to the residents."

MC leaned against the counter. "I can't think of a better way to start off the week. Any security cameras?"

"No." Jim Bob propped himself next to her, arms crossed against his broad chest. "There aren't any cameras. Maybe the management company in charge of the building should think about upping security...or installing any sort of security besides the lock on the outside doors. Do you think anyone inside has those Ring doorbells installed on their apartment doors?"

MC tilted her head to look up at the Jolly Red Giant. "Seriously? You're asking that question for real?" At five-foot-eight, she wasn't short by any means, but Jim Bob towered nearly a foot above her. Maybe that's part of his problem—the air was thinner up there. "Think about it. What good would doorbell cams do us? Unless there's an apartment right across from where the mailboxes are located."

"Ah, crap. I knew that." He whacked himself on the forehead. "I wasn't thinking clearly. Getting ahead of myself. I guess we'll have to settle for good old-fashioned gumshoe detection."

"Correct. Shall we get a move on?" She itched for a case all her own. This was her second week at work, and while she was glad for the excuse to be out in the field, Jim Bob, stumbles and all, was showing signs of being capable of handling things on his own. She wasn't a nanny, for god's sake.

"I'll sign out a car and grab the keys."

"Hold up, Red. I have an early afternoon appointment, so I'll drive separately and meet you at Winsome Garden. Text me the address."

"You got it, chief...ah, McCall. Sorry, I forget we aren't doing the whole 'chief' thing." Jim Bob lifted a shoulder.

"Remember to text me the address." MC retreated to her office. "Dear goddess, give me strength to get through this day."

MC located the building on the Eastside of St. Paul, south of

Interstate 94 and east of White Bear Avenue. Not a huge complex, about a hundred and twenty apartments and a slew of storage cages in the basement, according to the information Jim Bob provided. An outdoor parking lot for residents was behind the complex, and a small visitor parking area with about fifteen spaces was at the front of the building.

The shrubbery on either side of the front entrance resembled victims from *The Texas Chainsaw Massacre*. MC seriously doubted any of the dried up grayish-brown hulks would bud. The management company might want to think about sprucing up the grounds. Winsome Garden Apartments looked more like Bleak Acres.

MC parked her car, and Jim Bob swung an abused, faded charcoal-gray Crown Vic into the space to her right.

"Got the best car in the fleet, I see," MC said.

"Chelsea told me this was the only one available. I think she doesn't trust me to drive the SUVs. I don't know what she thinks I'll do. I'm not a stupid teenager." He stuffed the keys into his pants pocket. "I have visions of the tires coming off on the highway or even the engine blowing up on this dinosaur." He kicked a tire. "The car's gotta be older than me."

"Don't take it personally, Red. It's kind of a newbie rite of passage—count on always getting the crap car unless you're with a senior inspector. Anyway, let's get cracking. It's almost ten. I wonder how many folks are home at this time of the morning. A lot of people are probably at work. Do you have a contact here?"

"I have a name and phone number written down." He dug in his pocket. "Oh, better yet." A woman had just unlocked the front door to the complex as they walked up. "Excuse me, ma'am," he said. "Would you mind letting us inside?"

The white-haired woman, maybe in her seventies, was dressed in a flowered zip-up, hooded sweatshirt over neatly pressed tan khaki slacks and a pair of pristine black New Balance sneakers. She faced MC and Jim Bob. "And who might you two be?" She stood, a barrel-shaped obstacle blocking their way. "You don't live here, obviously. If you don't live here, then you need to have someone who does let you in. That's the rule."

MC said, "I'm Postal Inspector McCall and this is Postal Inspector O'Malley. We're here to investigate last week's mail theft." She and Jim Bob presented their credentials.

"Postal Inspectors, huh? Are you the same as police?"

"Very similar," MC said.

"You all carry guns and whatnot?"

"Yes, we sure do," Jim Bob said.

"Well, okay. I guess I can let you in."

Jim Bob reached over her head and held the door open for the lady. Then he and MC followed her.

MC asked, "Would you show us where the mailboxes are?"

"You bet. Come with me." She set off down a long, wide hall with apartments on either side. Her sneakers squeaked along the aged tile floor. About halfway through MC spotted an elevator alcove. Good to know they wouldn't have to schlep up and down the stairs between the five floors.

A shorter hall jutted off to the left and then they were at the rear of the building. A bank of silver mailboxes with apartment numbers lined one wall. To the left was an Electrical Room and another door directly across was probably a stairwell access. At the end of the mailboxes was a set of double doors labeled "Loading Dock."

"Here you go." The woman propped her hands on her hips.

"Thank you for your help," Jim Bob said. "Can I ask where this door leads?" He indicated the door across from the Electrical Room.

"Opens to the stairs down to the back door." She scooted over and opened the door to show them.

"No lock on this door?" MC retrieved her notebook and pen from her pocket.

"Not on this one, no. None of the stairwell doors have locks. But you have to have a key to get in the back door. Same as the front."

"What about the loading dock?" Jim Bob walked over to the wood double doors and pulled one side open.

"Those are the same. No lock on the inside doors. The only way to open the overhead door is from inside here. See?" She pointed out a metal box with a green open button and red close button. "Gotta come inside the building and through here to open the dock door. No other way."

MC scribbled notes. "Okay. So how do people who don't live here get access then? Say an appliance or furniture delivery?"

"Well," she peered up at MC, "that's simple, really. They go through the management company, and I imagine sign a bunch of documents and get issued a key. Or a resident meets them and lets them in and then makes sure the door is closed when they leave."

MC felt like she was being lectured by a teacher who thought the answer was so obvious MC shouldn't have needed to ask.

Jim Bob hit the open button, and the fiberglass door began to roll up in its tracks. Once it was fully open, they had a view of the loading dock to the blacktopped driveway and the resident parking area beyond. He pushed the close button, and then they were sealed inside once again. "I doubt whoever got in did so this way. Too much hassle."

No shit, Sherlock. MC bit her lip to stop the words from spewing forth. "Agreed. Were you a victim of the mail theft last week? Did you see or hear anything? Or talk to any neighbors who might have?"

"I checked after the mail delivery and my box was empty. And I hadn't stuck anything in the outgoing slot. As for seeing or hearing anything, I'm up on the fourth floor so I didn't witness any of the action." She crossed to the mailboxes, unlocked one, and peered inside. "Hmmm...nothing today yet." She closed and relocked the box. "You might try speaking with Mavis Schlotz in two-oh-one. She told me her mail had been taken. Maybe she's aware of who else was affected. Otherwise, there's not much else I can tell you."

MC said, "You've been so helpful. Could we get your name? For the record in case we have further questions."

"Sure. I'm Viv Smith. Not too hard to remember." She smiled.

"Viv Smith. S.M.I.T.H.?" MC asked.

"Correct. Typical spelling. I'm in four-oh-two."

"We appreciate you helping us out," Jim Bob said. "If you think of anything else we should know, please call." He extracted a business card from his pocket. "Office and cell phone numbers are on here." He handed Viv his card.

MC followed suit.

"I sure will. Have a great day, officers." She disappeared down the hall toward the elevators.

"Good job on the business cards, Red. Now what's our next move?"

Jim Bob beamed. "I say we head up to the second floor and see if Mavis is home."

Nearly two hours later they'd managed to knock on nearly every door on floors two through five. Mavis hadn't answered, so they continued on. Not one hit on the second floor. On the third floor halfway down the hall, a troll-like guy opened the door and mumbled a few swear words. When they produced their credentials, he slammed the door in their faces. No hits on four. On the fifth floor the last door they tried was that of the young twenty-something woman who reported the mail theft. She informed them on the day the theft occurred a guy wearing a dark gray hoodie and black jeans bowled her over as she attempted to come in the back door. She recalled he may have been wearing black sneakers but wasn't positive.

"Can you give us more of a description?" MC asked. "Was he white? Black? How tall? Old or young?"

"It was so quick I barely registered it was a man. I yelled at him for being rude, but he was sprinting away by then." She told them when she reached the first floor, she noticed mail and advertisements scattered all over the floor. A few rows of mailboxes were tilted open, as if the carrier forgot to secure them. No postal carrier in sight.

When they were finished, MC punched the elevator's down button. "Before we leave let's see if we can catch the carrier. If it's the same one, maybe we could get some info from them."

"At least we have a partial description of a person of interest now."

They disembarked from the elevator on the first floor to the sounds of thudding and scuffling. "What's happening?" Jim Bob asked.

MC glanced left, then right. Down by the mailboxes she saw what she thought was a postal carrier entangled with a person in a hoodie. "C'mon, Red." She took off.

Jim Bob overtook MC, threw himself at the hoodie person and MC tried to extricate the carrier. Mr. Hoodie slipped Jim Bob's grasp, bolted for the stairwell door, and blasted through it.

MC said, "You stay here. Make sure the carrier's okay. I'm going after this guy." She hit the stairs leading to the rear door and heard the outside door clang shut. She pounded down the steps and burst outside. Halfway down the loading dock driveway, she halted.

No one in sight.

She skipped the parking lot because she didn't hear any cars starting. At the street alongside the complex, she checked both ways. To her left, she picked up movement at the corner, a half block away. She took off. As she was about to round the corner, the toe of her shoe clipped a raised edge of the sidewalk, and she went down.

"McCall. What—?"

MC stood, picking gravel from her palms. "Don't even. I'm fine. Before you ask, yes, he got away." Her palms approximated mincemeat and her black twill pants and matching suit coat were dusty, but otherwise she was unharmed. Unharmed except for her ego. Face-planting during a foot pursuit was the last thing she had on her agenda for the day. "Goddammit. I saw him take a left at the corner here."

They surveyed the area.

Jim Bob said, "I don't see anyone or anything."

"Observant, Red." She delicately picked more rocks and sand from her hands.

"You need a First-Aid kit? Geez you got some intense sidewalk rash."

MC glared at him. "How's the carrier?"

"He's fine. Not injured. I told him to stay put. Man, I was freaked to find you picking yourself up off the ground. You sure you're good?"

She did a slow count to five, feeling the burn on her cheeks. "I'm dandy. But the suspect vanished into thin air. Well, not thin air. Probably he had a car stashed somewhere nearby and he's on the highway heading who knows where by now."

"Highway to hell is my guess." Jim Bob grinned.

"Funny guy." She winced and started toward the apartment building, half annoyed and half grateful the newbie cared about her well-being. "Let's get a statement from the carrier. Then I need to take off for my appointment. Can you handle entering all the notes into DigiCase when you're back at the office?" He had enough time on board that the case management system shouldn't be a challenge for him. "If you run into issues, I'll help you tomorrow."

"I can do it. No problem. Got all the details in storage right up here." He tapped his temple.

"Make sure the info transfers from your storage into the case system. In fact, I highly recommend you get in the habit of taking notes. You can't always rely on memory, Red."

MC made her 1:30 p.m. appointment with a few minutes to spare, so she quickly used the restroom next to the waiting area to thoroughly scrub the blood off her hands. It wasn't long before the doc invited her into the office.

Dr. Zaulk took a seat in an ivory-colored wingback chair, which matched the one MC occupied. Their usual setup. A small rectangular cherrywood table separated the two chairs on the "island," as MC referred to the eight-by-ten-foot area rug beneath them in the center of the airy first-floor office.

"Let's dive right in then, shall we? Starting with—what happened to your hands?" Dr. Zaulk asked.

"I was chasing a suspect this morning and tripped over a lip in the sidewalk. My hands took the brunt of the fall. Guess I left a few layers of dermis on the cement." She held her hands up and examined them.

Suddenly she was four years old again and holding her hands up in much the same manner but also crying. The swing twisted around on its chains after MC had jumped from it mid-air. "I'm telling mom and dad, Cindy. Why'd you make me jump?"

"Mary Catherine, you can be such a baby sometimes." Cindy stomped off.

MC trailed behind her sister sniffing snot and pressing her bloody palms against her pink shorts. "Cindy, wait for me. Please. I'll stop crying. Promise."

Cindy skipped ahead, arms swinging. Carefree. Alive.

"Cindy."

Dr. Zaulk's voice penetrated the cloud around her. "MC? Where'd you go?"

MC settled her hands in her lap. "I had a sister. Cindy. She died when she was eight and I was four. I worshipped her." She swallowed the lump forming in her throat. "She'd dared me to jump from a swing, and when I did, I landed hard and fell. My hands got cut up on the playground's crumbling blacktop." She held her hands up, palms facing Dr. Z. "Much like this. Seeing my hands just now threw me back to a day I haven't thought about in more years than I can tell you."

"Can you tell me more about Cindy? And that day?"

"It was the day she died." MC's voice faded away as the movie played in her head, clear as the day it all happened. "Oh my god. All these years I hadn't remembered the day I hurt my hands was the same day Cindy died. How can that be?"

"It's possible your brain suppressed the memory. A safety-switch of sorts. Do you feel up to sharing those memories?"

"I don't know." MC covered her face with her wounded hands as if she could block the memory from escaping into the light of day. *You need to get this out. You've buried it for most of your life and what good has it done you? The release might steer you on the path toward closure, finally.* She'd never shared this horrible part of her life with Barb and yet she was present to guide MC.

"Fourth of July. Our family and a bunch of other families had gathered at Minnehaha Falls Park for a picnic. Parents were grilling and all us kids had gone to the playground. I was on the swings with Cindy, and she dared me to jump. She was eight, and much bigger than me. A daredevil. She'd jumped from so high, I thought she was on the clouds. And she stuck a perfect landing." Climbing. Jumping. Soaring. Clips of Cindy flitted through MC's memory bank. "I was only four, but I didn't want to disappoint my big sister. So I jumped. It didn't end well for me." Once again, she'd not lived up to Cindy's expectations.

"How did you feel then? And now?"

"I was in pain. Crying. I was so mad at her. I blamed her, but then when she skipped off without me, I begged her to wait. My anger evaporated, replaced by a cold, paralyzing fear. Fear she'd leave me all alone. Fear I'd never be as good as her—at anything. Then later that day—she was dead. Gone forever. On a dare, no less. A stupid dare. Was it my fault? Was she trying to show me how to take chances, to live life on the edge?" MC took a breath and held it for a four-count. "I'd never be as daring as Cindy. I felt guilty for being angry with her."

"Do you still feel guilty?"

"I still feel inadequate. And guilty, I guess. Cindy's death. Barb's murder. Drinking. Worry that if I can't pull myself from under all the darkness, I'll lose the job I love." Would this be the end? Would Dr. Z decide she was too unstable to perform her duties after all? What had she done?

"MC?" Dr. Z laid her pen on top of her notepad. "MC, all those feelings are understandable. I think the injury you sustained today linked you to that faraway day with Cindy. I'm sure you're experiencing a waterfall of emotions and thoughts. Keep afloat. Don't let yourself drown. What do you need to do? I can give you some coping mechanisms to help you manage your thoughts."

"I don't know. The journaling has helped me process Barb's death and my recovery, I guess. But this…"

"Listen, we're at the end of our session today. Continue journaling. Try to add some mindfulness techniques. You might even find an app for your phone to guide you. You mentioned on the phone you're attending AA meetings weekly?"

"Yeah, I've been to a couple. Sunday evenings. I'm not sold on the whole concept. Not to be too cliché, but I'm giving it the old college try."

"Good. Keep up with the meetings along with the mindfulness and journaling. We'll delve deeper into these Cindy memories in the next session. I know we'd planned on every other week, but with this new development, I feel we should keep exploring the issue. Weekly sessions for the foreseeable future, and as we work through things, we can go to every other week. Do you think you can handle AA and seeing me weekly?"

Could she handle so much delving into her inner psyche?

"Yeah, I guess." Doc didn't need to know the AA thing was going to be short-lived. She'd fulfill her promise to Dara. Six and done. "Weekly it is. See you on the eighteenth."

She could use about a gallon of vodka right about now.

Chapter Six

Still slightly off-kilter from her appointment two days earlier with Dr. Zaulk, MC struggled to focus. She felt stuck in some weird time warp. Memories of Cindy's death mixed with memories of Barb's murder. Not the best recipe for concentration as she pushed through entering her notes from the mail theft field work with Jim Bob. DigiCase, their case management system, was straightforward, but she stuttered to a stop about a hundred times before she got the information entered.

A stiff drink. That would help clear the cobwebs. Perk her right up.

Her gaze landed on Pearl. "Hey, girl. I'm sorry I've been neglecting you. I wonder what you need." Chelsea's instructions said to water it every two to four weeks, and it'd only been a little over a week. She needed more details. Her fingers flew over the keyboard as she Googled how to take care of succulents. She chose a link near the top of the page and dove in, quickly learning that overwatering succulents could cause root rot. Yikes. Smaller pots, like hers, required more frequent watering, as the dirt would dry out quicker. But lack of sunlight meant less watering because it absorbed less water. "Pearl, taking care of you is going to be a lesson in contradictions."

"Good morning."

MC glanced up from her computer screen to find Jim Bob's jolly giant form filling her doorway. Why the hell was he so jovial on a Wednesday morning? Or any morning for that matter? "Morning, Red. How long you been standing there?"

"Just now. Why?"

"Never mind. What can I do for you?"

He plopped into a chair. "How're your hands? Are they healing?"

She peered over the edge of her desk to assure herself he hadn't destroyed the chair. "My hands are fine." Her voice cracked, throat parched, reminiscent of cotton-mouthed mornings after all-night benders. In the past, a shot of wheat-infused liquid fire fixed her. Hair of the dog worked wonders. Lukewarm coffee would have to suffice. "I finished entering case notes from Monday. Feel free to check it out and add anything."

"Will do. I was thinking about hitting up the postal stations in

35

the areas of the robberies. Talk to the supervisors and carriers and accountability clerks. I think the Arrow Key is key to the case. See what I did there?" He flashed his pearly whites.

Kid was so proud of himself. She, less so. "Yeah. I sure do. Funny. Enlighten me further. What's your plan of action?" More importantly, did it involve her having to accompany him? Hopefully not. Her head was too fuzzy, and she'd need to be on her toes if she were out in the field with him.

"I'm going to conduct a security review. Examine their key inventories. See what their process is for assigning and tracking building keys as well as Arrow Keys." He clapped his hands together. "Brilliant. No?"

"Most definitely. Sounds like a solid plan." She knew what he'd find. Lax, if any, accountability of those precious keys. Unfortunately, key inventories were a perpetual problem in the tens of thousands of post offices. But she didn't want to burst his bubble. Let him find out on his own. "Let me know what you learn."

"You don't want to come along?"

His hangdog face almost made her laugh. "I trust you to handle it on your own. But call me if you have questions. I'll keep my phone close."

He popped up from the chair as Jamie came in.

"Morning, MC. Jim Bob," Jamie said.

"Hey, Jamie. What's up?"

He nudged his glasses up his nose with a finger. "Got a report of a post office robbery."

"Holy hell," Jim Bob said. "Where?"

"Castle Cove. Up along the north shore. Robbed this morning. MC, I'm going to send you up there."

"I could go with her." Jim Bob bounced on the balls of his feet.

Jamie said, "I need you to deal with the mail thefts here in the Cities."

"You got it, boss. I'm out. Going to the stations. Key inventories. See ya." He waved and left.

Jamie took a deep breath. "He's a bundle of energy."

"Understatement of the century, but he's all right." She cleared a space on her desk and opened her notebook, the fuzz dissipating from her brain. "Tell me more about this robbery in Castle Cove."

"Happened this morning. Details are sketchy. Good news is no injuries. But I do need someone up there today." He sat in the chair Jim Bob had vacated. "You're the only inspector I can send. But I need to know you can handle this on your own. The last case you worked up there was traumatic."

MC said, "I understand your concerns, Jamie. First, let me

assure you I am one-hundred-ten percent up for it. Truth be told, I've been hoping for a challenge. The mail thefts are important, but Jim Bob's chugging along fine."

He set his elbows on the arms of the chair and folded his hands together. "I'm worried being on your own up there might be rough after all that transpired last time."

"I'm continuing to see my therapist and we're working through a lot. In addition, I've committed to weekly AA meetings as part of my post-rehab program."

"We have no way of knowing how long you might need to be in Castle Cove. Will you be able to continue with your AA meetings and therapist? Those are important appointments. I don't want to put too much stress on you, but we really need you."

"I'll find a local AA meeting in the area. I'll return on Sunday for the therapy appointment on Monday and then go back to Castle Cove. Or worst-case scenario, I can do a phone session. I'll save the agency money by staying at my place on Lake Superior near Two Harbors, so no hotel expense. That should sweeten the deal."

Jamie grinned. "I was hoping you'd offer to post up at your place. I didn't want to assume though. You're relieved from mentoring Jim Bob. I'll pair him with someone else."

"Red is a pain in the butt when he gets into dorky middle-school-boy mode. Which admittedly is more often than I'd like. But what I've seen so far, he's got the foundation for being a successful inspector. He's got a solid grasp of the basics. Between his bouts of squirreliness, he takes the job seriously. I really think he'll be okay working on his own." She wondered, though, who would have to suffer through his bad jokes and TV detective references.

"MC?"

"Sorry. Making a mental list."

Jamie stood. "Okay, as soon as you can button stuff up here go ahead and sign out a vehicle and be on your way. I'll let Jim Bob know the plan."

"If you don't mind, I'll drive my own car." She preferred driving her car when she went up north. "I'll let you know once I've packed and am ready get on the road."

"Copy that. Take whatever equipment you'll need. Safe travels. I'll await an update once you arrive in Castle Cove."

After Jamie left, MC straightened the chaos on her desk, packed her stuff, and set an "Out of Office" message for her email. She'd check her email while out of town, but since the main focus was going to be Castle Cove, other issues would take a back seat.

Before she vacated the building, she called Jim Bob to check-in a final time.

"Yeah, Jamie already told me about the assignment. So, I can call you anytime? Day or night?"

"Red, don't push it. If you get in a jam or really need guidance, let Jamie know. You got this."

"Roger, chief...uh, I mean, McCall."

She heard his laughter as she ended the call. Goddess help her, at this rate she'd be ordering a double.

No you won't. You can handle him and his shenanigans. He's harmless. Don't let him push your buttons. Do your job. Barb always knew how to talk her down.

MC made one final stop before leaving the city.

Zane said, "Hey, MC."

Dara wheeled around. "Hot snot boogerballs!" She clapped once, the sound like a firecracker. "McCall, nice of you to grace us with your presence."

MC met Zane's gaze, and they burst out laughing.

"What? What's so funny?" Dara asked. "Joke's on me." Hands on cargo pants-clad hips, Dara was a fireplug ready to defend herself.

"Ah, c'mon Dara," MC said. "No harm meant. You crack us up, even if you're a tiny bit over-the-top. Right, Zane?"

"Absolutely. What can I get started for you, MC?"

MC produced her travel mug. "Fill 'er up, high octane, please."

Dara grabbed the cup and went to a tall silver tower filled with a dark roast blend. "What brings you into our fine establishment in the middle of the day?"

"I'm leaving town for a while. Got a case up in Castle Cove. Post office robbery."

"Up north again?" Dara handed the cup to MC, brow wrinkled. "You ready to be up there so soon? I mean..."

"Dara, I know what you mean. I'll be fine. Unfortunately, I have no way of knowing how long I might be gone. I really wanted to be more available to help you and Meg."

"We're fine," Dara said. "Things are going smoothly. Zane has been a huge help here at the shop. Go. Do your job."

"You'll call or text if you need me or anything changes with Meg? I want to support you both as best I can. I'm not running away or finding an excuse to avoid you. I promised to do better, and I aim to keep my promise. You know that, right?"

"Whoa. Easy there, pal. We know you're here for us. I believe you. But I will caution you—don't miss those weekly meetings." Dara wagged a finger back and forth. "For your own good. I promise to keep you in the loop on Meg."

Zane added, "We'll miss you."

MC said, "I'll miss you all too. Now I have to get going. Take care."

"See ya," Dara said.

MC arrived in Castle Cove a few minutes before 2:00 p.m. She parked her Subaru on Main Street, in front of a post office the size of a trio of outhouses. The clapboard siding was bright white, and a postage-stamp-sized flowerbed had been planted in front.

A handwritten sign was taped to the front door, "No stamp sales or package drop-offs today. Post office boxes may be accessed as normal. Thanks for your understanding."

She entered and walked up to a counter about eight feet long abutting a wall of merchandise available for purchase. A wooden door prevented the average Joe from accessing the work area beyond. Ancient PO boxes lined the remainder of the wall.

A tall, gangly man with thin gray hair and a pair of caterpillar brows above eyes the color of a well-worn pair of blue jeans stood behind the counter with a stack of stamps. Behind him sat an iron rack with five canvas mail sacks used for sorting mail hanging from hooks.

"Excuse me." She flashed her credentials. "I'm Inspector McCall here to meet with Ned Hargreve."

"That'd be me. Glad to see you, Inspector. I'll let you in the door."

MC walked into a workspace containing six mail sorting cases. A black standalone safe about the size of a deep freeze was against the wall next to a desk. Transom windows with steel bars let light into the building. Double swinging doors in back, currently secured with a heavy chain and padlock, most likely led to the loading dock. A regular door allowed employee access.

A restroom was near a row of seven tall metal lockers. Next to them was a brightly lit breakroom with two tables, folding chairs, and a couple of vending machines.

MC said, "The office is much larger than it appears from the outside."

"We utilize every inch of space. Come on in the office and have a seat." He walked toward a doorway to the left of the safe.

The office was the size of a phone booth, when such things existed. A standard government issue gray metal desk faced the door, a more contemporary office chair behind it. Two visitor chairs were wedged in front of the desk. Two five-drawer metal file cabinets were crammed behind Ned's desk. A stunning picture of Split Rock Lighthouse surrounded by a kaleidoscope of Northern Lights was in sharp contrast to the dreary decor. The framed photo hung on the wall between the file cabinets.

"Nice shot of Split Rock." MC fished out her note-taking tools.

"Thank you."

"So tell me what happened earlier today."

"The incident occurred before I arrived this morning. My clerk Sophie Andersen was the only one on site."

"Is she still here?"

"Yes, she is. Do you want to speak with her now?"

"Yeah, that'd be good."

Ned led her to the breakroom. A youngish woman with light brown hair pulled back in a ponytail sat reading a paperback, *The Mortal Groove*, by Minnesota's own Ellen Hart. She wore an official light blue US Postal Service polo shirt, blue jeans, and sneakers and came across as unperturbed by what had transpired. But maybe it was a facade.

Ned said, "Inspector McCall, this is my clerk, Sophie. She was here at the time of the robbery."

Sophie's hands trembled slightly as she set the open book face down on the table.

MC said, "Thanks, Ned. I'll speak with Sophie and then I'll circle back to you."

"I'll be up front or in my office." He hustled out of the room.

"Nice to meet you, Sophie. I didn't see you in here when I arrived."

"I was using the restroom a few minutes ago."

"Ah, makes sense." She smiled. "I need to ask you about today's events, but before I do, how are you?"

"O-okay."

MC took her time opening her notebook and writing the date and time on the blank page. If she kept things slow and easy hopefully Sophie would absorb the calm.

"Would you please take me through your morning?"

"Um, well, I got here around five. No. Wait. It was earlier, yeah, four-thirty."

"How did you enter the building?"

"I have a key for the back door."

"Gotcha. All right. You arrived at four-thirty through the rear door. What next?"

"I switched on the lights in the workroom area, this room, and the restroom. I have a daily checklist of duties. Got those done, and the last was to move my assigned cash drawer from the safe to the register."

"Okay. Let me back things up. Is there a building alarm?"

"Geez. Yes. I completely forgot to mention the alarm. Duh." Her face flushed. "Yes. The keypad is to the left as you enter the door. I hit the lights and then entered the code. And *then* I did the other stuff."

MC wrote quickly, but precisely. "Good. You unlocked the safe?"

"I did. Anyway, I had set my cash drawer on the counter and was booting up the computer when I heard this loud noise…a clank." Her voice shook and she cleared her throat.

"Where did the noise come from?"

"It sounded like it came from the dock. My first thought was the driver delivering our incoming mail was early. Or maybe raccoons were messing with the trash container. I walked toward the back. Then a man…he came in through the door, like out of nowhere. I swear I locked it behind me. The door. I don't know how he got in." She began to hyperventilate.

MC feared Sophie was going to pass out. She popped up from her seat. "Let's stop there for a second. Take a couple slow, deep breaths." MC bought a bottle of water and set it in front of Sophie. "Drink."

Sophie drank. "Sorry about freaking." She took a deep breath and slowly released it.

"You feel able to continue?"

"Yeah."

"Okay." MC checked her notes. "The man entered through the same door you'd come in earlier, correct?"

"Yes. But like I said, I'm positive I locked it." She knotted her hands together on the table. "Maybe I didn't."

The last thing MC wanted was for the woman to beat herself up over locking the door or not. "Let's revisit the door after we've made it through the whole incident. What happened next?"

Sophie gulped more water. "He had…the guy…had this black knit face mask, like snowmobilers wear. Holes for his eyes, nose, and mouth. No, that's not right. There was no hole for the nose, only the eyes and mouth. Yes. I thought it weird because who wears a mask in the middle of May." She nodded. "And…and he had a…a gun." She swallowed hard. "Pointed at me."

MC watched Sophie's face go from slightly flushed to white as new fallen snow, freckles dark dots sprayed across her cheeks and nose.

"Okay. Easy. Breathe. In. Out."

Sophie clenched and unclenched her fists. "Whew. This is rough."

"I know. Take your time." She gave the young woman an

empathetic smile.

As Sophie pulled herself together again, MC jotted notes.
"Okay. I'm good."

"All right. Just let me know if you need a minute. Back to the gun. Can you describe it?"

"Black. Squarish. Not huge. But, honestly, staring at it felt like I was facing a cannon." Her eyes widened. "I've never had a gun pointed at me in my twenty-six years on this earth. It was terrifying." She took another swallow from the bottle. "Gloves. He was wearing gloves. Black gloves. Not winter gloves. But similar to what a nurse at the clinic wears when she's giving you a flu shot."

Nitrile or latex gloves, black, MC wrote. "Good. Can you describe him physically?" He had enough sense to wear gloves to avoid leaving fingerprints.

"He was tall, but not super tall. Maybe six feet or an inch or two more? Kind of Ned's height. I couldn't see his hair because of the mask. He was wearing blue jeans and a black nylon windbreaker. He had on work boots, maybe." Eyes narrowed, she gazed past MC. "I can't remember the color. Or maybe they were hiking boots. Sorry."

"You're doing great. This is a lot of good information. What else? What happened next?"

"He asked me if anyone else was in the building. I thought about telling him I expected Ned any minute, but it wasn't true. I wanted to avoid making him angry. I couldn't think what to do but tell him no. Then he told me to turn around and show him where the money was. But I noticed him scoping out the office. Like he was searching for something."

What, besides money, would a robbery suspect be after in a post office? She drew a circle around this question. Stamps? But selling stolen stamps is not a huge money-maker.

"He jabbed the gun into my back and told me to face forward and keep moving. At the counter he made me hand him all the paper money from my cash drawer. No coins. Only cash, he'd said."

"How much do you suspect he got?"

"A hundred twelve dollars. The paperwork from yesterday will confirm how much money was left in my drawer when I closed out."

"Excellent. What next?"

"He put one hand on my shoulder and kept the gun at my back. Then he did this weird thing—he had me dump out all the mail sacks behind the counter." She shook her head. "It was the strangest thing. He kicked the mail and parcels, scattering stuff every which way, and at the same time tried to keep the gun pointed at me."

MC stopped writing for a second. Sophie was much calmer, and the story was flowing freely. Too freely? MC studied the younger woman. She didn't detect any signs of evasive body language. "Kicking mail around and holding you at gunpoint?"

"Yeah. But then he suddenly stopped and waved me over to the mess. Told me to spread it all out so he could see it. I did what he told me. The mail was already everywhere, and I spread it out more. I wasn't about to try and run or anything anyway. He got kinda angry at one point and pushed the empty rack over. Then had me stand against the wall. He got down and flipped the mail over like he was looking for something specific."

"Did he say anything?"

"He told me a couple times not to move. Otherwise, no. Finally, he kicked aside the empty sacks heaped next to the file cabinet. Maybe he was frustrated? Then of all things, he told me to set the rack up and pick up the mail. So I did."

MC puzzled through the information. Was it some dumb ploy to cover the robbery, or something else? A lot of time for someone to waste and chance being caught.

"I kind of struggled to set the rack upright and he helped. He levered the end up next to the file cabinet and his foot got tangled in an empty bag. Then when he backed away his jacket caught on one of the hooks. He yanked on it and yelled, 'piece of shit,' and then he told me to never mind him, and to pick up the mail. Then he kicked the rack. Maybe he was ticked off because he didn't find anything or because his jacket was messed up."

"Did he find anything in the mail? Take anything?"

"At first, I didn't think so. But after I had all the pieces picked up he told me to move into the corner behind the counter and face the wall. He had a fistful of mail and more stuck out of his jacket pocket. He instructed me to count to one hundred, said if I stopped or tried to call someone he'd know and he'd shoot me. The whole scene was surreal, like a bad cop show." She sighed. "But I didn't want to take a chance he was watching me."

"You made the safest and smartest decision, Sophie. Let me clarify, he never asked you at any point whether you had a phone? Never searched you?"

"No. He never asked. He never searched me."

"Okay. So you're counting to one hundred. Then what?"

"I did exactly what he said. When I reached one hundred, I immediately called 911, and then I called Ned. I walked through the work area and noticed a trail of mail. More than a dozen pieces, he'd presumably dropped on his way out. When I reached the door, it wasn't quite closed. I peeked out, but I didn't see or hear anyone or anything."

"When did Ned arrive?"

"He got here probably five to ten minutes after I called."

"Who picked up those mail pieces?"

"I did. Deputy Kempffer said I could go ahead and clean up. Then he took my statement, and Ned told him he'd called you guys, the inspectors. He said the postal inspectors would probably want to talk with me too and so Ned had me stay until you got here."

Why the hell would Kempffer have anyone clean up an active crime scene? Made zero sense. A spark of anger ignited deep in her belly. She had half a mind to track down the idiot right away. Ask him if he'd attended law enforcement training with Barney Fife or what. Incompetent dolt.

"I don't want to talk negatively about cops," Sophie said, "but I have to say Deputy Kempffer wasn't too concerned about what happened. Especially after Ned told him he'd notified you guys. Kempffer acted like it was a waste of his time to even be here. My observation, or opinion, I guess."

"Thank you for your honesty. Is there anything else you think is relevant?"

What was the suspect's deal with the mail? Had he been hoping to grab credit cards? How would he know which pieces fit the bill? Maybe he'd been on something and was upset he didn't get as much cash as he'd hoped and thought there'd be some cash in the outgoing mail. But why not have Sophie lead him to more money in the safe? Why mess with the mail? So many of the pieces didn't fit into the puzzle yet. She didn't even have the edge pieces in place, much less the heart of the puzzle.

"No," Sophie said. "That's all I remember."

"All right. Thanks. You've been extremely helpful."

MC decided her first order of business after getting a statement from Ned would be to track down Deputy Kempffer.

After MC got Ned's statement, she retrieved her evidence collection kit from the car, slipped on a pair of nitrile gloves, and did a walk through. Sophie showed her specifically where the suspect had been. Her search didn't turn up any evidence.

Unfortunately, Sophie was unable to determine exactly which pieces of mail the suspect had handled. The suspect wore gloves, so no benefit in trying to get prints.

She took a few photos of the office with her phone, especially the front counter area where the suspect and Sophie had spent the majority of the time during the crime. She was interested in the set-up of the rack holding sacks for different types of mail.

What had the guy been after?

MC completed her search of the crime scene and drove to the Lake County Sheriff's Office in Two Harbors. She was familiar with the LCSO from her previous drugs in the mail investigation. She was still stunned to think that the drugs investigation ultimately led to her uncovering Barb's murderers.

MC parked outside the Law Enforcement Center. The sun was still bright, but evening would soon dampen the light. She patted her coat pocket for her notebook.

Inside, she approached the bulletproof glass at the front desk. The woman glanced up. "May I help you?"

"Yes. I'm US Postal Inspector McCall. I'd like to speak with Deputy Kempffer." She held her ID up to the glass.

The woman glanced at the identification. "One moment, please." She picked up a phone. MC couldn't hear what she said but detected a note of annoyance. Then MC clearly heard her ask, "Do you want me to call Gunnar?" A pause, and the woman's eyes flicked toward MC. "I thought you might say that. I'll escort the inspector to the conference room." She stood. "I'll buzz you in and take you to meet Deputy Kempffer."

"Thank you. I'm sorry, I didn't catch your name."

"Lynette."

MC followed Lynette through the squad room and down a hallway, past the frosted glass door of Sheriff Gunnar Tollefsen's office to a door labeled Conference Room. The room contained an oval-shaped wood table and eight rolling faux leather chairs. MC chose a seat on the far side of the table, facing the door.

"Tyler...Deputy Kempffer will be here shortly." She hesitated. "Piece of advice. He's a hard-ass so watch your six."

"Good to know. Thank you, Lynette." Well, that was interesting.

She'd no sooner opened her notebook when a man entered. She stood. "Deputy Kempffer?"

"Who wants to know?" He stood ramrod straight, thumbs hooked in his utility belt. He oozed hypermasculinity. The attitude, along with his straw-colored hair styled in an undercut parted on the left and a tight fade, and the spit-shined boots, were signals that caused MC to question whether she could trust him. His mud-brown eyes bore into her, mouth a thin hard line.

She moved around the table and offered her hand. "US Postal Inspector McCall." He was barely taller than her. Giant ego but not giant in stature.

MC sat down.

Kempffer stood in place. "What's this about?"

"Why don't you have a seat, and we can discuss it?"

"I'm on duty and need to be back on the street. You feds don't have a clue what real policing is about. Think we have time to chitchat?" He made a scoffing noise. "Well, we don't."

Jesus. What a condescending dickhead. She really wanted to say that part out loud. "I'm not trying to waste your time, Deputy. I've been assigned to investigate the robbery at the Castle Cove Post Office. Ned Hargreve informed me you were first on scene. I'd like to know what you found and what you heard." She picked up her pen and met his stone-cold gaze.

She waited.

The silence ticked on for ten. Fifteen. Twenty seconds.

"I talked to the girl and I talked to Ned. They said the thief got away with some cash and made a mess by dumping out mail. A whole lotta nothing."

This guy was light on respect, not to mention cooperation. Lynette had been right, she'd need to watch her six around him.

"Wow. Must've taken you about thirty seconds to get those details. What else? C'mon, Kempffer. Believe it or not, I don't have time to play your game. Did you interview any people outside the post office? Neighbors? Anyone?" MC could be a hard-ass too. She smiled at him. "Let's call a truce. Give me a copy of your report and I'll be on my way. Deal?"

"Fine." He whirled around and stomped off.

He returned right quick with a photocopy of his report, which didn't amount to much more than what he'd already told her. The document confirmed her suspicions. He'd not bothered to talk to anyone outside the facility.

"Thank you. If you remember anything more or hear anything, I'd appreciate a call." She tossed a card on the table and walked out. Guys like him gave law enforcement a bad rep.

Lynette wasn't at her desk at the front. MC checked her phone and discovered it was after five.

In her car, she stuffed the photocopy of Kempffer's report into the front pocket of her messenger bag. Thought about going back in and having a face-to-face with Sheriff Tollefsen but decided to give Kempffer some leeway. See if he'd hang himself before she went over his head. She'd dealt with her fair share of asshats throughout her career. She had zero fucks left to give. People like him made retirement appealing, no matter how much she loved the job.

As she drove the ten miles to her "up north" home, a cabin on Lake Superior, she was tempted to veer into the strip mall and load up on Grey Goose. Instead, she continued up Highway 61 to Betty's Pies and asked for a Beargrease Burger and fries with a slice of Great Lakes Crunch pie to go.

Ten minutes later she drove into her cedar-sided two-car detached garage. The cabin, also cedar, lay beyond the garage. A couple of years earlier, MC and Barb had invested in a major renovation, making the place suitable for year-round occupancy. The update included a suite off the kitchen for Dara and Meg. The suite was sweet. It included a bathroom and combination bedroom/den with a queen-sized bed, two armchairs, a cherrywood accent table, and a thirty-two-inch TV. In the main cabin, the loft space, serving as a second living room, was the best feature and where MC spent most of her time. Floor-to-ceiling windows with an office alcove faced the lake and allowed the morning sun to brighten the space. On the opposite end, a TV fit for a small theater hung above a gas stone fireplace. Two cocoa-brown leather recliners and a walnut table sat in front of three north-facing windows. A sand-colored fabric couch and low-profile walnut and metal coffee table faced the TV.

She unloaded her overnight bag, work bag, and food from the car and locked the garage. What little yard existed was greening up nicely. The sidewalk to the house was a mess of sludge left after the snowmelt. She made a mental note to have someone come out and do a maintenance check on the central AC. Once inside she set her supper on the kitchen counter and stowed her overnight bag in the bedroom.

While she ate at the kitchen table, she scrolled through listings to find an AA meeting. She doubted she'd be back in the Cities for the Sunday one.

Two down, only four more to go. Then she'd be done. Finito. Over and out.

MC quickly finished her supper after she discovered a Friends of Bill W. meeting in the area. Either she hauled her butt to the meeting or picked up a handle of Grey Goose from the local liquor store. The meeting won, this time.

Gravel crunched beneath the car's tires as she navigated the unpaved road that meandered west off Highway 61 north of Castle Cove. On her left, a giant cross loomed into view, surrounded by a mound of boulders. The orange-yellow of the sinking sun gave the cross an almost evil glow and dulled the pile of rocks at its base. Directly behind the cross was a gravel parking lot with a handful of cars. The place of worship was basically a pole barn building with a big wooden cross bolted to the side.

She drove past an old farmhouse and slowed to a crawl in a turnaround. A long narrow building was on her right. The sign identified it as Whispering Aspen Ministries Meeting Hall, which was where the AA session would take place.

MC parked and entered the Meeting Hall. When she opened the screen door, she noticed a weathered wood sign reading Mess Hall nailed above the entrance. She'd seen online the place had been a summer camp decades ago.

In the lobby a reception desk was off to one side and straight ahead a stone fireplace and two comfortable-looking sofas. Beyond the entry, MC entered the actual hall. The gleaming oakwood floors were beautiful. The far wall consisted of floor-to-ceiling windows facing the forest behind the building. A set of sliding doors next to the windows probably led to a patio. In the center of the large room, a dozen blue, cushioned chairs, like the kind you'd find in a doctor's office, were arranged in a circle. Four were occupied.

A stainless-steel counter divided the kitchen from the old mess hall's eating space. Lined up across the surface were the requisite coffeepot of battery acid and bargain basement snacks.

A voice from behind her caught her flat-footed. "Feel free to help yourself."

She pivoted and stood face-to-face with Ned Hargreve, Castle Cove postmaster.

Didn't that just figure.

"Ned."

"Inspector McCall. Nice to see you again. Are you here for the Friends of Bill?"

She appreciated the option to make like she wasn't seeking an AA meeting. "Ah, yeah. Yes, I am. This is a bit awkward."

"We're all here for the same reason. But I understand your hesitancy. I'm the leader, ah, Trusted Servant, of this group."

Great. Even more awkward.

Ned said, "I gather by your silence you're thinking you should leave. I encourage you to stay. We don't have to let anyone know we've met prior to this moment."

"I guess." No. This is not good. I can't deal with this.

Yes, you can. Give the meeting a chance.

"I'll grab a seat then. Thanks."

Five more people straggled in and then Ned began the meeting. MC was the only participant without a copy of *The Big Book* in hand. A couple of the tomes were beat up, like they'd been through hell and back, probably reflective of the owners' struggles. Hers was still on the back seat of her car, the spine pristine.

The meeting wasn't horrible. The meeting also wasn't great. It just...was.

After the closing Serenity Prayer the majority of the group made a beeline for the refreshments.

MC grabbed a chair next to Ned. "Ned, don't take this the wrong way, but this," she waved her arm around the room, "feels too awkward for me. We have a professional relationship I'd like to keep separate from—well, from this. I think it would be in our best interests."

"I respect your feelings. Tell you what, I know of another meeting in the area, in Two Harbors, on Thursday evenings at six thirty. The Senior Center on Main Street."

"I appreciate your consideration. I'll see you in the morning. I need to go over a few more questions." She began to stand but then sank back onto the chair. "Can you tell me what this church is like? I read online the place used to be a summer camp for kids."

Ned glanced around before responding. "To be honest, I'm not sure. I'm not much of a churchgoer myself, although Pastor Thackeray keeps hounding me to come to Sunday service. I haven't heard anything bad per se, but I find the atmosphere off-putting or maybe more to the point, the pastor is off-putting."

"Do you think it's cult-like or something?"

"I don't think so. But Thackeray isn't like any other pastors I've known in my life. He's way more into working out, flexing his muscles and stuff. He's very involved with the youth, I've heard. I know he's chummy with some of the town's big players. The town supervisor. The county sheriff in Two Harbors." He stood.

She took the cue and did the same. "None of those bigwigs are in your social circle?" Would Ned push back and ask her why she wanted to know about his friends?

"No. I pretty much keep to myself. I've found it's a better way to live. Can't get into much trouble if it's me and my fishing pole. Besides, after working with people all day, I relish the peace and quiet. I guess to some I may seem reclusive, but I enjoy my own company. I do interact with others once a week." He waved an arm around the room.

"I wasn't trying to pry. Just to get a lay of the land. Believe me, I totally relate with the need for peace and quiet after working with people all day." Silence and a few calming glasses of vodka used to be her self-medicating wind-down ritual. "Thanks for the info. I'll be on my way. See you tomorrow."

When MC reached the door, someone opened it. She stopped in her tracks as a man with longish brown hair showing off a mountain of forehead barreled inside. He halted when he noticed her.

"Pardon." He stuck out a hand. "Pastor Thackeray."

He sure didn't strike MC as the pastor-type. Eyes the color of river rocks creeped her out. He embodied fifty-something gym rat rather than religious leader. She quickly shook his hand and refrained from wiping hers on her jacket. "Nice to meet you, Pastor."

"Ah, so you don't want to reveal your name to me. I get it." He tilted his head toward the room behind her, where the last couple of attendees were assisting Ned with the post-meeting clean up. "It's in the name, right? Anonymous and all." He grinned, showing teeth so bright she was momentarily blinded.

"Yeah, something like that."

"Well, God bless. I wish you success on your journey. If the spirit moves you, please feel free to join us for Sunday morning services. We welcome all."

Creepier still. "Right. Well, if you'll excuse me, I was on my way out."

He pushed the door open for her. "Have a good evening."

She exited and walked down the steps. Something felt totally off about him.

With each step through the parking lot the temptation to pick up a bottle of Goose on the way home pecked at her. Peck. Peck. Peck. Step. Step. Step.

No.

Stay strong.

Why? What's the point?

You know very well what the point is. Living your life. Keeping your job. Honoring your promise to your friends.

All true, but she didn't have to like the truth.

On the drive home MC decided she'd best attend the meeting in Two Harbors the next evening. The pull was strong to leap off the wagon. Plus, attending the Thursday meeting would bring her total to four. Only two more and she'd smash the promised goal. But who was counting?

Chapter Seven

Day two of the post office robbery investigation yielded nothing new. Frustration weighed MC down. She'd spent the morning with Ned at the Castle Cove Post Office. He'd been able to confirm the person had gotten away with one hundred twelve dollars in cash. Scant return on investment.

MC mulled over the scene Sophie Andersen had described. Why was the suspect so interested in the mail? If it weren't for the possibility...probability?...the suspect had stolen mail, MC would be tempted to turn the case over to LCSO to pursue. The dollar amount wasn't substantial enough to warrant dedicated Inspection Service resources. Since she'd been unable to confirm or deny he'd left with any mail in his possession, she'd keep the case for now.

Next, she walked the neighborhood around the post office and knocked on doors, but no one was home. Or if they were, they weren't in the mood to answer their doors. Tomorrow was another day.

On her way to her car parked behind the post office, she came across a portly gent with a wild, cotton-candyesque head of white hair, walking in the opposite direction. He had a toy poodle with an eerily similar hairstyle on a bright pink leash. "Excuse me, sir?"

He stopped and completed a pirouette toward MC, pulling gently on the leash. "Come, Princess." The dog, wearing a gold collar with embroidered glittering crowns, trotted smartly toward its owner. "Yes? What can I do for you?"

"I'm US Postal Inspector McCall." She showed her ID. "I was wondering if you and Princess were walking here between five and six yesterday morning?"

"As a matter of fact, Princess requires her early morning constitutional between five and six. We take four walks a day. The next—"

"Excellent. Did you happen to see anyone entering or leaving the post office when you were here?"

"Does this have to do with the robbery? I heard from Buster Crumbly the post office was robbed."

"Yes, I'm investigating that." MC jotted Buster Crumbly's name in her notebook. "Mr....sorry, I didn't get your name."

He scooped the fluffy dog into his arms. "This is Princess. I'm Hobie Jenkins."

"Mr. Jenkins, did you notice anyone out and about during that time?"

"We did. About scared the bejesus out of Princess. A man with a dark-colored jacket bolted from behind the post office and ran around the corner." He pointed over MC's shoulder.

"He came from the building and took off in the opposite direction from where you were?"

"Yes. We were walking toward the post office when I saw him. Took me by surprise to see anyone come from back there, and he wore something dark over his head." He set Princess on the ground and used his hands to indicate a pulling motion over his face and head.

"I think I get your drift, Mr. Jenkins. Face mask?"

"Could be, yep. Which I found strange because the weather's so mild now." He retrieved Princess from the ground and stroked the poof of hair atop her apple-sized head.

"Anything else you remember? How tall? Shoes? Was he carrying anything?"

"Now that you mention it, maybe he had something in his hand. A book? But no, not a book, wasn't the right shape." He scratched Princess's head again. "A phone? I couldn't quite see. The ordeal happened so quickly."

"You've been helpful. Thank you, Mr. Jenkins." She handed him a business card. "Would you mind contacting me if you remember anything else?"

He tucked Princess in the crook of one elbow and accepted the card. "We sure will let you know if we remember anything else." He stuck the card in the front pocket of his faded corduroy pants. "Have a good day, Inspector. Hope you find the villain." Hobie set Princess on the ground and set off down the street.

"Mr. Jenkins, one more thing." Jesus. Did those words come out of her mouth? Was she now channeling Jim Bob? "You mentioned a Buster Crumbly. Where would I be able to find him?"

"Buster spends most days from about ten in the morning to close at two with his butt parked on a stool at the cafe's counter. Drinking coffee and spouting off about the goings on in Castle Cove. He's what you might call a know-it-all. Or at least he thinks he knows it all." Hobie chuckled at his own joke.

"What's the name of the café?"

"The only eatery worth patronizing in this hamlet is Castle Cove Family Café."

"Thanks. You have a good day."

Hobie and Princess scampered away, the dog trotting in front of her master. Then it struck her. Hobie reminded her of Danny DeVito.

Her next destination was Two Harbors. She stopped at the Law Enforcement Center to check-in with Deputy Kempffer. The front desk was unoccupied, but a female deputy sat at a desk directly behind Lynette's. MC knocked on the glass to get her attention.

The deputy got up and approached. She was about MC's height, maybe slightly taller. Considerably younger. Dark brown hair cut short with some curl to it. No nonsense. Athletic build. She could be a soccer or rugby player.

"How can I help you?"

MC presented her credentials. "US Postal Inspector McCall. I was hoping to see Deputy Kempffer."

"He's out on patrol." She checked her watch. "He might be on his meal break. Usually, he eats at Betty's Pies."

"Great. About the time I get out there he could be gone."

"Is there something I can help you with, Inspector?"

MC squinted at the name stitched on the deputy's shirt.

"Well, Deputy Ekstrom, unless you have knowledge pertaining to the post office robbery yesterday morning—"

"In Castle Cove? No. Kempffer caught the call. Wasn't happy about it either." She opened her mouth to say more but then shut it.

Had she detected a hint of scorn in Ekstrom's voice? Maybe she thought Kempffer was as much a dick as MC did.

"Guess I'll try and catch him. I wanted to see if he'd remembered anything more."

"I can give you a copy of the report he filed."

"He provided the document yesterday when I was here. Though I practically had to twist his arm. Thanks, though."

"Typical Kempffer."

A door slammed somewhere behind the deputy. She threw a quick glance over her shoulder.

"Sorry. Checking if anyone was coming."

Ekstrom seemed on edge. Of course, could be MC projecting her own sense of unease. What had her nerves jangling?

"No worries. So you don't know anything about the robbery?" *Or why your fellow deputy didn't even bother to check out the crime scene.*

"I don't. I'm fairly new. Kempffer was my field training officer." She leaned forward and lowered her voice. "I honestly learned more on my own than I ever did with him. I think he has issues with women on the job."

"That tracks."

"Wish I could help you."

MC fished a card out and jotted her cell phone number on the back then slid it in the shallow well beneath the bullet proof glass. "Take this. If you hear anything or see anything related to the robbery, give me a call? My cell's on the back."

Deputy Ekstrom nabbed the card and slipped it in her uniform pants pocket. "Will do. Nice to meet you, Inspector McCall. Maybe we'll get to work together sometime."

With the afternoon growing late, MC drove to Betty's Pies to try to catch Kempffer. A county squad car was parked near the restaurant entrance. She might be in luck.

MC parked next to the squad car and weighed the benefits of attempting a discussion with Deputy Bad Attitude when the restaurant's door opened, and the man himself strolled out. He walked to the squad car, bent toward the driver's side mirror, and smoothed his hair. He probably thought his reflection should thank him.

Before he could crawl behind the wheel MC got out and called over her roof, "Deputy. A moment of your time?"

He spun toward her. Kempffer opened the car door, put one foot in. "I'm on patrol. I don't have time to sit around, fed. I got nothing to say to you."

"We can play it like that if you really want." MC walked around to the open door but kept out of his personal space. "I can go through your superior and we can all have a sit-down about this investigation. Either way works for me. I need info on my case."

Kempffer slid behind the wheel, his duty belt creaking. One hand rested on the inside door handle, the other on the steering wheel.

If he put up a stink, she'd have a reason to discuss matters with Sheriff Tollefsen. She'd worked with him peripherally when Barb's killers Nick Wooler and Quentin Laird had been busted a few months earlier. MC had been wound so tight chasing them she'd barely paid attention to the local officers she'd worked with. She remembered Sheriff Tollefsen had cooperated with the Inspection Service and St. Paul PD. No pushback. Normal interagency cooperation.

The memories rolled around like dice tossed down a craps table.

"What the hell do you want from me? Seriously? I gave you a copy of my report. I don't have anything else to share."

"Why'd you tell the postmaster it was fine to clean up the place? From what I've heard from the witnesses as well as what's not in your nothing burger of a report, you did absolutely zilch in the way of crime scene investigation. Why?"

"What was there to investigate? No one was hurt. Nothing was busted up. The suspect had gloves on, so what would be the point of dusting for prints? Surely you can see the logic in not wanting to waste my time and resources."

Because your time is so valuable. Her ire dialed up to eleven. "You didn't think, at the very least, taking photos of the crime scene was necessary?" Basic crime scene procedure and this arrogant tool couldn't be bothered?

"Like I said, nothing looked out of place so what good would pics do?" He examined the nails on his right hand, then his left.

"What about the fact Sophie reported the suspect was armed and had dug through the mail he'd had her dump on the floor? Didn't that pique your interest?"

MC wanted to slap the shit out of this asshat who was completely unconcerned about a legit crime in his jurisdiction. How do people like him make it into any agency?

"Nope. Not at all. I never gave it one damn minute of thought. Truth be told, I don't care what you think. Now, if you don't mind, I need to get back on patrol. Go with God, Inspector." He slammed the door and within seconds had backed out and driven down the hill to the highway.

Go with God? What the hell? Rooted to the spot, she stared at the vacant parking space. Every fiber screamed for a barrel of vodka.

She put Kempffer on the back burner but fully intended to have a frank discussion with the sheriff very soon.

In her car, she did a quick Google search of taverns in the Castle Cove area. The Dirty Minnow topped the list. MC considered her options and put the car in gear.

A few minutes before 6:30 that evening, dressed in jeans and a lightweight flannel shirt over a white tee, she walked into the Two Harbors Senior Center for the AA meeting. Nearly a dozen people milled about. The requisite circle of chairs was set up in the middle of the tiny space. MC made a beeline for the table where a Harvest Gold colored West Bend coffee maker was set up and flanked by two towers of white Styrofoam cups.

She grabbed a cup and filled it with steaming brew. With only powdered creamer available she decided to take it straight. She moved away to allow others access and scoped out the room.

"Not half bad, huh?" said a voice next to her.

A woman dressed in a faded denim shirt and similarly faded jeans stood next to MC. Blond, wavy, shoulder-length hair framed an oval face, and hazel eyes lit up the room. The woman's hair color was nearly identical to Barb's. MC's heart fluttered.

The woman studied MC. Finished her coffee and set the cup on the table near a stack of napkins. "You okay? You're a bit pale. First time?"

"Not my first meeting, but my first time here."

"Figured as much. My name is Ellen."

"MC."

A short, wiry man with ice-gray hair shorn close to his scalp called out, "Okay, folks, let's gather. It's time."

"Welp. Ready or not, here we go." Ellen moved toward the circle.

MC dumped her half-full cup in the trash. She sat across the circle from Ellen, facing the door. Last thing she needed was a twinge of...what? Attraction? Guilt? Whatever had jolted through her moments earlier. Focus. She needed complete focus. Not to mention it was way too soon to even think about feelings for another woman. Barb had only been gone for six months. Jesus, McCall. What are you thinking?

Once again, she was the only one who hadn't lugged in *The Big Book*. She drifted during the opening prayer. Then the meeting leader, Trusted Servant, she reminded herself, asked a member to read through the twelve steps. Then he asked if anyone wanted to share about the step he'd chosen for discussion. Which step was it?

She'd not paid attention. Well, she had no intention of sharing anyway. MC tuned out the folks droning on about their addiction trials and tribulations. Her goal was to get through the hour and add to her tally.

Try to empathize. Learn from others' experiences and you might not feel so alone.

Barb was overridden by a softer, more present voice. "Step Six isn't so much about God removing the defects of my character. I'm not quite sure I believe in God, as you all have heard me say many times. I do believe in some higher power out there in the universe." Ellen swirled a hand above her head.

MC sat up straight. She couldn't meet Ellen's gaze. Instead, she stared at the wood floor where Ellen's feet rested. Nice Keen hiking boots.

Ellen continued. "What resonates for me is I choose to change. It's taken me a while to grasp it's not something I do once and move on. I wake up each morning and decide I will change. That day. The following day. The day after. Ad nauseam. Change is my life-long commitment. Because without the commitment, I'd dive right back into the bottle."

Each word Ellen uttered pierced MC's skin and rocketed into

her bloodstream. Ellen was the first person who'd said anything that made one scintilla of sense.

After the ending Serenity Prayer a couple people darted out, but the majority stuck around and pitched in cleaning up. MC hesitated but then decided to beat feet, her usual mode after a meeting.

Ellen came up to her, a folding chair in one hand. "Hey, MC, right?"

"Yup." She side-stepped toward the door.

"Wait. I was wondering if you wanted to go grab a cup of coffee at Harbor Java. They're open until nine during the week."

Alone? Nope. Can't do it. Bad idea.

"I…ah. It's not a good time. I've got…" Work. Laundry to do.

"Hey, it's okay. I thought it would be fun to get to know each other outside of this." She swept her arm around the room. "I don't know about you, but I can always use a friend."

Friend. Get a grip, McCall. What did you think she was after? Jesus.

"Sure. That'd be great. But not tonight. Another time?"

Ellen grabbed MC's hand and pressed a folded napkin into her palm and closed MC's fingers over it. "Another time would be awesome. Call me. Or maybe I'll see you here next week."

"Maybe." MC stuffed the napkin into her pocket. "Have a good week." She executed an exit stage-left, like old Snagglepuss, and was out the door.

The drive home was a blur. MC felt like a dislodged piece of space junk orbiting the earth, nothing tethering her. She pulled into the garage, and next thing she knew she was at her kitchen table. How had she gotten here?

Shock. Guilt. A slow burn built up inside her. An icy glass of the Goose would smooth out the rollercoaster ride.

No.

She jumped up from the chair and wrenched the fridge open. A can of sparkling water was the first item to catch her eye.

A better choice.

Her thoughts careened like an out-of-control Indy 500 car. Plenty of to-dos to keep her mind off booze. Castle Cove was a peculiar situation. Asshat Deputy Kempffer ought to be knocked down fifty notches, and she had no compunctions about tackling the task. Last, but far from least, how to handle the AA situation and the added complication of Ellen.

But was it a complication? Or was she making it a complication?

She leaned against the fridge and cracked the can open. What had happened? Was she a lunatic?

Who knew what Ellen thought. One thing was certain, she wasn't attending AA to find friends. AA was a task to be checked off a list of tasks. Two more meetings would take care of it.

You shouldn't feel guilty about making a connection. You need connections. That's how you survive. Don't wall yourself off from the world. She's nice. You can never have too many friends.

MC removed the napkin from her pocket and slowly unfolded it.

Ellen Bensen. 555-642-1022. Call anytime.

"Tyler, don't forget you need to get the kids' groups started at six-thirty. Then come back to the house." Pastor Thackeray, dressed head to toe in Under Armor, left his workout pals, Town Supervisor Bradford Symons and Deputy Tyler Kempffer, doing bench presses in the fully equipped gym in his basement. Not waiting for Kempffer's reply, he jogged across the wide yard to the rear entrance of the Meeting Hall. A quick stop in his office to don his 18k gold cross on a chain and pick up one of the kids' favorite items, his Star Wars Jedi Luke Skywalker Lightsaber, and he was ready to get the evening rolling.

The clock on his office wall showed 6:15 p.m. Up above, the steady murmur of voices rang out. He'd unlocked the three lower-level rooms earlier. The children's group, PreK to fifth, met in the Yellow Room with an older teen overseeing them. The youth group was broken out into two smaller categories. Sixth through eighth met in the Blue Room, and ninth through twelfth in the Green Room.

The adults met above in the Main Hall or Mess Hall as some still called it, for Bible study. Thackeray was trying a new spin this year, mixing the men and women instead of separate groups on separate days. With more adults present, he was allowed the flexibility to work one-on-one with the youth. The grade-schoolers especially. They were perfectly malleable.

Halfway through the evening, the adults would take a break and prepare snacks for the kids. The teens were in charge of hauling the snacks from the main-level kitchen to the three kids' rooms in the lower level. The rule was everyone helped clean up at the end. Sometimes it became quite a fiasco, especially with the younger ones if they were overtired, wound up, or cranky.

Thackeray passed a group of middle-schoolers shoving each other on their way down the stairs. The screwball antics quickly ceased when they noticed him coming up the stairs.

"Good evening, kids."

"Hi, Pastor." Several voices of varying octaves responded.

"Let's be careful on the steps. Keep in mind Matthew 7:12, 'So in everything, do to others what you would have them do to you, for this sums up the Law and Prophets.'"

"Law and profs? What?" A boy who Thackeray knew to be a class clown asked. His posse of friends snickered and high-fived him.

"Boys." Thackeray's voice reverberated. He caught a glimpse of a slender blond girl who sidled around the pack of boys and continued down the stairs. Gracie. Hmm. He knew who he was going to choose as the special guest tonight. First, he needed to insinuate the fear of God into the obstreperous kids. "There's a time and place for goofing, and scripture isn't one of them. Perhaps you all need to study the Bible more and play fewer games. Keep the devil at bay. I'll inform Youth Pastor Kempffer to let your group leader know tonight will be Bible-focused."

"Aw, Pastor..." The jokester zipped his lips when Thackeray stared him down.

"The point of the verse, boys, is I want you to be nice to each other. We don't want anyone to get hurt. No roughhousing on the stairs. Right?"

A chorus of, "Yes, Pastor," followed him up the staircase.

Then he heard one of the kids say, "What's up with the gold cross and the gym clothes? I think it's weird that he carries a stupid lightsaber. What's a toy got to do with religion? I told my parents I'm sick of this place. I don't need none of this God crap."

"Shut up, man. You want pastor to hear you and get us all in even more trouble?"

Thackeray reached the top of the stairs as Kempffer came in the front door. "Tyler, there's a handful of middle-school boys who are having doubts about their faith. See what you can do about getting them on track. I already informed them no games, Bible study only."

Kempffer blew out a long sigh. "I think I know who you're referring to. Little snots. I'll make sure to assign them a bunch of Bible verses to memorize. I'll let the room leader know they're not allowed any game time tonight. Who're you picking for special time?"

"I have someone in mind. First, I need to put in an appearance with the Bible study folks."

"Can't wait." Kempffer fist-bumped Thackeray and went down the stairs to get the evening rolling.

Thackeray checked in with the adult group. Once he made sure they were on track, he returned to the lower level and slipped into the Yellow Room. One of the girls who was due to graduate high school in June was instructing the kids on truth. Twelve kids sat on the floor in a circle around her. Room Leader girl—what was her name again? she asked for a volunteer to read a short prayer. Very few hands shot up, but most of them couldn't read yet anyway. PreK-fifth was a pretty wide span in ability.

Room Leader pointed at a tow-headed boy, and Thackeray's grip on his lightsaber tightened. His heart rate kicked up a notch. Cole Norberg. His voice warbled then got stronger as he recited, "God, we w-w-want to live by your truth. Help me—us—to have truth in our hearts and to believe and act on your words. Amen."

A chorus of amens followed.

"Excellent." Pastor moved toward the circle, lightsaber at his side. He saw some faces brighten. He wanted to believe he was the reason, but more than likely it was the toy sword. One face—Cole's—shut down. No light.

Room Leader girl said, "Welcome, Pastor."

"Thank you." He hit the switch, and the lightsaber blade lit up. "I bet you all know what this means." He waved it over his head.

Little hands clapped. Someone piped up, "Someone gets to go with the pastor."

"Exactly right. Pray with Pastor time." He paced around the outside of the circle. "Who will be the lucky one? I know, let's let the sword choose." He quickened his pace.

The pool of little faces watched in anticipation.

"Pick me!"

"No. Pick me!"

Room Leader said, "Shhh. Settle down and let's see who the pastor chooses." Her hands were folded in front of her as she smiled at the group.

"I feel the pull." Pastor Thackeray jerked forward as if the sword were dragging him. "It's getting stronger." He came to a stop directly behind Cole and placed the lightsaber on his thin shoulder blade. "Cole. I hereby knight you. You have been chosen."

Some clapping and some sniffling ensued. Room Leader kicked things into gear. She clapped her hands twice. "Quiet, please. We're all happy for Cole. Everyone over to the tables. We'll continue this week's lesson on truth."

Cole sat unmoving, staring at the floor, as the other children tore off in their assigned directions.

"Cole?" Pastor squatted in front of him. "Time for special prayer time with me. Come on. Youth Pastor Kempffer will join us soon."

Cole stood and meekly walked out with Thackeray. He didn't

utter a word as they exited the lower level via the rear door by the pastor's office and made their way across the wide yard to the pastor's home. The boy trudged along, head down.

Thackeray had half a mind to prod the kid with the lightsaber. "Come on, Cole. Let's move a little faster." Finally, after what felt like a forty-day walk, they entered the house. A door straight ahead led into the kitchen and another to the basement. Thackeray guided Cole down the stairs.

At the bottom of the steps to the left was an eight-by-eight carpeted area with a reclining gaming chair, an L-shaped couch, and a couple bean bag chairs. A flat screen TV was mounted on the wall, with a gaming system and controllers set out on a table beneath it. An iPad was charging next to the gaming system. The area was sectioned off by six-foot-high privacy screens.

To the right was a kitchen with a sink, refrigerator, and microwave. Cabinets above and below the sink completed the section.

The remainder of the basement, a huge space, maybe fifteen-by-thirty feet, was filled with free weights, a couple weight-lifting benches, a treadmill, a BowFlex, and two elliptical machines. Thick mats protected the concrete floor. A smaller TV was on the far wall with a news channel on mute.

Cole stood absolutely still. Thackeray pushed him toward the "game den" as he liked to call it. "You go get comfortable, Cole."

The boy's gaze was locked in on something behind Thackeray. He swiveled to see Bradford Symons emerge from a door at the far end of the basement. The town supervisor wore gym clothes and a Lone Ranger-type eye mask.

"Excellent choice, Pastor." Symons tipped a half-full glass of amber liquid in Thackeray's direction.

"What have I told you about imbibing in front of the kids?"

"Pardon my French, young man." Symons glared at Thackeray. "Fuck off. I'll drink what I want, when I want." And to prove his point he drained the glass and set it in the sink.

Thackeray clenched his fists and mumbled under his breath about language.

"What, Pastor?" Symons asked. "Watch my language? How about you don't worry about my language and get the praying done so we can get the games started? I've prepped the playroom." He rubbed his hands together.

"I was thinking of going back to get another lucky kid. I think Cole's tired." He glanced at the practically catatonic boy.

"Nah, next time get two. We've wasted enough time tonight. Let's get this show on the road." Symons rested a hand on Cole's knobby shoulder. "What do you say, fella? Ready for some fun with the Lone Ranger?"

Thackeray nudged Symons aside. "Cole?"

No response.

"Cole, let's pray." He reached for the kid's hands.

Cole flinched and backed up a couple steps. Still silent.

"Remember, Cole, we must all follow God's will. You don't want to disappoint God, right? You don't want to upset your parents because you're not obeying God."

"R-rright," The barest of whispers. Cole, eyes the deep vivid color of cornflower blooms, finally locked gazes with the pastor.

"Good boy. God speaks to me and what I tell you is what God has told me to tell you. Something for you to remember. Now let's have a quick prayer. Then we'll go play."

"But I didn't get to do any video games yet." Cole's bottom lip quivered.

"I know, son, but we're a bit behind tonight, so next time I'll let you have double the time. Okay? If you're good tonight, it may be the night you get your big reward. But only if you behave and do God's will. Remember, Jesus loves you and loves you even more when you obey. Right?"

"I guess." Cole's eyes filled with tears.

"Time's a wasting." Symons's tone indicated he was losing patience fast.

Thackeray made a mental note to remind Symons to dial it down and not freak out the kids. Otherwise their secret club could be unveiled, and they'd be toast.

"Cole, you know how this works. I'm going to blindfold you now, and we'll go to the secret playroom. Remember, this is God's will. You must obey and not talk about any of these special activities. Keep in mind, if you're extra good and pray extra hard, there will be a prize for you when you leave."

"Yes, Pastor." Cole's voice was barely a whisper.

"Let's go already," Symons said.

The two men guided Cole across the basement into the closet and flipped the light switch on. Once the door was closed, they moved to the backside of the storage room. Thackeray reached behind a metal shelving unit stocked top to bottom with cleaning supplies. He found the button and pressed it.

A door flush with the rear wall whispered open a few inches. Thackeray pulled the door wide revealing concrete steps leading down into a space dug fifteen or twenty feet below the basement level. In the 1950s, the original owner of the house hired a contractor to install a fallout shelter. The bunker was steel and concrete, possibly lead-lined, and measured thirty-by-thirty feet.

The room contained an ancient air return machine, a wall safe, shelving, and an escape hatch with a round steel cover. The hatch opened to a tunnel, which ended up in the backyard some seventy-five feet away from the house. A manhole cover hidden in a small grove of red pines marked the tunnel's exit.

Thackeray discovered this secret bunker when he'd taken over the church and the house. The previous pastor had never mentioned it. Thackeray wondered if he'd even realized the shelter existed. All wondering aside, he couldn't believe his luck in unearthing the hidden treasure. The perfect place for him and his friends to entertain themselves.

Symons descended first, followed by Cole, with Thackeray bringing up the rear. Once they were all on the stairway, he hit another button to close the panel.

At the bottom of the steps the threesome shuffled along a short hallway to a metal door. A black phone was mounted on the wall next to the door, with a matching phone on the inside. Probably for communication in the event of a nuclear threat.

He, Symons, and Kempffer had set up a mattress on the floor against a wall with a slew of stuffed animals arranged across the top. Behind it, they'd hung a black cloth to cover the concrete block. Two cameras on tripods, and lights on stands, were placed at different angles at one end of the mattress for video and still photos. Kempffer did most of the equipment setup and handling. As the newest member of the group, Kempffer was slowly allowed more playtime once Thackeray had convinced Symons he was trustworthy.

Thackeray and Symons had been actively building up their hobby for a couple years. A year earlier, they'd allowed Kempffer in. He was the one who'd suggested they could not only have their needs satisfied, but they could make a ton of money if they recorded their sessions and sold the images and videos to other like-minded people via the internet. He'd assured them there was a highly lucrative market for their type of entertainment.

Hence, the business was born. Who said you couldn't mix business with pleasure?

As added cover, Thackeray made Kempffer the youth pastor. The teens loved him because at age thirty, he was more than twenty years younger than Thackeray and appealed to them. He also played guitar, which the kids thought was cool.

Even though he was older, Thackeray was good at, in his mind anyway, luring kids in. All the "fun" they had access to as the pastor's chosen one on any given week made them want to return. Well, most of them anyway. Cole was his favorite lately, but the boy was exhibiting problematic behavior. Like how he and his sister Gracie, the little troublemaker, had acted in front of Ned last Sunday evening. Thackeray didn't need nosy Ned asking questions about those kids. He was more worried about Ned than Gracie and Cole's parents. They loved to leave their kids at the church so they could blow their paychecks at the Dirty Minnow, sucking down off-label gin and beer while losing even more money playing electronic pull-tabs. Not great Christian examples for their kids, but a great cover for Thackeray. Who would question the good pastor showing extra attention to the kids of chronic alcoholics?

Thackeray needed things to stay status quo now that he and his partners had built their predilections into a thriving side-hustle. None of them were great at manipulating and marketing photos and videos in their niche market, but Kempffer had discovered a young lad who was a tech wizard. Kempffer recorded all the playroom activities and then passed the camera SD cards to his minion, who handled all the finer details of production, marketing, sales, and distribution. Luckily with no questions. For these services they paid him handsomely. Kempffer was the go-between and kept Thackeray and Symons's identities secret, as well as not naming the tech guy. Plausible deniability kept the wheels in motion.

Chapter Eight

Jamie shuffled papers on his desk. "What's the latest on the Castle Cove situation?"

MC sat across from him mainlining caffeine. "Castle Cove. Zero physical evidence. A decent enough description of the suspect's clothes and general physical build from the clerk, the only employee on duty at the time. The guy was wearing a knit ski mask over his face, so we have no identifying attributes. Don't get me started on the deputy who answered the initial 911 call and his absolute lack of investigation." She set her cup on the corner of Jamie's desk and opened her notebook. "Deputy Tyler Kempffer. Guy has a chip the size of a boulder on his shoulder. Not sure why."

"Will he be a problem?" He met MC's gaze head-on. The overhead lights reflected off the lenses of his glasses.

"Don't worry, I won't lose my cool. At least not right away. He's totally non-cooperative. Tried to refuse to give me a copy of his report. In hopes of motivating him, I did mention a possible heart-to-heart with Sheriff Tollefsen. Then I got a copy of the report. But still, he's unprofessional and doesn't play well with others."

"You're nothing if not professional. So no leads at all?"

"Not currently. I've done a few knock-and-talks around the neighborhood, and so far no one saw anyone or heard anything suspicious. I'll revisit the houses where no one answered, but I'm not holding my breath."

"Keep me posted." He slipped a folder to the top of the stack in front of him. "Jim Bob is knee-deep in the mail thefts. Kid is holding his own though. I'm liking what I've seen."

Obviously, Jim Bob's infatuation with Columbo hadn't irked Jamie. "Good to hear. By the way, I need to get out of here. I have an appointment at one this afternoon. Then back to Castle Cove. I'll keep you posted."

Before she left MC gave Pearl a drink of water. "Keeping you fresh, girl." She was bemused by the one-way talks with Pearl.

Midday traffic to St. Paul was like driving in a live game of Frogger. MC arrived at Dr. Zaulk's office with two minutes to spare, her head aswirl. The robbery, Meg's radiation, getting through the AA meetings, and the possibility of a new friend as a result of the latest AA session. So much. Good thing it was Dr. Z time.

They'd both settled into their respective regular seats in Dr. Z's office. MC was less than settled. She crossed, then uncrossed her legs.

Dr. Z asked, "Would you like a bottle of water before we begin?"

"No, thanks." MC picked at her thumb nail. A new tic. Not something she'd noticed doing in the past. Why was she so nervous? Scared? Almost like a tweaker jonesing for the next fix. Drugs. Alcohol. Addiction was addiction.

MC did a deep, slow breathing exercise.

Dr. Zaulk asked, "Do you feel ready to begin?"

"As ready as I'll ever be."

"During our last session you shared a memory of four-year-old you and your sister Cindy. Specifically, the day Cindy died. Have you processed the feelings?"

"I came to realize why July fourth is a day I'd rather not think about. The reason has nothing to do with fireworks and drunk people."

"Can you tell me more?"

"Well, I was mad at my sister. I guess mad at my parents, too, because they wouldn't let me go with the big kids. But once Mom and Dad were busy with the other adults grilling and setting up the food, I snuck off anyway." She closed her eyes and drew in a deep breath, then exhaled slowly. "I tracked down the older kids by the falls. The footbridge at the top of the falls to be exact. They were taking turns climbing on top of the wall and scaling it the length of the bridge. Mostly the boys were doing it. I stood on the bridge, maybe ten feet away from the group. One of them I think got scared and said the wall wasn't safe, it was falling apart, and he hopped down fast. I think his name was Pete, and he was in Cindy's grade."

"What happened next?" Dr. Z's voice was low and steady.

"Cindy. She..."

"She what, MC?"

MC grasped the arms of the chair.

"Relax. Take your time."

She released her grip and continued. "Cindy scampered up the wall like nobody's business. No fear at all. At the top she proclaimed, 'You're a 'fraidy cat, Pete.' Then she twirled like a gymnast on the balance beam." The movie played in slow-motion behind her eyes. "I was proud, *my* big sister showed up a dumb boy. But then I saw him, Pete the wimp, creeping up behind Cindy. He reached toward her. At first, I froze. But then I yelled at her: 'Cindy! Watch out! He's gonna push you.' She turned toward Pete.

Or was it me she sought?"

MC's world then and now tilted. The sensation of free falling overcame her, much like when you're on the verge of falling asleep and the world drops away, jerking you awake.

Tears slid silently down her cheeks. "Cindy was gone. I couldn't see her. All the kids in the pack screamed. They wouldn't stop screaming. Pete, the little creep, I swear he had a smile on his face. When he saw me looking at him, the tears flowed like a faucet, and he ran yelling for his mom. I edged toward the wall. I had to find Cindy. But then someone scooped me up and hustled me to a car. Not our car. Neither of my parents was driving. They stuck me in the back seat. I closed my eyes. Must've fallen asleep because I woke up later on the couch at home. Chaos reigned supreme the rest of the day."

"I'm so sorry, MC. That is a horrible experience. But you must know you are not to blame for Cindy's death."

"How do you figure? If only I'd kept my big mouth shut, she wouldn't have lost her balance." MC wanted to smack her fists against the sides of her head and knock the memories out. "Or if I'd listened to my parents, none of it would've happened."

"Or it's possible Pete would've succeeded in pushing Cindy, resulting in the same outcome. Or they wouldn't have chosen to scale the wall and instead played tag. Or...and on and on. There are what-ifs and ors for every situation. We can only address what did happen. And you are not to blame."

All these years MC had vacillated between blaming herself and blaming Pete for Cindy's death. She'd never told anyone.

"It's peculiar, but right after it happened, I couldn't remember what I'd seen. Then one day at school a classmate said something to me. Pete's brother. He said Pete had told him Cindy's head had busted open like a watermelon on the rocks under the falls."

"Jesus," Dr. Zaulk said so quietly, MC wasn't even sure she'd spoken.

"But it didn't make sense. I remember him grinning then fake-crying and running for his mommy. He didn't look over the wall. Not that I remember."

"Did you tell your parents about this boy?"

"They're the ones who told me Cindy had died. I asked how. I was so confused. I didn't know if I was remembering what happened or making it up in my head. They sat me down and told me in monotone voices there had been a horrible accident. Period. They weren't going to talk about it anymore. Going forward, we never did. Then when Barb was killed, I blamed myself again. I should've been home with her. I could've saved her. If only I had…then Cindy would be alive. If only I had…then Barb would be alive. See the pattern?"

"MC, there is no pattern. You are not responsible for Cindy and Barb's deaths."

No one knew how gutted she was over those two intrinsically connected deaths in her life. Now as these memories unleashed, she felt flayed wide open. She swiped her shaky hands down her face to erase the tears. "If you say so." A couple gulps of air steadied her. "Whew. That was a lot, huh?"

"Yes. It was. But I'm glad you finally got it out. Progress only comes with hard work."

"Hard work. Yeah, story of my life these days." She gave a half-hearted laugh.

"Let's schedule again for next week. Continue journaling. Have you tried a mindfulness app? I advise you to keep up with AA too. I know it's a lot, but again, hard work."

"Not yet on the mindfulness thing. Truth be told, this past week I haven't done much journaling either. Work has ramped up. But I have managed to keep up with AA. In fact I did two meetings last week. The first one wasn't a good fit, so I opted for a different one in Two Harbors, which worked better." Not to mention I met a woman who I think was hitting on me. Or at the very least wanted to become friends. Guess what? I responded by running away like a scared kid. A story for another day.

Jesus, she could use about a gallon of vodka. Her mantra at the end of every Dr. Z session.

MC found both Dara and Meg inside Flannel. "You're both here. What a great day." Too much enthusiasm? The last thing she needed was for Dara to think she'd been hitting the bottle.

Meg hurried from behind the counter and wrapped MC in a bear hug. "I'm so glad to see you. I thought Dara said you were out of town for work."

"Yeah, what's the deal?" Dara's voice echoed across the cafe. Luckily the only two customers present were glued to their computer screens with headphones over their ears.

"Thought I'd pop in to say hello. Hopefully, you'll reward me with a vat of coffee for the road."

"Say no more." Meg clasped MC's hand. "Dara, get MC what she needs."

"I always do." Dara mumbled and slapped the tap of the dark roast urn to fill up a large cup. "So why you in town?"

MC peeked over the counter toward the kitchen. "No Zane

today?"

Dara said, "Not until later. He's closing tonight."

"Great. Well, tell him I said hello."

They gabbed about various and sundry bits of the latest in their respective lives. MC was glad to see Meg's energy level had picked up. The radiation was going well. Dara yammered about business being on an upswing, mostly, until MC's cell phone rang.

"Sorry, gals. Gotta take this." She pivoted away. "Inspector McCall."

"Inspector, Ned Hargreve here. From Castle Cove?"

"Hi, Ned. What can I do for you?"

"I think it might be more what I can do for you." A skim of static fizzed in her ear.

"I'm listening."

"Thought I'd lost you there for a second, not always the best reception up here. Anyway, the weekend custodian found a wallet behind the file cabinet up front by the window. The cabinet is next to the metal rack where we stage the mail sacks, the ones the robber dumped out. The wallet doesn't belong to anyone who works here."

Whoa. "Hold onto it. I'm down in the Cities, but I'm about to jump on the road. Should be there by six depending on traffic."

"Do you want me to have Deputy Kempffer pick it up and hold it at the sheriff's office for you?"

"No." Easy, McCall. No need to let Ned know about the beef between her and Kempffer. "Keep it at the post office, and I'll come directly there."

"I'll stick around here until you arrive then.

"Thanks, Ned." MC pocketed her phone.

MC reached for the cup. "Sorry to cut our visit short, but as they say, duty calls."

Dara said, "I already put cream and sweetener in, so you're good to go."

"You're the best. Thanks." She blew kisses, made like a baby, and headed out.

The coffee was exactly what the doctor ordered. The caffeine provided her with a burst of mental energy. But the rejuvenation did a number on her bladder about halfway into the drive.

She stopped at Toby's in Hinckley to use the restroom, fill the gas tank, and grab a bottle of water. She was about to pull away from the pump and get back on the road when her phone rang. Jamie's number filled the screen. "Hey."

"MC, I was hoping you'd answer. Didn't want to leave a long voice mail."

"What's up?"

"I've got something new. Our liaison inspector at the National Center for Missing and Exploited Children contacted us. They received a tip from someone at cloudvault dot com, a cloud storage service."

"Sounds ominous."

"A user stored Child Sexual Exploitation images in an account on the cloud."

"Jesus, CSE. What's wrong with people?" MC grabbed her notebook and pen. "Hold on a sec. I want to write this down." She pinned the notebook open against the steering wheel. "Okay, go."

"A manager at the company provided the email and IP address, which tracks to a location in Castle Cove. A church. I'll email you the details. I figured since you're already in the area you could check it out."

"Got it. I've an update on the robbery for you. The postmaster in Castle Cove called earlier. His custodian found a wallet behind a file cabinet while cleaning yesterday. My first stop will be to retrieve it. Hopefully, there's an ID. If I get a hit I can pay the owner a visit. Then I'll check into this new thing."

"Great. Keep me posted. If I hear any more from NCMEC, I'll pass it along."

"Copy that."

When it rains it pours. She'd been craving a more challenging case. Now she was up to her eyeballs in cases. All the better to keep her occupied and away from the liquid hellfire.

Ned stood inside the front door of the Castle Cove Post Office. MC pulled to the curb and gave the horn a toot to get his attention. He waved and came out.

"Sorry, Ned. I got here as quick as I could."

"Not a problem, Inspector. I needed a break and thought I'd check for you. And here you are." He held the door open for MC, followed her in, and locked up. "The wallet is on my desk. I'm closing today, so I have tasks I need to attend to. Feel free to use my office as long as you need."

"Thanks. But first, could I bother you to show me where the custodian found the wallet?"

Ned walked her behind the counter past the sack rack the suspect had dumped over. Next to it was a four-drawer, gray metal cabinet.

MC asked, "What's in the cabinet?"

"Office supplies. Files not requiring secure storage. Some decorations. Miscellaneous stuff."

"Does the custodian always move the cabinet to clean?"

"I think she has it on a once per month rotation. It so happened yesterday was the due date."

"When had the previous cleaning happened?"

"April nineteenth. Third Sunday of the month."

"No wallet in April. Wallet shows up in May. Lucky break. Hopefully." But how could the wallet have ended up where it did?

She moved the mail rack aside to get closer to the cabinet, which wasn't flush against the wall because of the molding along the floor. She took out her phone and snapped several photos. "All right, got 'em."

"Let me know if you need anything."

"Sounds good. Thanks, Ned."

MC sat at Ned's desk, grabbed a pair of gloves from her pocket, and pulled them on. The slate gray nylon wallet was a bifold with a Velcro flap closure. Inside she found fourteen dollars in cash, a Visa credit card in the name of Caleb Lewis, a Mastercard debit card for First Bank of Two Harbors also in the name of Caleb Lewis, a stamp card for Two Harbor Sub Shop, and an opaque plastic photo sleeve containing a few photos of a woman and a young boy. Likely the same twosome, taken over the years, showing age progression of the boy from a chubby baby, to a toddler, and the latest, elementary school-age. She extracted each photo and flipped them around to find only blank white space. No identifying information.

Wife and son of Caleb? Girlfriend and son?

Surprisingly, no driver's license. She prodded every nook and cranny and slot of the wallet and found nothing more.

Caleb Lewis. She had a name. Better than nothing.

She jotted a note in her notepad and then stuck the wallet in an evidence bag in case it ended up being actual evidence. Then she followed the screech of equipment being moved around in the rear of the building. Ned stood in the center of a herd of empty hampers and carts.

"Hey, Ned? Sorry to interrupt."

"Not a problem. What do you need?"

"Do you recognize the name Caleb Lewis?"

Ned stroked his short-cropped silver beard. "Doesn't ring any bells. I can ask around tomorrow when Sophie and the carriers come in if you'd like."

"Yes, please. Call me...well, no, I'll stop in at some point during the day tomorrow."

"Okey dokey. Finished for now?"

"I am."

"I'll let you out the back door." He struggled through the maze of equipment, his arms flailing about like an aged version of the scarecrow in *The Wizard of Oz*.

"Can I help you move some of this stuff out of the way?" MC asked.

"No, thanks. I'm nearly finished, then I'll be out the door myself. You have yourself a good evening. I'll keep an eye out for you tomorrow."

"Thanks, Ned. See you then." It never ceased to amaze her the amount of work being a postmaster entailed. She doubted she'd have the fortitude to take on the job.

Not a complete bust, but she'd sure been hoping for more than a name. Progress, albeit slow.

Every nerve ending itched like crazy. She rubbed her hands together to try and alleviate the sensation. One drink. Just one would alleviate the craving.

Her stomach growled as she walked around the corner to her car. MC secured the evidence bag in a lockbox in the rear of the Subaru. Lucky Lucy's Bar across from the post office advertised pizzas to go. Kismet. At the bar she placed her order for a small pepperoni pizza to go and a Diet Coke. Perched on a stool, she surveyed the multitude of bottles arrayed on the backbar. Her palms were sweaty, and heart rate kicked up.

No. Action would help. She needed a break in the case. She needed to practice the patience she'd preached to Jim Bob earlier. Or enlist the help of someone else. She called LCSO and asked for Deputy Ekstrom. "Hey, McCall here. Can you do me a solid? Run a name for me, Caleb Lewis. I need an address." Ekstrom had to finish something she was working on but promised to get back to MC with the information.

Her pie came out as she drank the last dregs of soda from the glass. She bid a reluctant farewell to her clear-liquid nemesis across the bar, then paid her tab and left before her inner demons could override her decision.

MC hit the unlock button and put the pizza box on the floor behind her seat. Out of the corner of her eye she noticed *The Big Book*. How could words in a book help her?

Despite the difficulty, all signs pointed toward maintaining her state of un-inebriation.

"Hell, and it's only Monday."

Thursday is only a few days away. You can do it, MC. Believe in yourself. I do.

If Barb believed she could hold out until the next AA meeting, she'd dare not disappoint.

Chapter Nine

The next morning, MC's phone shimmied in the cup holder.
Ned. She pulled to the shoulder and hit the hazards.

"Hello?"

"Inspector McCall," Ned said, "we have a young man here asking
about a wallet. Could be the guy you're after."

"Keep him there as long as you can. I'm about five minutes
away."

"He's jittery. Not sure he'll stick around."

"Use whatever delaying tactic you can come up with. See if he'll
give you his contact information. I'm on my way." She punched the
hazards off and got back on the highway.

Two minutes and twenty seconds later MC rolled up in front of
the post office. Ned greeted her at the front entrance. "Morning,
Inspector. You made good time, but unfortunately you missed him
by about one minute. The guy was very antsy. I've been asking
myself since he exited the building whether I believe in ghosts."
He stared down the block.

"I'm sorry. What?"

He held the door open, and she crossed the threshold. "I was
hot on his heels when he left. Thought I'd get a license plate
number or at the very least a description of his car. But no such
luck. Nothing and no one in sight. Poof. He vanished."

"Weird and disappointing. Let's go to your office and you can
fill me in on the details."

Coffees in hand, they settled in the cramped office. MC flipped
her notepad to a fresh page. "From the top, please, Ned."

"Sophie found me in the back. She had a customer, a young guy,
who'd said he thought he may have lost his wallet here last week
when he brought in some mail. I had Sophie stay in the work area
and sort mail while I went up front to find out what was what.
When I got up there he was pacing, so I called him over to the
counter."

"Did Sophie recognize him? Like she may have recognized him
from the day of the robbery?"

"She didn't say anything, so I don't think so."

"What did he look like?"

"He wore a jean jacket over a gray hoodie sweatshirt with an
image of that Pokémon character, blue jeans, and he had on Vans
shoes. I remember the shoes because I notice shoes. I'm a shoe

geek. Anyway, the Vans were blue/black with a white stripe. He was rumpled, like he'd just crawled out of bed. He had short dark hair sticking up every which way. May be his style, I don't know."

"Good," MC said. "This is good. He said he thought his wallet may have gotten mixed in with some mail. Wouldn't you or the clerk notice a wallet as you sorted the mail?"

"Exactly. Say it did get into one of the mail bags, then how'd it get behind the file cabinet?"

"Good question. What'd you do next?"

"I asked him to describe it. He said it was a gray nylon wallet, not much inside it. I asked him if there was an ID, like a driver's license. Told him if I did have the wallet, I couldn't give it to him without some kind of proof it was really his."

"Excellent." MC jotted down the details.

"He told me there was some cash, two fives and a couple ones. A bank debit card and a Visa credit card too. No mention of a driver's license or any other form of ID."

"Interesting, especially when you asked him specifically about an ID."

"Very unusual. People will tell you right off the bat their license is in the wallet and give their name and address to prove it. Not this kid. I told him to stay put and I'd go check a couple places where we stow lost and found items."

"How was he behaving during all this?"

"At first, he seemed like everything was copacetic. But then a few customers entered behind him, and I called for Sophie to come and wait on them. I asked him to step aside, to come to my office to wait while I checked for the wallet."

She was impressed with how Ned had worked to keep the individual around as long as possible.

"But that was the straw that broke the proverbial camel's back. Kid got skittish. Said, 'Nah, if you don't have the wallet, I'll go check the bank and some other places.' Then he hopped from foot-to-foot, nervous-like. I told him I didn't know if we had the wallet, and that's why I asked him to wait in my office. Then I grabbed paper and a pen from the counter and asked him to write down his contact information if he didn't want to wait and we'd call. He bolted out the door, like a track runner off the starting block. I already told you the rest."

MC drank the lukewarm coffee bean-flavored water. She sure missed the good stuff at Flannel. "He didn't give his name?"

"Not to me."

"Let's go ask Sophie. She spoke with him first, right?"

"Yes, she did."

They waited while Sophie finished a stamp sale to a spritely octogenarian woman who wished them all a wonderful day.

"Sophie," MC said, "Ned told me you talked to a customer earlier about a lost wallet."

"Yeah. A guy. Probably my age. I didn't know if I should say anything, so I went to get Ned."

"Good plan. Did this man happen to give you his name or any other information?"

"He did say his name. Caleb something. I should've written it down." She rested a hand on her chin.

MC remained silent. If Sophie gave her the same name on the credit cards, she'd have a solid launching point.

"Did you recognize him?" MC couldn't keep quiet any longer. "Do you think he may have been the robber?"

Sophie said, "Maybe. I think the robber was taller though."

MC's hopes were dying a slow death with every answer from Sophie.

"Lloyd. No, wait that's not right. Lowell. Hmm, no that doesn't sound right either."

"Take your time." MC held her breath, crossed her fingers, toes, and eyes.

"Lewis. That's it. Not sure of the spelling. I'm pretty sure he said Lewis."

MC pulled her notebook from her pocket and wrote down the name. "Thank you, Sophie. You did great."

The name Sophie gave was a match for the name on the credit cards in the wallet. Now she had a name and a physical description. Caleb Lewis was now at the top of her persons of interest list.

MC decided as long as she was in Castle Cove she'd knock on some more doors. Maybe her luck would change.

Midday traffic southbound on Highway 61 from Castle Cove was almost non-existent. After another round of unsuccessful interviews, MC needed something to cleanse her mind. She tuned into a true crime podcast for the drive to Betty's Pies. *Undisclosed* was hosted by three attorneys who were reexamining the conviction of Adnan Syed. The podcast did a much deeper dive into the case first covered in *Serial*, with the aim of uncovering evidence to support a post-conviction hearing for Syed. MC was impressed by their commitment to helping Syed.

The sign for Betty's Pies loomed in no time. The parking lot was jammed, which explained why the road was deserted. Everyone and their sister were at Betty's for lunch. MC took a seat at the counter and ordered, then flipped through a left-behind copy of the *Minneapolis Star Tribune*. She read the front-page article about Governor Dayton and the fight over funding for early education. When the server slid her bowl of chicken wild rice soup in front of her, she set the newspaper aside.

While she slurped soup, she scanned the restaurant. Deputy Ekstrom still hadn't got back to her. Hopefully, she'd had a chance to run Lewis through the system. After lunch she'd pay Ekstrom a visit at the station. Kempffer had been a huge disappointment. She'd held out a modicum of hope he'd have a change of attitude and be cooperative. But that hadn't panned out. She'd stick with Ekstrom going forward.

Still hungry MC ordered a slice of strawberry rhubarb pie and a cup of coffee. The perfect cap off for the chilly spring day.

She paid her bill and walked back to her car. MC returned to the podcast as she drove the few miles to Two Harbors.

She hung a left at the Dairy Queen onto 6th Street, then a right onto 3rd Avenue and parked in front of the Courthouse.

Inside, MC walked up to the window and was greeted by Lynette's smiling face. "Inspector, good afternoon. What can I help you with?"

"Hi, Lynette. Nice to see you. Any chance Deputy Ekstrom is around?"

"Let me check the roster and see where she might be. Okay, let's see. Ah, yes, she's actually in the building. I'll give her a call. Come on in and have a seat." She hit a buzzer.

MC walked into the office area.

"Grab a chair at one of the desks." Lynette picked up the phone.

Within two minutes MC saw the deputy striding her way.

"Hi, Inspector McCall. Sorry. I meant to call you earlier but got tied up. Lynette, okay if we use the conference room?"

Lynette said, "Conference room is free all afternoon. Have at it."

MC followed Ekstrom past the sheriff's office into the conference room. "I thought I'd stop by and see what you found on Caleb Lewis."

"He doesn't have any priors. I just emailed you his address. I knew him from school and church. He's a year older than me. Kind of a loner. I remember when we were in high school he was really into video games and computers. Total geek. Nerd. Whatever you want to call it. Why? Has he done something?"

"His name came up regarding the post office robbery last week." MC paused. "What you're telling me doesn't really fit the bill of someone who robs a post office though."

"I haven't seen him for a while. But I do think it would be a reach, from what I remember of him, to be involved in something like that. We knew each other at Whispering Aspen and at school, elementary and middle school. I think Caleb stopped going to church at the beginning of high school, same as me."

"Was there no youth pastor after Thackeray became head pastor?"

"Nope. Thackeray did it all."

"Is there a youth pastor now?"

"Yeah. You'll get a kick out this," Ekstrom said. "For the past two years, Kempffer."

"No way. He doesn't strike me as someone who'd enjoy spending time with kids of any age. I envision him with a group of bros drinking beer and harassing women."

"Well, he does that too. I think the big draw for kids is he's good at playing guitar, and at sports, so he connects with some of them on that level. I don't go to church anymore, haven't since before high school. I told my parents it was too creepy, and my best friend and I were always getting in trouble for hiding out in one of the abandoned bunk cabins instead of participating in Youth Group."

"Creepy how?" Goosebumps popped up on MC's arms.

"I was in a place where I wasn't sure I believed in God, and Whispering Aspen did nothing to help bring me closer to a belief. The place was cloaked with negative energy. Around Pastor Thackeray for sure. He's skeevy. Cared more about working out than pastoring and paid way more attention to us kids than necessary. Don't get me wrong. He preaches Jesus all day long, but it feels more like an act than a calling."

"I've met him briefly." The memory of shaking his slimy hand made her want to run to the restroom and scrub her hands raw. "Yeah, I got total gym rat from him in the few seconds I was in his presence. He also invited me to Sunday service, which I can tell you I did not attend."

"I don't blame you one bit. Steer clear is my advice."

"I'll take your warning about Thackeray under advisement. But back to Caleb."

"You really think he robbed the post office?"

"I'm not sure. But his wallet was found wedged behind a file cabinet a couple days ago. Coincidentally, today he stopped by the post office to ask if anyone had found it and gave some story about it getting mixed in with some items he'd mailed. Which wouldn't at all line up with his wallet ending up behind a file cabinet. I'd really like to speak with him."

Ekstrom said, "Christ. I nearly forgot. When I was riding with Kempffer during my field training, I remember we stopped Caleb one night. Like my second week on. He'd been speeding, barely. Anyway, we got out of the car, I went along the passenger side of the vehicle, and Kempffer hit the driver's side. I didn't realize at first it was Caleb because I hadn't seen him in years. Kempffer asked for his license and registration, the usual. Well, Caleb didn't have his license on him. Kempffer about blew a gasket. I think he was already pissy because he had me along, but that's another story."

"Sounds like a gem in more ways than one, our Kempffer. What happened? He give Caleb a ticket?"

"I thought that's what was coming, but he didn't. We'd pulled Caleb over like two blocks from where he lived, and he begged Kempffer to follow him to his house and he'd produce his license. Said if he got one more speeding ticket his insurance would skyrocket. We got back in the car, and I said something to Kempffer about letting the guy go. I didn't let on I'd recognized Caleb, figured Kempffer would've gone ballistic and done something more off the books."

"This is some TV cop drama you're telling me right now."

"I know. We rolled the two blocks behind Caleb's car. He lives in a garage apartment. Anyway, Kempffer told me to stay put. After about ten minutes I was ready to decamp and walk up the stairs to the apartment when Kempffer came out. He clomped down the stairs, a half-assed grin pasted on his face. When I asked him what happened, he told me to mind my fucking business. He 'took care of it' and I didn't need to get my panties in a twist."

Christ on a cracker. MC hated Kempffer more with every word Ekstrom spoke. How could a guy like him be a youth pastor?

"You've no idea what happened in the apartment? What Kempffer and Caleb discussed?"

"Nope. Nada. Not a clue. All I know for sure is Kempffer didn't write a ticket or a warning because there's nothing in the system. Not the way I like to do police work. Honestly, I'm suspicious of what Kempffer may have been up to. I don't like him, but more importantly, I don't trust him. I don't trust him to have my back."

"Have you broached the subject with Tollefsen?"

"No. I'm the newest deputy and the only woman. I don't want to rock the boat."

"I know, but you can't do your job if you can't trust your backup."

Like you've got room to talk, McCall. Remember the risk you put others in during Cam's raid a few months earlier? How could they trust her to have their six when she could barely function because she was so obsessed with tracking down Barb's killer most of the time, and the remaining time drowning herself in a vat of vodka?

"Things have sort of fallen into a monotonous pattern since then. I avoid Kempffer when and if I can. Keep my head on a swivel and do my job. I wanted to get a couple years under my belt before I considered making waves."

"Well, if there's anything I can do, call me."

"Thanks."

"Do you have his address for me? Caleb's, I mean. I'd really like to speak with him."

"Got it right here. And his record is clean, except for a few speeding tickets over the past couple years." Ekstrom slid a note to MC. "Don't suppose you'd like backup for that visit?"

"As a matter of fact, I would. Especially if he remembers you. Might put him at ease and make the interaction less adversarial from his perspective."

"I can scope out the place once we get inside. See if there're any clues. He'll be distracted by your questions and less likely to notice me noticing things."

MC liked this young deputy's tenacity.

Fifteen minutes later, Ekstrom had cleared giving MC a hand with Chief Deputy Johnson.

MC followed Ekstrom. On the western part of the city in a residential area, they drove up a windy gravel driveway about twenty-five feet long, past a two-story white clapboard house to a two-and-a-half car detached garage. The drive curved left onto a blacktopped area about twenty feet wide by ten feet long in front of the overhead door. A sturdy wooden stairway on one side led to the above-the-garage apartment.

Ekstrom waited for MC at the foot of the steps.

"Not bad digs. At least from outside," MC said. "Yard is neat. House well-maintained."

"Yeah, the old couple who own the house are sticklers for keeping up the property. Shall we?"

They climbed the stairway. MC pounded on the door with the side of her fist. They waited a couple minutes, and MC banged again. With no window to peer inside, she surveyed the large yard that abutted a wooded area.

"No cars in the driveway," Ekstrom said. "Guess he's not home."

"Let's walk around the garage and see what we see," MC said.

They descended and walked around. On the opposite end of the garage from the apartment entrance was a concrete slab with an overhang. Probably an extra parking spot, but it was empty.

"Well, that's a bust," Ekstrom said.

"Yeah, but at least you got me one step closer by giving me his address. Sorry to waste your time."

"Nah, it's all good. If you want, when you decide to try again, give me a call. If I'm able I'll meet you."

"It's a plan. Thanks again. Stay safe." MC backed down the driveway. At least she was one step closer to questioning Caleb Lewis. Forward momentum was imperative.

The thought of a drink crept in, disguised as a reward. She put the car in drive and aimed for home.

This shit sucked.

Keep it together, McCall. Worst case scenario she could hit up the Wednesday evening AA meeting out at Whispering Aspen Ministries. But then there was Ned. But it would be one more meeting ticked off the checklist. Truthfully, working a case involving the AA meeting head honcho was a whole other level of discomfort she didn't need. She'd hold out and go to the Thursday meeting.

At home she pulled a can of sparkling water from the fridge and climbed the stairs to the loft and her office nook. She fired up her laptop to check her email and saw an email from Jamie.

Crap. In her preoccupation with Caleb Lewis the CSE thing slipped her mind. The email address specified was pixie.dust1@cmail.com. The cyber gurus had provided an IP address linked to a church. The church listed was Whispering Aspen Ministries.

Whoa.

Could it be a coincidence Whispering Aspen Ministries was entwined with both of her investigations? One was indirectly, while the other very directly.

Of one thing MC was certain. She didn't believe in coincidences. Maybe she'd hit the Wednesday AA meeting after all. The meeting would be perfect cover for her to be at the church and track down the pastor for a conversation.

Chapter Ten

Several vehicles were parked in the Whispering Aspen Ministries parking lot. MC had decided to show up twenty-five minutes early for the seven o'clock evening meeting. She planned to scope out the Meeting Hall, maybe scoot downstairs on the off chance she'd run into Pastor Thackeray. And possibly locate the church's computer or computers. The IP Address Jamie shared in his email traced to the church, but not to any specific computer.

She passed through the empty entrance area with the fireplace and two couches. The fireplace provided a barrier between the lobby and the main room where the AA meetings and other events took place. Lights blazed, so she figured there was at least one person already in the main hall.

The sound of chairs scraping along the wood floor confirmed her assumption before she reached the fireplace. She peeked around the stone facade. Ned Hargreve, his back to her, worked a group of chairs into a semblance of a circle. No one else was present. But she'd seen at least half a dozen cars in the parking lot. Maybe something was going on in the church?

The stairway down to the lower level was on the opposite side of the fireplace. She trod carefully to avoid Ned's attention. She'd worn a pair of black New Balance running shoes, jeans, and a lightweight olive drab-colored vest and a thermal long-sleeve shirt. The shirt and vest were loose enough to conceal the paddle holster at her back securing her service firearm. Normally, she wouldn't carry at a meeting, but tonight's meeting was a cover. Mostly. She was ready to do some business. She dipped down the stairs, making sure her shoes didn't squeak on the shiny wood opened-back steps.

At the bottom two short hallways jutted to either side. A longer hall loomed straight ahead. MC chose the left hall and discovered two restrooms. Women's. Men's. None of that "all gender" choice for the holy members of Whispering Aspen Ministries.

Across from the bathrooms was a supply room about the size of her office in the Cities. Shelves lined two walls and contained all manner of arts and crafts materials along with copier paper and Bibles, of both the children and adult variety. A fancy copier sat on a table against the rear wall.

A twinge of jealousy bit her.

The copier was far nicer than the one the Inspection Service provided. She backed out of the room and crept over to the hallway on the other side of the stairs.

On the right side was an open door. A quick peek inside revealed a single toilet bathroom with a sink, soap, and towel dispensers. Opposite the restroom was another door. On the wall to the left of it was a gold-plated plaque.

Pastor Thackeray.

Ah, the head guru's office. She knocked lightly. No response. She checked the hall. Saw no one. She twisted the knob. Locked.

To the right of the pastor's office was an exit. The metal door had a small square window crisscrossed with wire mesh. Nothing out there but grass trying to throw off the last vestiges of winter and a wood gazebo, bleached gray by the weather, about a hundred feet beyond the building. The gazebo abutted a wooded area. Not a soul in sight.

She checked the time on her phone. She'd been down here nearly five minutes. It felt like hours. The last area to scope out was the longer hall.

Signs on the wall indicated room names: The Blue Room, Green Room, and Yellow Room. All were securely locked. The lower level was secured like Fort Knox. Geez.

MC thought for a half-second about going upstairs for the AA meeting. Instead, she opted to investigate the outside. Even though she could've ticked off another meeting, she wasn't thrilled about Ned being the leader.

She headed for the exit door and reached for the handle as someone yanked it open from the outside, almost knocking her off her feet.

"Whoa. Can I help you?" Pastor Thackeray dressed in workout clothes blocked the exit. "What are you doing down here? Who are you?"

The questions fired at her like artillery shells on a battlefield. He sounded annoyed and concerned. His stringy, longish hair and high forehead, wide enough to project a movie on, were his most striking features.

"Pastor Thackeray?" She wondered if he remembered meeting her last week.

"That's me. You still haven't told me who you are." Apparently, she hadn't made an impression.

"Do you have time for a few questions?"

"You want to join the church?"

"Yeah. Maybe." When hell froze over.

He yanked a ring of keys from his pants pocket and unlocked the office door. "Come in. Have a seat." He flipped the light switch.

MC followed him inside the devil's lair and took a seat in one of the chairs in front of his massive desk. A computer and keyboard sat atop a desk she'd expect to find in an office in downtown Minneapolis rather than up here in the north woods. "Interesting room."

"Back in the day it belonged to the camp counselors. Used to be two sets of bunk beds, one on either side of the room." He waved an arm around. "I left the study area in front of the windows because sometimes the kids need to come in and use a computer."

A wooden built-in desk and two chairs faced the windows. On one end a laptop was plugged in. Shelves were attached to either side of the desk. Probably so counselors could do paperwork or whatever camp counselors did other than monitor other people's kids all day and night.

At the opposite end of the room, the pastor's monolithic desk sat between built-in cabinets on one wall and built-in bookshelves on the other.

Thackeray sat in a black-leather executive chair, fancier than she'd expect in a backwoods church. "I'm Pastor Thackeray. Welcome to Whispering Aspen Ministries. We love to see new folks join up. What's your name?"

"MC."

"MC? What do the initials stand for?" He folded his hands together and rested them on his desk.

"Let's leave it at MC."

He opened his mouth. Closed it. Opened it again, like a fish out of water. "As you wish." He pulled a drawer open on the right side of his desk. Grabbed something and slid it closed.

MC watched him closely. The ticking of the second hand traveling the circle of the clock above the windows behind her grew louder.

Thackeray leaned forward and shoved a colorful trifold pamphlet her way. "This will give you a general overview of Whispering Aspen Ministries. We're a welcoming, all-inclusive community." He pulled the computer keyboard toward him. "If you'd like I can start a new member file for you."

She flipped through the glossy pamphlet showing pictures of kids playing outdoors and others sitting in a circle praying. Adults in the big room upstairs, in a circle with what she assumed were Bibles in their hands. Brief statements about the community groups: adult Bible study; youth group; teen group; taking care of tots group, which was basically a babysitting service during church. The whole thing made her want to run screaming for the hills.

"I'd like to take this and give it some thought."

"Fine. No rush. Maybe you'd want to attend Sunday morning service? We have two, eight fifteen and eleven. You're welcome at either one. We also have our weekly adult Bible study on Thursdays. Actually, as you can see in the brochure, all groups gather on Thursdays. We like to fill the place to the rafters whenever we can."

"I'm sure you do, Pastor. Unfortunately, I have a prior commitment on Thursday evenings." For once she was glad to have an AA meeting on her docket. What she'd really like was for the pastor to leave the office for a minute or two to give her a chance to look at his computer. "Could you tell me more about the community and staff? These pictures show lots of kids' activities." She opened the brochure.

"Do you have a lot of kids in the congregation?" Ease up, McCall. Don't show too much interest in kids, or he might get spooked. She was stymied on how to get him to leave the room. No way could she outright ask about CSE because he could be involved.

"You sure have a whole lot of questions. Thinking of becoming a pastor and replacing me or something?" His mouth formed something between a sneer and a grin.

MC checked out the ceiling, noticed a brownish spot in one corner. Water leak? She was pretty sure the kitchen was above them. "Well, now that you mention it. I might be thinking of a career change in the next couple of years, but I'm not sure I'm cut out to lead a church. Maybe you could share some insight?" Pile it on much, McCall?

"I can give you some reference material. Steer you toward theological courses that would be beneficial. My recommendation is to start by attending a service." Thackeray stood. "Well, if there's nothing else then, MC, I do have some work I need to attend to." He stepped around the desk and waited near her chair.

For now, she couldn't get at them, but at least she'd located two of the ministries' computers. She pushed herself up from the chair and followed Thackeray to the door. "Thank you for your time."

"Don't mention it. Hope we see you on Sunday. You know your way out? Up the stairs and you'll see the front door. There's an AA meeting still in session, so you may run into some folks up there." He tilted his head to one side. "You look familiar. Weren't you here last week for the meeting?"

Those muddy dull eyes of his bore into her. Her gut clenched like someone had her in a vise. She shrugged. "Thanks for your time, Pastor." Thanks for a whole lot of nothing. She climbed the stairs.

A negative aura surrounded Thackeray. She couldn't pinpoint

why, other than he wasn't what she'd expect a pastor to look like. He hadn't even quoted any Bible verses to her. Didn't they all spew Bible quotes every chance they got? Was he the culprit though? The one who'd saved images to the cloud account? Maybe someone used his computer.

On the main floor a wave of recovering addicts' murmuring voices carried her out the door.

The thirst flickered in her mind like a dying ember, but she smothered it before it could spark again.

When she arrived home, she checked email and surfed the web. A light glinted off a framed photo of Barb on the shelf next to her desk, distracting her. Time to call it quits with work. She closed the laptop and killed the lights in the loft.

At the bottom of the stairs she veered left and went out the sliding doors off the kitchen. The sun had set. A bruised sky hung solemnly over Lake Superior.

MC settled into one of the four Adirondack chairs on the patio next to what used to be Barb's garden. Which also happened to be where MC, Dara, and Meg had spread some of Barb's ashes several months ago.

Bits of untended growth popped through the patch of dirt. What would she do with the garden? She wasn't a green thumb like her late partner. Barb could coax the most vibrant and luscious vegetables to grow from the driest, least habitable earth.

Tears blurred her vision. Memories came, a slideshow in her mind.

Somewhere in the distance an owl hooted, and the chirp and squeak of a bat or two echoed in the night. She'd had all she could handle of fresh air and the nocturnal orchestra and went inside to bed.

Chapter Eleven

Freshly showered and dressed in her usual twill pants, button-down shirt, and blazer cut specifically to accommodate her holster on her belt, MC made her way to the kitchen for her first cup of coffee. The best of the day.

She reached in her blazer pocket for her phone and realized she didn't have it. Back to the bedroom where the charging cable lay across the nightstand naked as the day she'd unpacked it.

After a moment, she realized she'd probably left the phone in the office alcove up in the loft. MC retrieved the phone and was relieved to not have messages to respond to. She toasted a bagel and smeared cream cheese on the two halves, then settled at the kitchen table with another cup to consume her breakfast in peace. Her plan for the morning was to bring Jamie up to speed on her visit to Whispering Aspen. Then she'd, once again, visit homes around the Castle Cove Post Office on the off chance anyone had seen or heard anything suspicious the day of the robbery. Like a dog with a bone, she'd not give up until she'd made contact at every house around the post office. She'd round out the day with a visit to Buster Crumbly's hangout to find out what he knew about the robbery.

MC rolled up in front of the Castle Cove Family Cafe at one thirty. She had half an hour until they closed. Hobie Jenkins had told her she'd find Buster Crumbly perched on a stool at the lunch counter. A tiny tinkling bell announced her arrival. All faces turned toward her like she was Norm entering the bar in *Cheers*. All faces totaled six. An older couple at a table up front near the windows, and four at the lunch counter.

She nodded toward the couple in the front and made a beeline for the cluster at the counter. Four guys, Vietnam Vet-aged, swiveled around on their stools, eyeing her approach.

"Afternoon. US Postal Inspector McCall." She flipped her credentials open and panned it for the four sets of eyes to see. "I'm looking for Buster Crumbly."

The guy on the last stool slapped a hand on the shoulder of the man next to him. A grin split his face. "Here he is."

Buster Crumbly unfolded to about six-feet-five inches as he stood. MC craned her head back to meet his gaze. Not at all what she'd expected. Based on Hobie's appearance and the name, somehow, she'd envisioned a mix of Tweedle-Dee, a munchkin from *The Wizard of Oz*, and Humpty Dumpty.

Crumbly's forehead was heavily lined. A few wisps of gray hair were neatly combed from left to right. Washed-out brown, watery eyes had deep saggy pockets beneath them. He had a schnoz to rival Jimmy Durante for sure.

"Here I am. Postal Inspector, huh? What could a postal inspector want with me?" His long arms with hands the size of dinner plates hung easily against his sides.

"Well, Mr. Crumbly, Hobie Jenkins told me he heard about the recent post office robbery from you. I'm investigating that robbery. I wonder if you might shed some light on how *you* heard about it?"

The other three men eyeballed Buster. Not a peep from any of them.

A massive crash came from the kitchen area. Someone had dropped a load of something resulting, MC guessed, in a mess of shards based on the language emanating from the area. At the counter, all eyes remained on Buster.

"I heard it from my neighbor. He happens to be a deputy with the Lake County Sheriff's. I'd seen him the evening of the day it happened. Guy was kicking stuff around his garage and swearing up a storm. I walked up his driveway and asked if he was all right, knowing full well he wasn't, mind you."

MC wanted to tell him to get to the point. But it was obvious Buster was the type who took his time telling his stories. He no doubt embellished them with each telling.

"And?" She asked.

"Long story short…"

Please dear God.

"He told me he'd had a shit day. Some woman fed had yanked his chain and he didn't appreciate it. I'm thinking now, with you right here, you must be that person."

You think, Captain Obvious? MC suppressed a smirk.

"I asked why a federal agent was in Castle Cove. He told me the post office got robbed early that morning and he'd caught the call. But when he got to the post office nothing was out of place, and when he heard the postmaster had contacted the," he waved a hand in MC's direction, "Inspection department he said screw it, let them handle it."

"Inspection Service," MC said.

"What?"

"You said Inspection Department. Just clarifying that the agency I'm with is the US Postal Inspection Service."

"I stand corrected." He half-bowed. "Anyway, he went on and on about how the fed showed up at the station wanting to interview him. And asking for a copy of his report. There were some swear words mixed in, which I'll keep to myself. But you get the drift." Oh, boy, did she.

"This deputy named Kempffer, by chance?"

"Yes, indeed."

"That's all you know regarding the robbery?"

"In a nutshell." He folded himself onto his perch, a physical period at the end of a sentence.

"Anyone else have any more to add?" The crew shook their heads.

"Well, I appreciate your time." She slipped a card onto the counter. "If anyone thinks of anything else, please contact me. Enjoy the rest of your day."

Back in her car, MC made a few quick notes in her notebook and stashed it in her pocket. Sounded to her like Kempffer had given this civilian as much information about her case as he'd shared with her.

Another fruitless day of investigating passed. Nothing Buster Crumbly shared advanced any theories, other than that Kempffer was an adversary. The few people she'd found home earlier in the day had nothing to add either.

She pondered next moves. Forward motion eluded her, like a car with bald tires on an icy road, unable to gain traction. Even though the case stalled, she decided to cruise by Caleb's address. No car occupied the slab on the far side of the garage. Note to self, call Deputy Ekstrom and see if she'd be up for another knock-and-talk attempt tomorrow.

MC sat in her Subaru on the street in front of Caleb's place. The engine idled along with her mind.

You wanted more to do. Remember? You specifically said you needed a case you could sink your teeth into. Now you have that, plus some. You can do this.

If only she had as much confidence in herself as the spirit of Barb did, then she'd be right as rain. That was a long shot. MC McCall was about as far from right as rain as she'd ever been in her nearly fifty years on planet Earth.

She slipped her notepad from her blazer pocket and flipped through the pages. She breezed past the notes about Jim Bob's mail theft investigation. The Castle Cove post office robbery was anything but handled. Outside of having possession of Caleb Lewis's wallet and Sophie's vague physical description, she had zilch. Nada.

MC put the car in drive, and her mind shifted gears too. A tornado of thoughts swirled in her head. She contemplated how she might be able to approach Pastor Thackeray. Somehow, she needed access to both computers in his office. Could be other computers located in the Meeting Hall. She'd only laid eyes on the two in Thackeray's office. Maybe she'd have to ask him outright. Let him know there'd been a report, and it traced to Whispering Aspen.

But if she did that and Thackeray was involved, she'd be giving him the opportunity to destroy evidence. Something she wanted to avoid.

She checked her phone and saw there was enough time to stop at the cabin, change into more casual clothes, and make the 6:30 AA meeting at the Senior Center.

MC halted inside the entrance of the Senior Center and surveyed the room. About eight or ten people, including the leader, were conversing and devouring treats. The local bakery's goods were probably a draw to this meeting.

Ellen Bensen stood next to the goodie-laden table. "Hi, MC."

"Hey, Ellen." MC reached for a cup. She filled it and was pleased to find a carton of actual cream sitting in a dish of ice. A hefty dollop of creamer sure beat the powdered alternative from last week. Her stomach gurgled, reminding her she'd not eaten since breakfast. She grabbed a jelly-filled donut with a napkin, hoping to silence the complaining beast, which also served as an excuse to avoid making conversation with Ellen. *Why am I afraid of Ellen? Get a grip, McCall.*

Ellen asked, "Have you had a good week?"

A blob of chewed donut lodged halfway down her throat. MC took a couple swallows of coffee, thankfully cooled enough by the creamer it didn't scorch her mouth. Finally, the food dislodged. "I, ah, yeah, okay, I guess." Wow. Articulate much? She felt like a junior high wall flower. Jesus.

Ellen pulled at MC's arm to guide her away from the table as a couple members leaned in to grab snacks. "Let's sit. We still have about five minutes before the meeting."

MC stumbled along behind Ellen like a lost puppy hoping for a home. No. She wasn't searching for a home. Snap out of it.

Ellen chose two chairs on the far side of the circle. "This okay?"

"Sure." MC took the final bite of her donut. "My god, this donut is like crack." She clapped a hand over her mouth realizing what she'd said.

Ellen laughed. "Don't worry. I don't think anyone heard you. Besides, I'd bet nearly everyone in the room would agree with you. Be forewarned, if a person isn't careful, they could pack on the pounds from the treats served at this meeting. Max, our leader, he and his brother own and operate the bakery."

"No, I wasn't aware. I didn't even remember his name was Max." She really should pay more attention. "These snacks are dangerous."

"Absolutely. The last thing we need is another addiction to replace the one we're recovering from," Ellen said.

Come on, McCall. Do the adult thing. "So how was your week?" That wasn't so difficult, was it?

"Long. With summer fast approaching, I'm going in eighty different directions, prepping for, hopefully, a major tourist influx. Gift shop needs to be adequately stocked. Brochures. Advertisements. Programming. Sometimes I feel like there aren't enough hours in the day."

"Sounds overwhelming. What is it you do?"

See you're doing well. Good job. Keep going.

"Oh, hell. I didn't mention?"

"No." Or had she and MC missed it like she missed Max's name?

"I'm the site manager at Split Rock Lighthouse."

"That's cool. I bet it's challenging. I haven't been out to Split Rock in years. It used to be..." One of Barb's favorite spots.

"Used to be what?"

"Okay, folks." Max stood in the middle of the circle. "Gather round. We'll get the meeting started."

"To be continued," Ellen whispered to MC.

At the end of the hour, after the Serenity Prayer was recited, the flock dispersed.

MC and Ellen folded chairs and stacked them against the far wall.

Ellen leaned toward MC. "Would you like to go get a cup of coffee with me?"

"Now?" MC asked. Of course now, you idiot. She could be so dense.

"Yeah. Well, after we finish here. Harbor Java is open until nine. Are you familiar with it?

"No, I haven't been there."

"It's not far past Judy's Cafe on Seventh Avenue, aka Highway Sixty-one."

"That's on my way home. I...here's the deal, Ellen. I'm not in the market for an AA sponsor."

Ellen grinned. "Oh, no. I'm not offering to be your sponsor. I haven't volunteered for that role. Not sure I'd be able to handle it, to be honest. This would just be a chance to enjoy conversation without the dozen or so sets of ears around. No pressure. If you'd rather not, I totally understand."

This was moving so fast. MC felt like she was in a fighter jet going supersonic, heading quickly for hypersonic.

Let go, MC. Have some fun.

"Okay. You talked me into it."

"Great." With a wave, Ellen headed toward her truck.

MC's thoughts reeled as she drove. The assurance Ellen wasn't trying to wedge herself into MC's life to keep her on track had tilted her no to a yes. That and Barb.

But what would she tell Ellen?

What would Ellen share with her?

What the hell was she thinking? She almost veered into the parking lot of Harbor Liquors, even lightly touched the brakes. The quick toot of a horn behind her snapped her back to reality. She pressed down on the accelerator and continued on to the cafe.

MC entered Harbor Java with Ellen right on her heels. So many businesses in the area were named Harbor whatever.

They placed and picked up their drink orders and chose a table in the farthest corner at the rear of the shop. The lake country decor was way different from what MC was used to at Flannel, but she found it soothing. Welcoming, even.

Ellen set her latte aside. "Needs to cool down." She gazed at MC. "So, thought about ditching me at Harbor Liquors, huh?"

MC choked on the liquid going down her throat. "What?"

"I was the car behind you. The obnoxious horn-honker." Ellen picked up her cup and took a tentative sip. "No judgment, MC. We've all been there. Won't be the last time you'll be lured. Drinking will be top of mind for a long time."

Why didn't Ellen tell her something she didn't already know? Alcohol was the first thing she thought of, after Barb, every morning when she woke up and before she fell asleep every night.

"I don't suppose you'd believe I was trying to avoid hitting a squirrel in the road?"

Ellen let loose a guffaw. A foursome at a nearby table briefly paused their conversation.

MC took a couple deep breaths and held up her mug. "This is pretty damn good. So, site manager. Do you enjoy the job?"

"I do. What could be more fun than living at an actual lighthouse? Not to mention the scenery and the amazing hiking trails. But before I give you my complete autobiography, what about you? What do you do in life?"

Nicely played, MC thought.

"I'm in law enforcement."

"Really?" Ellen studied MC. "I can see that."

Now it was MC's turn to laugh. "I'm not sure if that's good or bad."

"It's good. I have nothing but respect for people who put their lives on the line every day. Are you with the sheriff's office? You're not familiar to me."

"Actually, I'm from the Cities. I'm with the US Postal Inspection Service. A postal inspector."

"Never heard of postal inspectors. What exactly does a postal inspector do? How are they—you—law enforcement? You have a badge and gun and the whole shebang?"

"Yep. The whole shebang. I'm on assignment investigating the recent robbery at the Castle Cove Post Office." She decided to leave out the child exploitation investigation but made a mental note she might be able to glean some information from Ellen about Whispering Aspen Ministries.

"Are you staying at the Shady Inn Motel in Castle Cove? I mean, if you don't mind my asking. As far as I know it's the only motel in the town. Unless you're staying here in Two Harbors?"

"I own a cabin, well, it's a year-round place now. I'm between Two Harbors and Castle Cove on Lake Superior. I stay there. Helps the agency's budget and I get the comforts of my up north home. Win-win."

"Look at me, sitting across the table from a real-life cop...sorry, inspector. I have to tell you, when you said inspector my mind went immediately to Inspector Gadget."

MC rolled her eyes, driving Ellen to bust a gut.

"You're offended. I'm sorry. My sense of humor gets the better of me sometimes."

"No offense taken. I guarantee you I am human. No part of me is cyborg. I have no gadgets hidden in any part of my body." She spread her arms wide. "Fully human sitting here in front of you. I don't have a niece named Penny solving my cases behind my back."

"Impressive. You are more familiar with Inspector Gadget than I thought possible. Cheers." She raised her cup.

MC knocked her mug against Ellen's. "Cheers." She had been insulted, but she washed that bitter pill down with smooth coffee, which could only be improved with a shot of— stop thinking about booze.

Ellen was entertaining and MC was convinced they played for the same team. She'd picked up on it the second Ellen spoke to her a week earlier. The more time they spent together, the more positive she became.

"So, do we move on to more personal questions and revelations now? Or is it too soon?" Ellen asked.

MC set her cup on the table and swirled the liquid around. How to answer Ellen?

She flipped her phone over to check the time. Still thirty minutes until the place closed. She felt trapped. Maybe she could make up something about needing to be on a phone call for work. Or to check in with her friend about her cancer treatment?

She's nice. She's not being invasive. She's trying to be—a friend. Take a breath.

After sucking in a deep breath and a slow release, MC took the leap. "What would you like to know?" Before Ellen could respond MC interjected, "Within reason."

The two shared their respective ages, MC was older by a year, and where they grew up, MC in St. Paul and Ellen in Grand Marais. Opposites on that front.

Ellen asked MC if she wanted to hear how she'd landed in the AA program. "I don't want to bore you or foist more AA on you." Ellen set her mug aside and folded her hands on the table. "Please don't be insulted, but you remind me a lot of me when I first joined the program."

MC swallowed the final dregs. What the hell had she gotten herself into here? "Really? How so?"

"You don't want to be at the meetings. Maybe you think you don't need the meetings. Possibly you're angry. More probably every fiber of your being screams for a drink every waking moment. How am I doing so far?"

"You get all that from meeting me twice?"

"I have pretty good addiction radar. I've had lots of experience. Ten years sober and I still fight the demon every day. The fact of the matter is I will for the rest of my life. Not hyperbole. I lost my partner because I loved alcohol more than I loved her, or at least that's what she told me on her way out the door."

Addiction radar.

Gaydar.

Jesus. Any other "dars" coming her way?

"I appreciate you sharing your story. I'm working on getting a handle on my situation. I've committed to six weekly meetings, and I've completed five, so one more to go."

"What happens next? After number six you are free and breezy? All healed? No more help needed? Believe me, it doesn't work that way. At least not for me it doesn't. Listen—"

"Those meetings are like sitting in the seventh circle of hell. It's not been lost on me I've been living a trope—the dingy church basement, the store-bought cookies dry enough they crumble at the touch, and worse yet trying to wash them down with coffee that would give battery acid a run for its money. All these backdrops for the circle of damaged humanity gathered to try and gain some control over their out-of-control lives. Please, I don't need a lecture." MC pushed her chair away from the table.

"Wait." Ellen held up her hands palm out. "My bad. Sometimes I start to sound like a sponsor when I get wound up. No lectures. Promise. Though yours was worth listening to. Maybe hear this one thing? From a friend."

Surprisingly, Ellen's soothing voice did something to her she wasn't prepared for, and she halted the urge to bolt like a wild mustang in the Montana mountains.

Ellen stood and moved around the table to face MC. "What helps me on this journey is to think in terms of making positive connections in my life instead of fixating on the state of sobriety. So blasé the word—sobriety. Many people associate negative connotations with even the word, much less the actual work involved, which caused me to struggle when I first embarked on the new life adventure of living without alcohol. Until I heard someone mention connections. That clicked for me. Positive connections, cultivating and maintaining them, is how I live my life. Thus ends my Ted Talk. Thank you for listening." She smiled. "See, no lecture."

Connections.

Ellen said, "Good grief. Store-bought cookies? Dingy church basement? Where have you attended meetings?"

"In St. Paul my meetings were in an actual dreary church basement and the java was undrinkable and the cookies dry as sandpaper. Not hyperbole. Similar story at a church in Castle Cove. A decent meeting hall, but in a creepy, old summer camp converted to a church."

"Whispering Aspen Ministries?"

"That's the one."

"Pastor Thackeray gives me the willies. I went to one service there when I first moved up here a couple years ago. I got a cult-like feel from the setup. I question the pastor's commitment to being in service of God and the community. He exudes an unsettling aura, a slickness. Enough to get me to swear off religion. But he filled the church, so enough people around the area must believe his preaching. Someone mentioned he's been around for a long time. Started as a youth pastor and climbed quickly to the top spot."

"Interesting. I met him after the one AA meeting I attended up there. I'm on board with your assessment." Maybe she and Ellen connecting...no pun intended...was meant to be in more ways than one. She might be able to glean some insight about Whispering Aspen and the pastor.

"MC?" Ellen touched her arm lightly.

"Sorry. What did you say?"

"I asked if you'd be interested in a hike over the weekend. A short out and back hike. I could show you some awesome trails now that the weather is warming up. Granted the trails will be somewhat muddy in spots, but worth the muck. We could hike around Split Rock, or if you want I could show you a well-hidden gem near a section of the Superior Hiking Trail which happens to abut Whispering Aspen Ministries."

"Nothing too challenging, I hope."

"I promise this trail is easy."

"I'm willing to give it a shot. Although, be forewarned. I haven't hiked in a few years."

"Deal. Wear hiking boots, if you have them, or sturdy trail shoes. Come to Split Rock Saturday morning, say nine? I'll make us some coffee and have muffins before we head out. Enter the lot for the Visitor Center and when you get to the Keeper's Cottages, I'll have the gate open so you can drive right in. Go all the way to the end and park in front of the garage."

"Sounds like a plan." She actually felt up-lifted at the prospect of doing something normal. Fun. Especially since they'd be right by her quarry.

Chapter Twelve

MC's day started off on a serious note.

The phone rang, interrupting MC's first cup of coffee. "Hey, Jamie. Must be something important if you're calling me at seven on a Saturday morning."

"Hey, MC. I know, sorry. I was hoping to get a run around Lake Harriet this morning, but before I head out, thought I'd check in with you. I ran out of time yesterday."

Keeping tabs? Making sure she's bright-eyed and bushy-tailed on the weekend and not hung over? Or was she being overly paranoid and he truly was doing a status check?

"Well, I don't have anything new to report on either investigation. I was up at Whispering Aspen earlier in the week. Met with the pastor, who's a very odd duck, but wasn't able to get at any computers. In his office he has a desktop, and a laptop on a spare desk he claimed was for the youth group kids to use. Probably for homework or Bible study or more likely to play online video games. I'm not sure how to get at either computer. When he's not in the office, it's locked. I might have a couple of people I can pump for more information on him though. A local deputy and someone who said she attended service at the church but stopped because she was creeped out. The place gave her cult vibes."

"Interesting. Tracks with CSE, if I were a betting kind of guy. Keep on it and let me know what you dig up. Any movement on the post office case?"

"I have a person of interest I'm trying to nail down. Need to have a conversation with him. His wallet was found wedged behind a file cabinet at the post office and believe it or not, he came into the post office, asking if anyone had found it. Either he's a ditz who can't keep track of his wallet or he's brazen as hell, and he knows he had to have lost it when he robbed the place and figures no one would suspect him if he showed up inquiring about it all innocent-like."

"I'd vote for the brazen as hell option. Stay on him."

"You got it. How's Red doing?"

"He's like a pit bull puppy with a bone...not about to let go. I have a feeling he'll get some positive results soon. I like what I see. He's able to work independently, but also with others on the team. Maybe a bit overzealous, but he'll learn to temper that as he matures as an inspector."

"He's annoying as hell most of the time but definitely has potential. I'll be in the Cities late tomorrow. I have a therapist appointment on Monday, and I'll stop by the office before the appointment."

"Sounds good. Have a good weekend. See you Monday."

MC put on her Merrell waterproof hiking shoes and grabbed a water-resistant shell jacket from the mudroom closet. She had twenty minutes to get to Split Rock.

She drove past the first of the three Keepers Cottages, the one tourists could walk through to see how Lighthouse Keepers lived when the lighthouse was active. She rolled through the open gate, past the second cottage, and finally parked in front of the garage behind the last cottage as Ellen had directed her. She'd no sooner exited her car when the rear door of the middle cottage opened wide. Ellen was framed in the shadows of the doorway.

MC wondered why Ellen had instructed her to park behind the last house instead of the one she lived in. She walked along the cracked asphalt toward Ellen's abode. The sun-dappled brown starting to green grass and the sparkle of light off Lake Superior on the other side of the cottage brought MC a sense of newness. Freshness. She imagined bears emerging from their winter hibernation into the warming days and bright light felt much like she did in that moment.

"I had you park down at the end so I can get my truck out of the garage when we leave. Welcome to Spilt Rock, my humble home."

Ah, mystery solved.

"Thanks. I'd forgotten how beautiful it is out here. You must have a stunning view from the front of your place."

"Come in and see for yourself. Warning, though, it's tight quarters here, not like big old houses in the city." Ellen stood aside as MC climbed the couple of steps up to the concrete porch and entered through the rear door.

The smell of fresh-baked muffins hit her as she walked into a cozy kitchen. Despite her unease her mouth watered.

After a tour of the two-story house and a quick bite to eat they were ready to embark on the day's adventure.

Ellen rinsed their cups and plates. "I thought we'd go down to Castle Cove. Figured you'd be interested in a closer look at the Whispering Aspen compound. We're lucky the temp is supposed to hit seventy by noon and not a cloud in the sky. I have a couple of water bottles for us to take along."

"Perfect. Thank you." She'd not even thought about a water bottle. Where the hell was her head? "I can follow you in my car."

"Or I can drive and bring you back afterward. I know a secret spot to park, and it isn't big enough for two cars. Besides, it's a better option than the trailhead lot which might be full already. You won't tell on me, will you? Or are you ethically bound to report such incidents to the local sheriff?" She grinned as she dried her hands on a towel and hung it on the oven handle.

"I'm all for finding the best parking, so your secret's safe with me," MC said.

They exited via the rear door and loaded their water bottles and Ellen's daypack behind the driver's seat of her Toyota Tundra pickup before getting in the cab. Ellen rolled down the cracked asphalt driveway toward the gate. About ten feet shy of the fence she slammed on the brakes. "Quick. Get out."

"What the?" MC stared as Ellen scrambled from the driver's seat leaving her door ajar. Alarm dinging and dome light lit.

"Hurry. Before it's too late. Come on." Ellen waved a hand at MC.

MC popped her door open and met Ellen at the front of the truck.

Ellen grabbed MC's wrist, not exactly a grip of iron, but one that brokered no argument. With her free hand she pointed toward the lighthouse. "Check it out. Up at the top, the rail along the spire. See it?"

"What am I supposed to see?"

"She's beautiful."

"Who's beautiful?" Was she supposed to find some woman on top of the damn lighthouse? What was happening?

"There." Ellen continued to point. "On this side of the lake on the rail."

Then MC's eyes locked on the visage. A majestic peregrine falcon perched on the thin iron rail. "Now I see what you're so excited about. Regal. Like she's sitting on her throne observing her kingdom."

"Exactly." Ellen's voice floated on the breeze. "She's been visiting frequently this spring. Sometimes I get my binoculars out and watch her from my front porch. I feel like I'm an audience of one. I find the encounters calming. Meditation in nature. Did you know when peregrines go into their hunting dive, they can reach speeds of over two hundred miles per hour? Fastest animal on planet Earth. Well, shall we hit the road?"

Ellen's sudden exuberance whacked MC upside the head. Was this how being around Ellen would be? Calm and one second later an explosion of energy, like lighting a sparkler on the Fourth of July. Not a bad thing. Different.

"Wait." MC asked, "How can you tell that the peregrine is a female?"

"Males and females are nearly identical. Females tend to be nearly thirty percent larger than males, with a wingspan between twenty-nine and forty-seven inches. I can't be sure that's a female, but I like to think she is."

"Good enough." MC got back in the truck.

They parked in Ellen's secret spot, which was little more than a cleared dirt patch off a gravel road near the trail. The space was large enough to stow the truck, and the surrounding foliage, though not fully bloomed, acted as a decent camouflage.

Ellen grabbed her daypack and beckoned MC to follow her. After a struggle through some blossoming brush, MC was surprised to see a decent trail open before them. She followed Ellen along the pathway, minding the exposed tree roots and peaks of rock poking up through the earth. "Is this part of the Superior Hiking Trail?"

Ellen paused. "I'm not sure if they consider this part of the official trail. I like to think it's a well-kept secret only a few dedicated hikers and maybe some locals know about. I rarely see anyone when I'm out here. The trail meanders around and we can access the trailhead a couple miles from here. I'll show you the sign when we get there. Next time if you're up for a longer hike to Gooseberry Falls State Park we can start at the trailhead. There are some spur trails with astounding overlooks on the way to Gooseberry. We'd be able to glimpse Lake Superior, waterfalls along Gooseberry River, not to mention Crow Valley. The forest is spectacular." Ellen took a breath. "But like I said, next time."

Ellen was an enigma. How could she be so confident there would be a next time? MC was mostly ambivalent and a tiny bit curious about this new person who'd inserted herself in her life. For now she'd allow some leeway, see where they ended up.

"So where does this hidden gem of yours lead us, again?" MC was most interested in seeing Whispering Aspen Ministries property.

"In about two miles we'll come up on the backside of the old summer camp, now Whispering Aspen. The trail isn't on their land, but it's easy enough to skip over the invisible property line from the forest onto camp land."

"Lead the way Macduff."

"Ah, a fan of Macbeth, are you?"

"What?"

"Lead on Macduff. It's a reworking of a phrase from a combat scene in *Macbeth* where he, Macbeth, lures his opponent into combat by saying something like "Lay on, Macduff" blah blah blah. I can't remember the exact quote."

"Huh. No, I am not a Shakespeare fan. I'm more of a mystery

novel type when I do read. I'm not even sure where I picked up the phrase. Something I heard at some point in my life, I guess. But interesting its roots are in Shakespeare's work." MC pointed to a stand of tall pines bare of branches about two-thirds of the way up. "Those are Red Pine, right?"

"Yep. Also known as Norway Pine."

"Minnesota state tree. I read that in a Department of Natural Resources pamphlet. Or maybe I heard it on Minnesota Public Radio. I can't remember for sure." Enough, McCall, you're babbling.

"Either way, you are correct. It is our state tree. Watch this rotted birch log coming up. Argh. So much mud." Ellen scraped her boots against the aforementioned log.

MC skirted the whole mess, uncapped her water bottle, and drank while Ellen finished cleaning globs of muck from her footwear.

About forty-five minutes later Ellen veered to the right onto a less-worn trail near a grove of quaking aspen trees. Then it hit her. They had to be near or on Whispering Aspen Ministries land.

Ellen stopped. "What's that smell?"

MC didn't detect anything other than normal forest smells. Possibly a hint of rotten eggs.

They weaved their way through trees and brush and stopped short of a partial clearing with a dilapidated cabin or maybe an old woodshed. The building was about fifty feet from where they stood.

Maybe it was an outhouse. But no, the ramshackle whatever it was measured about twelve feet by twelve feet, too large for an outhouse, unless someone was into group bathroom sessions.

On the side facing them was a window with planks nailed across it. The planking was newer than the grayish blackened wood of the actual structure.

"What is that?" Ellen asked. "I've never noticed it before, but I haven't really come along this trail. It's got to be one of the original cabins from the old summer camp. Or maybe a relic from the old logging days?"

MC picked up the scent of rotten eggs with an overlay of sweet tones the closer she got to the place. "Whatever it used to be, I think it's being used for something different now. Not sure what. Hang tight. I'm going to go see what I can through the window."

"Are you crazy?" Ellen whispered. "We should get outta here before someone sees us."

Before any more discussion ensued, MC went for it. She avoided as many sticks or other debris as she could that would announce her approach. The smell of sulfur got increasingly stronger as she neared the structure.

There wasn't enough space between the slats to see inside so she skirted the building. The rear wall had no door or window. The far side had another window with wood nailed across it.

No gaps there either. She came around to the front. A door was smack dab between two windows. Of course, these windows were also covered. She pressed lightly against the wooden door, even though she fully expected it to be locked. The door moved about two inches and a screech loud enough to wake the dead emitted from the hinges.

MC froze, heart racing like a thoroughbred at the Kentucky Derby. She stole a glance at Ellen, whose face was as white as a full moon.

Nothing happened. No one came to the door. No one yelled. Emboldened, MC pushed the door open enough to get a glimpse inside.

A wood-burning stove took up the center of the space. Firewood was stacked along the back wall. On one side five-gallon opaque containers of clear liquid were lined up. Water? On the other a roughhewn wood counter and cabinets beneath and above took up the whole wall. A stainless-steel sink sans faucet was set into the counter. A copper container with a stainless-steel bottom rested on the counter. The contraption didn't look like a cooking pot. She wasn't quite sure what it was, but it was shaped somewhat like a smokestack.

She backed out and ran into Ellen, who'd come up behind her.

"What the hell?" Ellen asked.

"I'm not positive, but I think we've found ourselves a distillery operation. I'm ninety-nine percent certain it's not a meth lab. Maybe moonshine or whiskey. Any of which is illegal to make outside of a verified distillery business." She pulled her cell phone from her jacket pocket.

"What're you doing?" Ellen asked.

"I'm calling a local deputy to let her know. The sheriff's department will want to put an end to whatever this is. Crap I have one bar, and it's blinking in and out. How far do you think we are from Whispering Aspen?"

Ellen moved past their secluded spot, off toward the east. "I'd guess the old camp cabins are maybe a quarter mile to the east and the Meeting Hall and church farther east down the same trail."

MC said, "We should walk the trail until I get a better signal."

After they reached the first of the camp bunkhouses, her cell service jumped up to three bars. She contacted Deputy Ekstrom and was pleased to discover she was on duty. She quickly summarized what they'd found. MC told her the best ingress would be to park at the Meeting Hall and hike the trail past the camp cabins to find them. Ekstrom said she'd be there to check it out and asked if they'd mind hanging out until she arrived.

"Will do." MC ended the call. "This little haven will no longer be a secret. Deputy Ekstrom is on the way."

"Do you think someone from the church is behind this setup?" Ellen asked.

The thought had occurred to MC. "I'm not sure. Can't even be sure this shack is part of their property. But if I hear I'll let you know. If I can."

"You law enforcement types are great with keeping your lips zipped when you want to. I hear it all the time on TV shows and movies. 'Sorry, I can't divulge information on an ongoing investigation.' It's not like I'd be blabbing to anyone."

"We law enforcement types take the sanctity of our investigations seriously. But trust me, it's for your own safety as well as the integrity of the investigation when we don't share information."

Even though this wasn't part of MC's ongoing investigations, she was intrigued. The last thing she expected on a hike in the northern Minnesota woods was to uncover a still. What next?

Forty-five minutes later, Ekstrom appeared. MC and Ellen filled her in on how they happened upon the moonshine distillery in the woods behind Whispering Aspen.

Ekstrom didn't know whether the land was part of the state forest or part of the church's property or owned by someone completely different. She hazarded a guess the cabin predated even the summer camp, now church community. Maybe it was someone's hunting shack a hundred years ago.

Deputy Ekstrom said, "Johnson said a team will confiscate all the stuff and we'll hold onto it. Anything hazardous will be disposed of safely. This is a first for me. Never seen anything like this."

"Me neither," MC said. "Good luck finding the master distillers."

"We'll monitor the area and review public records. If we can track down the owner, it's a starting point."

MC's gaze bounced between the distillery setup and Deputy Ekstrom's note pad. Doing a double check, ensuring everything got recorded. Sometimes she was beyond anal.

Ekstrom stowed her notes and took out her phone. She shot

photos outside and inside the still. "Someone may come and mess with the place before we can do a teardown."

Ellen cleared her throat. "Sounds like a lot of work for you all." She glanced at MC, one eyebrow hitched upward.

MC had almost forgotten Ellen was there. Shitty move on her part. She pulled Ellen aside. "Hey, I need to stay. I don't know how long it'll be. You can wait, but it might be a long while. I'm really sorry."

"No worries. We can always try again. Maybe we'll stick around the lighthouse trails. I can pretty much guarantee there aren't any moonshine stills there. Maybe some fermenting mushrooms, but no alcohol."

"I'll have Ekstrom drop me at Split Rock when we're done so I can collect my car. Okay?"

"Sure. No problem. Take your time. If I don't see you later, I'll see you on Thursday?"

"Yep. Thursday." MC heard the scuff of Ekstrom's boots behind her. "Hey, Deputy, Ellen is going to take off. I'll stay and assist until backup arrives."

"Great. You can tag along when I talk to Pastor Thackeray too."

"I like the sound of that."

Ellen adjusted her daypack on her shoulders. "I'm off then. See you later, MC. Nice to meet you, Deputy Ekstrom. Good luck with this mess."

"She seems nice." Ekstrom said as Ellen returned to the trail and disappeared.

"Yeah, she is. I haven't known her long. She runs Split Rock."

"The lighthouse? I had no idea," Ekstrom said. "That would be one giant job. So many people go through that place every year. So how do you two know each other? What happens on Thursday?"

MC hadn't realized Ekstrom overheard that part of the conversation. Should she reveal the truth or evade? Did she need one more person to know about the devil on her shoulder? Would the truth cast any doubt on her professional capacity?

"Sorry. I'm not trying to be nosy. You don't need to tell me anything you don't feel comfortable sharing. I was curious because I heard her say something about seeing you on Thursday. No harm. No foul."

"I met her at an AA meeting in Two Harbors."

"Good for you." Ekstrom's cheeks took on a rosy hue.

"I don't usually share personal information with anyone outside a very tight circle of friends and my bosses. Because we have a professional relationship, I trust you'll be discreet and not turn me into a topic in the local LE gossip mill." MC stood her ground with bated breath. Defensive much, McCall?

"You can count on me." Ekstrom responded. "My lips are zipped. Ah, geez."

"What?" MC about-faced in time to see Deputy Kempffer and another familiar face, Chief Deputy Luke Johnson, walking westward along the trail from Whispering Aspen.

"Inspector McCall," Chief Deputy Johnson said. "Long time no see. What brings you to our neck of the woods this time? You investigating illegal stills in the northland?" He grinned.

"Nice to see you again, Chief Johnson." She eyed Kempffer who stood seething behind Johnson. "Deputy Kempffer." A little poke of the bear.

"What have we got here?" Johnson asked Ekstrom.

She filled him in with a quick comment here and there from MC. Ekstrom ended with, "I thought once someone arrived, I'd head to Whispering Aspen and discuss matters with Pastor Thackeray."

"Yeah, probee, why don't you leave that to the more experienced officers," Kempffer piped up.

MC stiffened. Kempffer was a loudmouth waste of oxygen. His condescending, misogynistic tone was undisguised and inappropriate.

"I was first on scene. Inspector McCall was the one who notified LCSO. She volunteered to assist with interviewing the pastor and any other folks on-site up at the church."

"Kempffer," Johnson said, "I want you to call in a hazmat team and when they arrive, you supervise and take an inventory of the shack. Ekstrom and Inspector McCall can handle the interviewing. We clear?"

"Crystal." Kempffer yanked his cell phone from his pocket and stomped to the far side of the clearing to make the call.

MC said, "He's not too pleased."

"Doesn't matter. He was unprofessional. He's a decent enough deputy, but loves to delegate more than his fair share," Johnson said. "That goes no further than the three of us though. Understood, Ekstrom?"

"Understood, chief."

"Then off you go to find out what you can from Thackeray."

It didn't slip past MC that Johnson had left off the good pastor's title. Maybe she should loop him in on the images traced to Whispering Aspen? On the other hand, Johnson and his crew had enough on their plate with the illicit moonshine setup to disassemble, so she tabled the idea for the time being. Hopefully, something would shake loose when she and Ekstrom spoke with Thackeray.

Luckily, MC had stuffed her badge in the inside zip pocket of her jacket. She fished it out and hung it around her neck as she and Ekstrom walked the trail toward the church grounds. They passed six dilapidated summer camp cabins huddled along the dirt path leading to the Meeting Hall and church.

MC and Ekstrom had little trouble locating Thackeray. He was in the Meeting Hall. They'd not seen another soul, as they entered through the main door and cut through the entry way to the stairway leading down.

Thackeray waited at the bottom of the staircase. "What can I do for you officers?"

MC's heart pounded. "Jesus." Had he materialized out of thin air?

"No, I'm a pastor. But Jesus is always with us." He fingered the gold cross hanging around his neck.

What a nutjob.

Thackeray said, "Little Riley Ekstrom? Is that you? I haven't seen you since you were what? Twelve? Thirteen? I recall that being around the time you stopped coming to church. We sure do miss you. God's door is always open."

MC, one step behind Ekstrom, noticed the deputy's entire body stiffen.

"It's Deputy Ekstrom, Pastor. Do you have a few minutes to answer some questions?"

The tangible chill in the air was equivalent to the gales of November blowing off the great lake. MC half expected to see icicles form on the railings.

Pastor Thackeray was shocked to hear a distillery was being operated out in the woods. Swore on his Bible he had no idea the shack even existed. "Honestly, I don't remember ever venturing past our group of cabins. I'm not big on the outdoorsy stuff, more a homebody."

MC swore he flexed his biceps when he said homebody. For Christ's sake, what a douchebag.

Ekstrom, seated in one of the two chairs facing Thackeray's desk, scribbled in her notebook. "Do you know where Whispering Aspen's property ends?"

Thackeray folded his hands over his not-quite-flat belly and sat back in his executive chair. The gold cross and chain glinted under the florescent lights. "Far as I know, the last cabin on the trail is the end of our property. If I'm not mistaken, the state forest takes up from that point on." His gaze zeroed in on MC. "Weren't you here a few nights ago asking about becoming a member? I didn't realize you're a deputy."

"I'm not a deputy. I'm federal law enforcement. US Postal

Inspector."

"Hmm. What does a postal inspector have to do with investigating a moonshine hut in the woods? Did someone send jugs of moonshine through the mail?"

"I happened upon the still when I was hiking earlier today. As a professional courtesy, I offered to assist Deputy Ekstrom with interviews."

"Given any more thought to joining our little community here at Whispering Aspen?" Thackeray leaned forward and rolled his chair up close to the desk.

MC thought he was getting ready to launch himself at them. God, he was slimy. "No, but I still have the pamphlet you gave me."

He huffed and stood. "Well, if you don't have any more questions for me, Deputy and Postal whatever, I'll see you out. I have a sermon to write." He came around the desk and stood waiting, negative vibrations emanating from him.

He was on edge. But why?

Thackeray opened the door to usher them out.

MC stopped in her tracks. "Is that a lightsaber?" She pointed to a toy lying on the built-in desk under the windows. On Wednesday she'd noticed a laptop on that desk. Now the laptop was gone, but the lightsaber glowed green.

"One of the kids must've left it in here. We have a ton of them. The little ones sometimes get them as rewards when they've completed special tasks or done a good deed." Thackeray strolled over and flicked a switch to turn it off.

"Right. Well, thank you for your time." MC handed him a card with her contact information. "Please call if you think of anything you forgot to mention today."

She and Ekstrom no sooner exited, and the door banged shut behind them.

"He's utterly repulsive," Ekstrom said. "You got to see firsthand what I've been saying about him. He puts on an act to get you to believe he's a holy roller, but then the mask slips and the true Thackeray sticks his head out. I've always thought something about him was off."

They climbed the stairs and exited the Meeting Hall. Ekstrom's cruiser was parked in the roundabout between the Meeting Hall and the church.

"I'll bring you back to Split Rock, then I have to write up my report on this situation."

"Any chance you'll have time when you're finished to meet me at Caleb Lewis's? I'm thinking Saturday might be a good day to execute a knock-and-talk."

"Sure. I'm on the six-to-six shift so I have a few hours left."

"Great. Text when you're done, and I'll head to Caleb's and wait for you."

Ekstrom texted MC about three. The report was done, and she was good to go.

Twenty minutes later, MC pulled her car behind the LCSO marked unit.

"Ready?" Ekstrom asked.

"Let's do it."

Ekstrom headed for the outside staircase leading to Caleb's apartment door.

MC touched Ekstrom's elbow and pointed to their left where a bright red Dodge Charger was parked in the car port on the far side of the garage. "We might get lucky."

At the top of the stairs MC pounded on the door.

A minute later, the door opened halfway and a twenty-something man with short dark brown hair, wearing a hoodie, faded jeans with a hole in one knee, and Vans sneakers peered out at them. "Can I help you?"

"Postal Inspector McCall. This is Deputy Ekstrom from Lake County. Are you Caleb Lewis?"

His brown eyes were wide as dinner plates. "Um, yeah. I'm Caleb. What's this about?"

MC said, "Mr. Lewis would it be okay if we came inside and asked you a few questions? It shouldn't take very long."

"Am I in trouble? I mean. I'm kind of busy. I was working on a project for work."

MC shuffled half a step forward. "I promise we won't take up too much of your time."

"Okay. Come in." He moved aside and MC and Ekstrom entered. Lewis closed the door and pointed for them to go right toward the sofa in the living room.

On the left was a nook with a dining table, junk scattered across the top. The dining area connected to a small galley kitchen. A hallway ran straight back from the door and MC glimpsed three doorways. A couple of bedrooms and a bathroom? Nice lodging for a young single person.

The living room was decked out with a fifty-inch TV on the wall and a sound bar and cable box on a shelf underneath it. The couch and a recliner were directly across from the TV. A game controller had been tossed onto the seat of the recliner.

Ekstrom said, "Nice digs."

"Yeah. So what questions do you have?"

MC said, "Why don't you take a seat?" He chose the recliner, pushing the game controller to the floor. MC sat on the couch not far from him and where she had a sightline to the rest of the open space and the start of the hallway.

Ekstrom strolled by the kitchen table, checked out the kitchen, and repositioned herself at the beginning of the hallway.

Caleb cracked his knuckles and asked again, "What questions do you have?"

"Here's the deal, Caleb," MC said. "I'm investigating a recent robbery at the Castle Cove Post Office. I'm real interested in why you thought your wallet might've been found at the post office."

"How do you…?"

"How do I know you're looking for your wallet? Because the postmaster informed me you showed up asking if anyone had found your wallet. Your inquiry happened at a point after the robbery. Why, Caleb, would your wallet be at the post office?"

Caleb jumped up from the recliner. Immediately sat down. His leg jiggled as if it wanted to perform River Dance for them.

Ekstrom had eased into the hallway, craning her neck.

"What's she doing?" Caleb pointed at Ekstrom. He moved to stand up. "What are you doing?"

MC said, "Caleb, stay seated."

Ekstrom edged into the living room. "Take it easy, Caleb. Mind if I use the bathroom?"

"I guess."

"Why so twitchy, Caleb?" MC asked. "I'd swear you're trying to hide something."

He shook his head and jammed his hands into the pouch of his hoodie sweatshirt.

"Cat got your tongue?" MC asked. "No reason to worry if you tell the truth. No one present but the three of us, well right now the two of us, and the four walls of your humble abode. I'm not trying to trap you." She spread her hands out as if to say, see, nothing here. "I'm hoping to get some simple answers."

"I don't know anything about the robbery."

"I didn't ask if you knew anything about a robbery. Why would I think you might know something about the robbery?" MC was on high alert now. "I asked about your wallet you claimed to have lost at the post office. The post office which happened to be robbed." This interaction was going in circles.

"All I know is I lost my wallet and the last place I remembered having it was when I brought a bunch of mail to the Castle Cove Post Office. So why wouldn't I show up to ask about it? I got nothing to hide." His bouncing leg told a completely different story.

"Why the Castle Cove Post Office, Caleb?" MC asked.

"What do you mean?"

"I mean, you live here," she stretched her arms wide, "in Two Harbors. Why wouldn't you mail your items at the Two Harbors Post Office? Why drive up to Castle Cove?"

Caleb's jitters amped up to DEFCON five million. "I dunno. Because I was driving up that way and then I remembered I had stuff to mail?"

"Are you asking me or telling me?"

"Telling."

Ekstrom re-entered the room. MC sensed something was afoot.

"Tell you what, Caleb. Why don't you come down to the Law Enforcement Center here in town? Maybe we can reconnect you with your wallet. Sound like a plan?"

"Why can't someone bring my wallet to me? If someone has it? Why do I need to go to the police station?"

Ekstrom said, "We gotta do the right paperwork and stuff."

"Okay. When should I come in?"

MC exchanged glances with Ekstrom. "I'd imagine you want your wallet. Right? So you tell us."

"I guess I could do it today. Or maybe tomorrow. But tomorrow is Sunday. Should I wait until Monday?"

"Monday is fine, Caleb. If you can wait, we can too." MC stood. "Deputy Ekstrom, do you have any questions?"

"Not at the moment."

Caleb rocketed up from the recliner and launched them out the door.

MC said, "We'll see you Monday, Caleb."

The door closed behind them, and she heard the snick as the deadbolt was engaged.

They descended the stairs and walked to their parked vehicles.

"He's wound tight," MC said.

"He's going to be wound tighter soon. When I went to use the bathroom, I accidentally wandered into the other two rooms down that hall. One was a home office setup. Fancy desktop computer. Laser printer. Tons of DVDs, postal shipping boxes, and padded envelopes on a small plastic table. In the midst of all that I saw a shrink-wrapped DVD, the movie *Cars*. Out of place in the middle of all the blank, or assuming they're blank, DVDs and jewel cases."

"Okay. We know he works from home. So?"

"It's what I saw on his computer. It was horrible, McCall." She shuddered. "I saw a naked boy. He couldn't have been more than eight or nine. Holding one of those lightsaber toys like we saw in Thackeray's office earlier. He wasn't looking at the camera. He looked spaced out, and the sword was hanging from his hand. Naked, McCall. The boy was NAKED. I cannot unsee the image."

"Did you touch anything?"

"No. The image was in plain view. Kept my hands in my pockets. Should I ask for a search warrant?"

MC thought about it. Then she did a search of the United States Code on her phone. The language of the federal statute indicated if the image were on Caleb's computer they could assume it had been sent to him via another computer, which would make it federal jurisdiction. "I'll handle the search warrant."

"But there's no mail involved. So how does that fall under your agency?"

"The USC states there is federal jurisdiction over possession of CSE materials via the internet. The US Postal Inspection Service has developed a national expertise in this type of investigation. We've partnered with NCMEC since their inception."

Ekstrom said, "This just got a whole lot messier than a robbery."

MC wondered if there could be a connection to what Ekstrom saw on Caleb's computer and the tip USPIS received from NCMEC. "My boss got a call that someone from a cloud storage service reported CSE images had been uploaded on their server and the photos initiated from an IP address associated with Whispering Aspen Ministries."

"Holy shit," Ekstrom said.

MC said, "From your lips to God's ears."

"I have another interesting tidbit." Ekstrom pulled her phone from her pocket and swiped the screen. "I found this on the kitchen table, so I took a quick pic." The photo showed a scrap of paper wedged beneath a stack of mail. A phone number and the initials T.K.

"T.K.?" MC asked. "Do you recognize the initials or the number?"

Ekstrom said, "Only T.K. I know is Tyler Kempffer. The number doesn't match the one I have for him, but I only have his work contact. I'm sure he has a personal phone too."

"The plot thickens. Caleb is deep into something scummy. His story about his wallet might be partly true. His wavering and agitation scream he's not being totally forthcoming."

The day was getting more bizarre by the minute. Everything was clear as the mud stuck on the soles of her hiking shoes.

She thought about how a couple shots of Grey Goose used to

help. Then she snapped out of it. "So that was interesting. Did you believe any of what he said?"

"Nope. Guy's twitchy as hell. And he doesn't know yet what I saw on his computer. We need to move fast on the search warrant."

MC said, "The connection to Kempffer is perplexing. Why does he have Kempffer's phone number? Or what we assume might be Kempffer's phone number."

"A possibility is that Kempffer may have written it down the night we pulled Lewis over. I'll ask around. See if anyone can connect them. Other than the time we pulled Caleb over during my field training, I haven't personally seen them together. That incident was absolutely out of line. What Kempffer did, following Caleb here and making me wait in the squad car, was not right. He was up to no good. I'd bet my next paycheck on it."

MC opened her car door. "You'll let me know if you find a link? Meanwhile, I'm going to the Cities to see about a search warrant. Once it's approved, I'll let you know, if you want in."

"You betcha."

Back home MC packed her bag and grabbed her laptop. Then she called Assistant US Attorney Vince Long in Minneapolis. She quickly explained her situation, and what she and Ekstrom had observed at Lewis's apartment. "I know it's Memorial Day weekend, but any chance we can meet tomorrow and swear out an affidavit for a search warrant?"

"I could spare some time late afternoon. Say two o'clock. My office. We'll hash out the affidavit. Then we'll go to see the judge. I know one who will allow us to show up at her residence, even on a long weekend. She has a special distaste, as we all do, for child predators."

"Time is of the essence here, Vince. I appreciate you meeting on a holiday weekend."

"See you tomorrow, MC."

She packed the car and drove to St. Paul. Instead of checking in at Flannel she went to her apartment.

Seven p.m. Saturday night wasn't a busy time in her building's laundry room, so she was able to toss in a load. While the wash cycle ran, she did some forensic digging on Caleb Lewis and Tyler Kempffer.

Not long into her sleuthing, she found Kempffer's bio on the Whispering Aspen Ministries website. A photo of him out of uniform loaded on the screen. Youth Pastor Kempffer. She already knew he was involved with the whack-a-doodle church, so nothing new there.

The next hit she got was a public records entry for a divorce. Interestingly, he and his now ex-wife had only been married eighteen months. MC tracked down his ex via Facebook. She took a chance and reached out to her through the message app.

She explained who she was, that she was working on an investigation in Castle Cove, and was hoping for some insight into Deputy Kempffer. She pushed the envelope and got a little personal, asked why they'd divorced less than two years after getting married. And further, why had the ex-wife relocated?

What were the chances she'd respond? Close to zilch, MC thought. That done, she ran down to put her clothes in the dryer. The last thing she wanted was someone to throw them in a wet mound because they were impatient to use the washer.

Chapter Thirteen

As promised, AUSA Vince Long was at his desk when MC arrived promptly at two p.m.

MC said, "Thanks again for coming in on Sunday, Vince."

"I really didn't have anything big planned anyway. Happy to help. Let's set you up at the conference table."

MC set her laptop on the table.

Long sat next to her. "You know the drill. Write everything you and the deputy observed during the interview visit with the guy, what was his name again?"

"Caleb Lewis." Her fingers flew across the keyboard. "The warrant should cover the computer, hard drive, and any records relating to the production, distribution, and mailing of any child sexual exploitation materials. Correct?"

"Exactly."

After about an hour of back and forth and running spell check for the nine hundredth time, they had a solid Affidavit in Support of a Search Warrant printed out.

"Let me check Judge Linch's address." Long scrolled his phone screen. "Okay, got it. You want to follow me or ride with me? Either way works."

"I'll follow you. We can go our respective ways afterward. I don't want to inconvenience you any more than I already have."

He gave MC the address.

"Deephaven. Nice," MC said. The city was located about twenty miles west of Minneapolis, so not too long a drive. The map app directed MC to I-394 West to I-494 South, and then onto Highway 7 West for approximately four miles before exiting and winding through residential streets. Finally, she hung a left on Bramble Road and found Judge Linch's house near the end of the cul-de-sac.

MC pulled into the driveway behind Vince's black Audi Q7. Snazzy ride. Maybe it was time to let go of Barb's Subaru Forester and move on to something different.

She joined Vince on the flagstone walkway leading to the dark wood front door. He rang the bell. Almost immediately the door opened.

Judge Edith Linch wasn't more than five feet tall with shaggy-short iron gray hair and was dressed in blue jeans and a denim shirt with smudges of dirt along the front and the sleeves. "Come in. Come in." She shifted aside. "Pardon my appearance. I was working in the yard."

The semi-open floor plan was bright and airy. White walls, trim, and molding, and light oak flooring. A direct contrast to the darker nautical blue of the exterior.

"Go ahead and take a seat." The judge ushered them into a long room with white built-in bookshelves and a glass-topped table that faced the front windows. MC envied an oak window seat spanning the length of the windows, white storage drawers underneath. Three chairs were arranged around the table. A laptop and printer sat on one end of the table along with a scattering of pens and eyeglasses.

Vince said, "Thank you for seeing us on a Sunday, Judge Linch."

MC withdrew the affidavit from her bag. "We appreciate you taking time to help us, Judge."

Linch put on a pair of bright-purple-framed reading glasses. "You're welcome. When it comes to these types of crimes, I'm available any time. Let me see what you have there, Inspector McCall." She quickly read the document. "Everything seems to be in order. The warrant would cover the computer, hard drive, other memory/storage devices, and any other CSE on the premises." She peered over the tops of her glasses. "There's nothing worse than these child abusers. Fries my bacon."

MC swore to the contents of the search warrant and signed the affidavit. The judge then signed and issued the search warrant. MC stuffed the document into a file folder.

"Best of luck dropping the hammer on this guy." Judge Linch escorted them to the door.

"Thank you," MC said. "Enjoy the rest of your weekend."

Vince said, "Really appreciate you, Judge. See you next week."

The judge closed the door behind them and MC said, "I'm so glad you could make the time today. I really didn't want to wait on this."

"I get it. Not a problem. Good luck. Let me know if you have any questions. Be safe out there."

MC drove back to St. Paul, her mind afire with plans for the following day. Before heading home, she planned to stop at Flannel and check in with her people. A decent cup of coffee and a biscotti sounded perfect.

Chapter Fourteen

Despite the success with AUSA Long and Judge Linch the previous day and with the warrant in hand, MC felt like she'd been slammed to the ground after someone jumped off the opposite end of the teeter totter. Her edges were frayed. She showered and dressed in her St. Paul apartment, packed her clean clothes and work paraphernalia, and stumbled out the door. The Monday morning doldrums were probably partly due to the overcast skies and the fact she'd not had any caffeine yet. She was fried from driving from up north and then running around securing the search warrant. But then the prospect of what she might uncover at Caleb's pumped her up a few notches.

She pointed the car in the direction of Flannel. While she wanted to see her friends, MC actually hoped that this time Zane would be opening and not Dara. Her sluggishness would be a red flag, and Dara was always on high alert.

The Flannel sign came into view, and it almost felt like the beginning of a transformation.

Dara was behind the counter and brightened when MC entered. "Well, good morning, sunshine. Happy Memorial Day. Joyful beginning of summer and all that bullshit." Dara paused and squinted at her. "Why are you so ragged? Cripes, you looked better last night when you were here." Dara's voice enveloped MC in a blanket of dread. Exactly what she'd hoped to avoid.

"Hey, Dara. I'm just exhausted. Maybe I'm coming down with something. Been working a lot, and the drive back and forth every weekend is wearing me down. No rest for the wicked. I'm even working the holiday."

"Hmmm." Dara helped the customer in front of MC and then without asking what she wanted grabbed the largest cup and filled it with the daily dark roast blend. The aroma hugged MC. "You got a set of luggage hanging under your eyes. You didn't get into the devil juice last night, did you?"

Jesus. "No, Dara. I did not drink." But thanks so much for pushing that thought to the forefront of my brain. She swallowed her annoyance with her good friend. "How's Zane?" A change of topic was in order.

"Zane is good."

Meg came out from the kitchen area. "I wondered what all the commotion was out here. Whenever I hear Dara's voice all the way in the back, I know something's up. Nice to see you again this morning, MC."

"Meg, you're looking better every day." Yesterday they'd updated her on Meg's radiation regimen. Meg was tolerating the sessions well. Thank God.

"What's going on?"

"I was telling MC she looked like death warmed over. Then I asked if she'd slipped on the proverbial banana peel and fallen into a barrel of booze."

Meg smacked Dara on the arm. "Stop. You're incorrigible. Why can't you be nice instead of stirring the pot?"

MC took a sip to cover the grin she felt coming on.

"How are the cases? Last night you didn't say anything. How's it going?" Meg asked.

MC was glad to have a snippet of time with them when the focus was on them and not her. "Yep, juggling two investigations. The robbery and the other is child exploitation. The worst."

"How horrible." Meg shook her head. "I can't even imagine."

"Can you tell us more?" Dara wiped the counter and stacked empty cups near the urns.

"No. Sorry. I really can't talk about it. And believe me, you don't want to hear it anyway."

"I guess now I understand why you might be feeling so rough," Dara said. "You're dealing with a lot of shit. You keeping up with the weekly meetings?"

MC took a deep breath and held it for a four count, then released it slowly. "Yes. Every week. Haven't missed one yet. In fact, this week will be my sixth meeting." And last. But she didn't remind Dara of that fact because the last thing she wanted to do was get into an inevitable argument.

"Okay, gals. Nice to see you both again this morning. Miss you like crazy. But I need to get some work done in the office before my therapist appointment and then it's back to Castle Cove."

Meg came around from behind the counter and hugged MC. "You have a good week. Safe drive. We love you."

Dara, in an unusual break from her norm, also embraced MC. "Be strong. You got this."

The positive words and contact from Dara were a welcome change from other utterances in the past. MC took the win.

"Stay in touch. Let me know if anything changes?"

"I will," Dara said.

MC said, "Good morning, Pearl. You're looking well. I promise as soon as this case is done, I'll be more attentive."

She fired up the computer and made quick work of her emails. The building was eerily quiet, but she reminded herself this was a holiday. Most of her co-workers were probably off.

A knock on her door startled her. "Come in."

Jamie opened the door. "Hey, good to see you. Got a few minutes?"

"You bet. Grab a chair." She gulped her now cooled beverage, but she needed the caffeine. "Yesterday AUSA Long and I got my affidavit for the search warrant on Caleb Lewis's residence completed, and Judge Linch issued the warrant. Can I get a Digital Evidence Tech to meet me in Two Harbors later this afternoon? I know it's a holiday, but I want to execute the warrant ASAP." She reiterated the in plain view image Ekstrom saw on Lewis's computer, as well as her own suspicions about his being the elusive post office robber, though the search warrant was specific to CSE.

"I'll call in Felix Phelps. What time do you want him at the site?"

"I have an appointment at one. I should be on the road by two and could meet Felix at Lewis's place around five. Plenty of time to ensure we start during daylight hours, as required," MC said.

"Sounds like you're on the right trail. Does Lewis have any ties to Whispering Aspen Ministries? We know the images reported on the cloud storage service initiated from Whispering Aspen."

"I haven't uncovered any connections yet. The couple times I've been at the church, I haven't seen him or heard his name mentioned. I can check with Deputy Ekstrom. She's a contemporary of Lewis's who attended the church up until her teens, when she stopped going. That's about ten years ago. A connection would be one more nail in his coffin." She stifled a yawn. "Sorry. The whole scheme is wretched. Why do people do this to kids?"

"Lots of sickos in this big bad world." Jamie nudged his glasses up. "MC, listen, I'm concerned the robbery investigation might be stalling. It's been almost two weeks. You mentioned this Lewis guy possibly being a person of interest in both cases?"

Ah, crap. Was Jamie worried about her capabilities out in the field? Her own self-doubts were gremlins roaming rent-free in her head. The investigation was dragging at a snail's pace, but not for lack of effort on her part. She'd been feeling mostly good about her work.

Hopefully, he wasn't going to tell her he thought she'd been faulty in her mentoring of Jim Bob as well. There was only so much "concern" for her work she could take in one sitting.

Take a breath, MC. Have a conversation. Don't jump to

conclusions and go on the defensive.

MC took her dead partner's advice to heart. "Jamie, I know it's been slow-going on the robbery thing. I've been running into roadblocks trying to interview people in the area. Door knocks haven't produced any viable leads. Lewis, the most likely suspect, has been slicker than frog shit in eluding me. Until Saturday when we finally caught him at home. I partnered with Deputy Ekstrom because she has familiarity with the town and somewhat with this Lewis character. As for his being involved with both cases, it might be wishful thinking on my part. I haven't seen any proof he's involved with Whispering Aspen Ministries, so maybe he's got a fetish and it's nothing to do with the investigation. If so, we'd have an additional CSE investigation." God help her if that proved to be the case.

"But on the other hand, I don't believe in coincidences. So when Ekstrom saw, in plain view, the image on his computer, well, it upped the ante." As she'd spoken the words a realization sunk in. If Caleb Lewis had no ties to Whispering Aspen, he couldn't have sent those images to the cloud storage service from the church site. Still. The image on his computer warranted an investigation just as much as the photos on the cloud storage service did, and she'd follow her nose and see what she could turn up.

"But with the robbery, I'm worried the amount of time we're investing doesn't correlate with the amount of money taken. Maybe we'd be better off turning the case over to LCSO because the cash taken was only slightly more than a hundred bucks, right?"

"Well, yeah. The thing is the thief grabbed a bunch of mail at the very end. No way of knowing how much or exactly what. The whole scenario is a steaming pile of stink. My gut tells me there's more to it than the cash. I get a sense the culprit, whether it's Lewis or someone else, isn't a career thief. Lewis agreed to meet us at the sheriff's office today. But now with the search warrant in hand, I can just haul him in and go at him hard about everything."

"Makes sense. Continue with what you're doing. I trust your instincts. But I'm really hoping for some results soon."

"You and me both."

Jamie stood. "You've got a full plate. You hanging in?"

"I'm doing all the things I should be doing. I'm good."

He rested his hands on the top of the chair. "Keep me updated."

She had time before her therapy appointment, so she logged into DigiCase and updated her case notes. Afterward she checked Facebook hoping Kempffer's ex had responded. Lo and behold there was a message waiting. She clicked it open. The ex-Mrs.

Kempffer informed her she'd be more than happy to discuss Tyler.

The divorce was recourse for his physical abuse. She'd also found a shoebox full of kiddie porn in their closet and confronted him. His defense was to beat her and threaten to kill her if she told anyone. His words were, "I'll hunt you down and end you." That was the last straw. The wife left town, hired an attorney, got a divorce, and never saw or spoke to Tyler again.

"I want to keep it that way." The ex-Mrs. Kempffer wrote. She also informed MC that Tyler had issues with women, especially women in positions of power. Her final comments were ominous. "Be careful. Do not trust him."

MC wanted to write back and tell the woman that porn implied consent, but a child can never give consent. The proper terminology for what Kempffer possessed was Child Sexual Abuse Material. A crime.

Kempffer was proving to be so much worse than MC first thought. A human abomination.

MC wondered if Ekstrom knew about Kempffer's history. If not, she'd fill her in. All this brought up an even more disturbing question. Could Kempffer be involved in the Castle Cove child exploitation activities? He had a connection to Whispering Aspen. He was the youth pastor. Things could get real ugly, real fast. Nothing scarier than a bad guy with a badge.

Riding high and anxious from the latest revelations, MC headed to her appointment. On the way to Dr. Zaulk's office, a call came on her cell. MC checked the screen. Unknown. She figured it was a cold call, so she let it go to voicemail.

By the time she found a parking spot around the corner from Dr. Z's building, a red dot with a two hovered above the phone icon. Unknown's call and voicemail. As usual, MC was early, so she listened to the voicemail. The gist of the message was for her to stop poking her nose where it didn't belong. Whoever left the brief message had disguised their voice with a modulator. When she tried to call the number, she got a no longer in service recording.

A burner, no doubt.

What the hell?

She'd have to deal with this later. Time to get inside.

Dr. Z's waiting room was empty. She sat and rehashed the information from Kempffer's ex. He was worse than she'd imagined. Abusive and into CSE. How the hell had he passed muster to get into law enforcement?

Dr. Zaulk's voice interrupted the whirling dervish in her mind. "MC, come on back."

She followed the doc in. A part of her wondered what, if any, reaction Dr. Z might have if she plopped herself onto the bean bag chair instead of the ivory-colored armchair she'd chosen from the very first session.

"Would you care for some water?" Dr. Z asked.

MC picked at her thumb nail. Déjà vu. "No. Thank you."

Dr. Z settled into her chair and opened her notepad. "So last time you shared in a huge way about Cindy's death and your guilt. I'd like to delve deeper if you're feeling up to it. I'm optimistic that putting voice to those memories will help set you on the path to healing."

"I don't know." How could she ever heal from all the trauma? She was still shocked she'd spilled the beans about Cindy in the first place. The event had been buried so deep. Locked away. Yet last week, out it came without any warning. Unleashed like a monsoon ripping through her.

"Tell me what you're feeling. What you're thinking. You're clearly processing something," Dr. Z said.

I feel like I need a barrel of booze.

Stop.

"I remember." She picked at the thumb nail some more, drawing a tiny bead of blood.

"You remember what?"

Without warning a torrent of words poured out of her. "Before Cindy died one of the things our mom used to do was help us take care of wounded animals we'd find." She gazed off into the distance.

"One time we found a baby robin. It had fallen from the nest in the tree in our backyard. The momma robin wasn't around. Cindy scooped up the baby bird, the tiniest bird I'd ever seen, and brought it in the house. I thought for sure Mom would be upset with us for bringing it inside. Instead, she found an eye dropper, an empty shoe box, and some newspaper to shred. She set the baby bird on top of the shredded paper inside the box. Then with the dropper, she taught us how to feed it drips of water."

"That's a wonderful memory. Why are you frowning? Is there something about the memory that puzzles or upsets you?

"I didn't realize I was frowning. I'm not puzzled or upset. Maybe sad. Because after Cindy died, Mom no longer paid attention to wounded animals, or to me really. I never bothered to try and rescue any creatures either. Nothing was the same without Cindy. Life radically changed."

She dragged in a ragged breath. A searing pain gripped her from head to toe.

"Take your time. No need to rush," Dr. Z said.

"Remember I told you my parents forbade any mention of Cindy's death? They'd told me to leave it alone." She'd obeyed. She always obeyed. "It was almost as if Cindy never existed. I missed her every day. But I learned to keep that secret buried deep and to never voice my feelings or ask questions. Until my last couple appointments here." When it all tumbled out like rocks rolling down a crumbling cliffside. She'd unleashed the memory and there was no way to cram it back in the box.

After her parents were killed in a freak car accident, there wasn't anyone left to share memories with or ask questions of anyway. MC sealed everything in a vault inside her and went about living her life.

Then she met Barb, and a light had shined again. Though she'd never told Barb about Cindy.

"What's going on, MC? Talk to me."

"Nothing."

"I don't believe you."

"Regret. I am regretful. My immediate regret is I never had the courage to entrust Barb with this part of my life. I'm guilty of keeping this secret from her. I feel like I betrayed her trust. Or maybe I unconsciously questioned whether I could entrust her with these parts of me?" Her tongue stuck to the roof of her mouth. "Maybe I will take a bottle of water, please."

Dr. Zaulk retrieved a bottle from a small fridge behind her desk and handed it to MC.

"Thanks." She twisted the cap off and drank deeply before putting the cap back on. "I have these...not really sensations...more like film clips. Sound bites from that day. Cindy's final day. But they're out of order. I see a boy reaching for Cindy's leg. I'm screaming. Then a boy, not sure if it's the same boy, is laughing and taunting me."

MC's heart pounded so loud her body shook. "Then more screaming, but I don't know if it's me or other kids. Cindy's grin turns into a rictus of fear—her hand reaching out, grabbing thin air. Had she called my name? Someone, an adult, scooped me up. I tried to break free. To go to Cindy. She'd already disappeared. I squirmed to get down. I had to help Cindy. But whoever held me kept telling me I couldn't help her. The last visual I remember is my arms outstretched...reaching toward the wall and my sister. A kaleidoscope...colors and movement then nothing."

She drank more water. "This endless yowl, like a cat on fire— was me, four-year-old me, wailing into the abyss. Then blackness. Silence. Nothingness."

In the ensuing years she'd had nightmares about stone walls, waterfalls gushing, and a little girl toppling off a wall. Every time

MC made it to the wall to peer over, everything went black. The actual memory had been buried so deep in her psyche she'd not been able to coax any of it out until now.

"We're at the end of our time, MC. You've shared a lot of heavy stuff again today. I'm going to recommend something to help you process the guilt you feel over not telling Barb. You can share those memories with her now, by telling them to her, out loud." She held up her hands as if to ward off imminent protests from MC. "Hear me out. It works. Communicating with our loved ones who have passed. Or if that's too uncomfortable for you then journal the memories, along the lines of writing a letter to Barb. Do whichever resonates for you. Trust me. You'll purge some of the guilt."

As if anything could help purge the load of guilt she carried. A tsunami might wipe out the level of guilt she held.

Or a two-day bender.

"Journal. Talk. Ugh. I don't know, doc." Was her aversion to voicing the memories to someone other than Dr. Z? Maybe. Would Barb have been supportive had MC had the courage to tell her? Of course. No question. She wouldn't have allowed MC to hold onto the guilt. Barb always had the solution to whatever was MC's problem.

"Give it a try, MC. Don't let it fester any longer. I'll see you next week. Same time."

MC left Dr. Z's office wrung out and thirsty for some liquid therapy to augment all the talk therapy. Instead, she put the pedal to the metal, headed for Two Harbors and Caleb Lewis's apartment.

A little after five she was in Two Harbors, having just filled her gas tank before continuing to Caleb Lewis's residence.

Her cell buzzed. Unknown. Again.

Time to answer. "Who is this?"

The same modulated voice said, "If you know what's good for you, you'll stop meddling where you don't belong. Mind your own fucking business. Get the hell out of town. You'll regret it if you don't."

"Who the—" MC stood, phone gripped so tight she thought she'd bend it.

Her new phone pal had already hung up.

She tried to call the number, which was different from the earlier call. Same result though. No longer in service.

Another burner.

Someone was being very careful. But who? And why?

For the time being she shelved the phone calls issue and called Deputy Ekstrom.

"Ekstrom. Inspector McCall here. I've got good news on the Lewis search warrant."

"Well, hold up a second. I've got updates too. Are you up here?"

"Yeah, I'm in Two Harbors at the gas station. What's up?"

"Good. Last night, sometime before nine o'clock, Caleb Lewis was the victim of a hit-and-run accident. Right in front of his house. His landlord came home from an evening out and found Lewis splayed out unconscious in the street. He was mangled."

"What the? Witnesses?"

"No witnesses. Last I heard he's in the hospital, unconscious. Bruised ankle and knee. Busted wrist. A bunch of cuts and contusions. Not great."

"Oh my god. Totally sucks, especially if he doesn't pull through. Christ. Well, the search warrant is approved so we can execute, and I have a Digital Evidence tech, Felix is his name, meeting us at Lewis's place. But what the hell happened? I mean the street he lives on is off the beaten track. Was he out jogging in the dark?"

"I doubt he was jogging. He was dressed the same as when we saw him, hoodie, jeans, and Vans shoes. Not the usual attire for a run. His apartment door, it wasn't just unlocked, it was wide open. Lights on inside. Almost like he'd heard a noise and went to investigate."

"Can we get in to see him at the hospital? Maybe he'll come around. I'd love to be there to get first crack at him. No doorbell cameras on neighbors' houses caught any of what went down?"

"A lot of the neighbors are old, been in their houses for thirty, forty years. Probably don't know anything about doorbell cams. McCall, there's something else you need to know. I had a bit of a run-in with Kempffer on Friday. He was coming off duty and I was going on. He cornered me in the stairwell and told me I'd better mind my own fucking business."

"Mind your own business about what?" A phrase very much like the two anonymous calls she'd received. Could it be Kempffer?

"I have no idea. But I suspect it's something to do with Caleb Lewis because I'd asked our front desk person, Lynette, if she or anyone knew if Kempffer was friends with Lewis. One of the guys possibly overheard me and blabbed to Kempffer. Bro culture, ya know?"

"Yes, I know. Something's going on with your co-worker. I could feel the undercurrent of something brewing the first day I met him and asked about his report on the post office robbery. He's a bully with a short fuse and it's been lit. And I got a couple threatening phone calls today from an anonymous jerk using a crappy voice modulator, warning me to mind my own business and get the hell out of town."

Ekstrom asked, "Do you think Kempffer is involved? The messages sound similar to what he said to me the other day."

"I don't know but we should both watch our backs. I did track down his ex-wife. She had quite the story to tell about him being abusive. More importantly to our current investigation, she found a shoebox of, as she said, 'kiddie porn,' stashed in their closet. When she confronted him, he beat her and threatened to kill her if she said anything. I almost wrote her back to correct her use of 'porn.' Children whose sexual abuse has been produced and distributed deserve to be protected and respected. And the seriousness of that abuse shouldn't be reduced to words like porn." MC crawled off her high horse. "So ask me again if I think Deputy Kempffer might have something to do with Caleb Lewis's accident."

"I did *not* see that coming." Ekstrom's voice was barely audible. "I had no idea. I mean, I'd heard he'd only been married for a short time and the ex-wife had moved away. Fast. Here one day, gone the next. But. Wow. His threat to me in the stairwell tracks with that past behavior."

"In any event, we should probably get over to Lewis's apartment. The warrant has to be executed during daylight hours. I mean, as long as we start while it's daylight, we're fine." Geez ramble much, McCall? "Do you by any chance have a connection at the hospital? Someone who could let us know if Caleb regains consciousness. It's going to throw a wrench in the works if we can't interview him."

The cogs clicked in MC's head. She tried to align the gears, but they weren't quite meshing. Was Kempffer the culprit behind the images sent to the cloud? Or was it Lewis? Or both? Or Thackeray? Or someone completely different? Was the post office robbery connected to the CSE?

MC paced near her car.

"I don't really know any of the nurses or docs at the hospital, but I could stop by and ask them to place a note in his file for someone to call me when he comes around. I'll say it's involving an ongoing investigation."

"That'll work. Then meet me at Caleb's apartment."

"Ten-four."

MC stopped at the cabin and changed into BDU pants, black tactical boots, navy T-shirt with the US Postal Inspection Service logo on the left chest, and as a precaution, a tactical ballistic vest with Police US Postal Inspector in yellow lettering on the back. She tucked two spare magazines in the built-in ammunition holder just in case. A black duty belt secured her firearm at her hip. She stuffed her badge into her pocket.

Twenty minutes after her call with Ekstrom, MC was parked at the top of Lewis's driveway. Felix Phelps, parked on the street, exited the navy Ford Explorer he'd signed out for the trip north. She'd worked with him before. He was a wizard with technology.

MC saw Caleb's car parked on the far side of the garage, which made sense as he was laid up in the hospital.

The evening was mild with cloud coverage blocking light from the setting sun. "Hey, Felix. Thanks for making the trek. Sorry to ruin your holiday."

"Not to worry, MC. I didn't have anything going on anyway. Happy to be of service."

Felix had a mop of black hair that reached his collar. His uniform of choice was pressed khaki pants and a light blue button-down oxford shirt. Sometimes he'd wear a plaid button-down for shits and giggles. A true geek. He wore round John Lennon-style glasses, which were cool.

"Yeah, what did we drag you away from?"

"Nothing much. I was binging *Dr. Who* and crocheting a scarf for my mom. I know it's spring but wanted to get a head start on my holiday gifts."

Crocheting? Did he say crocheting?

Felix laughed. "You should see your face right now. I find it relaxing. Try it sometime, you might be surprised."

Ekstrom arrived and parked behind MC's Subaru.

"Here's our county partner," MC said.

Ekstrom exited her car and joined them. "Hey, McCall."

"Hey, thanks for the assist. This is Felix, he's our Digital Evidence tech."

"Nice to meet you, Felix." Ekstrom shook his hand.

"You too. I'll be in my car 'til you guys clear the apartment."

MC said, "Sounds good."

They watched him climb back into the Explorer. MC wondered if he'd brought his crocheting along.

"All right," Ekstrom said. "Do you need anything? Evidence bags? Gloves? Foot covers?"

"Nope. Got an evidence collection kit in my car. Help me haul the stuff?" She keyed the back hatch open.

"Will do. I stopped at the hospital. Guess who I saw slinking away as I got to Lewis's room?"

MC handed Ekstrom a stack of evidence bags. "Who?"

"Kempffer. I came around the corner to Lewis's room, which is third from the end of the hallway. At the end of the hall is a stairwell and Kempffer was going through the door. I ducked around the corner in case he happened to turn around. Waited until I heard the door latch closed, then I made a beeline for Lewis's room. He's still out of it. I tracked down a nurse, told her Lewis was a person of interest in an investigation and to notify me when he wakes. She said she'd make a note in the chart."

"Kempffer, huh? Guy's everywhere and nowhere. I'm beginning to suspect a connection between Kempffer and Lewis and the child exploitation images."

"Do you think Lewis is in danger? Or was Kempffer just stopping by to see how he's doing?"

"Not sure." MC grabbed her kit, which contained crime scene markers, latex gloves, evidence collection kits that included swabs and containers for biological samples, if needed, a measuring tape, flashlight, and fingerprint lifting kits. She patted the side pocket of her BDUs to make sure she'd stuck her notebook in there. "You ready to see what's going on in Caleb's apartment?"

"Let's go."

MC went up the stairs first.

They set the gear on the landing.

Then MC knocked on the door. "Law enforcement. Search warrant! Open the door!"

No answer, as expected with Caleb lying unconscious in the hospital.

She knocked a second time and then twisted the doorknob. "Door's unlocked. No one locked up after he was transported last night?"

"The door should've been secured by whoever handled the call. Johnson won't like to hear someone dropped the ball."

MC said, "Or maybe they didn't."

They both drew their weapons.

MC glanced over her shoulder at Ekstrom. "Ready?"

"Yes. Go."

They stormed the apartment, moving rapidly through, room-by-room. Once they'd cleared the place, they regrouped in the dining area.

MC holstered her gun. "Hard to tell if anything's missing."

"Agreed. Oh, shit."

"What?" MC asked.

"I wonder if Kempffer was one of the responding deputies."

"Was he working last night?"

"I think so. I'll check the log when I get to the station."

"We'll note it in the report."

Ekstrom waited out on the landing and MC returned to her car and waved Felix over. "All clear."

Felix joined them on the stairs with his satchel of super-secret tech gear.

MC said, "Okay, everyone suit up out here. Shoe covers. Gloves. Let's get to work. Ekstrom, you start in the kitchen, dining room, and living room. We're gathering anything related to CSE, so be sure to look in every nook and cranny, and beneath stuff too."

"You got it." Ekstrom pointed to the stack of evidence bags. "Want me to grab some of those?"

"Yeah, that'd be great."

Back inside, Ekstrom headed for the kitchen/dining room.

MC said, "Felix I'll show you the office. You can set up at the computer. I'll go through the office space while you work your magic."

"Lead the way," Felix said.

MC started for the hall when Ekstrom said, "Huh. Weird."

MC stopped. "What?"

"Remember the pic I showed you with the slip of paper and the initials T.K. and a phone number?"

"Yes. Why?"

Ekstrom waved a hand toward the pile of crap on the table in the dining room. "To my eye, the same stuff is still here with the exception of that scrap of paper." Ekstrom took a couple photos. "I'll sift through everything piece-by-piece, but I think it's gone."

"Could be Lewis tossed it or moved it. Or he had it on him when he left the house last night. Check the garbage. I'll keep an eye out for it too. Remember our focus with this warrant is CSE materials."

She proceeded down the hall to the office. The room was barely big enough to accommodate a computer desk, printer stand, and a four-by-two-foot portable table holding all the items Ekstrom had mentioned on their previous visit. Not the fanciest of offices.

Felix stood beside the chair. "I'm jealous. This chair is awesome. Probably the most expensive item after the desktop computer and twenty-seven-inch monitor. This guy knows his stuff. I bet he's a gamer."

The chair was fancier than anything MC had ever used. The tan and black leather high-backed chair had a lumbar pillow, another pillow below the headrest and some type of release to recline with a footrest that would raise.

"This is the Cadillac of office chairs." He settled into it and wiggled the mouse to wake the computer.

The screen came alive, revealing a photo, probably a canned image and a logon box. "Will that be a problem?" She pointed at the screen.

Felix flipped the keyboard up and peeled something from the underside. "Nope." He showed her a strip of torn index card. "Got what I need right here. Even savvy users can sometimes forget their passwords. Guy probably thought no one would ever have cause to access his computer so wrote down the username and password." Felix wove his fingers together, stretched his arms in front of him and cracked his knuckles. He leaned forward, eyes fixed on the screen as his fingers pounded the keys.

She was going cross-eyed watching him. "You got this, Felix?"

"Yep." He leaned over and pulled a small box from his black bag. "New external hard drive. We use clean storage media to ensure no contamination during transfer to keep the original pristine. Then I mirror and download the files."

"You go ahead. Work your magic."

MC tackled the DVDs. There were two in jewel cases on the desk next to the computer. Both had labels stuck to the outside titled, "Behind Closed Doors." She could only imagine. She sealed them in evidence bags and labeled the bags. Pushed farther back on the desk was a used padded envelope. She picked it up. Empty. She flipped it over and found it addressed to Jimmy Lewis. She bagged the empty envelope as well.

Three cylindrical plastic containers of DVDs sat on the small table. She suspected they were blanks ready to be used. To be safe, she gathered them and placed them in a larger evidence bag. Sealed and labeled it.

None of the Priority Mail boxes were put together, so nothing to see there. The padded envelopes were empty except for the top one. MC spread the opening wider and used two fingers to tweezer out a commercially packaged DVD. The movie *Cars,* shrink-wrap sealed tight. She stuffed the DVD back inside the envelope, flipped it, and read the address. Jimmy Lewis in Rochester, MN. Same as the empty padded envelope she'd bagged minutes earlier.

Was Jimmy Caleb's son? She assumed Jimmy was a kid as the movie was a kid's movie. Why was the empty envelope also addressed to Jimmy? Had Caleb decided to send a different movie at the last minute? Another question to add to the growing list.

Ekstrom stopped in the doorway. "Didn't find anything interesting in the kitchen or living room. The mail was mostly junk with a couple of bills mixed in. I'm guessing we don't need it?"

"If the items aren't related to CSE leave, them. Check this out." She showed Ekstrom the kid's movie and the empty envelope addressed to the same person. "Do you know if Lewis has a kid? I'm assuming Jimmy is a kid because why would he be sending a kid's movie to an adult?"

"I'm not aware of him having a kid. I know he has an older sister. She's like four or five years older than him. Maybe it's her kid?"

"Do you know where the sister lives?"

"Nope. Sorry."

"I sure hope Lewis regains consciousness because I have a shit ton of questions for him," MC said. "I'm done in here. Everything is bagged and tagged." She stacked the stuff she'd collected into a cardboard box for easy transport. "Felix, where you at in the process?"

"I'm installing write-blocking software on the external drive so the data can be viewed but nothing can be added, deleted, or changed. The external drive is our working copy. When I'm finished with that, I'll seize the computer and load the hardware in the car for transport to the office. Then I'll get to work parsing the data."

"What all will you be able to see?" Ekstrom asked.

He adjusted his glasses. "I'll use extraction software and be able to view all the files on the drive. If he's hidden any files, I'll be able to see them. If he deleted files, I can restore them if they're not overwritten. Then I'll review what resides on the Internet. Chat rooms, messaging, websites, and on and on. I might be able to put together a decent picture of his Internet activity using email headers, time stamps on messaging, and encrypted data. Lots of options."

"Jesus. Mind-blowing," Ekstrom said.

MC said, "Okay. I'm going to the bedroom next. You want to check the bathroom?"

"Yep." Ekstrom walked out of the office muttering incomprehensibly.

"I think you broke her brain, Felix," MC said. "Mine too."

"Thanks. Just doing my job."

Caleb Lewis's bedroom was surprisingly tidy, except for the dresser, which was an inexpensive four drawer particle-board dresser covered with a mishmash of crap. Crumpled receipts. Coins. Pens. Gum. Gum wrappers. A fistful of bills crushed into a ball. MC photographed the mess. Could the cash be from the post office robbery? In any case, it wasn't covered by the current warrant. She added another question to the ever-growing list in her notebook. She and Caleb Lewis were going to have quite the conversation when he woke up. If he woke up.

Daylight faded into evening. MC and Ekstrom had gone through Caleb Lewis's place with a fine-toothed comb. When they finished, MC left a copy of the search warrant, and an inventory of items seized on the kitchen counter. She pushed the button lock on the doorknob and closed the door.

Felix had already loaded the computer, printer, the new external drive, and his black bag into the Ford Explorer. "I'm off. I'll get to work viewing the contents tomorrow morning."

"Thanks, Felix. Safe travels. Keep me posted."

"Will do."

MC and Ekstrom loaded all the boxes of remaining evidence into her car. "I'm not driving to the Cities right away, so we need to store this in your department's evidence locker. Who do I need to call to get the okay?"

Ekstrom said, "Chief Deputy Johnson or Sheriff Tollefsen. I'll follow you to the station. We can make the call from there, then unload and secure it."

They reached the Law Enforcement Center and to MC's surprise Sheriff Tollefsen was in his office despite the holiday. She laid out the situation and he immediately approved her request.

"Always happy to help the Inspection Service, McCall. I'll call down to the Evidence room and the duty officer will provide you a locker where you can store everything. Once it's logged and loaded in, he'll provide you a receipt. No one will be allowed access to the locker except you."

"I appreciate you, Sheriff. Deputy Ekstrom has been extremely helpful. Would you be able to spare her to continue assisting me?"

"Yep. When she's on duty she can assist, unless of course we have a situation that calls for all hands."

"Absolutely. Again, appreciate your help."

MC and Ekstrom cataloged and stored the evidence. MC got her receipt from the duty officer after the locker was secured.

"Ekstrom, let's call it a night. I cleared it with Tollefsen for you to keep working the case with me unless they need you for something locally."

"Roger that," Ekstrom said. "Thanks. I'm about done in."

MC raked a hand through her hair. "It's been a day. If you hear anything about Lewis from the hospital, you'll let me know?"

"Yep. I'm off tomorrow and Wednesday, but I'll be around. So if you need me call or text."

"Sounds good. Otherwise enjoy your days off."

MC was exhausted. She sure wouldn't want to be in Felix's shoes. The idea of having to sit and scroll through innumerable visual depictions of sexual child exploitation made her ill.

She grumbled to herself on the drive to her cabin, imagining the ways she could torture the abusers. If she could shed the mantle of law enforcement long enough to administer punishment for the crimes, she'd happily slide back into her proper role afterward. Her heart rate increased with the hum of the tires on the pavement.

The rapid pace of the blood hammering through her heart was making her eyeballs throb. She slowed her roll. Took a deep breath. In for four. Out for four. In for four. Out for four.

The controlled breathing barely worked. She completed several more reps to flush out the bad juju. Either that or—don't even think it, McCall.

She switched on the *Undisclosed* podcast. Her self-restraint was commendable.

Chapter Fifteen

Pastor Thackeray called Tyler Kempffer bright and early. "My house at nine this morning. Basement. Workout. No excuses. Be there."

"Whoa. Good morning to you too, Pastor. No can do. I'm on duty seven to seven today."

"You get a break, right? I'm serious, Tyler. Tell your boss you have some church business with me this morning. You *are* the youth pastor, last time I checked. I'm sure Tollefsen won't mind. He's a religious man."

"It's not Tollefsen I need to worry about so much as Chief Deputy Johnson. He oversees schedules and roster changes. He's always on my ass for something. I don't need any attention on me right now. Get my meaning?"

"Mind your manners. You're speaking to a man of God." He was ready to crawl through the phone and throttle Kempffer. Lately he'd descended to a whole new level of disrespect. The cash flow from their side hustle had trickled to near nothing the last couple of weeks. He wanted to know why.

"We have some business to discuss. So do what you have to do to make sure you're here at nine. Don't be late." He disconnected.

More than two hours later Thackeray finally heard Kempffer's squad car in the driveway. He threw open the front door. "You're fifteen minutes late, Kempffer."

"Yeah, tell someone who cares. What's got you all hot and bothered anyway? Before you go on, I don't have time to work out. I gotta get back on patrol."

"Get in here already." Thackeray held the door open. "Go on through to the kitchen." He knew Kempffer wasn't used to coming in through the front, so he directed him. "Grab a chair at the island. Want coffee?"

Kempffer sat on a swivel chair at the center island. "I didn't know you put such poison in your sacred vessel."

"Sarcasm will get you nowhere. Coffee, or no?"

"Yeah. Black."

Thackeray filled two Whispering Aspen Ministries emblazoned mugs.

"Tyler, let me ask you…are you happy with your position here at Whispering Aspen Ministries?"

"Sure. Why?"

"Are you enjoying the perks of your position here? The extracurriculars I allow you and Symons to participate in—to profit from as well as participate in. You're liking everything, correct?"

"Yeah. Yeah. Praise be and pass me the little kiddies."

"You're satisfied with the extra income, the benefits you're reaping. Symons doesn't care about a share of the money. He's all about getting his rocks off with the little ones and maybe having an image or two to relive the experiences later. He's not concerned about our little business operation. With that said...I am wondering why the side hustle has suddenly slowed to a side shuffle. Where's the money, Tyler? Why has it suddenly dried up?"

"Well, I've run into a bit of a roadblock. See..."

Thackeray rounded the center island, clamped a hand on Tyler's shoulder, and spun him around so they were face-to-face. "No, I don't see. That's why you're here and why I'm asking you questions. Are you getting cold feet? You playing me? Setting me up? What the hell is going on?" He slammed his other hand onto Kempffer's other shoulder. His hands were like iron, weighing Kempffer down.

"You're getting red. Shoulders starting to ache?" He increased his vise-like grip. "Don't even think of trying to throw me. You answer to me."

"Let me go already." Spit flew from Kempffer's lips. He grabbed Thackeray's arms, which didn't do much more than try to loosen his hold.

Thackeray's body thrummed with power. Electrifying in its intensity.

Kempffer strained against him. "Jesus. C'mon. Your fingers are digging craters into me. Lemme go."

"You going to be straight with me?"

"Yes!"

Thackeray released him and pushed him aside. He sauntered around to the other side of the counter and grabbed his cup. "Spill it." Eyes on Kempffer, who alternately rubbed his shoulders and patted his straw-colored hair into place. "Stop messing with your hair. What's with that style anyway? Are you trying to signal that you belong to one of those fringe extremist groups? Maybe you just wish you did."

"No, I don't belong to...you know what, I don't need to explain my friggin' haircut to you. Besides, you don't have room to talk. You do know having your hair long doesn't compensate for the receding hairline, right? Does God approve of your vanity? I bet not. In fact, you resemble someone who's a kiddie diddler."

Thackeray's face heated up and not from the steam coming off his coffee. "Enough bullshit. What's going on?"

"The kid I had working the computer, compiling our images and videos and burning DVDs to sell online, well, he's run into some trouble. With the law.

"There's been a slight snag in the distribution. He's not been able to get anything done for over a week, so the money has slowed. Honestly, we might have to find someone new to handle that end of the business. Doesn't mean we have to stop the other though." He grinned. "Can I get a warm up?" He held the mug out.

Thackeray stared at him. "What kind of trouble with the law?" If this guy, who Thackeray had chosen not to know, had been busted for child pornography it could be the beginning of the end for all of them. They'd fall like dominoes.

"Ah, something about being a suspect in a post office robbery. Nothing to do with us. I caught the call to the post office when it happened. Had no idea he was involved. But I guess there's been some evidence uncovered that points at him. I shut him up, for a while anyway, until I can figure out how to proceed."

"Tyler. What. Did. You. Do?"

Kempffer set his cup on the countertop. "He had a little accident and is out of commission for a while. By the time he's up and about, I'll have figured out how to make sure he doesn't say anything about working for us."

"Working for *you*." Thackeray corrected him. "I don't know this guy from Adam or Cain or Abel. You see? So he's *your* guy. Working for you. Getting paid by you."

"Yeah, but..."

"No buts. I don't like surprises. I am not a fan of disruptions. Even more, I abhor even a hint of being caught. You better take care he doesn't squeal about any of the work he's done for you. You could end up not only out of a job, but your ass could end up in prison. Kiddie diddlers, to use your terminology, don't fare well in prison, I hear."

"If I go down, we all go down." He stood and jabbed a finger at Thackeray's face. "You and Symons. What will the town think about its supervisor and pastor being involved in a kiddie porn scandal?"

"Easy junior. No need to get your tighty-whities in a twist. Remember who's the respected member of the community and who's the asshole cop whose wife divorced him because he beat her. You're such a dumb prick."

"Ain't no way for a pastor to talk. Chill." Kempffer was up and pacing the faded to no-color linoleum floor. "I'll figure something out. In the meantime, we need to get some new stuff tomorrow night. A couple of new kids this week. Cole is getting too weird. I think his big sister, Gracie, suspects something. She's been paying way too close attention lately."

"You let me worry about which kids are picked. You don't care one way or the other once they're down in the fun room. You and Symons will be happy with whomever I choose, or you can take a hike. Besides, Cole is a perfect little angel of God. Gracie doesn't know what she doesn't know. I choose him because the parents can be counted on not to be involved. They're either at the Dirty Minnow drinking pisswater cheap beer or out in some shack in the woods sucking down homemade moonshine."

"Got it. So that hooch hutch found on Saturday is the brainchild of the Norbergs? I'm not surprised. Well, in a way I am. Didn't think Pete and Alicia had enough brain cells to cobble together a moonshine business. Wonder if Chief Deputy Johnson has figured out they're the culprits. Guess I could get some brownie points by telling him."

"No. Do. Not. Tell. Anyone. Let them be. Why do you think I didn't spill the beans when that woman deputy and postal cop were asking me questions? The Norbergs' preoccupation works to our advantage. That's why I invite Cole so often. No parents asking questions if he shows up a little late or if he's extra quiet after youth group or special church events. They're too sauced to even realize."

"That's all well and good. But like I said, the sister is paying attention. You best be on your toes around her. The older she gets, the wiser she'll get."

"Point taken. Maybe we need to find something to steer her off course. Let's think on that. Maybe it's time for her to shadow to become a room aide for the little ones or something. You're the youth pastor. Figure it out."

"Sure. I'll figure it out. But for now, I'm out. I don't need Johnson breathing down my neck. See ya tomorrow night."

Thackeray watched Kempffer execute a three-point turnaround and drive toward the county road. The situation was less than optimal. He needed to keep Kempffer on a short leash.

In the kitchen he snatched his cell off the counter and called Symons. "Hey, Bradford, it's Curtis. We got us a situation." He filled Town Supervisor Symons in on the online shop being shut down because Kempffer's guy was in hot water with the law. "I've had a deputy, not Kempffer, out here along with a postal investigator asking about some moonshine shack they found out west of the church property. Postal investigator left her business card. We gotta play things cool, but I think we'll still be okay for tomorrow evening's playtime."

Symons said, "I'll get with Tollefsen and see what's going on. Maybe there's a way we can divert attention away from Whispering Aspen. A way to warn off the wolves sniffing around."

"Yeah, the last thing I need is to get busted," Thackeray said. "Let me clarify, the last thing *we* need is to get busted."

He couldn't lose his church or the special bonds he had with his favorite kids. They needed him. He was their guiding light toward a life with Jesus Christ as their Lord and Savior.

Chapter Sixteen

MC was in her loft office finishing some work emails before she was due to be at the weekly AA meeting, when her phone pinged.

A text from Deputy Ekstrom: *Lewis is conscious. On my way to the hospital. Meet there?*

Hell yes. She fired off a reply. *Leaving my place now. Ten minutes.* A glimpse at her phone and she realized it was nearly six p.m., which meant she'd miss the AA meeting. It would've been number six too. Now she'd have to wait and finish next week either here or in St. Paul, depending on how things played out.

A call came in as she was getting into her car. Her new friend, Unknown. "What?"

"Get the fuck out of town." The deep modulation of the voice changer made whoever was on the other end sound like a robot. "Sooner rather than later. I guarantee you don't want to find out what happens if you don't fucking leave."

"Who is this?"

Of course she was talking to dead air, as with the previous calls. Was this number four? She'd lost count. The phone number was always different and always no longer in service when she checked. The calls had to be connected to one of the two investigations. She'd put money on the CSE case. But who the hell was calling? Kempffer was high on her list with his disdain for her, plus he had a history of having a stash of explicit pics. Lewis was in the hospital unconscious, so he was out. Or he had been until now. MC shoved the call out of her mind.

She concentrated on a plan to question Caleb Lewis.

An LCSO squad car was parked in front of the hospital when MC rolled up. She parked behind the tan Chevy Tahoe and hoped another squad car wouldn't cruise by and ticket her for parking in a no parking zone.

Ekstrom said she'd wait on the second floor. When she got off the elevator, Ekstrom was leaning against the wall facing the elevators.

"Hey. I haven't gone into Lewis' room yet. You'll never guess who I saw skulking through the stairwell door near Lewis' room."

"Who?"

"Kempffer. That's the second time. Freaking weird. Why's he acting so sneaky?"

Why indeed. "A question I'll add to my list for Caleb Lewis. Did Kempffer see you?"

"Nope. He didn't turn around. Went on his merry way through the door."

They entered Caleb's room and found him propped up in bed with the TV tuned to the local evening news, gnawing on his thumbnail, oblivious to the anchor spouting all the day's tragedies. On his left arm, a cast extended from knuckles to elbow.

"Caleb Lewis," MC said.

He pulled his thumb from his mouth. "You two again. Did you find my wallet?"

MC glanced at Ekstrom. "He wants to know if we found his wallet."

"I'd think he'd be more concerned with who landed him in the hospital," Ekstrom said.

MC approached the side of the bed, Ekstrom beside her.

"Caleb, someone did a number on you." MC pointed at his cast. "Did I hear you have a broken leg too? Tough times." She couldn't see the outline of a cast beneath the covers. Though it was difficult to see because the rolling tray table had been pushed to the end of the bed directly above Caleb's feet. A plastic pitcher of water and a cup sat next to a box of cheap tissue on the surface.

Why would the tray be so far out of the patient's reach?

"No broken leg. Bruised ankle and hip but not broken." He squirmed as if trying to find a more comfortable position. Fiddled with a button on the remote hooked to the bed and adjusted the head of the bed so he was more upright. Then he started messing with the covers. Anything but acknowledging them.

They made him nervous. Or he was off-kilter after a visit from Kempffer.

"In any case," MC said, "lots of scrapes and bruises, like you went up against a truck and the truck won."

"Funny. Why are you here? I already gave my statement to another deputy."

"Did you now? Which deputy?" MC asked.

"Don't know." Caleb stared at the TV. "Didn't get his name."

Ekstrom leaned over the bed. "Hey, Caleb, did I see Deputy Kempffer leaving your room right before we came in?"

"Who?" He shifted and cleared his throat.

MC moved around to the other side of the bed and rolled the tray table toward the head of the bed. She picked up a plastic tumbler with a bendy straw stuck in the lid. "Want some water?"

She handed him the cup. "Maybe after a nice long drink your memory will be refreshed. Deputy Kempffer. We know you know who he is, so stop playing dumb. He's been seen at least twice leaving your room since you were admitted after your accident."

"Accident? That was hardly an accident." Caleb sputtered water all over himself. "Fine. You want to know the truth?"

"Yes, please." MC locked eyes with Ekstrom, eyebrows raised. This was bound to be interesting. She thought about a line from *A Few Good Men,* something about not being able to handle the truth. "Lay it on us."

He glanced back and forth between them. "You going to do some "good cop, bad cop" routine?"

MC said, "Caleb, we don't play games. This isn't a TV show or a movie. Tell us what you're going to tell us. Mind if I mute the idiot box so we don't miss anything?"

He flipped a hand toward the television. "I don't need to hear it anyway." Then he took another slurp of water through the straw and set the cup on the tray table. "Here's the deal. It was no accident what happened to me. Kempffer called me, sometime in the evening, and told me to meet him outside my place because he wanted to talk to me in person, not on the phone. I'm out there waiting, and next thing I know I hear an engine revving behind me. I started to turn and realized it…a truck I think…it was coming straight at me. I tried to jump to the side. Then everything went black until I woke up here today."

"Are you trying to tell us that Kempffer purposely hit you?" MC wrote fast and furious in her notebook.

"I don't know." He scraped his uninjured hand through his rat's nest of hair. "All I know is he called me. I'm pretty sure it was a pickup that hit me because the lights were in my eyes. Maybe he never showed up after calling me. Or maybe he was the one who ran me down. I don't know. But this is shitty." He held up his left arm. "How'm I supposed to work now?"

Ekstrom, who'd also been taking notes, said, "I think work is the least of your problems right now, Caleb."

"Why? I don't have any other problems. Except for my lost wallet. Hey, you never answered my question about my wallet."

MC paused in her notetaking. "Caleb why did Kempffer want to talk to you Sunday night?"

"I don't know. He told me to be out front when he got there, that we couldn't talk on the phone. All clandestine and whatever."

"Clandestine indeed. Sure would help us to know what he wanted to discuss. Are you two friends? Hang out at the bar? What's the connection?"

"I wouldn't exactly say we're friends. Like we know each other.

But not to hang out or anything." He messed with the remote again, not meeting MC's gaze.

He's hiding something, MC thought. "In any case, while you query your memory banks to figure out why the cloak-and-dagger approach for meeting with Kempffer, I have some updates for you. While you were unconscious, a search warrant for your apartment was approved and issued. On Monday evening Deputy Ekstrom and I executed the search warrant, and we took possession of your computer, DVDs, and other evidence. Left a copy of the search warrant on your kitchen counter along with a list of items we took."

The color of Caleb's face faded to match the whitish gray of the hospital sheets.

"So you won't be able to work anyway, what with us having possession of your computer. But before we take this discussion any further, I'm going to quick read you your Miranda rights."

She slipped a small, laminated card from her wallet. "You have the right to remain silent. Anything you say can and will be used against you in a court of law. You have the right to an attorney. If you cannot afford an attorney, one will be provided for you. Do you understand these rights as I've read them to you?"

Caleb looked at MC. Then he looked at Ekstrom. And back at MC.

"Mr. Lewis?" MC went all formal on him. "Do you understand these rights as I've read them to you?"

"What the hell." His face went from pasty white to overripe tomato, quickly heading to plum-colored. The machine monitoring his pulse beeped like a countdown timer on a bomb. "Why?"

"First, you need to answer my question, Mr. Lewis. Do you understand—"

"Yes. Fuck's sake." He shifted restlessly.

MC wondered if he was seriously considering making a mad dash from the room.

"Do you wish to have an attorney present or are you willing to answer our questions?"

"I guess I should get an attorney."

"It is your right," MC said. "In which case we'll need to formally arrest you and continue this at the sheriff's office once we can get you cleared medically for transport."

He slammed his head against the pillow. "What the hell is even happening?"

A nurse dressed in a set of pale blue scrubs and bright blue Hoka sneakers walked into the room, clipboard in hand. "Time for vitals. Officers, if you wouldn't mind stepping aside?" She clamped a stethoscope in her ears and listened to Caleb's heart. In a blur of button-pushing she set the machine to take a blood pressure reading and miraculously the incessant beeping was silenced too. "Heart rate is elevated. Blood pressure slightly high." She stuck a thermometer in Caleb's mouth. "No fever. Good. Did you place an order for dinner? I suppose not if you weren't awake earlier in the day. I'll contact the cafeteria and have some soup, crackers, and Jello sent up."

"Great thanks." Caleb stared at the ceiling.

"Are you in pain, Caleb?" The nurse charted her findings on her clipboard.

"I'm good."

"Okay. I'll get the food ordered. Someone from the cafeteria will bring it directly to your room, so expect it within the next fifteen minutes." She patted Caleb's right forearm. "In the meantime, try to rest." Her gaze flicked between MC and Ekstrom. "Hopefully, you won't be too much longer."

MC said, "We're not sure how much longer we'll be, but please be assured we're not roughing up the patient. We're simply asking Mr. Lewis questions."

The nurse's shoulders stiffened, and a frown creased her brow. "I'll leave you to it, but he needs rest."

"One question, if I might?" MC asked.

The nurse stopped, her hand on the door pull. "Yes?"

"When would be the earliest Mr. Lewis could be released from the hospital?"

"You'd have to ask the physician on duty. I don't have that information."

"Great. I'd love to ask the doctor. Would you mind letting whoever know I need to speak with them?"

"Sure." The nurse left the room.

Ekstrom adjusted her duty belt and cleared her throat. "So, where were we?"

MC flipped through her notes. "I think we were waiting for Mr. Lewis to decide if he wanted to talk with us or if he preferred waiting until he had representation. Mr. Lewis?" She folded her arms, notebook and pen in one hand.

Caleb shut his eyes. Opened his eyes. Glanced from Ekstrom to MC. Brought his thumb to his mouth and chewed some more on the battered nail and skin.

Silence tended to be an uncomfortable commodity for the likes of Caleb Lewis.

The barely perceptible tick of the clock on the wall above the door was the only sound in the room.

After about eight million minutes Caleb said, "My head is really pounding. Can we do this another time?"

His pallor had a tinge of green about it, with deep dark pockets beneath his eyes. MC decided to give him the benefit of the doubt. "We'll let you rest for the night. Eat some food. But Caleb, know this. I will be speaking with the physician on duty before we leave. We'll be back in the morning. At that time, depending on your condition, we'll conduct our interview either here or at the sheriff's office."

"Understood." His voice sounded as if he'd gargled with gravel.

As soon as the door clicked closed behind them, MC made a beeline for the nurse's station. "Ekstrom, I'd feel a whole lot better if we could put a guard on his room. I don't really expect he'll try and make a run for it. I'm more concerned someone may try to get to him. Gut feeling, and I've learned to listen after all these years."

"I got you. Kempffer's been here at least twice. Lewis was sketchy about Kempffer. I don't think we have enough staff to post someone all night though. We have two people on leave so we're a bit strained right now."

"All right. Let's hope for the best and meet here in the morning. You go ahead. I'm going to track down the doctor and see if they'll give me any indication about when Caleb will be released."

MC left the hospital after a ten-minute consult with Dr. Hersh, a thin man of indeterminate age. She explained the situation.

The doctor assured MC that Mr. Lewis was on the mend and though he couldn't share specifics of his medical history, he was able to let her know he fully intended to discharge him in the morning. Mid-to-late morning once all the paperwork was settled.

She texted Ekstrom to update her and they decided to regroup at the hospital at ten the following morning and either transport him to the station for questioning or question him at the hospital if he wasn't discharged.

In the car, MC fired off an email to Jamie to update him on the very confusing but possibly progressing state of the post office robbery and the probability she'd get more information on the child exploitation case. Nothing definitive yet.

Her stomach growled, and she realized how hungry she was. Pizza sounded perfect. She could take it to the cabin and draw up a game plan for tackling Caleb while she ate. Plan solidified, she was about to turn the car on when she received a text.

Ellen. *Missed you at the meeting this evening. Hope all is well.*

MC's first reaction was annoyance. Was Ellen tracking her attendance? She didn't need another Dara to get on her ass about making it to meetings.

That's a bit dramatic, no? She's being a friend. Showing concern. Take a breath. Try being a friend.

Of course, Barb's voice knocked her upside the head and clued her in on the appropriate response to Ellen's text. *I'm fine. Dealing with a work-related issue.*

The three gray dots floated on the screen. *If you're finished, care to meet? Same place as last week?*

Did she want to meet? Was Ellen hitting on her or was it really a friend thing? Ah, hell, why not? At least she'd have someone other than herself to talk to. *Does Harbor Java have food? I'm starving.*

They have snack stuff. Bakery items. If you're wanting something more, we could meet at Wheelhouse Pub. Two doors down from the coffee place. They have Heggies Pizzas. Bad news is it's a bar. Don't want to put you in temptation's way.

MC was enveloped by temptation every second of every day no matter her location. *Wheelhouse works for me. I do enjoy Heggies in a pinch.*

Twenty minutes later MC parked in a side lot next to the Wheelhouse Pub. Two pickups and a rusted sedan occupied the minuscule lot. MC recognized Ellen's cherry-red Toyota pickup truck. She did a round of box breathing and then another.

Inside, two grizzled old codgers sat at the bar on the end nearest the door. Their faces tilted toward their beer mugs, well-worn and stained ball caps pushed back on their heads. She wasn't sure if they were concentrating on their malt beverages or catching a catnap.

Booths lined one wall. She caught sight of Ellen in the last booth.

The bartender drifted toward her. "Take a seat anywhere." He reminded her of Cliff Clavin on *Cheers*. His thinning, graying-whitish hair and bushy mustache were near exact replicas of the character's.

"Thanks." She waved a hand at him. "I see my friend is already here."

She slid into the booth opposite Ellen, a bit uncomfortable with her back at the door. Should she ask Ellen to swap spots? Then again, it wasn't like she was surveilling anyone, so maybe this one time she could relax and go with the flow. "Hey."

"Hey, yourself." Ellen drank from what appeared to be a glass of ice water. "Rough day? Evening? Whatever?"

MC grabbed a laminated card from behind the metal napkin

holder. "Yeah, it's been a busy day." The menu was thin. Pizza. Pepperoni. Sausage. Cheese. Supreme. All ten-inch size. All Heggies. "What's your poison?"

"Whatever you like. I'm not picky."

"Pepperoni it is then. I'm assuming in this establishment I go to the bar to order?"

"Indeed, you do. No waitstaff here. Bill runs a low-key business. Yes, the guy behind the bar is Bill. Owner and bartender all rolled into one."

"Does he remind you of—"

"Cliff Clavin?"

"Yes."

Ellen laughed. "He gets that a lot. Mind grabbing me a Diet Coke? Water isn't cutting it for me."

"You got it."

MC headed for Cliff and placed the order for a pepperoni pizza and two Diet Cokes.

"Should be about twelve to fifteen minutes on the pie." Bill filled two tall glasses with ice and squirted Diet Coke in before sliding the glasses across the bar. "Napkins on the table. I'll bring the pizza to you when it's ready."

MC was mesmerized by the lineup of liquor bottles on the backbar. All those hues.

"You want anything else besides the sodas?"

That was a loaded question. Of course she wanted something else...anything else. "Ah, no. Thanks." MC grabbed the drinks and headed to the booth.

The place was eerily quiet, except for the TV on in the front corner. Not even sports. The box was tuned to a reality show, which no one was paying the slightest attention to.

Once MC and Ellen had demolished the pizza and gotten a refill on their sodas, they settled back.

"How does it feel...being in here?" Ellen waved an arm to encompass the bar.

"Fine as frog hair," MC said. What the hell, McCall? Weirdo.

"Good. I know it's not easy. But hopefully it will get easier each time. Change of topic. Whatever happened with the moonshine place? Any news?" Ellen took a drink of her Diet Coke.

"The case is with the sheriff's office, I haven't heard where they're at with it. Pretty wild though that we discovered it." MC poked at the ice cubes in her glass with a straw. She watched the tiny bubbles fizz in the dark brown liquid. Her mind wandered to Caleb Lewis, the robbery, and the exploitation case.

"Penny for your thoughts," Ellen said.

"Oh god. Sorry. Caught up thinking about my cases."

"Dare I ask?"

"I really shouldn't talk about anything. I mean, I could but then I'd have to kill you." Jesus, McCall.

Ellen burst out laughing. "Same tired cliche heard in how many different cop movies and shows. Admittedly, it sounded fresh and new coming from you. I'll refrain from pressuring you for details you shouldn't divulge. Moving on to safer topics…if you'll be around this weekend, we could hike again. Only if you want. No pressure. Either Saturday or Sunday morning works for me. Whaddaya say?"

Another hike would probably do her body and mind some good. Especially after she massacred half a pizza. "Sure. I'm up for it. Maybe the trails near Split Rock. I think it's a safe assumption we won't uncover any hidden moonshine stills on state land. Well, I hope not anyway."

"Nine Sunday morning? Same plan as last time, meet at my place?"

"Works for me." MC flipped her phone over to check the time, surprised to see it was nearly nine p.m. At that moment, the phone shimmied on the table. She about jumped out of her skin. At least it wasn't from Unknown. "Hey, Red. Kinda late for a call." She held the phone away from her ear for a second. "Whoa. Slow down and maybe bring the sound down about eighty decibels. You're about to blow my eardrum. Are you all right?" She paused. "Okay then, I'm in the middle of something so let me call you back."

Jim Bob was wound up like a top about to spin off a table.

"I'm so sorry, I've got to return a phone call." MC slid from the booth. "This has been great. Thanks for the invite. I'll settle the tab."

Ellen pulled her wallet from her jeans pocket and tossed a ten spot on the table. "That enough to cover half with tip?"

"Close enough." MC picked up the cash and went to settle the bill with…Bill.

In the parking lot they said their goodbyes. Though they'd be traveling in the same direction, north on Highway 61, MC's trek was much shorter than Ellen's.

She punched the gas, keeping her speed a few clicks above the limit. The darkness was thick, the stars bright pinpricks poked into the black sky. Her mind was awhirl, wondering what cluster mess Jim Bob had gotten himself into.

MC rolled down her driveway and hit the garage remote. As soon as she was parked, she hit the button again, and the door rumbled closed.

She gathered her belongings, and exited, locking the door behind her. She scanned the gravel road and woods surrounding the cabin. Nothing was amiss, but the calls from Unknown warranted some extra caution.

Inside the house she engaged the deadbolt and quickly checked the sliders to ascertain no one had attempted to gain access in her absence. MC cleared the house and was satisfied her fortress was secure. Then she climbed the stairs to the loft.

Phone in hand, she took a deep breath and called Jim Bob back. He answered before the first ring had finished.

"Okay, Red. Lay it on me. What's the crisis? Wait. Before you dive in, tell me have you or anyone else been hurt?" She held her breath. "No? Good. Now tell me what has you in such a tizzy."

Jim Bob dove into a diatribe that made MC dizzy. He'd been on surveillance duty by himself earlier in the evening. "First, let me give you a synopsis of the previous two evenings. I spotted a person who resembled the suspect I've been tracking. That was Tuesday. I got out of the car to approach the person, and they sprinted away. I gave pursuit but lost 'em. Never saw their face. The person had a hood pulled low on their forehead. I think it was a man, but not a hundred percent on that. Similar scenario occurred on Wednesday. "Same bat time, same bat channel," Jim Bob's voice increased in volume again.

"Take a breath, Red. I'm not hard of hearing. Try and use your inside voice."

"Sorry. So tonight I posted in the exact same spot."

"The third evening in a row you've staked out the area? Were you alone?"

"Yes. Third night. No one with me. Some hot button case popped up the day before yesterday, so I was on my own. Which is fine. I got some pictures on the first night, before I attempted to approach the person."

Jesus. MC wished he hadn't been doing surveillance on his own. But learning on the job was part of the deal. He had to go solo at some point. Better a mail theft case than a murder.

Jim Bob continued. "Tonight, I was in my usual spot. After about an hour a St. Paul PD patrol car rolled up behind me. Cop got out, approached my position, shined his flashlight in my face, the whole nine yards. He asked why I was parked there. I explained who I was and what I was doing. Told him I was going to reach into my pocket for my ID and that I was armed."

"Red, did you not call SPPD and give them a courtesy heads up you were conducting surveillance?"

"Uh, no. Guess I should have, huh? The cop told me they got a call from a mother whose seventeen-year-old son was scared because for the past couple of nights when he came home from his pickup basketball game, some guy followed him. The mom said her son described the man as a red-haired giant who chased him."

MC bit back a laugh. "An accurate description."

"Funny. The cop suggested we visit the mom together so I could explain to her and the kid what had happened."

"How'd it go?"

"Embarrassing as hell. But at least I got a good look at the kid without a hood over his head, and he didn't fit the description. He's tall, probably six feet, but scrawny. I apologized to them for freaking him out. They accepted it. Well, I hope so anyway."

"What's the issue? Why are you so riled?"

"Geez, McCall. I scared the crap outta a teenager. I guess it messed with my head. Not to mention I'm worried Jamie is going to ream me a new asshole for the whole ordeal. I know you're not my mentor now, but I wanted to run it down with you."

"I get it. Here's what you do. Write it up in DigiCase. Include the SPPD officer's name and names of the mom and kid. Talk to Jamie first thing tomorrow. Be honest. Keep doing what you're doing. Except maybe don't scare the bejesus out of any more teens."

"Aye, aye, Cap—"

"Nope. Still not doing that. Good luck."

"Got it," Jim Bob said. "One more thing."

"Listen, Red, it's getting late, so can we not do the whole Columbo schtick?"

"Thanks for talking me off the ledge, McCall. Night."

He hung up.

Crisis averted, she moved on to planning how she and Ekstrom would deal with Caleb Lewis the next day after they retrieved him from the hospital.

Chapter Seventeen

Arriving at the hospital promptly at ten Friday morning, MC got through the front desk and took the elevator up to the second floor. The doors slid open, and MC had a moment of *déjà vu* when she laid eyes on Ekstrom leaning against the wall. "We gotta stop meeting like this."

"Right? This time I waited here in case Kempffer showed up."

"You been here long?"

"No, maybe a couple minutes. So what's the plan?"

MC said, "Here's what I'm thinking, as soon as the doc clears Caleb, we give him a ride to the station. We get him in an interview room and see what we can learn."

"Okay, sounds like a solid plan."

They entered Caleb's room and discovered an orderly stripping the bed.

MC halted in the doorway. "Good morning. We're here for Caleb Lewis. He was in this room."

"No one was in the room when I got here." The orderly stuffed sheets and blankets into a rolling hamper.

"Discharged?" MC asked.

He shrugged. "Guess so. I do what they tell me. They told me to strip and put fresh sheets on the bed."

Unfortunately, he didn't have much to share. MC walked over to the nurses' station, Ekstrom on her heels. "Hi, excuse me. We're here for Caleb Lewis. Has he been discharged? We were told yesterday he'd probably be discharged this morning."

The middle-aged nurse sitting in front of a computer glanced up. She tucked a pencil into a giant graying squirrel's nest of hair piled on top of her head and adjusted her eyeglasses, the colorful beaded chain swaying with the movement. "Yes, he's been discharged. Well, now that's interesting because another deputy claimed he was supposed to give Mr. Lewis a ride home."

MC asked, "Did you speak with the deputy? It was a man?"

"Yes. And yes."

"Do you remember what time the two men left?"

The nurse wrinkled her nose. "It was a frickin' goat rodeo in here earlier. Must've been a full moon last night or something. They left here around thirty minutes ago. Don't hold me to that, but close to, and yeah, the deputy was a man. Average height. Had wet-sand-colored hair with one of them razor-sharp parts, shaved on one side and longer on top. I think of that as military style. Ya know?" She leaned forward and lowered her voice. "I admit I didn't like his attitude. He was clean-cut, especially with the haircut, but he was rude." She straightened in her chair and her voice rose. "I don't appreciate rude."

Ekstrom said, "Kempffer. No one else in the department fits that description and no one else would've come here. Sheriff Tollefsen cleared me to work with you, and I'm pretty sure he didn't assign anyone else."

MC checked the plastic ID hanging from the nurse's neck. Mary Kline, RN. "Mary, I'm US Postal Inspector McCall." She presented her credentials for the nurse. "This is Deputy Ekstrom. We were scheduled to either pick up Caleb Lewis and take him in for an interview or conduct an interview here if he wasn't well enough to be released. Can you share with us exactly what transpired with the other deputy?"

"Nice to meet you both. You're much more polite than that man. Didn't even bother to tell me his name. Anyway, he came in all nice. Said he was here to help a citizen who'd been hurt in an accident. Then he told Mr. Lewis he needed to get a formal report on file about his hit-and-run. Mr. Lewis said he didn't want to go, but then the deputy got kinda rough and grabbed him by the arm. I told him the doctor hadn't signed the discharge papers yet, so they had to wait. But right at that moment Dr. Smith showed up with the signed documents. I'd barely handed Mr. Lewis his copies before the deputy hauled him away, not carefully either, if you get my drift. I'm concerned about Mr. Lewis's broken wrist." Her penciled-in eyebrows rose halfway up her forehead.

"Thank you so much, Mary," MC said. "I appreciate you taking the time to answer our questions."

"You're welcome. I hope Mr. Lewis is okay."

"We'll find him and make sure he is." MC pulled a card out of her pocket. "If you think of anything else related to this morning's incident, please contact me." She considered for a moment how many of her business cards she'd left all over Two Harbors and Castle Cove. Probably everyone and their sister had her phone number by now.

Ekstrom and MC made a beeline for the elevator.

MC jabbed the down button, and the doors opened. "Can you call the station and find out if it was Kempffer who took Caleb?"

"On it." Ekstrom pulled her cell from her pocket. "I'll check with Lynette. But I'd bet my next paycheck it was Kempffer."

"Something's fishy. Why is Kempffer messing with Caleb? Is he trying to sabotage my investigation? Or is something else going on?"

The elevator doors slid open and Ekstrom waved her on. "I'll catch up with you outside."

Ekstrom met up with MC outside the hospital. "Lynette said Kempffer was in earlier. She said he'd made an arrest this morning, a suspect in the post office robbery, according to him. As far as she knew, he was out on patrol. I could've asked her to track him down, but I don't want to give him any warning we're aware of his shenanigans. Whatever he's playing at, it's not by-the-book."

"Good call. But wait. He arrested a suspect for the post office robbery? Who? Caleb? Why wouldn't he have contacted me? This is devolving into a major clusterfuck. We need to track him down." She had almost as many questions for Kempffer as for Lewis. "It's imperative we find Caleb."

His wallet found at the post office was solid evidence. Her gut told her he was also involved in, at the very least, receiving and distributing images. Either related to the images from the Whispering Aspen IP address or of his own.

"What do you want to do?" Ekstrom asked. "Split up? I could go to the station, check who was processed and stuck in holding on the robbery. You could swing by Caleb's place, see if he's home."

Fat chance she'd find Caleb in his apartment. "That might be the best option. Something tells me Kempffer is purposely messing with the robbery as a red herring to keep us from discovering what he's really up to." Why the hell does Kempffer want her chasing her tail? What purpose did it serve? "I'll give you a call when I get to Caleb's. If you have anything for me before that, give me a ring. Okay?"

"Will do. Be safe."

"You too."

MC pulled into the driveway at Caleb's address. The bright red Dodge Charger was parked at the carport. After a quick walk around the garage and not finding anything unusual, she hustled up the outside stairway to the apartment.

She pounded on the door. "Caleb Lewis. Law enforcement. Open up." After about ten seconds she knocked again, ratcheting her voice up a notch.

Nothing.

She tried the door handle. Locked.

She scoped out the area. Not a soul in sight. MC descended the stairs and walked across the gravel driveway, through the side yard, and around to the front of the house. She knocked on the door.

Within seconds the door creaked open, and a slightly stooped white-haired man leaned forward. "What can I do for you?"

"I'm US Postal Inspector McCall." She showed him her badge. "I need to speak with Caleb Lewis. He lives in the apartment over the garage. He's not answering his door."

"Well, Caleb's been in the hospital. Someone ran him down right out there." He pointed a knobby-knuckled finger toward the street behind her. "Happened Sunday night."

"Right. I've been to see Caleb in the hospital. He was discharged this morning. I was supposed to meet with him, but when I got there he was gone. Have you seen or heard from him?"

"Haven't seen him since the medics loaded him into the wagon Sunday night. Wasn't conscious. I was fearful he wasn't gonna make it. Glad to hear he pulled through. You find who hit him?"

Christ on a cracker.

"No, Mr....sorry, I don't know your name."

"Arne Ogren. I own this here house and rent the apartment over the garage to Caleb. Originally, my wife Mildred and I had the apartment built because our grandson was going to move in and go to college nearby. But he decided he wanted to go somewhere warmer. California won out. So now we rent the apartment to Caleb. He's a hard-working computer guy. Real smart cookie, that one. He helps me when I have trouble with my machine."

"I see. Well, nice to meet you Mr. Ogren."

"Arne. Call me Arne. I'd introduce you to Mildred but she's in town at the beauty parlor getting gussied up."

MC pulled a card from her pocket. "Could I leave my business card with you? Should Caleb show up or you hear from him, have him contact me. Or you contact me."

Arne popped the lock on the screen door and accepted the card. "Can do, inspector. Is there a problem with Caleb's mail? Because we aren't having issues with ours. Our delivery person is the best."

"I'm sorry, Mr. Ogren, but I can't discuss an ongoing investigation. I am happy to know you and Mrs. Ogren are satisfied with your service. I can pass that along to the postmaster."

"Yeah, sure. You betcha." Arne waved a hand. "Never heard of a postal inspector, much less have one show up at my front door. What do you do?"

MC wanted to reel in the exchange and get a move on. "We're federal law enforcement who investigate crimes involving the US mail. That's the short version."

"Okey dokey. If I see Caleb, I'll tell him you stopped by."

"I appreciate it. Thank you for your time, Mr. Ogren...Arne." She corrected before he could chime in. "You have a nice day."

"You too."

Well, that was a disappointment. Now what? Where the hell did Kempffer take Caleb?

MC headed to her car and called Ekstrom. "Hey, Caleb's not at his residence, but his car is. His place is locked. I spoke with Mr. Ogren, the homeowner. He's about a million years old, but he's sharp. Told me he hasn't seen Caleb since the hit-and-run Sunday night. As far as he knew, Caleb was still in the hospital."

"I found out the guy Kempffer brought in for the post office robbery is none other than our local wino, Gimpy Sutherland."

"Gimpy Sutherland? Seriously, that's his name? Gimpy?"

"I think his actual name is Richard, but he's been known as Gimpy as long as I've known him because he has a permanent limp. Suffered an injury during combat in Vietnam. Shrapnel in his leg, I think. McCall, I'm telling you, no way Gimpy is the guy you want for the robbery. He's like seventy. Nearly bald. He's five-foot-six and thin as a whip. I swear he subsists on wine. He's still passed out from last night's bender. Apparently Kempffer said he got an anonymous tip. Someone saw Gimpy wandering around the dumpster behind the Castle Cove Post Office the morning of the robbery. "

"Dumpster-diving does not make Gimpy the robber. I don't know the town very well, but I think the postal clerk would be able to identify him." What fresh hell was Kempffer up to? "This makes no sense. But now we know he didn't arrest Caleb." MC leaned against the car door. "Any word on Kempffer's or Caleb's whereabouts?"

"Nothing."

"I'll meet you at the station. Maybe Gimpy will wake up soon and we can feed him and pump him full of caffeine, get some info from him about what transpired this morning."

"I'll get caught up on some paperwork until you get here."

The call no sooner ended than another call came in.

Unknown.

Of course.

"McCall." She'd had about enough of the intimidation tactics. "Who is this?"

"Never mind that. Pardon my French, but I've told you several times now to mind your fucking business. Don't make me take it to the next level," the robotic voice crackled.

"Your voice changer must be a cheap version, hard to understand a word you're saying. Man up and come talk to me face-to-face. Otherwise stop these ridiculous threats." She ended the call, not giving him a chance to respond.

She felt some sense of satisfaction after going on the offense with the faceless assclown.

Thackeray was furious when he glanced out his window and saw Kempffer pull to a stop in his driveway. He hurried onto his front porch as Kempffer came around his squad car and unloaded a young guy who looked to be early-to-mid-twenties and was unsteady on his feet. He was restrained and blindfolded, one arm in a cast.

"Christ. Are you out of your mind? Why'd you bring him here?" Thackeray felt his face heat up. He forced himself to dial it down a notch. He didn't want to blow a gasket in front of the kid. And even though whoever he was couldn't see Thackeray, unless he was deaf, he damn well could hear.

"Needs must. My work with my friend required somewhere we wouldn't be disturbed. I'm going to take him to one of the buildings."

A light went on. The guy had to be the distributor for their entertainment business. "Who is he?" Thackeray held up his hands. "Never mind. You can use the far one. But he stays blindfolded."

Kempffer said, "You want to sit in?"

God help him, Kempffer got on his last nerve. He counted on Kempffer to be a loyal and trusted follower—and business partner. Now he doubted everything about the deputy. Kempffer was on the brink of losing his shit and that would not do. Not at all. "Get a move on before someone sees you." He surveyed the church grounds, thankful it was mid-morning and no one else was on site. He wasn't about to say out loud he wanted to witness whatever Kempffer had in store for the kid, even though he intended to get a glimpse of what was to come.

Kempffer pushed the young guy ahead of him along the dirt trail west to the farthest old summer camp cabin. Nothing but woods and animals around them.

Thackeray followed them into the cabin and closed the door as Kempffer shoved the kid onto a moldy mattress on the bottom bunk, its metal frame rusty and pitted.

Thackeray put a finger to his lips to indicate Kempffer should keep quiet about his presence. Plausible deniability all the way. He was beyond pissed Kempffer had brought the kid here. Maybe it was time to push Kempffer out of their special club. He and Symons would be fine enjoying their hobby without him. Sure, the money had been good. Who didn't like a little extra cash? But this was way the hell out of hand. How had Kempffer lost the plot? One day things were humming along nicely and then out of nowhere, wham.

"Where are we, Kempffer?" the kid asked. "Who's here? How many people?" His voice was hoarse, his head moving back and forth despite the fact he couldn't see. "This is bullshit." He yanked his arms as if he could break free. "Why'd you blindfold and put this arm contraption on me, at gunpoint? What the hell? If I'm under arrest take me to the jail."

"The contraption is called a hobble restraint. In case you forgot you have a busted arm, so cuffs won't work. Don't worry about it. Your only job right now is to tell me what I want to know." Kempffer dragged a rickety wood chair from a corner of the cabin and set it down, facing the kid.

"Was it you who ran me down Sunday night? You trying to kill me? I waited for you like you told me. I know a truck hit me. Was it you?" The young man coughed. "Could I get some water?"

"C'mon, buddy. You know me. Why would I call to meet with you and then try and run you over? Think." He poked a finger at the kid's temple. "Does that make any sense on any level? Dumbass."

Thackeray raised his eyebrows at Kempffer. Had the idiot gone totally rogue?

Kempffer shrugged at Thackeray as if to say, I did what I thought I had to do. Live with it.

"Can you answer me?" Caleb asked.

"I was running late. I had some things to do and by the time I got to your place, you weren't there. I saw an LCSO patrol car driving down the street, but no lights or anything. Figured they were on regular patrol. I didn't know what happened until later."

"Okay. What did you want to talk to me about that night? Why couldn't we talk on the phone or you come inside my place? Why'd we have to meet out in the street?"

"First of all, I didn't say meet on the street. I said to meet out in front of your place."

"What else would 'out front' mean if not the street? It's not like there are any sidewalks."

"You asked what I wanted to talk about, then shut up and let me tell you. Jesus." Kempffer glanced at Thackeray. "You've been lagging on the distro of our stuff. The money is barely trickling in. You haven't posted anything new. What the fuck you been doing, bro?"

"I've had some personal shit to deal with too. You're not the only one. Can we leave it at that?" The kid shifted on the bunk. The metal frame squealed in protest. "My arm's killing me. Can you let me loose?"

"Tell you what, I'll decide what we can leave it at, dipwad. And no, I can't let you loose. How stupid do you think I am?" He scoffed. "I'm going to need more answers than you're handing out. I don't want this to get ugly. But it will. You feel me?" He poked the young guy in the chest with his gun.

Thackeray made a move to intervene. The last thing he needed was for Kempffer to lose his cool and shoot the guy on Whispering Aspen property. Sweat trickled down his back. He needed to put an end to Kempffer's Gitmo interrogation techniques and get them both gone before anyone else showed up.

The kid sucked in a breath. "I don't know what more you want me to say. I've answered your questions."

Thackeray crept forward and nudged Kempffer's shoulder. He inclined his head toward the door.

"You sit and think about what else you need to tell me. I'm going to step outside for a minute. Don't try anything funny because I'll have my eye on you the whole time." He rested the side of the gun barrel against the guy's cheek. "You feel me?"

"Yeah, I got it." The kid tilted his head away from the gun.

Thackeray exited and Kempffer tromped out the door. He had no more patience for whatever game the deputy was playing. They moved down the path away from the cabin. "What is wrong with you, bringing him here?" He kept his voice low. "I don't want to know him. I most certainly don't want him to know me. He's your problem. You created it. You fix it."

"Nah. I'm going to need some time with him. He and I have some issues to work through. No one ever comes out this way, so we'll be golden. Give me through the weekend."

Thackeray's gut somersaulted. He needed to pray. Lift some weights. Yeah, a solid session with the free weights would help clear his head. Once his vessel was humming, his mind would follow. Then he'd be able to process the situation and write a sermon for Sunday's service.

"Fine. Through the weekend. I want him gone by Monday. No trace of him left behind." He stood toe-to-toe with Kempffer.

"Yeah, yeah, I'll let you know when we're finished."

Kempffer disappeared into the cabin, the screen door slapping shut behind him.

Ekstrom and MC were holed up in a conference room at the

station. MC reviewed notes from their earlier and very brief interview with Gimpy Sutherland. The poor guy was barely cognizant of the fact he was in jail.

He vaguely recollected that a bulky deputy, white guy with a funny haircut, had hauled him in real early that morning. He'd been asleep on a park bench in Castle Cove. "Minding my own business," Gimpy'd said. The deputy had handcuffed him and put him in the back of his truck. "Had to hoist me up into that monstrosity he drives. I couldn't keep my balance too good."

Gimpy reeked of stale wine and sweat. His nearly bald head was dotted with dime-sized age spots. Criss-crosses of red threaded the whites of his hazel eyes. His nose was a plump purple bulb stuck in the middle of his thin stubbled face.

All the deputy had told him was someone called the sheriff's office anonymously and reported Gimpy was the guy who robbed the Castle Cove Post Office a couple weeks ago.

"I didn't rob no post office. I know Ned. I get my Social Security check by mail. Why would I go and rob a place I like? Don't make no sense."

No, it sure didn't make any sense. After they gave Gimpy about ten gallons of black coffee and half a dozen donuts, they cut him loose and had someone drive him to Castle Cove. Ekstrom filled Sheriff Tollefsen in on the situation, and he supported the decision.

MC got a call as she finished reading about the Gimpy saga. "Inspector McCall."

"Yes, hi, Inspector, this is Arne Ogren. You were at my house earlier asking about Caleb?"

"Yes, hello, Mr. Ogren."

"Please, Arne."

"Arne. Is there something I can help you with?"

"You said to contact you if I heard from Caleb."

MC snapped her fingers to get Ekstrom's attention. "Have you heard from Caleb, Arne?"

Ekstrom wheeled her chair closer to MC.

"Not exactly. See, when I picked up Mildred from her hairdresser appointment, I told her about your visit. Mildred was all atwitter about you stopping by. Asked if I was cordial. Did I invite you in. Offer you something to drink. And—"

"Mr. Ogren. I mean Arne. Do you have news about Caleb?"

"I do. Sorry. Mildred told me that while I was out on my morning stroll, Caleb called from the hospital. He asked if we'd be able to pick him up when the doc discharged him. Of course, Mildred, being the mothering type, she promised we'd be there as soon as he called."

"You're telling me Caleb asked you to drive him home from the hospital?" The plot thickened. Caleb knew MC and Ekstrom were going to return to the hospital this morning. He'd planned on ditching them. As if they wouldn't put two-and-two together and check his apartment first thing when they found him gone.

"Yes, ma'am. I'm as surprised as you sound. Surely. But Mildred, well me too, we're worried about Caleb. Because he hasn't called us to come get him. Then you showed up asking for him. Where's that young man gone off to?"

The sixty-four-thousand-dollar question.

"Arne, I have no idea. We'll investigate and see what we come up with. Would you please let me know if you hear from him or if he shows up at home?"

"I will, indeed. I hope he's okay." Arne's voice wobbled.

"I hope so too, Arne. Thank you for the call. You take care. Bye."

MC set the phone on the conference room table. "Houston, we have a problem."

Ekstrom said, "I caught some of it. Caleb asked the Ogrens to pick him up this morning."

"Yes. Exactly. Except Mildred forgot to tell Arne. When I spoke with Arne earlier, he had no clue. He thought Caleb was still at the hospital. When he picked up Mildred from the hair salon and told her about my visit, she informed him Caleb had called early and asked for a ride home. He was supposed to call them when he knew what time."

"The call never came?" Ekstrom asked.

"Correct."

"Well, fuck a duck. What the hell is going on? Did Caleb do a runner?"

"I don't think so because his car is still out at the Ogren place. We have confirmation Kempffer took him from the hospital."

"Right. I thought he'd bring Caleb home at some point. Do we track down Kempffer and ask him Caleb's whereabouts?"

"I'm not inclined to go down that road." She halfway suspected Kempffer was Unknown, her phone stalker.

"I've got a few hours until I'm off duty. I can keep an eye out for Caleb or Kempffer. I'll run through Castle Cove too."

"Good idea. I'll do a pass-through myself. Good to have a soft vehicle tooling around too. If someone were trying to fly under the radar, they'd get spooked by a marked squad car but probably not care one bit about a Subaru."

"Okay. We'll stay in contact and decide next steps as stuff happens?"

"Yep, I think that's the best plan," MC said.

Chapter Eighteen

Sunday morning a few minutes before the eleven o'clock service, Gracie and Cole tumbled from the back seat of their parents' beat up Hyundai sedan. "Mom? Dad?" Gracie leaned her head back inside the car. "Won't you come to church with us? If you do, then Cole can sit with us." She kept her voice quiet. Polite. Best not to upset the applecart.

"Gracie, we have business we need to attend to," her dad said. "Maybe next week. You two kids go on in." He tilted his head toward the church. "We'll pick you up after donut and juice time."

"But..." Gracie suspected her parents' business was conducted on bar stools at the Dirty Minnow. Was the bar even open on Sunday mornings? She'd overheard them talking many times about the place and when they came to pick up her and Cole, they smelled funny. Sickening fumes wafted from them, giving Gracie a headache. Booze. Gross. She swore she'd never drink.

Her brother never said anything. He followed her lead. Cole was blond-haired and blue-eyed like his sister. But he was a tender soul. He was small for his age. He was nine, almost ten, but could pass for seven or eight. She had to maintain enough strength and courage for both of them. He trusted her to take care of him, watch over him. Today she was on a mission to do just that.

"No 'buts.' Do as your father told you, Gracie. Unless you want to be grounded." Mom squinted and her face turned red, which was never a good sign. Pushback often ended with some form of punishment. Grounding was the best of the worst. The slapping, or swatting with her dad's belt, those were bad. Being locked in a closet in the basement overnight with no supper was the worst. But at least they had a roof over their heads and food on the table.

"Yes, ma'am. Come on, Cole." She grabbed her brother's hand and half dragged him from the turnaround to the church.

"Gracie, will they have chocolate-frosted donuts today, do you think?" Cole trotted beside her to keep up.

"Hope so. They're the best. You behave during service, and I'll be waiting for you in the lobby afterward. If we hurry maybe we can get to those donuts before everyone else. Deal?"

"Deal," Cole said quietly.

Inside the church Gracie delivered Cole to the Quiet Room where parents with infants, toddlers, and pre-k kids sat, along with kids ages six to nine who were unaccompanied by an adult. Two video screens and speakers hung from the corners on either side of the door. She nudged Cole into the space. "Go on now. Sit quiet and follow along. Then we'll get our donuts."

"Okay." Cole went to the farthest corner of the room and sat in a chair against the wall.

Gracie saw Youth Pastor Kempffer to the right of the door with the teen group leaders in charge of the unaccompanied kids. Gracie had witnessed how the teens operated. They spent more time on their cell phones than paying attention to the kids.

Youth Pastor Kempffer gave specific instructions to the teens about corralling the young ones and making sure they paid attention. No running around. Some parents had complained last week that kids were being disruptive. He'd said that the room was called "Quiet Room" for a reason.

Everyone in the church understood Pastor Thackeray didn't enjoy disturbances during his sermons, hence the need for the Quiet Room. Gracie didn't quite get why the space was called the Quiet Room. The room was never completely silent. Babies cried. Kids got restless. She thought it should be called the Noisy Room and that parents shouldn't complain about disruption because at least it was contained.

Gracie being twelve was allowed to sit in the actual church by herself. She chose a seat closest to the exit and in the furthest corner from the stage, which had a cross the size of King Kong as a backdrop.

Today was the day she'd try to get inside Pastor's house and into the basement, determined to see where kids were taken during Youth Group nights. She suspected bad things were happening to Cole and other kids, but she needed proof. Cole had absolutely shut down and refused to tell her anything. On evenings when he'd been to Pastor's house, he was even more withdrawn than usual. Even after Cole was given one of the much-coveted lightsabers, he couldn't be coaxed to engage. The toy laid abandoned on the floor of his closet, untouched since the night he brought it home.

When everyone stood for the opening hymn, Gracie snuck out the door. Outside the church there were tons of cars and trucks lined up in the parking area. But no one was outside. She crossed the turnaround to the Meeting Hall and skirted along the east side toward the grassy area and the gazebo. She was pretty sure when Pastor took the kids to his house on Thursday evenings, he used the back exit from the Meeting Hall. If he used the main front entrance, he'd be exposed to the adults on the main level having Bible study. Probably best to follow suit. She envisioned herself as a solo Nancy Drew out to solve a mystery.

Gracie reached the rear of the Meeting Hall. The gazebo stood in the middle of the large grassy yard area straight ahead. To the left of the gazebo was the ancient archery target, made from an old tree. To the right an expanse of yard, as long as a quarter of a city block, lay between the hall and Pastor's house. To the far left another pathway led westward to the six cabins that were used when the place had been a kid's summer camp, long before she was born.

She sprinted to the gazebo and hunkered down behind it. A quick survey of the area and she determined no one else was around. Gracie began to stand when she heard the squeal of the rear door of the Meeting Hall. She ducked down and peered around the gazebo. Youth Pastor Kempffer stood outside the door, and he slipped the straps of a bulky black backpack onto his shoulders.

Kempffer adjusted the pack and checked out the area. When his head turned toward the gazebo Gracie went flat on her belly and held her breath. After a count to ten she got to her knees and zeroed in on Kempffer walking west along the trail to the cabins.

Now she had a conundrum. Should she stick with her original plan and try to get into Pastor's house? Or follow Youth Pastor Kempffer? She chose to follow Kempffer. Next youth group night she'd try to sneak into Pastor's house.

Gracie, thankful she'd worn sneakers, hustled into the woods parallel to the path. Careful not to step on branches and give herself away she half-jogged until she reached the first cabin. She caught a glimpse of Kempffer nearing the last one.

To, hopefully, avoid detection, she crept to the rear of the first cabin and quickly made her way to the sixth building. She stood on a giant rock under a window on the backside of the cabin and snuck a look inside.

Kempffer shrugged the backpack off and talked to someone she couldn't quite see. She braced herself against the cabin's outer wall and leaned further right.

A man sat on the bottom of the first set of bunkbeds. She was pretty sure it was a man. He had something wrapped around his head. A scarf? No, not a scarf a blindfold. He was handcuffed to the bunk's metal post. Also, there was a strip of duct tape over his mouth.

She'd seen enough cop shows on TV to believe he'd been kidnapped.

Holy crap.

What was going on? Kempffer jabbered, but Gracie couldn't

hear the words. She decided to take a huge risk and after moving around to the front, she squatted next to the steps at the door. She had no sightline from her vantage point, but she could hear Kempffer's words.

A muffled thud made her gasp. She clapped a hand over her mouth.

Kempffer's voice traveled through the partially open door. "Okay, pal. Got a sandwich and some water here for you. I'm going to remove the tape, but if you make one sound, I'll shoot you."

The situation was messed up. Kempffer had a gun. Of course he did. Gracie knew he was a deputy and deputies had guns. Was the other guy a deputy too? But why would Kempffer kidnap another deputy?

Kempffer said, "Here goes. Remember what I said. Feel the gun in your chest? Yeah. Good."

A ripping sound followed by a muffled groan reached Gracie's ears.

"Man, I gotta pee."

The voice was softer, not as deep as Kempffer's. Gracie figured it was the other guy.

"Jesus. You are a pain in my ass. I don't have much time so I'm going to take off the restraint, but the cuff stays on your right wrist. I'll walk you outside. The blindfold stays on. No funny business or fast moves. Got that?"

"Yeah. Yeah. Can we hurry? I really have to go."

Scraping sounds and thumps followed.

Holy crapola. Gracie scrambled backward and ducked around the rear corner. The slap of the screen door was followed by feet thudding down the wood steps. Then she heard crunching. Probably leaves and sticks on the ground. They must have gone to the right toward the tree line.

"Hurry up, man. Pee already."

"It's kinda difficult with the cuffs hanging from one wrist and a cast on the other. Give me a second."

Sounds of scuffling and then a thump.

"Ow. Why'd you do that?"

"I told you no funny business. You try to run, I'll shoot you. If you want to stay alive hurry up and pee. Otherwise I'm putting you inside and you can piss your pants for all I care."

"I didn't try to run. I slipped because I can't see. Jesus, you ever tried to pee blindfolded?"

Gracie heard running water. Probably the guy had finally figured it out and was peeing.

"Okay, numbnuts, zip up. Let's go. I have barely enough time for you to scarf the sandwich and drink some water."

As soon as the screen door snapped shut Gracie returned to the steps.

"Hurry up and eat. Good boy. Now drink some water. All right that's enough. Time for the hobble to go back on. Last, but not least, tape. See that wasn't so hard, was it?" Kempffer laughed. "Forgot you can't answer. Here's the deal, I have church duties to handle, but I'll stop by later to chew the fat. I want you to behave while I'm gone. Believe me, I'll know if you don't. I have eyes everywhere."

What did he mean? Gracie scuttled to the back again, wondering if there were other people in the area. But she hadn't heard or seen anyone. Someone would have stopped her if she'd been spotted. Maybe he had a camera set up inside the cabin.

The thunk of the inside door and the smack of the screen door closing caused Gracie to jump and her heart to pound. Kempffer came into view stuffing things into the backpack and zipping it closed before slinging it over one shoulder. He fast-walked down the trail toward the Meeting Hall.

What would Nancy do? Think, Gracie. Think. She sat on the ground behind the structure. Glanced at her cheap plastic watch. In twenty-five minutes, the service would end.

Gracie decided she'd wait ten minutes to make sure Kempffer didn't return. Then she'd enter the cabin. The man inside couldn't hurt her because he was restrained. He also couldn't see her or say anything, so she felt pretty safe going inside.

Once time was up. Gracie rose to her feet. Checked the area. Birds chirped and a slight breeze ruffled the newly leafed trees, but no one was around. She crept to the front of the cabin and climbed the three steps to the door. Before she could reconsider, she opened the outside door and then pushed the inside door open enough to wedge inside.

She closed the door and faced the guy on the bunk. His head tilted toward her. Then he grunted and mumbled. What was he trying to say?

"Hi," Gracie said in her most calm voice, trying to sound grown up. "I'm going to take off the tape so you can talk. Okay?"

He nodded and gave her a thumbs up from the cuffed hand.

She inched forward, staying out of reach even though he couldn't touch her. Gracie leaned in and tore the strip of gray tape from the guy's face.

"Ouch."

"Sorry."

"It's okay. Whew. Thank you. My name is Caleb. Who're you?"

"I don't want to tell you my name because I don't know you."

"Smart. But I can't hurt you, right? I'm locked up tight. I wouldn't anyway."

"Yeah. But I'm still not going to tell you. Why are you here? Have you done something bad?"

"No. I haven't done something bad, but the man who forced me here, he's bad."

"But he's a deputy and a youth pastor," Gracie said.

"You know him? Did he see you? No, he couldn't have, or you wouldn't have gotten in here. You're right, he's a deputy. Didn't know about the youth pastor gig. He's not a good guy. He kidnapped me and I think he tried to run me over with his truck. I was in the hospital, and he showed up there on Friday. He told the nurse he'd give me a ride home then he drove me here. Wherever here is."

"You've been in this place since Friday?"

"Yeah. What day is it today?"

"Sunday."

"Where are we?"

"The old summer camp. Whispering Aspen Ministries. What's going to happen to you?"

"Listen, whatever your name is, I need you to call the police for me. Tell them where I am. Kempffer is a bad man. I'm not positive, but I think he might be planning to kill me."

Gracie sucked in a breath. "Kill?"

"Yes. Kill. So would you please, I'm begging you, please call the police?"

"What did you do to make him want to kill you?"

"We had a business deal that went sour and now he's angry. So angry he'll do anything to keep himself out of trouble. Including killing someone."

Time was running out. Service would be over in ten minutes. She still had to hike to the church without being seen.

"Please." His voice was soft. Pleading. "You're my last hope."

"I don't have a phone. But when I get to the church, I'll find one and call the police." Gracie wished more than ever she owned a cellphone. So many of her classmates already had one. Her parents told her they couldn't afford one for themselves much less for her.

"Thank you. I hope someday, when this is over, I'll be able to thank you properly."

"I gotta go." Gracie opened the inside door.

"Wait a second. You should put the tape over my mouth. He might return before you can call someone."

Gracie bent and picked up the gooey strip and pressed it over the guy's mouth. He nodded his head.

Once outside she checked the time. Only seven minutes. She booked it down the trail, not caring how much noise she made now. When she reached the edge of the grassy yard behind the Meeting Hall, she stopped to be sure no one was around. She walked calmly around to the front of the hall where people would soon gather.

She slipped through the door, the sounds of women's voices emitted from the kitchen area. Gracie walked toward the front counter where she'd only ever observed someone sitting or standing when there were special events and people were required to check in. Kind of like at a motel.

On the far-right side she spotted a phone. She picked up the handset and at first heard nothing. Her heart skipped a beat. Then a dial tone sounded. Gracie punched in 911.

A woman's voice answered, "911 what's your emergency?"

What was her emergency? Something banged in the kitchen, Gracie jerked and almost dropped the phone. "Ah, hello," Gracie said.

"Hey, hon. What's the emergency?" The woman's voice was nice. Calm.

"There's a man. He's kidnapped. He needs help." Gracie stooped down and cupped her hand around the receiver, whispering.

"A man kidnapped and what? Can you speak louder, hon? It's hard to hear you."

"I don't want anyone to hear me. The old summer camp. The last cabin on the trail. Please send someone to help him."

Gracie heard voices outside. Service was over. She peeked through the front windows and saw Kempffer walking across the turnaround, heading for the Meeting Hall.

"Sorry. I have to go. Send someone quick." She returned the handset to the cradle and ducked down behind the counter as the front door opened.

She heard heavy footsteps and more voices outside. After an eternity but was probably thirty seconds, she stood up and came face-to-face with Kempffer. "Hi, Pastor Kempffer." She edged around the counter.

"Gracie Norberg. What are you doing?" His gaze drilled into her, making her breath catch. She coughed. "Um. Sorry. I lost a book. I thought I left it here after youth group Wednesday."

"Did you find your book?" Kempffer stared at her empty hands. His eyes were slitted like a snake's.

"No. Maybe it's down in the Blue Room?"

"I'll go check. Where are your parents?"

"They couldn't be here today. But they'll be here soon to pick us up." She hoped. Oh, crap, Cole. She'd promised to wait for him in the church. "I have to get Cole and we'll be back for donuts and juice. Thanks for checking on my book." Gracie flew out the door without waiting for a response. Her main concern was to find Cole.

Gracie ran through the oncoming throng of parishioners, like a salmon swimming upstream. She craned her neck every which way searching for Cole. By the time she reached the church only a few people milled around. No sign of Cole in the lobby. Her heart thundered in her bony chest. She peeked inside the main church. A couple of women stood conversing in the aisle. No Cole.

Next she checked the bathrooms. No luck.

Finally, she went to the Quiet Room. Gracie pushed the door open and found her little brother cowering against the wall next to the door, Pastor Thackeray's hand on his slim shoulder.

"Ah, there she is. Good morning, Gracie. God bless." Pastor Thackeray sneered. "I was asking Cole if he was here alone. Thought I'd have to bring him to the house until someone came to pick him up." He smiled and fingered the gold cross necklace he wore.

Not on your life, she thought. "Afternoon, Pastor. C'mon, Cole." She held her hand out for him. Cole ducked from under Thackeray's grasp and slid his hand into Gracie's.

"Enjoy the donuts, kids," Thackeray said. "Remember to study your Bible verses for next Youth Group."

Gracie pulled on Cole's hand. "Let's go get us some chocolate-frosted donuts." She hoped the police would show up soon to rescue the kidnapped guy in the woods.

Helping others. That's what Jesus would do. Surely, not whatever Pastor did. He acted like he helped, but he was nothing but a creepy-crawly, mean person. Not mean. Evil. He was evil. Maybe even the devil disguised as a pastor.

Her next mission was to prove her point. And keep her brother safe.

◆

MC and Ellen had hiked a portion of the Split Rock River Loop Trail. Around noon they'd made it to Ellen's truck in the parking lot off Highway 61, three miles south of Split Rock Lighthouse.

Ellen lowered the tailgate, and they hopped up to rest and drink some water.

"I think I scraped most of the mud off my shoes on those rocks." MC checked the soles of her hiking boots. "I expected some muck, but a couple spots were super swampy."

Ellen grinned. "You don't enjoy hiking through bogs?" She dug into her daypack. "Want a granola bar?"

"Yes. Thanks." MC accepted the snack. "Bogs, not my favorite, but I was astounded by the Split Rock formation. I've been coming up this way for most of my life and never knew the source of the name for the state park. Despite some tricky areas, I really enjoyed the views. Waterfalls. River. Shale. Beautiful vistas. Thank you for showing me the beauty."

"We only saw half the trail. The river crossing can be challenging and the only way to complete the actual loop. Two bridges have bit the dust over the years. Washed out. You take your life into your own hands attempting to cross the river. Unless it's dry as a bone, I'm not brave enough to wade through the water to get to the other side."

MC took a bite of granola and chewed. "I'm even less brave. The thought of finishing the hike in wet boots is far from appealing."

"Too true," Ellen said.

MC got a call. "Hey, Ekstrom. What? Where? When? Okay. I'll need to go home and change. I'll meet you there in an hour. Maybe less." She ended the call.

Ellen finished her snack and stuffed the wrapper in her daypack. "Sounds like work."

"Yes. I'm sorry, but I need to pick up my car and head home."

They slid off the tailgate and Ellen pushed it up. "No apologies necessary. Work calls, you gotta answer."

A couple minutes before one p.m. MC pulled into the driveway at Whispering Aspen Ministries. Two LCSO-marked units were parked in the turnaround. People milled everywhere. Probably members of the church sticking around to see what brought the cops out to their church.

MC was dressed in her field gear, tactical boots, BDUs, T-shirt, tactical vest, and nylon jacket. Badge in her pocket. Her gun on her right hip. She called Ekstrom's cell as she walked toward the Meeting Hall. "I'm here. Where are you?"

"Last cabin."

"On my way."

A tall man, well over six feet, light brown hair, dressed in a white button-down shirt and black dress pants approached her. "Excuse me. Officer?"

She didn't bother to correct him. "What can I do for you, sir?"

"Can you tell me what's going on? Why the deputies and

whatever agency you're with...what you all are doing here?"

"Who are you?" MC clocked him to be early-to-mid fifties. He had an air of businessman about him.

"Bradford Symons. I'm the Castle Cove Town Supervisor."

MC had no clue what a town supervisor's role encompassed, so she wasn't about to share any details with the guy. "I'm sorry, sir, but I cannot discuss an ongoing investigation. You'll have to contact Sheriff Tollefsen." She found the path and continued to the cabins.

"Hey, McCall," Ekstrom strode toward MC as she approached the cabin.

A couple of deputies MC didn't recognize were staged in front of the cabin. All guys. But thankfully not Kempffer. "Heya. So, where's Lewis? Is he all right?"

"He's still inside the cabin with Johnson."

"Johnson's here too? Good. No Kempffer though? He must be the only one not here."

"Not quite the whole station, but a lot of us. No Kempffer. Word is he'd been around earlier."

"He's the master of vanishing into thin air."

Ekstrom said, "He was seen at the Meeting Hall right after church service ended. One of the kitchen ladies saw him speaking with a young girl. But no one's seen him since. Johnson called, but Kempffer's not answering his cell."

"Puts a pretty bright spotlight on him then." Why would Kempffer not respond? Unless he had something to hide. MC hadn't liked the deputy from day one. The current situation was proving her instincts accurate.

Ekstrom said, "I overheard Lewis tell Johnson that Kempffer dragged him here under false pretenses. Says he's been held here since Friday."

"How long have you all been on site?"

"One of the guys got here within ten minutes of the call to dispatch." She inclined her head toward the deputies standing outside the cabin. "I was farther away. I got here about fifteen minutes after him. Johnson arrived right before you."

If MC was tracking the timeline correctly, Kempffer had last been seen right around the time the call came into dispatch. He had about an hour head start, give or take a few minutes. He could be anywhere.

"I'm going inside," MC said. "I want to hear for myself what Lewis has told Johnson." She took a step, then she pivoted back to Ekstrom. "You know who else I've not laid eyes on since I arrived?"

"Who?"

"The pastor. Thackeray. Something this scale happening on his church's property I'd expect him to be doing...well, pastorly things. Asking questions. Offering assistance. Singing God's praises. At the very least providing calm and comfort to his flock."

"Good point. I haven't seen him either. But I didn't go inside the church or the Meeting Hall. Maybe he's holed up in one of those places doing what you mentioned."

"Maybe." Unlikely. Something wormed around inside MC. Suspicion was its name. Pastor Thackeray and Kempffer. Two peas in a pod?

MC entered the cabin. Caleb was seated on the bottom of the first bunk bed, cuffs and a hobble restraint next to him. Johnson sat on a rickety chair facing the bunk.

Johnson stood. "McCall. Glad you made it."

"Sorry it took so long. I had to make a stop. What happened?" MC met Lewis's gaze. "Mr. Lewis. We've been looking everywhere for you."

"Mr. Lewis told me one of my deputies, Tyler Kempffer, kidnapped him from the hospital. Why don't you tell Inspector McCall what you've told me so far?" Johnson said.

Lewis took a swig from a bottle of water. "Like I told the sheriff"—

Johnson said, "Chief Deputy. Don't think Tollefsen would appreciate being replaced without an election."

"Sorry. Like I told Chief Deputy Johnson, I was waiting to be discharged from the hospital on Friday when Kempffer showed up and told the nurse he was giving me a ride home. I knew you were coming with the lady deputy, so I told him I didn't need a ride." He drank more water and dragged his hand across his mouth. "The nurse told him, Kempffer, I couldn't go anywhere until the doctor signed my papers. I thought I was safe from having to go with him, but then the doc showed up with my stuff and said I could leave. Next thing I know, Kempffer's dragging me out of the hospital. He tossed me in the back seat of his squad car, put that torture device around my arms, and blindfolded me. I asked where he was taking me and why. He told me to shut up. Then we ended up here, although I didn't know where here was until this morning."

"That's quite the story," MC said.

"I'm telling the truth."

Johnson said, "Matches what he told me before you got here."

Caleb's gaze bounced between MC and Johnson. "Honest. Kempffer has it out for me."

Like he has an honest bone in his body, MC thought. Time to relocate Caleb Lewis to an interview room.

MC said to Johnson, "I need more time with Mr. Lewis. Can one of your deputies transport him to the station and allow me the use of an interview room?"

"I'll have Ekstrom take him in and reserve a room for you. Audio and video recording?"

"Absolutely. Thank you." To Lewis, MC said, "Deputy Ekstrom will be in to take you to the Law Enforcement Center in Two Harbors. I'll be there shortly. Sound good?"

"Do I have a choice?" Lewis tossed the empty water bottle onto the bed.

"No, Caleb, you don't," MC said. "Maybe you'd prefer to wait here for Kempffer to return?"

"Nope." He held up his good hand. "If I never see that guy again, it's too soon." He cradled his cast on his left arm. "Any chance I can have some pain reliever? My arm is throbbing."

"We'll see what we can do. Sit tight and Deputy Ekstrom will be by in a minute," MC said.

By early afternoon all the necessary players were gathered in the dimly lit observation space next door to an interrogation room at the Lake County Law Enforcement Center.

MC and Ekstrom huddled at the round table in a corner of the room with a few evidence bags spread across the tabletop. They'd both be in the interrogation room, but MC would handle the questioning. She wanted Ekstrom to backstop her if she needed additional information or required clarification on an issue.

A jailer entered the interrogation room with Lewis in tow. MC stood at the one-way mirror and observed the interaction. Lewis was a ghost against the pale gray walls in the harshly lit room. The one-way glass and difference in lighting allowed observers to see the interrogation without being seen by the person being questioned. The jailer brought him around the rectangular metal table, so he was facing the door to the room, the one-way mirror to his right. The guard removed the soft wrist-to-waist restraints. MC had asked that Lewis not be cuffed during the interview. She wanted him as relaxed as possible in hopes he'd be more forthcoming with information.

MC checked the computer screen. The cameras in the other room captured Lewis and the two empty metal-framed chairs across from him where MC and Ekstrom would take up positions. No recording of video or sound would occur until MC initiated it by pressing a button on the wall outside the interrogation room door.

She did an about-face and asked Ekstrom, "Ready?"

Ekstrom gathered the slew of evidence bags and her notebook. "Yep."

The two paused outside the interrogation room. MC did a box breathing rep then pushed the button on the wall, opened the door, and proceeded with Ekstrom to sit in the chairs facing Caleb.

MC placed her notebook, pen, phone, and file folder on the table.

Ekstrom piled the evidence bags on the corner near her and aligned her notepad squarely in front of her.

A cop after her own heart. Organized. "Good afternoon, Caleb. This is a formal interview. We are recording. Let me begin." MC recited the date, time, and location of the interview. "Present are myself, US Postal Inspector MC McCall, Twin Cities Domicile." She paused and inclined her head toward Ekstrom.

"Deputy Riley Ekstrom, Lake County Sheriff's Office," Ekstrom said.

"Caleb, would you please recite your name for the record?"

Caleb cleared his throat and sat up in his chair. "Caleb Lewis."

MC said, "Next, I'm going to read you your rights. It's protocol. Caleb Lewis, you have the right to remain silent. Anything you say can and will be used against you in a court of law. You have the right to an attorney. If you cannot afford an attorney, one will be provided for you." MC stared Lewis in the eyes. "Do you understand these rights as I've read them to you?"

"Yes." He rested his injured arm on the table.

"Do you want an attorney or are you willing to talk with us without one?"

"I guess go ahead and ask your questions. I can stop and ask for a lawyer anytime, right?"

"Do you want a lawyer, Caleb? We have a lot of questions. Hopefully, you can shed some light on a few things." She paused. "But we can put it on hold until an attorney can get here. It's Sunday. Not sure how quickly you'll be able to raise someone on the phone and how fast they can get here. Might mean we postpone until tomorrow." She jotted a note on her pad. "What's it going to be?"

"I'll talk to you. For now."

Good enough. MC opened a file which contained pages of questions she'd been compiling on the post office robbery, the child exploitation, and the accident that landed Caleb in the hospital.

"First, how's the arm?"

"Better. They gave me some ibuprofen."

"Good to hear. Let's move on to what brought me to your neck of the woods to begin with." MC held out her hand.

Ekstrom dropped an evidence bag onto MC's open palm.

"You recognize this item, Caleb?" MC pushed the clear plastic bag across the table toward him.

Caleb grasped the bag. He flipped it over. "Yep, it's my wallet. I mean I'm almost one hundred percent positive it's mine. Where'd you find it?"

Jesus. Was he really going to play dumb?

MC allowed him to hold onto the bagged wallet for now. "Where were you on the morning of Wednesday, May thirteenth? Early morning, to be more specific."

MC checked off each question she asked on a page in the file folder.

His knuckles turned white as he clutched the crinkling plastic bag.

"Caleb?" MC said softly.

"I don't remember. That's a couple weeks ago." A tremor shook the hand holding the wallet.

"When was the last time you visited the Castle Cove Post Office? Was it on May thirteenth by chance?"

"Possibly. Yeah, I stopped there to mail some stuff, then later I realized I'd lost my wallet. After a few days I returned to ask if anyone had seen it." He set the package on the table. "Then you two showed up at my house to ask about my wallet. I told you I thought maybe I'd left it at the post office. So obviously someone found it, which is great." His body vibrated.

"Again, that was on May thirteenth that you left mail at the Castle Cove Post Office?"

"I guess. I don't know for sure."

MC pulled back slightly from the table and quickly checked underneath. Caleb's leg jackhammered. He'd behaved similarly when they talked with him at his home a week earlier.

"Why so jittery, Caleb? Just answer the questions. Be honest." MC scooted her chair closer to the table. "What if I were to tell you we have a witness who can place you at the Castle Cove Post Office on May thirteenth?" They didn't, but he didn't know that.

"Who? They'd be lying." He shot straight up in his chair. A wild light lit his brown eyes.

"Nice try. You may as well confess. We know it was you." MC laid her pen aside and folded her hands on the table.

Ekstrom had remained silent, but a quick side glance assured MC the deputy's attention was riveted on Lewis. Pressure was their friend.

MC drilled her gaze into Caleb. "We can sit here all day and all night if that's what it takes for you to tell us the truth. Trust me, you'll feel much better once you offload the weight you've been carrying around. The truth, Caleb. It's the right thing to do." Should she be more forceful? But she didn't want him to clam up.

Elbows planted on the table, Caleb leaned forward, not meeting her gaze. He gnawed on the thumbnail of his uninjured hand.

"Caleb? Come on. Whaddaya say? Man up?" She hated the phrase, but who knew. Maybe it'd work on him. "We know you don't have a history of robberies. I checked your record. Tell us what compelled you to do what you did. Let us help you." Help him. That was a laugh. She wanted to nail him, but she dangled the carrot anyway.

"Help me? When has any law enforcement in this town ever helped me?"

The barb flew across the table.

"You've had unpleasant run-ins with local authorities? With whom, specifically? Tell us about it."

"You don't care. All cops care about is getting criminals, and if they can't get the criminals, they force innocent people into saying they're criminals."

MC checked in with Ekstrom. "You have any idea what he's going on about?"

Ekstrom said, "Possibly. Can you be more specific, Caleb? We aren't the bad guys. I promise we aren't going to pin something on you if we don't have proof to back it up. You have my word. And I'm from here. I grew up here."

"Maybe I need a lawyer," he said.

MC stood and retrieved the wallet. Gathered her file and notepad. "Absolutely your right, Caleb. In which case this interview is over. You'll be escorted to a holding cell. At some point the jailer will get you to a phone, and you can hopefully track down an attorney. We won't be able to meet with you again until after you've had a chance to speak with whomever you hire or are appointed to if you can't afford to hire someone. Maybe sometime this coming week. Until then, you'll remain in custody."

MC and Ekstrom exited. MC hit the button to stop the recording. Inside the observation room they stood at the window and watched Caleb mumble to himself. He plowed his good hand through his messy brown hair, making it stand up in every direction. Her patience had worn thin.

Ekstrom said, "I think he's more afraid of Kempffer than what we've got on him. Because so far, we've only mentioned the post office robbery. He might think he can dance around that and slip through. But Kempffer has proven he'll go to extremes to keep

Lewis quiet about whatever's going on between them."

"Maybe. The kidnapping has got to be playing on a loop in his head. But he asked the girl to call us. So why not talk? I was sure he'd cave on the robbery and then it would've been an easy segue into the CSE crime. I expected when we mentioned the images on his computer, that would be the point where he'd lawyer up." MC shoved away the cloud of self-doubt threatening to bog her down. Determination bolstered her. "Maybe we can use the robbery charges as a bargaining chip to get more on the exploitation." She ruminated on the possibilities, reminding herself to keep her cool. "Let's give him a few minutes to stew. Then have someone take him to holding."

Caleb Lewis's eyes were glazed. Like a rat in a maze trying to find the cheese but running into walls.

She hated these roadblocks, but also acknowledged the interview hadn't been as smooth as she'd have liked. She could've been more nuanced in her approach. She felt apprehensive. What if she had lost the ability to efficiently probe and ferret out information. To do the job effectively. At a time when the stakes involved child victims.

Her mind spun with images of children being exploited for the perverse pleasure and profit of entitled men. Men who had control and power over the kids. Men who used verbal coercion and intimidation to convince them if they didn't obey and keep their mouths shut then something bad would happen to them...to their families...and it would all be their fault.

MC was determined to shut down the operation, arrest, and charge as many dirtbags as possible. She imagined herself as Bigfoot stomping the assholes into oblivion.

Justice. She wanted to enact justice.

Her thoughts were interrupted by a phone call. "McCall." She exited from the observation room.

"Why are you still here? You've been warned. Now you'll pay the price." The voice modulator crackled and fizzled, making the caller's words sound like Rosey the Robot from *The Jetsons* cartoon when she went haywire.

"Do tell. What's the price? Why don't you come talk face-to-face instead of these empty cowardly threats by phone?"

"Be careful what you wish for, bitch."

Before she could retort, the call ended. She stood with a handful of dead air.

Back inside the observation room she motioned Ekstrom to join her at the round table. She opened her notebook and recorded the date and time of this latest call. "I just got another call from Unknown. That's number five by my count."

"You still think it might be Kempffer?" Ekstrom asked.

"If I had to bet. He's the only person who's had attitude with me. I might've considered Mr. Lewis," she inclined her head toward the one-way glass, "but obviously he's been out of commission, and we know he doesn't have access to a phone right now." Caleb sat in the interrogation room where soon a jailer would retrieve him and stow him in a holding cell. Until he came to his senses or rounded up an attorney, whichever came first, he could mull over his circumstances.

Pastor Thackeray left the Quiet Room at the church. He'd been so close to an unplanned special session with Cole Norberg, until his meddlesome big sister Gracie showed up. The girl should know her proper place in the hierarchy. To respect those more important than her.

After Gracie dragged Cole out of the church Thackeray followed. His flock would be waiting for him at the Coffee and Donut Fellowship in the Meeting Hall. Congregants expected him to show up, say a short prayer, and pronounce the people and the snacks blessed.

He hurried out the door and found a LCSO SUV parked in the turnaround. Some people hung around outside, while others continued into the hall. Why the hell were the cops here?

Within minutes two more squad cars rolled in. The now-forming crowd parted like the Red Sea in Exodus 14 to make room for them. What on earth was going on at his church? He sidled around the periphery and slipped into the Meeting Hall. No sign of deputies.

A good number of the community occupied the tables or stood talking. Undoubtedly, they were discussing his amazing sermon from this morning. Thackeray caught sight of Gracie and Cole, each with two chocolate-frosted donuts stacked on napkins.

That's right, kiddos. Grab nourishment. Especially little Cole. Boy was angelic, but a stiff wind could blow him away. Nothing but air. It wouldn't hurt for him to chow down a few extra donuts.

He half-expected a pack of deputies to come traipsing in. Cops could sniff out a donut like no one's business. So far, no sign of any of them though. Thackeray moved into the kitchen and grabbed a cup of coffee. He said to one of the volunteer women, "My good sister, can you tell me what's going on?"

"Pastor, I'm not sure. I heard people saying there are deputies outside, but I didn't hear any sirens."

"Have any of them, the deputies, come inside?" He scanned the hall, hoping to spot Kempffer.

"No. But I've been busy, so I may have missed them."

"Have you seen Youth Pastor Kempffer?"

"I did. Earlier. Before all the hubbub. He was conversing with one of the young girls. I'm not sure of her name. But then she left, and I didn't see where Youth Pastor Kempffer went." She scanned the crowded hall. "Oh."

Thackeray joined her in the doorway. "What is it? Do you see Kempffer?"

"No, but that girl there," she pointed to a spot at the end of the table where the donuts were set out, "she's the one he was with earlier."

He followed the direction she pointed. Lo and behold, the child in question was the bane of his existence, Gracie. He studied her and Cole as they consumed their treats.

"She's the same girl Pastor Kempffer spoke with?"

"I'm pretty sure. I need to fill the sugar bowl and set out more creamer. Excuse me, Pastor."

"Have a blessed day." He fingered the gold cross necklace. Dare he try and corner Gracie and find out what happened between her and Kempffer?

Too late. Gracie and Cole were in motion, shoveling the remainder of their donuts in their mouths as they moved toward the door. Too many people around.

He chose not to pursue her now. From inside the door Thackeray watched as Gracie and Cole skipped down the steps and into their parents' sedan. Wednesday night during Youth Group he'd sit Gracie down for a one-on-one meeting about minding her business. God didn't abide busybodies.

While his flock enjoyed their post-service social hour, he went downstairs to his office. He quickly checked all the rooms, but no sign of Kempffer. Maybe he'd gone to the house. Sometimes Kempffer liked to get a workout in instead of attending Sunday service. Or he could be resolving the situation in the last cabin. Thackeray didn't want any part of whatever that entailed. He escaped out the rear door and jogged to his residence.

Inside he found the kitchen as he'd left it. He opened the door and descended to the basement. The kids' play area was a dead zone. The TV was off. All the games were stacked neatly on the shelves. The kitchenette was tidy, except for a cupboard door ajar. He opened it and took in the multiple boxes of fruit snacks and granola bars. There was an empty spot where the granola bars were stored.

He clocked that one of the plastic-wrapped cases of bottled

water had been ripped open. Four bottles were missing.

He wondered if Kempffer had pilfered supplies for the situation.

The workout area was in order. All the equipment was in place. The television at that end of the room was off.

He opened the door to the storage closet. The cleaning supplies were in order on the shelves, but several packages of rags were scattered across the floor, and the button to open the secret door was in plain sight.

Thackeray pushed the red button and the door, which was flush with the wall and undetectable, opened a couple of inches without a sound. He grasped the edge and pulled it far enough to walk through, then left it open because no one else was around to discover the hidey-hole. He descended the concrete stairs leading into the secret bunker and moved quickly down the short hall to the metal door.

"Kempffer? You down here?" Thackery called out as he closed the metal door.

"Yeah." Kempffer paced in front of the mattress set against the far wall. A box of granola bars and crumpled wrappers lay on the mattress. On the floor next to it were four bottles of water.

At least Thackeray knew who'd pillaged his snack and water supplies. "What the hell is going on? Why are you holed up in here? What about your...situation?"

"Are you shitting me? Did you see all the troops out there? I swear Tollefsen sent every deputy in the tri-county area. I need a gun. Do you have any guns?"

"Take a chill pill. No, I don't have any goddamn guns. Jesus."

"Great language coming from a pastor," Kempffer said. "You learn that from your Holy Bible?"

"I can boot your ass out of here. I don't need all this heat on my church." Not to mention his extremely important extracurriculars.

Kempffer picked up a stuffed teddy bear and ripped its head off. He threw it across the bunker.

"I thought you were going to handle the situation with your guy. I can only assume the all-hands law enforcement presence is because someone found him."

"That's my guess too. When the squad cars started to roll in and I saw Johnson, I dipped. I've been wracking my brain, trying to figure out who called it in."

"Maybe the post office cop who's been here the past couple weeks? She's been a thorn. I don't even know why," Thackeray said. "Left me her card the last time she was here. When was that?" He paused. "Ah, yes. The day the moonshine shack was discovered out in the state forest. She was asking questions. What, may I ask, does a postal cop have to do with a non-postal crime? The woman needs to mind her own business. Do her job and get gone."

"She's here because of the post office robbery," Kempffer said. "She's a massive pain in the ass. All snooty, like she's better than us local cops. Asking me questions like I'm a suspect, then demanding a copy of my report. Who does she think she's dealing with, Barney fucking Fife? You're damn right she needs to get the hell out of town. How hard can it be to solve a simple robbery? I even tossed her a freebie. I grabbed Gimpy Sutherland off a park bench and booked him for the crime. Put in my report an anonymous witness called in a tip."

"If she's investigating the post office crime, why has she been out here? Other than the moonshine still, I can't fathom what interest she has in our community."

"I don't know." Kempffer stopped pacing and faced Thackeray. "You tell me. Are you a suspect? Did you rob the post office, Pastor?"

"Don't be ridiculous. Of course I didn't rob the post office. Thou shalt not steal is one of the Ten Commandments, need I remind you."

"That's rich. You citing a commandment. Do you recite them all while you diddle the kiddies down here?" He kicked a Pokémon stuffy off the mattress.

"Don't be crass, Tyler. Please stop destroying the toys. I don't want to spend more money because you're having a temper tantrum."

"Whatever. Listen, I'm going to need to hang here until the heat dies down."

"You sound like every bad nineties TV cop drama."

"You're a laugh a minute. Can you go to my place later and grab me some clothes and my gun?"

"What? I'm your errand boy now? Where's your truck? How about I kick you out, and you figure what to do on your own? Keep me out of it."

"My truck's parked out of sight on an old logging road a half mile away." Kempffer poked a finger into Thackeray's chest. "You have a lot to lose if I'm caught. Because I believe I've told you before, if I go down, we all go down. You. Symons. Our computer boy wonder. All of us. I know you don't want to lose your little kingdom here." He waved around his arms. "Not to mention your little lambs."

Kempffer was right, the insufferable ass. He regretted ever involving him in his and Symons's hobby. For the foreseeable future he needed to devise a way to rid himself of Kempffer and keep the aforementioned heat off himself.

A thought trickled from the far recesses in his brain. He could kill Kempffer. If he did it down here in the fallout shelter, no one would know. He could bury him deep in the state forest. By the time anyone found him, he'd be a pile of bones picked clean by the carnivores in the woods.

Thou shalt not kill.

Damn commandments.

"Let me think about it, Tyler. You can stay here tonight. But I am not going to your house to get you anything. The last thing I need is for someone to see me going in or out of your place, and then I'm right in the soup with you. You'll have to concoct another plan. Stay down here until tomorrow morning. I can feel the law breathing down my neck. Either that postal cop or a deputy is bound to show up here thanks to you."

"Can you at least get me some real food? A pizza or burger and fries? Something? I can't eat these cardboard-tasting granola bars. They suck. I don't get why the kids like them. Taste like crap."

You've tasted crap, Thackeray wanted to ask.

"I'll think about it. I need to assess the situation you've created on my property. So stay put and shut up."

"Whatever." Kempffer stalked to the opposite end of the shelter and grabbed his guitar off the stand. He sat in one of the two armchairs set up in the area where whoever wasn't enjoying their time with the kiddies could relax and observe the action. He strummed the opening chords for "Mr. Misunderstood" by Eric Church.

Thackeray hated country music.

The less than productive first interview with Caleb Lewis had MC eager to have another go at him. After instructions for the jail to contact her should Caleb by chance come to his senses and want to talk, she and Ekstrom left the station.

Ekstrom bid her farewell for the moment and went out on patrol duty.

MC went home to the cabin. The sun was high in the western sky, the day waning. A can of Diet Coke in hand, she settled at her desk. The icy cold soda was a poor substitute for her old pal Grey Goose.

She reviewed the notes from Caleb's interview. Full of contempt, what she'd really wanted to do was rip into him about the image on his computer—one image for sure and more than likely many more. Where there was one photo exploiting a child there were always more. Like Lay's Potato Chips, scum couldn't have just one.

Disgusted by the thought, she'd wanted to drill Lewis. Pump him to find out if he'd been to Whispering Aspen Ministries lately. If she could get an admission, then she'd be one step closer to tying him to the IP address and the images on the cloud server too.

The level of self-control MC exercised during the interview had been far from easy. But the last thing she needed so soon after returning to the job was to fly off the handle. Ekstrom's presence helped reel her in, kept her on track. She was eager to push though. To get beyond the robbery and move on to the sickening images. But today wasn't going to be the day.

She held out hope he'd change his mind about the attorney and talk with her again. Maybe tomorrow. Or Tuesday. Waiting sucked, but she didn't have much choice.

With crimes against children foremost in her mind, the issues with her sister Cindy roiled around too. A cauldron of evil boiled and bubbled into a toxic brew inside her.

Something else wiggled around in the deepest recesses of her mind. She stood and paced the length of the loft, notebook and computer open on her desk. Drank Diet Coke. Paced some more. What was trying to wend its way through her brain?

A maelstrom of images and words.

Child.

Children.

Crimes.

Abuse.

Death.

Adult men.

Power.

Control.

Sexual dominance.

Taking advantage of children. Using and tossing them like throwaways as if they were of no value in the world.

Then a faraway memory, warped and fuzzy at first, began to solidify. Before she knew it, the event crawled into her head like a worm burrowing into the earth and slithering home so easily.

The year was 1975. MC was a week from her tenth birthday. A

warm August night in St. Paul. She'd begged her mom, Dad was at his Tuesday bowling league, to allow her to walk to the corner store two blocks from their house.

The evening air was thick, darkness encroaching. All MC wanted was to buy a grape popsicle to help cool down. She'd made the trek a million times. Their neighborhood was safe. Her mom acquiesced without hesitation.

MC made it to the store minutes before the 9 p.m. closing time, bought her popsicle, and said good-bye to Old Joe, the owner. Outside the store she cracked the popsicle into two, tore open the wrapper and pulled out the first stick. She walked down the side street toward her block where she'd cross her street and go left half a block to her house.

The popsicle was refreshing and super grape-y. Precisely the way she liked it. MC slurped the treat, enjoying the freeze on her lips and tongue. She crossed her street and was about to head left down her block when she heard a whistle behind her. Then a man's voice calling a name. Half a popsicle in her mouth, the other half still in the wrapper, she swung toward the voice. Half a block up the side street she'd just traversed, near the mouth of the alley, a tall bulky shadow figure stood outside the pool of light from the streetlamp.

Was that Mr. Lemon their across-the-street neighbor? His wife was a teacher at MC's school. In fact, Mrs. Lemon had been MC's second grade teacher. The Lemons had a miniature white poodle named Snowball.

"Hey, you." The man—was it Mr. Lemon?—called out. "Can you come help me? My dog got off her leash." Something rope-like dangled from his hand.

MC squinched her eyes to slits. Was that Mr. Lemon? He seemed the right height. She sucked on the frozen treat, almost finished with the first half.

The man sounded a lot like Mr. Lemon.

"Please?" he asked.

She bit off the last chunk of popsicle from the stick, shrugged, and recrossed the street. Her mother's voice popped into her head, "Do not follow strangers." But this probably wasn't a stranger. She was pretty sure he was their neighbor. Mom would want her to help Mr. Lemon find Snowball.

"Mr. Lemon?" She continued to walk toward the man with the leash in his hand.

"Yes."

As she neared, she saw the guy had a mustache. That sealed the deal. Mr. Lemon had a mustache. Her nerves calmed. "Did

Snowball run away?" MC drew closer.

"I'm afraid so. Can you help me find her?"

MC was happy to help. She was perhaps five feet from the man when he stepped backward into the shadows of the alley.

"I think she ran down here. Let's go check." He let go of the leash and reached for MC's hand, and getting ahold of her wrist. He'd angled away enough so half his face was buried in inky black and half in the pale glow from the streetlight.

MC's heart tumbled like a boulder in a rockslide. The remaining popsicle half slipped from her hand. This was NOT Mr. Lemon. She'd never seen this man before. But by then he had an ironclad grip on her left wrist.

The shadows swallowed them. With his free hand he began to unzip his pants. He pulled her hand toward the dark opening. "My dog's not lost. But I have something else you can help me with." He tugged harder on her wrist.

Her eyes felt like they were going to pop out of her skull.

MC gathered her breath.

She should scream.

Then on the ground at his feet she noticed, not a leash, but a piece of rope, maybe a clothesline. Her heart kicked into overdrive, the scream swallowed.

"Come on. Be a good girl. Help me. I got something real nice for you. You'll like it. I promise." He fumbled the zipper all the way down and unbuckled his belt. He drew her hand to the cave of darkness.

"No!" MC wrenched her wrist, trying to free herself from his giant hand. "No. No. No. Let me go!"

"Shush now. Don't make me hurt you."

MC was icy with sweat. Her heart thudded like an elephant thundering through the jungle. She leaned forward and then pulled back hard using her free hand as added leverage. Because her arm was slick with perspiration, her wrist slid out of his grip.

Without another thought she ran full tilt for home.

The porch light was on, and MC barreled through the front door out of breath, sobbing. The story poured from her as she fell into her mother's arms. Her mom guided her to the couch and sat next to her. MC recalled shaking so hard her teeth clacked together. She stuck her hands in her armpits and rocked back and forth.

Then her mother called the police. After she hung up the phone, she locked MC in the house, alone, and drove the neighborhood, searching for the attacker. MC had never seen her mom so furious. At her? At the stranger? Both?

Two police officers showed up at the same time as her mom.

Mom hadn't seen anyone on her drive. One cop left to conduct a search of his own. The other cop, an older man with thick gray hair, bulldog jowls, and a band of flab exploding over his shirt collar, listened to MC's story. He lectured her.

"Mary Catherine, you should never approach a stranger. I'm sure your parents have told you this. In fact, I bet your teachers have too. Now I'm telling you. Never, ever, approach someone you don't know. Even if you think they might be a neighbor. You come home and tell your parents. Do not go to strangers." He jabbed a thick finger at her as she observed him from the couch. "You got lucky tonight, young lady. You shouldn't have even considered responding to the man."

MC bowed her head in shame, sucking back the tears threatening to unleash. The cop blamed her. She'd been the bad one.

The second officer returned. He was younger. Tall. Thin. Black hair and super blue eyes. The bluest she'd ever seen, like sapphires. Much bluer than her own. He'd driven around the area. Drove down the alley where MC said the nasty man had been standing.

He said, "A guy was in his garage working on his car, but he didn't fit the description. Said he hadn't heard or seen anything. Had a radio playing loud inside the garage. He'd been out there about two hours."

The police and her mom discussed the situation by the front door. MC remained statue-still on the couch. The more they talked, the more MC shutdown. This was her fault. She was to blame—she'd done something stupid.

The old cop told her mom MC shouldn't be allowed out unchaperoned after dark. Was he scolding Mom now?

Yikes.

He went on to say MC obviously couldn't be trusted not to go off with any weirdo who called out to her. "I'd keep her on a short leash," he'd advised. "Make everyone's life easier. We have real crimes we need to handle."

Times were different in 1975. Here she was now, nearly forty years later, following the digital trail of the unspeakable, unraveling the lives of those who preyed on the most vulnerable. Defenseless children exploited by emboldened, entitled adult men. Times had changed. But they also stayed the same.

MC shook herself out of her memories. She was pissed, shocked, and incredibly repulsed.

She'd had enough.

MC plucked her phone and car keys from the desk and fled to her car. She drove a few miles south on Highway 61 to the Wheelhouse Pub. The very establishment where she and Ellen had eaten pizza not long ago.

Inside the crowd was thin, three patrons. All old-timers. Two set up on the first two bar stools. The other at the far end. She chose the middle ground and bellied up to the bar.

"What can I get you?" Bill the bartender/owner slid a coaster in front of her.

"Vodka tonic with lime. Make it Goose." She pointed at the tall opaque bottle, black eye staring her down, standing watch on the backbar.

"You got it." Bill mixed the drink and set the tall glass on the coaster. "Anything else?"

She shook her head without lifting her gaze from the drink.

Bubbles rose in constant motion.

MC stared.

Hypnotized.

She wrapped her hand around the tall slim glass.

Didn't lift it.

Sat transfixed.

All the memories, past and more recent, rolled nonstop in her head like Skee-balls at an arcade.

Cindy's death—MC's fault.

Man who tried to make her touch him when she was ten—MC's fault.

Her parents dead because a drunk driver obliterated them—not MC's fault. Maybe.

Barb murdered in their home six months ago—MC's fault.

A second-grader dead from an opioid overdose. A student of Barb's—MC's fault.

Currently, young children being sexually exploited and possibly abused—she'd not found the offenders. The kids probably still suffering at the hands of their abusers—MC's fault. She hadn't nailed the bastards yet. Too slow.

Solution to all the above?

The drink in her hand.

Take a breath. If you drink, what will you gain? What will you lose? Temporary numbness from the pain. But you'd risk solving this case, possibly lose your job. More importantly you may lose your life.

MC lifted the glass. Stared at the lights reflecting through the liquid. Slowly brought it toward her face. She leaned over the glass, eyes closed, and stuck her nose close to inhale the essence.

Can anything stop the past from haunting the present?

"You all right?" Bill asked.

She opened her eyes. Almost lost in the sight and feel of what she perceived to be the only remedy for what ailed her. "I'm not sure. Let me ask you a question, Bill. Can anything stop the past from haunting the present?" She peered at him over the top of the drink.

"Well, that's a big question. I ain't no head-shrinker, but I can tell you this much. That there," he pointed at the glass in her hand, "surely is not the answer. If anything, I'd say drinking only enhances the haunting. Numbs us. But doesn't remedy us." He grabbed a white terrycloth towel from beneath the bar and wiped the already pristine wood. "But I'm a lowly bartender. What do I know?"

MC set the glass onto the coaster and nudged it toward Bill. "How much do I owe you?" She pulled her wallet from her pocket.

"Nothing. Glass is still full. We're good. You have a good evening now." He tapped a knuckle on the bar and went to pull a draft for the loner at the far end.

She folded a twenty and slid it half under the coaster. "For the therapy." Her voice was barely audible.

A newfound determination flooded her veins.

For once, satisfyingly, a thirst for justice overrode her thirst for liquor.

At the cabin she packed an overnight bag and drove down to the Cities. Originally, she thought she'd stay put in case Caleb wanted to talk. In light of what she'd almost done at the Wheelhouse Pub, she had to make her Monday afternoon session with Dr. Zaulk.

Chapter Nineteen

Exhausted from the night's drive, MC rummaged for pajamas: plaid flannel shorts and a T-shirt. She plugged in her phone, fell into bed, and let sleep take her away.

The blinding white antiseptic space MC existed in offset the suffocating darkness that constricted her heart. Blood flow inside her slowed to a trickle. Her breath, dense as a London fog.

She half-recognized the place. She'd been here before, but not in nearly two months. Why now?

A voice erupted from her left. One she'd not heard in more than forty years. The voice called to her. "Mary. Mary Catherine. Grab my hand. Don't let me fall. I'm sorry I was mean to you at the swings. Please?" A small pale hand reached through a throng of eight-year-olds clambering around a low stone wall where rushing water was a background soundtrack.

MC slugged her way through the scrum of kids. It was imperative she reach Cindy. A collective gasp and a cacophony of high-pitched screams propelled her forward, as the wall loomed, a foreboding barrier.

Someone pushed her from the side.

She sprawled on the ground, scrambled up, called out for Cindy. She was Cindy's last hope. Only she could save her big sister. If she failed, everyone would blame her.

"MC, help." Barb's voice sounded from her right.

MC froze.

Should she go toward Cindy or go to Barb?

She had to choose or lose them both.

Someone or something shoved her from behind. She reached to steady herself against the wall and her hand encountered—nothing.

Air.

Inky, empty air.

Then she was in free fall.

She sensed, rather than saw, the ground rushing to meet her. The point of impact was nearly upon her.

A scream wedged in her throat.

MC convulsed and awoke, arms and legs flailing. After a second, she realized she was in her bed in her St. Paul apartment. A glance at her phone showed it was nearly five a.m.

May as well get the day started.

The vestiges of the nightmare clung to her like a shroud. A warm shower did nothing to revitalize her.

What a rude awakening.

She dressed and repacked her bags, then made a pot of coffee. She sat at her kitchen table, hands wrapped around the hot mug, reflecting on the glass she'd held the evening before. Her gaze tracked the swirls of rising steam, and she brooded over her current situation.

The weight of her circumstances was a heavy burden. A list formed in her head. The recently unlocked memories, Barb's murder, rehab, AA meetings, Meg's cancer, returning to work, and two cases she struggled to solve. All those things wrapped around her neck like an anchor, sinking her faster than the Edmund Fitzgerald on stormy Lake Superior.

Lately, she'd been confident her life was on track. But the constant pull for booze was like a battering ram against her brain. Yesterday she'd nearly capitulated. Would she be able to walk away next time? Doubt clouded her vision. Hopefully, Dr. Z would help her see more clearly.

MC wondered what Dr. Zaulk's reaction would be if she chose to throw herself onto the green bean bag chair and sink into oblivion. Probably the good doc would be unfazed, so instead MC chose her usual seat.

"How are you, MC?"

"You know, partly cloudy with a chance of headache." She squirmed, trying to get comfortable. Drummed her fingers on the arm of the chair.

"You seem preoccupied today."

"Might be the understatement of the year." MC opened the bottle of water she'd accepted upon entering the office and took a swig.

"Lots happened this past week?"

"Where do I begin?" She twisted the cap on the plastic bottle, then loosened it. Back and forth. "I didn't journal at all. No time. I didn't talk to Barb." But she spoke to me, awake and in a dream.

"Thank you for your honesty. Tell me what has you on edge. Is it work?" Dr. Z's gaze fixed on MC's hands messing with the bottle.

Should she set the bottle on the table? But then she'd end up fidgeting some other way. In the end she set the bottle in her lap, hands loosely around it. A touchstone of sorts.

"Here's the deal. Work is complicated. Well, the two cases I'm working are complicated. I missed an AA meeting because of work. I think…let me back up. The memories I shared last time of Cindy, I think what happened was there was a vacant spot where my memory of her dying should reside. For all my life I followed my parents' example and never spoke about it. Not ever. Not to my friends. Not to Barb."

"The memory was too complicated and all-encompassing for you to process as a child. You continued the same track into adulthood. I think you sealed yourself off from the pain. Perhaps even from guilt. Until now, after you've had so much more lived experience from losing Barb, going through rehab, battling back. The dam burst and the memories demanded to be let out."

"But there's more. Another long locked away memory blew me up yesterday."

She laid out the memory from the summer when she turned ten. The man. The leash. No dog. The fear. The shame. The treatment by the police.

"Another example of something I never spoke about again after it happened. Neither did my mom. I'm not even sure she told my dad about it," MC's voice cracked. She refused to cry. Instead, she gulped some water, wishing she could wash the vile memory away.

"MC, that's a lot. I'm so sorry that happened to you. I'm appalled at the way the police handled the situation. Did your mom ever take you to talk to anyone afterward?"

"It was the seventies, so I think cops weren't as savvy as they are now. Maybe savvy isn't the right word. Mom never brought me to a therapist. Again, it was the seventies. What happened at home, stayed at home."

"Even so. You were a child. You should've been believed and comforted, not lectured and threatened."

"Well, hold on to your hat because there's more. Last night I had "the dream" again. But an expanded version. This time I was trying to save both Cindy and Barb. No, let me rephrase that, I was forced to choose which one to save. I had to either go left and save Cindy or go right and rescue Barb. How could I make that choice? Before I could, I came crashing back to the land of the living."

"The grief and guilt you continue to carry, along with the new unlocked memory, more than likely resurrected the dream. Your mind may have reached a breaking point, and this was the way it handled the situation."

"Let me ask you the question I asked Bill the bartender. Does our past inevitably haunt our present?"

"Before I delve into the past or present question, I have one of my own. Bill the bartender?" Dr. Z arched an eyebrow.

"Yeah, about that. After I remembered about 'not Mr. Lemon

and the non-existent dog' I hightailed it to a local pub. Ordered a vodka tonic with lime. Any good drink needs a bit of color." Her attempt at humor flopped like a fish out of water. "I held the drink, doc. Mesmerized by every bubble floating inside the glass. Listened to the tink of the ice cubes against glass. Breathed in a good dose of the essence. Holy shit did I want to guzzle the liquid and feel the burn all the way to my toes." She took a couple deep breaths, gaze fixed on the rug beneath her feet. "I held the drink and asked the bartender, 'Do you think anything can stop the past from haunting the present?' He basically told me drinking wasn't the answer." MC faced Dr. Zaulk. "I did not drink."

"Good for you, MC. That had to be a very difficult decision. But you know it was the right choice. Even if Bill hadn't told you drinking wasn't the way to go, I'd bet you would've come to the same conclusion on your own."

"Maybe. Maybe not." Probably not. Given the opportunity to quench her thirst unhindered, she would've downed it. "So, the haunting thing?"

"The past informs the present. There's no way around it. We are who we are because of the life we've lived. But I don't believe the past haunts the present. If you meet these memories and process them and accept them for what they are...memories...you can move on. They'll never go away. They're an inherent part of you. But you can put them in perspective and choose to live your life to the fullest."

"Sounds like a tall order." How she wished Barb were here.

I'm always here. You are stronger than you think. Live your life. Don't let the memories live for you.

"I have confidence in you, MC, and now we're at the end of our time. This has been another packed session. I'm proud of you." Dr. Z leaned toward MC. "Journal. AA meetings. Friends. Utilize all the tools you have at your fingertips. That's how you move on."

"I'll do my best." Would she? Could she?

"I know you will."

There was her answer.

"Thanks, doc. See you next week."

Still a bit wobbly from the past twenty-four hours, MC walked to her car, rehashing Dr. Z's analysis and instructions. A Herculean undertaking. But at least Dr. Z had pulled her from the brink, for now.

In her car MC wrestled with whether to stop at Flannel and check in with Dara and Meg or get on the road to Castle Cove. A phone call and the name on the screen decided for her. "Hey, Ekstrom. What's up?"

"McCall, Caleb Lewis wants to talk."

"Awesome. I'm leaving St. Paul. I'll be there in about three hours." She queued up a podcast and shifted the car into drive and her mind toward making a breakthrough with Lewis.

And finding justice.

Ekstrom met her at the front entrance of the sheriff's office and let her inside. "How was your drive?"

"Uneventful. I had plenty of time to mull over questions for Mr. Lewis. He wants to talk sans attorney?"

"Yep. He's more…resigned, maybe? I'm not sure. But that's how I'm reading him. I guess a night in a holding cell gave him time to really think about his options."

"Maybe it gave him time to decide to do the right thing. Best-case scenario."

"What would be the worst case?"

"I ask a question or make a statement that tips him over the edge and he for real lawyers up. Then our job becomes more cumbersome. Not impossible. But more arduous for certain."

"I've had him brought up. Same room as yesterday. The observation room is ready, all systems go."

"Excellent. Let's stop there first so I can leave my stuff."

After a brief confab, MC and Ekstrom entered the interview room. Ekstrom pressed the button on the outside wall before the door closed behind her. Caleb occupied the same chair as the previous day. MC and Ekstrom took up their preordained spots across from him, backs to the door. Pin-sized red lights blinked on the cameras set up high in the corners. The recording equipment was rolling.

"Good afternoon, Mr. Lewis," MC said. I was told you expressed a desire to speak with us?"

Caleb's pallor was nearly translucent, like a vampire had sucked all the blood from his body overnight. He sat hunched, head nearly on the table. "Yes."

"Sorry, I couldn't quite hear you. You'll need to speak up." MC wanted every word to be clear on the recording.

He ran a hand through his dark brown hair, leaving it a riotous mess. Straightened. "Yes. I asked to talk to you."

MC ran through reciting the Miranda Warning again. Then she moved on to chronicle the date and time and who was present at the interview.

"Now that all the housekeeping tasks are completed, let's get started." MC reviewed her notes. "We've got a lot of ground to cover. I want to thank Deputy Ekstrom for stocking a supply of water so we won't get parched."

"Caleb…may I call you Caleb?"

"Yeah, that's my name." He unscrewed one of the bottles of water, the flimsy plastic crinkling in his hand.

"So, Caleb, would you be comfortable sharing information with me…us," she waved a hand to include Ekstrom, "about your activities on the morning of Wednesday, May thirteenth?"

"I don't really remember what I did specifically. That was a couple weeks ago. Probably I got up and ate breakfast and took a shower, same as I do most every day. Then I probably worked."

"Where do you work?"

"At home. I'm a contract computer software engineer. My work is all remote."

"I see. Does your work require you to bring packages or other forms of mail to the post office?"

"Sometimes. Well, not my work so much as personal stuff."

"Do you remember if you visited the post office on May thirteenth? For personal stuff?"

"No. Maybe. I don't remember." Caleb scratched the tabletop with a fingernail.

"How often do you go to the post office, Caleb?"

"Depends. Maybe once a week or once every two weeks. Varies, I guess. Why does it matter how much I use the post office?"

Scratch. Scritch. Scratch.

Caleb exhibited nervousness, but he was cooperating.

"Which post office do you use?" A fast pitch straight over the plate.

"Two Harbors. I live here." He spread his arms wide.

"Yes, we've established where you live—that's helpful. Any information you share with us will be helpful. Thank you. Now, have you used any other post office?"

"You mean like ever? In my life? Probably. I guess? I can't really think of specific times or places off the top of my head."

Time for a curve ball.

"Listen, Caleb, I'm going to show you something and I want you to tell me if you recognize it. Okay?"

"Sure."

Ekstrom handed the wallet enclosed in an evidence bag to MC. She slid the item across the table to Caleb. "Is this familiar?"

"It's my wallet. I told you yesterday."

"Yesterday was yesterday, Caleb. We're going to cover all the bases again today, so please bear with me. You're certain this is your wallet, correct?"

"Mostly."

"Let me clear up any doubt you may have. Inside that wallet," she pointed with her pen, "are credit cards with your name on them. Photos, a young woman and a small child, a boy I think."

"Great. Can I have it? My wallet?"

Ekstrom reached across and retrieved the evidence bag. "Afraid that's not possible," she said. "We'll keep it safe though."

MC said, "Let's discuss how we came to be in possession of your wallet. I hope you can enlighten us on how it came to be in the location where it was found. Would you be comfortable engaging with us about that?"

"Yes. If I can answer, I will."

"We want to talk about your activities on the day your wallet went missing. Caleb, if I get to a point where you don't feel comfortable, you can tell me you don't want to talk about it. Or if you decide you want an attorney present, let us know that too. Okay?"

He nodded.

"Tell us about your activities on the day you lost your wallet from the time you got up until you went to bed."

"I noticed my wallet was gone probably a couple weeks ago."

"Would it have been May thirteenth?"

"I'm not sure. But maybe."

After Thackeray's conversation with Kempffer the previous day, he'd secured the shelter access and returned to the main level of the house. Thackeray was restless. To cure his bout of unease, he'd strolled to the Meeting Hall to see if the action had died down. To avoid detection by any remaining law enforcement officers, he'd crossed the road and walked along the church side.

A few vehicles remained, so there were still folks on the grounds.

Thankfully all the cops had cleared from the area, and he'd successfully avoided talking to them. For now. He'd thought about walking to the cabins to see if anyone lingered where Kempffer had left his hostage but decided against it. No sense getting himself in the middle of Kempffer's situation.

He hustled to the house. After another discussion with Kempffer, they concluded the best thing to do would be to drive him to his house after dark. Thackeray would drive him in his Jeep and wait for Kempffer half a mile down the road.

Once he drove him to his place, Kempffer gathered some clothes and other necessities that Thackery didn't want to know about. Then Kempffer slept on the mattress in the fallout shelter.

Thackeray was restless. Morning had blended into afternoon. Monday was typically Thackeray's chore day. He washed clothes, cleaned the house, then treated himself to an intense hour-long workout. The afterglow left him invigorated and ready to face the rest of the day.

Having avoided the situation long enough, he went down to the shelter. Kempffer sat in one of the chairs playing his guitar. Some song Thackeray didn't recognize. Probably country. Thackeray was more a metal head, which surprised many people. No one could wrap their head around a pastor liking "that kind" of music. No skin off his nose.

"You come up with a game plan yet, cowboy?" Thackeray removed the towel from around his neck and wiped a sheen of sweat from his face.

Kempffer strummed the guitar. "Nope. Thought I'd hang here. Good a place as any to chill."

"Like hell. Tyler, they'll come for you eventually. Especially when you don't show up for work. I'm sure your friend has spilled his guts about how he landed handcuffed and blindfolded in one of my cabins."

"Tell 'em you don't know nothing. You haven't seen me since before service yesterday. Yada yada. Blah blah."

"You have to leave. The sooner, the better. Get far away. Do not contact me."

"Where do you propose I go?"

"Canada. Mexico. The moon for all I care, as long as it's far from here."

"I'm sure they have a BOLO on me which will include the borders. I was supposed to work this morning. Shit's hitting the fan." He set the guitar on its stand. "Hey, does Symons know anyone with a private plane? Someone who could fly me to like Montana or Idaho, someplace out west where no one knows me."

"You have money, Tyler? How do you propose to pay for a private plane?"

"I wasn't planning on paying for it, Curtis. You and Symons should be willing to help me get out of Dodge no matter the cost. I mean, with what I know." He made a tsk tsk sound. "You two would go away for a long time if I spilled the beans. How about it? Give Bradford a ring-a-ling and see what you two can come up with, eh?" Kempffer stretched his legs out in front of him, arms behind his head. "You know where to find me."

Thackeray felt the heat building from his toes. His hands curled into tight fists. He retreated before he did something he'd regret. He fingered the gold cross on the chain around his neck. Surely Jesus would forgive him for the murderous thoughts in his head.

Should he call Bradford Symons? Maybe the town supervisor did have connections with someone who owned a plane.

After a brief restroom break and sodas all around, MC, Ekstrom, and Lewis reconvened the interview and recording.

MC shifted papers around on the table. Opened a file folder. Picked up a sheet of paper. "Caleb, how tall are you?"

"Almost six feet."

"Do you own a black lightweight jacket? Like a windbreaker?"

"I used to. I don't know if I still have it." He pushed his chair away from the table and stretched his legs.

"How about boots? What kind of boots do you have?"

"You mean like snow boots? I have a pair of Sorel snow boots. I help Mr. Ogren by clearing snow during the winter."

How thoughtful, MC thought. "Any other boots? Hiking? Work boots? Anything like that?"

"I'd have to check my closet at home. Why do you need to know about my boots?"

Why do you think? MC felt her composure begin to slip and reined herself in. She took a swallow of Diet Coke and set the can down. A slow, measured movement.

"Do you own a gun, Caleb?" MC asked.

"I don't feel comfortable answering that right now."

"Okay. Do you feel comfortable answering why you robbed the post office? We know it was you. Evidence shows it was you."

He straightened in his chair. "Why would I rob a post office? I make good money doing my job."

"We're asking you the question. Why? You're the only one who can answer."

Caleb's leg jumped up and down like a frog on hot pavement. "Maybe you should worry about getting Kempffer. That asshole. He's the one who tried to kill me last week. Then he kidnapped me and kept me chained up in the woods. He's got some serious issues. Psycho. He should be in jail right now for kidnapping."

"We'll get to all that, Caleb. As soon as you come clean about the post office robbery." MC tapped her pen on the evidence bag holding his wallet. "See, we found your wallet behind a file cabinet at the post office. In the area behind the counter where you made the clerk give you the cash from the till and then had her dump out mail so you could go through it."

Caleb's leg stopped and then ramped up. MC worried he was going to launch himself right out of the chair.

He said, "I didn't—"

MC closed the file folder. Stacked the loose papers on top. "Caleb. Do yourself a favor and come clean. You robbed the post office."

Caleb crossed his arms and remained mum.

Time to shift gears.

"Deputy Ekstrom, would you hand me those other evidence bags?"

Ekstrom slid the items toward MC.

"Let's talk about the images on your computer, Caleb. The piles of DVDs we found in your office." She waved the bags holding the *Cars* DVD and the opened padded envelope with a Castle Cove, MN, postmark. "Who is Jimmy Lewis in Rochester, Minnesota?"

Caleb froze. "Are you referring to pictures of my nephew? Because I've been working on a digital scrapbook thing for my sister as a surprise."

"I doubt the images we're referencing are those of your nephew, unless you and your buddies have been exploiting him too."

"Maybe I need an attorney?"

"Are you requesting an attorney? You did the same thing last time we talked." MC held his gaze. "Let's be clear. Because we'll need to talk with you about charges involving the sexual exploitation of children, robbery, mail theft, and whatever other charges we can put together."

He froze, eyes wide.

Ekstrom said, "Caleb, don't take the fall for all of this on your own. Tell us who else is involved. Was it Kempffer? Were you being coerced? Threatened? Do you remember when you were pulled over for speeding last year?"

"Yeah. What's the speeding got to do with anything?" His gaze slid away from them.

MC said, "If you talk to us, I'll inform the US Attorney you cooperated. I can't promise anything, it's their call, but trust me, they take a favorable view upon people who are cooperative and help us get other bad guys off the streets. There're some serious CSE charges coming down the pike."

Caleb slapped his palm down on the table. "I'm not going down for shit I didn't do. I'm pretty sure Kempffer was the one who tried to run me down. Guy is stone cold. He could be a serial killer." He raked his hand through his hair again. "This was never going to end well. I wish some other deputy had pulled me over last year."

MC opened her notebook. "Let's begin there, Caleb. The night you were pulled over."

He told the story, much as Ekstrom had told MC, about being pulled over by Kempffer for speeding. "I swear I was going like three miles over the limit. Couldn't believe I was being pulled over. I knew another speeding ticket was going to kill me with the insurance company."

"So Kempffer pulls you over. What happened next?"

"I didn't have my license on me. Had the other stuff, insurance and registration. But my license was at home. I thought for sure he was going to yank me from the car and take me in. He was furious, ready to put some hurt on me." He waited for a beat. "Now I think about it, his behavior was extreme for the situation. Anyway, I figured I'd get ahead of it and told him I only lived two blocks away and if he followed me home, I'd show him my license."

The story checked with Ekstrom's account, point-by-point.

"The weird part happened when we got to my place. First, only Kempffer came up. You," he pointed to Ekstrom, "didn't. I thought that was strange. I went into my office because my license was on my desk next to the computer. Kempffer saw my set up and asked what I did. Told him I was a software engineer and did contract work for various companies. And I was a gamer too. He asked me what I knew about photos and videos and making DVDs. I told him that was easy work. Next thing I know, he's telling me I'm going to be a production and distribution person for a side hustle he and some other guys had going."

Kempffer was neck-deep in CSE. The information from his ex-wife plus what Caleb was spilling now nailed Kempffer's ass.

Who could the "other guys" be? She thought back to the original report of CSE images originating at Whispering Aspen.

Holy shit.

And the image Ekstrom saw on Caleb's computer showed a child holding a lightsaber. She'd seen a lightsaber in the pastor's office when they were talking with him about the moonshine shack. Was Thackeray part of this?

The Magic 8-Ball would show—a fucking strong possibility. The way the cards were stacking up now, she believed that Kempffer, Caleb, and Thackeray were connected to the child exploitation crime. But who else? Caleb had stated other guys. Plural. She tuned back in to him.

"He told me if I didn't agree, he'd add a bunch of other charges and make them stick, and I'd find myself without a license, maybe serve jail time. I couldn't be without a license. My sister and nephew live in Rochester and are basically my only family. How would I go see them if I couldn't drive?"

"Let me make sure I understand the situation. Kempffer coerced you into joining a CSE enterprise with 'some other guys'?"

"What's CSE?"

"CSE is Child Sexual Exploitation," MC said. "People in your world probably use the term 'porn.' That's a term that can never apply to children, Caleb. Adults engaging in consensual sexual acts and distributing the materials to the public for their sexual gratification, that's porn. The keyword being consensual. Kids can*not* give consent. See the difference?"

"Got it. So, yes, Kempffer made me work for them making CSE stuff."

"Who were these other guys?"

"I don't know. I only ever had contact with Kempffer."

MC leaned forward. "Have you been out at Whispering Aspen Ministries lately?"

"Hell no. I haven't been at Whispering Aspen since before high school. I remember you now," he pointed at Ekstrom. "You were there then too."

MC set the hook. "What did you exactly do for this side hustle, as you called it?"

"I received photos and did any clean-up to make them sharp, then burned them to DVDs. Same with videos."

"Then what?" She needed the distribution admission too.

"Sold them via a website I designed. The proceeds automatically went into an account Kempffer controlled. He paid me twenty percent and split the rest with his partners, I guess. Or maybe he kept it all for himself."

Rage and disgust battled inside MC with each word out of Caleb Lewis's mouth. These were children. Innocents. Not some random inanimate objects for sale on eBay.

MC showed Caleb another evidence bag with a plastic DVD case. "Recognize this, Caleb?"

He looked at the plastic pouch.

"A DVD of *Cars*. It's a movie I bought for my nephew's birthday. Why is that evidence?" He was genuinely puzzled.

MC ignored his question and moved on to the next item in the pile. "This?"

"That's an envelope to mail..."

MC could almost see the light bulb blink on above Caleb's head. "Please, go on. To mail what?"

Caleb sagged, back bowed. "I was going to mail the movie to Jimmy, my nephew. But I screwed up. Man, did I screw up. I was running behind on projects for my job, and I also had to get a bunch of DVDs out for Kempffer. I worked all day and then right before the post office was due to close, I brought a bunch of discs in. I went home and continued to work." He guzzled nearly half a bottle of water. "After dinner I organized my work documents and found the *Cars* movie under a stack of printouts. Then I remembered one of the padded envelopes I'd mailed had Jimmy's name on it."

"What did you mail to Jimmy if you still had the *Cars* DVD?" MC knew before he even uttered the words.

"One of the DVDs I'd burned for the online business. Had to be." He didn't meet her gaze. "I panicked. The post office was closed. It was after seven p.m. Then I got an idea."

"You thought you'd show up and rob the post office?" MC asked.

"Well, yes and no. I only wanted to see if I could retrieve the package addressed to Jimmy. I thought if I showed up real early, there'd only be one person. I figured if I waved a gun and scared them, I'd be able to get inside. I had an old knit ski mask to cover my face and a BB pistol that looks a lot like a real gun."

MC asked, "But why not wait until they opened and ask if they could check to see if your envelope was still there?"

"Honestly, I don't know. Like I said, I panicked. On so many levels. I had to get that DVD. I couldn't have my sister and nephew see what was on it. Not to mention how much trouble I'd be in with the law." He spun his hand in the air. "With all of you."

"Yet here you are in all kinds of trouble with us." And not a modicum of common sense in you. "What happened? You got there and waved your BB pistol at the poor clerk. Then what?"

"I saw the drawer with money. I ordered her to give me all the paper money and stuffed it in my jeans. I wanted her to believe it was a real robbery."

"Caleb, let me clue you in. When you entered the facility wielding a firearm it became a real robbery."

"I know. But finding the envelope was all I could think about. The metal rack with those big bags was right there by the counter. I saw mail inside the bags. I made her dump it all on the floor, and then I went through it." His voice hitched up an octave. "Wasn't finding the damn thing. I got mad at one point and kicked something. Then my jacket got stuck on a hook and tore. I was about to give up, dip out, when I spotted the package. I grabbed it and a bunch of other pieces as a decoy, I guess. I held onto my envelope and tossed the rest of the mail as I ran from the building. I didn't want to be stealing someone else's mail."

"That's very thoughtful of you." She bit back the sarcasm. "You kept the cash."

"I did. But I swear to God I was going to mail it to the post office anonymously. It's on my dresser at home. All of it."

Was this guy for real? Mail it back?

Caleb continued. "It wasn't until later I realized I'd lost my wallet. I'd had it in my jacket pocket when I arrived. I figured it had to be at the post office. I waited a few days and then went in and asked. Things got kind of weird. They wanted me to wait and then to write down my information. I freaked out and took off."

MC said, "Don't you think running was a bad idea? Innocent people more than likely wouldn't beat feet when asked for contact information."

"I dunno." He slumped. "Didn't think about it."

"We're going to step out for a few minutes, Caleb. When we return, we'll pick up where we left off. You need the restroom? A soda?" She stood and Ekstrom followed suit.

"Another Coke would be great," Caleb said.

"Someone will bring it soon."

MC left the recording on after they left the room. Who knew. Maybe Caleb would talk to himself, and they'd get more information.

Inside the observation room, MC texted Chief Deputy Johnson, asking him to stop in when he had time.

Ekstrom asked, "Plan?"

"Has anyone seen or heard from Kempffer? Lewis implicated him. We need to have a sit-down with him ASAP."

"He didn't show up for work this morning. Johnson was less than pleased. I heard someone went to his house, but no one answered the door. His phone goes right to voicemail."

"He's off the grid." MC paced the room. "I think we should ring up Pastor Thackeray as well. See what he knows about his youth pastor's whereabouts. What he has to say about a kidnapping victim being found in one of the camp cabins. And if he knows anything about the CSE images."

"You think he's involved?"

"I strongly suspect so. The initial report we got indicated images were sent from the church's IP address. And the lightsaber."

"The image I saw on Caleb's computer. The kid had a lightsaber."

"Yes. And when we were in the pastor's office asking about the moonshine distillery, I saw a lightsaber."

"I forgot about that," Ekstrom said. "Should we finish with

Lewis and then drive out to Whispering Aspen?"

The door opened and Chief Deputy Johnson stepped inside. "Ekstrom. McCall. You wanted to talk to me?"

MC said, "We got Lewis to confess. To the post office job and to distribution of CSE material. I want to finish up with him in a minute but wanted to update you. He's pointed the finger at one of your own as an accomplice."

"Let me guess...Kempffer," Johnson said.

"Yes, sir. According to Lewis," MC said. "You don't seem surprised."

"Kempffer has been dodgy, not much of a team player."

"I heard Kempffer hasn't reported for duty today."

"That's correct. Did I mention his disregard for rules? No one's managed to track his ass down. I've got orders out for anyone who lays eyes on him to notify me immediately."

MC said, "When we wind up the Lewis interview, I'm going out to Whispering Aspen. I have questions for the pastor. Will it be a problem if Ekstrom comes along? I don't want to leave you short-staffed, especially considering Kempffer's absence."

"It's fine. We'll manage. Do what you need to do."

MC stopped at the cold drink vending machine and got a couple Diet Cokes for her and Ekstrom and a regular Coke for Caleb before going back into interrogation.

"Here you go, Caleb." MC set the can on the table in front of him.

"Thanks." He awkwardly braced the can between his chest and busted arm and popped the tab.

MC consulted her notes and got down to business. The gears clicked.

"You gotta believe me," Caleb said. "I don't rob places. I've never done anything like that in my life."

MC heard a ring of truth to his story. She'd already searched the databases and found no priors. No indications of criminal activity. Well, except for the giant-ass red flag of CSE images waving in the prevailing winds.

"Caleb, you act remorseful...for the robbery anyway. Although you did travel a very long and winding road to get there. The idea Kempffer threatened you and bullied you into working with him is a little less believable. Are you the type who has issues finding a girlfriend?"

"What? No. I don't...it was about money. A business venture. I have a seven-year-old nephew who I love. I'm *not* into kids. Nope. Absolutely not."

"Did you touch any of them? You've admitted to having the images. Following that trajectory would lead us to ask if you'd also had physical contact with the victims."

"No." His eyes teared up, face turned the color of a plum. "I'm not some weirdo child abuser."

MC hit her stride. Not reacting to his discomfort.

"What you want us to believe is you fell into some get-rich-quick scheme after Kempffer promised to nix the speeding ticket? Sounds far-fetched to me. And the church? You a member?"

He scrubbed his face with both hands. "I don't belong or go to any church. Not since I was a kid and my parents made me go. I told you, I stopped going when I was like twelve or thirteen. Thackeray was a scuzzball. I couldn't stand the place or him. Why do you keep asking me about the church?"

The details didn't quite add up. MC was missing information integral to solving the case, like a baker missing flour when making a cake. She had confirmation that sexually explicit images of kids had been uploaded to a cloud-based storage service from Whispering Aspen. The IP address was proof. Caleb worked with images he got from Kempffer. Created DVDs and sold them. However, there was a disconnect between the front-end and back-end of the business.

Were the two not related after all?

"You gotta believe me. I was only in it for the easy money and the ticket thing."

"Caleb," MC said, "how did you receive the images and videos?"

"From Kempffer. He supplied them to me."

Was he being purposefully obtuse?

"*How* did he supply them? File transfers? What exactly was the process?"

"He showed up at my place with SD cards. I'd download the stuff, and he'd take the cards with him when he left."

SD cards didn't correlate with images being uploaded via an IP address. What was the missing link to connect the chain?

"You didn't use a cloud-based service to pull images down to your computer?"

"I mean, I have a cloud storage account. Two. One for work and a personal one. But I don't use either one for the thing with Kempffer."

"Okay, Caleb. We're done for now. Finish your soda and the jailer will take you back to your cell. Interview ended at," MC checked her phone for the time, "eighteen-twenty-two."

Chapter Twenty

Ekstrom drove to Whispering Aspen, MC in the passenger seat. The temperature tipped back into the fifties after a high in the mid-sixties. The sun was on its westward trajectory. Sunset would be a few minutes before nine p.m. There was enough darkness in her life, so she appreciated the lengthening of the daylight hours as the calendar plodded along toward Summer Solstice.

Ekstrom said, "Do we need a game plan going in?"

"This is no game. Trust me. People involved in crimes against children, they're the bottom-feeders of society." She stared out the windshield. "Sorry, I didn't mean to be snarky."

"I get it. So do you think Thackeray is one of those bottom-feeders? Or are we just trying to find Kempffer?"

"Excellent questions, Ekstrom. You sure you're new on this job?"

Ekstrom's face tinged with a pinkish glow in the evening light. She showed all the trappings of a great detective. Or postal inspector.

"In answer to your on-point inquiries, we are most definitely searching for your co-worker. I'm not sure if Thackeray's a child predator or not. You know him better than I do. Or at least longer than I have. What's your take?"

"Thackeray has always made my skin crawl. Working out has always been his main thing. Goes against how you'd think a man of God would present himself. He also pays a lot of attention to the younger kids. I mean, I guess that's why the old pastor gave him the Youth Pastor position and pretty much groomed him to take over."

"So you think Thackeray could be a predator?"

MC leaned heavily toward the affirmative on her own question.

"I guess that's my long-winded way of saying yes. It's a possibility. He's always favored Kempffer. There's a camaraderie between them. Or maybe a mentor-mentee relationship is a better assessment."

"Good to know."

They pulled up in front of the old white farmhouse and got out of the squad car.

The church was visible further down the road on the left. The Meeting Hall was across from it on the right.

The house's front porch light was on, though not needed yet.

Maybe Thackeray left it on all the time. A guiding torch for lost souls?

"Sure is quiet out here." As if in response to MC, the wind kicked up and the shushing of the aspen trees filled the air. "Except for the aspens. Listen to that. Sounds like the fluttering of a million butterfly wings. I heard once, on public radio I think, Native Americans could tell when they were closing in on aspen trees by the sound way before they saw them."

"Interesting." Ekstrom tilted her head. "When I really concentrate, I can pick up on the butterfly wing sound. Cool."

"Sometimes we need to take a breath and be one with our surroundings."

"Can I help you?" Thackeray's voice pierced the air, scattering any good vibrations to the winds.

"Evening, Pastor," Ekstrom said.

"Pastor Thackeray." MC walked over to the porch where the barrel-chested man stood, as if guarding his castle. "We'd like to ask you a few questions. Mind if we come in?"

"I figured someone would be out to see me at some point. We can talk right here on the porch."

"Wind's picking up. Maybe inside would be more suitable," MC's voice was firm. "Or we could take a ride to Two Harbors and converse at the station. Completely up to you."

A burst of red crept up Thackeray's thick neck and suffused his face with a fires-of-hell glow. "Fine. Come in. We'll talk in the kitchen. But I have somewhere to be in less than an hour, so can we make this quick?"

"Not a problem. Mind if we sit?" MC asked.

"Have at it." He waved a hand at the chairs around the center island. He went to the opposite side of the counter and slid onto a seat. A tall glass of something was in front of him. "You have the floor. Ask your questions."

Abrupt. A hint of aggravation?

MC pulled her notebook and pen from her blazer pocket. Interesting he didn't have any questions for them. Like what was the hullabaloo at my church yesterday?

"You must be aware by now there was an incident on church property yesterday." She studied his demeanor. "A man was found blindfolded and restrained in one of the cabins. Had you heard?"

"I think I recall someone mentioning something."

"What can you tell us about what happened?"

"Me?" He pointed a thick finger at his chest. "I can't tell you anything. I haven't the faintest idea what happened." He fingered the gold cross necklace. "I conducted the eleven o'clock service and waited with one of the children for someone to pick him up. By the time I arrived at the Meeting Hall, I think all the officials had departed. Perhaps you could fill me in on the details."

"The man who was held hostage was brought there by your youth pastor, Tyler Kempffer. Did you see Mr. Kempffer yesterday?"

"I saw him prior to the start of service. He rounded up the under-twelves to sit in the Quiet Room, which is a space delegated for parents with babies and kids under twelve not accompanied by an adult. Then there's no disturbance in the main church during the service. Children tend to get restless, which leads to rambunctiousness, and I can't have that in God's sacred house."

"I see. You didn't see Mr. Kempffer after service ended?"

"Like I said, I was otherwise occupied."

MC changed tracks. "What did you do the rest of the day yesterday?"

"My usual. I locked up the church once everyone was gone. The ladies tidied up the kitchen in the Meeting Hall after fellowship ended. I may have spent some time addressing church business in my office at the hall. Then I was here," he waved a hand around, "in my home."

"Were you home alone?" MC asked.

"I was."

"No one stopped by? You get any phone calls?"

"No visitors. No calls. Just little ole me." He snapped his fingers. "Ah, I did do a pretty intense workout in my home gym. But, again, I was alone."

"Wow. You have a home gym? Must be convenient. I'd love to see it. Some days I can't make it to the gym. A home gym would be so great."

"Well, I don't know."

"Maybe I'll get some ideas from your setup. What can it hurt?"

Thackeray huffed and slid from his chair. "Fine, it's in the basement. This way." He headed for the back door.

MC eyed Ekstrom, who nodded. Her hand drifted to her right hip where her firearm was holstered. She flicked the snap open. Behind her she heard Ekstrom do the same.

The door to the basement was by the back door. Thackeray flicked on the lights and descended the stairs. At the bottom he flipped a few more switches and lights blazed to life, revealing a setup to match many fancy health clubs. Elliptical machine. Treadmill. BowFlex machine. Free weights. A couple of benches.

What took MC more time to absorb was a shadowy area to the left. "What's this?" She stepped toward the corner.

"The children's play area. I spend time here with kids during youth group nights. They are tasked with reciting Bible verses they've memorized, and we do prayer sessions. If they behave and get the Bible verses correct, they're allowed time for video games or to use the iPad. Spiritual motivation. Did you want to check out the machines?" He motioned toward the workout area.

"Yes." MC and Ekstrom walked around the vast space. "Nice machines. Must've cost a small fortune." How did a small-town pastor afford all this? By partnering in a lucrative online business distributing CSE images and videos?

Thackeray strutted, proud as a peacock. "I got them about six months ago. Top of the line. I use them every day. Sometimes I have a couple of friends join me. With the amount of use they get, it was worth the extra money."

He ran his hand over the treadmill rail as if caressing a lover.

In a corner at the far end of the basement MC spotted another door, slightly ajar. "What's in there? Don't tell me you have a sauna too." She headed for the door.

Thackeray jumped in front of her and slammed the portal closed. "No sauna. I wish. Just a supply closet. Maintenance and cleaning supplies. Have to keep the equipment in tip-top shape."

"Makes sense. Mind if I sneak a peek? I'm also interested in the best cleaners to use. I'd want to keep my gym equipment in as good condition as yours." She crossed her fingers she hadn't overdone the syrupy praise.

Thackeray reached behind him and twisted the doorknob. "Sure. Not much to see but go for it." He switched on the light.

MC entered the space, Ekstrom on her heels. "Very impressive."

Black metal shelving lined the walls. Stacks of white terry cloth towels. Bottles and cans of various sorts arrayed the shelves. "You sure are well-stocked."

A package of towels lay on the floor. "Here, let me get this for you." MC reached for the package, but Thackeray beat her to it.

"No need. I got it." He grabbed it, bobbled it, and finally settled the package of towels on a shelf.

MC spotted a cover plate on the wall, like that over a light switch or outlet. What an obscure place for either one.

"That's about all there is to see." Thackeray herded them into the gym area. "If there's nothing else, I really would like to get to making dinner." He steered them back up the stairs.

"Thank you for your time, Pastor. If we have further questions, we'll be in touch. You have my card?"

"You gave me one last time we met, Inspector. I still have it somewhere." He ushered them out the door. "You two have a nice night."

MC slid into the passenger seat of Ekstrom's patrol car. "Talk about the bum's rush."

"Shifty man, Pastor Thackeray," Ekstrom said.

"You believe him about Kempffer? Not seeing him since before Sunday service?"

Ekstrom started the vehicle. "No. He kept touching that cross every time he answered a question. Was that a tell? Like he was lying to us and asking for forgiveness at the same time?" She put the gearshift in drive and pointed them toward the road.

MC said, "Thackeray's cagey. What's the deal with the kids' play area in the basement? Why bring kids over to his residence when there are multiple areas that would work at the Meeting Hall?" Questionable behavior at best. Debauched, sinful, and criminal behavior at worst. "He's separating specific kids. That sets off alarms and bells and whistles and red flags."

She was convinced he was coercing minor children by promising them rewards if they performed.

Ekstrom said, "Individual Bible study or prayer sessions. Alone with young kids."

"Exactly. A trusted adult. Someone in power, alone with defenseless children in his home. Inappropriate at the least, add in coercion and escalation to debased immoral actions, and we have the recipe for a child predator."

"Yep, totally suspect. He's off his game this evening. No preachy stuff. In a hurry to get rid of us, especially at the end."

"He's hiding something. But what?"

"Or who," Ekstrom said. "No one has seen Kempffer since church yesterday. Is Thackeray providing Kempffer cover?"

"But why give Kempffer sanctuary? He'd be putting himself at risk for aiding and abetting because we know Kempffer kidnapped Lewis. Would the pastor risk his own freedom to protect Kempffer? What exactly is their relationship?"

"I know they've always been close. But to me Thackeray has always been more concerned with himself. Self-centered. Now that I think about it, I doubt he would risk it all to protect Kempffer. If anything, he'd throw Kempffer under the bus."

MC gazed at the white clapboard house. "Narcissistic for sure. My gut tells me something's amiss. Think about how he reacted in the storage closet. When I attempted to pick up that pack of towels, he about knocked me over. Ekstrom, there was a faceplate like you see over an outlet or light switch on the wall behind the shelving. When he put the package in place it obscured the switch or whatever from view."

Ekstrom stopped at the intersection of the Whispering Aspen entrance and the highway. "Could've been another light switch."

"But why have a light switch not easily accessible? With only one light in the room, it doesn't make sense. Also, there was a discrepancy between what he told us when we first arrived and then at the end. Did you catch it?"

"No. What do you mean?"

"When we first asked to come in and talk, he said he had somewhere to be in less than an hour. Then at the end as he ran us out of the basement, he said something about making dinner."

"Good point."

MC couldn't let go of the feeling she'd missed something. "Humor me. Or do you have to get back to the station?"

"What're you thinking?"

"Ten or fifteen feet behind us I noticed a spot where I think you could back this rig in, facing the road leading to Whispering Aspen. We could stand watch for a while."

"Sure. I'm technically off the clock now. But why not? Maybe we'll catch him doing something he shouldn't be doing."

Thackeray stood at his front door. He tracked the movements of his two departing visitors as they drove toward the road. Then he locked the door and hastily retreated to the secret room.

"This is a less-than-optimal situation," Thackeray paced the concrete floor of the fallout shelter.

Tyler Kempffer sat in an armchair acting cool as a cucumber. "Curtis, you need to calm the hell down. You'll give yourself an aneurysm at the rate you're going. Did they mention me? I told you they'd come, didn't I?"

"I think I told *you* they'd show up. Anyway, they asked when I last laid eyes on you. I told them I hadn't seen you or heard from you since before the service yesterday. Tyler, you have to leave. Put distance between yourself and the church."

"Did you talk to Symons? See about a plane?"

"Symons has zero connections with a plane. None. No one. He doesn't even have a friend of a friend of a friend who owns a private plane. He's a big mucky-muck here in Castle Cove, but outside of town he's virtually unknown. Big fish in a small pond."

"Well, sonofabitch. I can't take my truck. They'll be watching for it. I should ride out the storm right here. I mean, there's no facilities down here, but otherwise I have everything else I need. I could use your bathroom when I need to. You can bring me food. No one knows about this place."

"In your dreams, Tyler. Not a chance. First off, how would I keep Symons from finding out you're here? He'd turn you in faster than anyone if he thought it would save his ass."

"You and I both know if that were to happen the dominoes would fall for all of us. I've made that clear. At this point you really don't have a choice. Well, I guess you could always kill me. But I'm pretty sure you don't have it in you." He smirked. "I'll hang out." He picked up his guitar, picked the strings.

Thackeray clenched his fists. A red haze filled his vision. He eyed Kempffer's gun on the table between the two chairs. Was Tyler right? Did he not have it in him to kill?

"You're leaving tonight, Tyler. Pack up. I don't want to know what you decide to do or where you decide to go. Just go."

"If I don't?" He pressed his hand against the guitar strings.

"Do you really want to gamble and find out?" Again, his gaze fixed on the gun.

Tyler followed his gaze. "Are you brave enough, Curtis?"

"Here's something to ponder, Tyler. I can walk up those stairs. Lock down the shelter and camouflage the entrance. No one would ever know it existed. Let you waste away down here." And go insane, he thought. "Sound good?"

Kempffer's mouth tightened. "You wouldn't."

"Wouldn't I? What's it going to be? You ready to shove off tonight or disappear into oblivion down here all alone? I'll give you an hour to decide. When I return, I expect to see you and your duffel waiting at the door. We'll discuss next steps."

Thackeray hurried to the black metal door and slammed it shut, locking Kempffer inside the underground shelter. He hated the thought of losing the playroom and the cameras set up inside but needs overruled wants.

Thackeray fully expected Tyler would be waiting impatiently on the other side of the metal door, eager. He wanted to get Kempffer out of his house and on the road to wherever he was going to go. Far away, hopefully. Never to be seen again, preferably. He picked up the handset for the phone and called Kempffer. Surprisingly the Cold-war era system still functioned. After about thirty seconds he hung up and tried the phone again.

Kempffer finally responded. "Let me out."

Thackeray said, "Here's the deal, I think you should drive down to Duluth and rent a car. Probably won't be able to get one until morning, but as soon as a place opens. Then head to the Cities. You could hop a bus or Amtrak for somewhere. Go West."

"I'm not leaving," Kempffer said.

They argued for a solid five minutes. Screaming through the phones on either side of the black metal door that sealed Kempffer inside the bomb shelter.

How had this gotten so cocked up? His only concern now was self-preservation. Kempffer would get what was coming to him. This was all his fault. "You fucked up everything," Thackeray said. "Got big ideas for making money, and your greed created an exposure risk for all of us. Jesus Christ."

"You didn't complain when the dough rolled in, and you were able to buy all the fancy gym equipment. A great pastor you are. Maybe practice what you preach for once."

"I'm sorry, Tyler. If I can't trust you to do the right thing and leave town, then I've no choice but to keep you where I know you can't cause any harm. I'll check with you again in the morning, see if you've changed your mind."

Thackeray climbed the concrete steps up to the basement closet, nudged the secret door back into place, then shut off the light.

For the time being he'd keep Kempffer locked up. Not really a prisoner. Surely after another night in the bunker, he'd come to his senses.

Thackeray locked up the house and poured himself a whiskey, neat. Something to take the edge off after a highly energized couple of days. He was about to flip on the TV to catch the late-night news when he heard a loud squeal like nails across a chalkboard multiplied by a thousand. Had some woodland creature just been murdered?

He doused the lights inside and out and retrieved his shotgun from the front closet. Yeah, he'd lied to Kempffer the previous day about not having a gun. What an idiot. A man needed to protect his home and property, especially a man of God.

At the back door he shoved his feet into an old pair of sneakers he wore to mow the lawn. He opened the door and slipped into the mild night.

No sounds.

No birds, no insects, no nocturnal soundtrack played.

Someone lurked out there in all that silence.

Back up against the farmhouse wall, he waited. He panned his gaze across the expanse of yard and the encroaching wood line abutting his property. Every so often the aspens quaked.

When he was about to give up and go inside to finish his drink, he detected movement. Straight back from where he stood. Near the group of red pine and ground cover.

He took a few tentative steps away from the house. Stopped. Listened. More rustling from the same area.

A muffled voice uttered something.

Thackeray rushed for the pines, shotgun ready.

In the copse he found Kempffer dusting himself off. His duffel bag was on the ground at his feet.

He'd forgotten about the escape hatch in the fallout shelter.

"What ya doing there, Tyler?" Thackeray leveled his shotgun at Kempffer.

Tyler lurched toward his bag on the ground.

"Nope. Don't even think about it. I know you have your pistol in there. In fact, toss me the bag and step away. Don't fucking do it, Tyler. I'll blow you to fucking kingdom come."

"Let me go, man. Come on."

"Too late. Can't trust you now. Psalm 118:8: 'It is better to trust in the Lord than to put confidence in man.' You've proven that to be true."

"You're going to quote a Bible verse to me while holding me at gunpoint. That's rich, *Pastor*." Kempffer bent over and grabbed something from his bag and then threw the bag at Thackeray.

"Now we're on a more level playing field." Kempffer aimed his handgun at Thackeray.

"I wish you hadn't done that, son." Thackeray pulled the trigger.

The repercussion reverberated like the opening salvo at a Fourth of July fireworks show.

Kempffer made an "oomph" sound and tried to bring his gun up. Thackeray blasted another round into him.

Kempffer landed on his back, his gun flopped out of his hand.

Thackeray took three strides and stood over the still figure. "Why'd you make me do that, Tyler?" He paced. "Didn't have to end this way."

◆

The sun crept below the trees in the western sky. Shadows segued into darker shades of night. Owls hooted. The sound bounced around MC and Ekstrom in the darkened car. Over the past two hours, they'd shared small tidbits about themselves. MC that she was almost fifty and could retire but set her sights on maxing out by staying on until fifty-seven.

Ekstrom that she'd been a deputy for about fourteen months and in a couple of weeks would turn twenty-four.

"Geez, over a quarter century span between us," MC said. "I'm old. What do you like to do off the job?"

"Hiking and weather-permitting wind surfing on the great lake. Love to read. Thrillers and true crime. Well, anything crime-related. How about you?"

"Used to be a runner. Lost that passion last year after a...bad patch in my life. So now I've been giving hiking a go. Been out twice. First one was when we found the moonshine still. Thought that hiking, being out in nature, would give me a break from the job, silly me. And then there's AA." She raised her hand. "Alcoholic here. Wow. You're the first person I've said those words to. Haven't even said them to my best friends."

"I'm honored you trust me enough to tell me."

"Ekstrom, beware what the job and life can do to you. Addiction is deadly. Even when I knew it was killing me and I was on the verge of losing my job, I couldn't stop. I'm lucky. I had friends, a co-worker and his wife, who saved my ass. Even now, in the quiet moments, I can feel the call of the bottle, a whisper in the back of my mind. It's not easy." She couldn't believe she'd unloaded on Ekstrom. They barely knew each other.

"That is intense, McCall. But I sense that you're strong. Like I can see your strength, and I feel like you got a handle on it. Or at least a grip on the handle. So like, don't let go. Hold tight. You got this."

They sat in silence as the woodland creatures and insects began their nocturnal concert.

MC nodded, cleared her throat, and said, "How long has Thackeray been here? At Whispering Aspen? Is he from Castle Cove?"

"All I know for sure is he was here before I was born, so before nineteen ninety-one. Not from here, though, out-state. He came to train with the old pastor, who was an old-fashioned fire-and-brimstone type I was told. After a year, the senior pastor got sick with some horrible cancer and died a year later. The community loved Thackeray. He was super young, connected with the kids, and was respectful with the elders. Thackeray slid into the position, and he's been pastor ever since. But like I said, I never connected. Didn't like him. Don't like him."

MC was about to suggest they give up when an explosion cracked the night. She and Ekstrom looked at each other.

Ekstrom sat up. "Was that—"

"A shotgun," MC finished. "Call it in. Do you have an extra Kevlar vest?"

"Should be one in the back." Ekstrom radioed in the alert, possible shots fired at Whispering Aspen Ministries, near the pastor's residence. She requested backup and informed them that she and Inspector McCall were going to investigate.

MC used her phone light to search the rear of the SUV. She spotted a vest and grabbed it, then rejoined Ekstrom at the front. "Keep the volume low on your portable." She shrugged out of her blazer, tossed it on the hood, and put the vest on. Her shirt was already sticking to her from sweat. "I'll take lead."

Another shot rocked the night. She pulled her gun from its holster and stuck her phone in her pants pocket.

They ran along the forested road, back up to the driveway that led to the front of Thackeray's house. Woods surrounded the property along the side and rear. MC held up her hand to signal stop. She scanned the landscape. No lights on inside the house. No outside lights either. Earlier the front porch light had been on.

MC said, "No lights. I don't detect any movement. Let's check the backyard. You go left. I'll go right. Use the house for cover."

"Ten-four." Ekstrom crouched and ran like a duck to the left side of the white farmhouse.

MC followed suit on the right side. She kept her back against the wall on the side of the house. No lights on behind the house either. She surveyed the periphery. Nothing moved. Wide open space on Ekstrom's side. The distance between the house and the back wooded area was probably seventy-five or a hundred feet. No patio. No lawn furniture. The grass was mowed but no indication that Thackeray utilized the yard.

A shadow moved out near a group of mature red pines. The stately trees soared about sixty feet into the air. MC picked up more movement and muffled sounds in the same area. She signaled Ekstrom to go around and come up behind her.

Ekstrom joined MC. "Did you hear voices? Over by the big pines."

MC whispered, "I picked up mumbling or grunting. I had visual of one person."

"Now what? Johnson radioed he and another deputy are enroute. Johnson's ETA is ten minutes. Don't know about the other unit."

"Let's snug up against the tree line on the right and wind around toward the patch of red pines. Ready?"

"Ready."

A couple of minutes later they hunkered down behind a huge red pine. *She's an old one*, MC thought. The trunk was a good five feet in diameter. The matriarch.

The peaty smell of the ground wafted around them, the spring night cool against her sweaty skin. She concentrated on where she'd seen the shadowy specter.

There.

She elbowed Ekstrom and pointed to a male about Thackeray's height and build. His back was to them, and she made out a long gun in his hand. He was pacing.

MC whispered "I think it might be Thackeray. Whoever it is, he has a shotgun or a rifle. I can't tell if he's alone or with someone.

Situation unclear."

"Do we alert him we're here?" Ekstrom asked.

"Yes. Let me do the talking. Be ready for anything." They worked out a two-prong plan of attack, and Ekstrom faded into the night.

Fingers crossed, MC hoped Johnson and the other deputy arrived soon.

MC did a rapid round of deep breathing as she gave Ekstrom time to get into position. She stood and pressed tight against the mother tree, absorbing her strength. Her handgun, pointed at the man, was rock steady. *Time's up.* She shouted, "Law enforcement. Drop your weapon and step away with your hands up."

The mumbling ceased. The man stood stock-still but held onto the gun.

"Do it now!"

"If I don't?" the voice thundered.

MC recognized the voice. "Thackeray," she shouted, "you don't want to know what happens if you don't. Lay the gun down and step away, hands in the air."

"This is all his fault." He kicked something on the ground. "Look what you made me do, dipshit." More kicks thudded into something solid, but not too solid. A human? A deer?

"Who made you do what, Pastor? Lay down the weapon and we can talk." MC moved a few feet closer and shielded herself next to a smaller tree. "Is someone with you? Someone injured?" If there was a person down, rendering aid was critical.

"Injured? Nah. He's a goner. Made sure of that, didn't I?" Another thump like he'd punted a football. "Roasting in hell."

MC advanced. Gun zeroed in on Thackeray. "Let us check him out. You come away. Relinquish your weapon and walk backward toward me. You don't have a choice here, Pastor. Do what I say." She moved closer yet.

He remained still as a statue. His back to her. Now she was close enough she could make out a dark-colored bag near his feet. Then he craned his neck and looked behind him. "Postal cop. What the hell are you doing out here in the middle of the night?"

"I have the same question for you, Pastor." She continued forward, knowing Ekstrom had her covered. MC prayed he wouldn't do a one-eighty and try and shoot her. Not great optics being shot dead in the woods behind a pastor's house.

"You should've minded your own fucking business. Left us alone." He shifted to face MC, raised the barrel of the gun.

Her finger tightened on the trigger.

He lowered the weapon. "If you'd left town when you were

warned and left us alone, none of this would've happened." Thackeray slowly raised the gun again, stopping halfway up.

MC's mouth went bone-dry. She was on the verge of shooting him.

"Fucking drop it, Thackeray." For the eight hundredth time the words ripped through the night. Was he dense? Maybe he simply didn't care. "You're surrounded," she bluffed. "You may get one of us, but you won't have time to get all of us."

MC made out Ekstrom in the shadows, her gun also trained on Thackeray.

If he thought he was going to try out the suicide-by-cop thing, he had another think coming. "I don't want to shoot you, Pastor, but I will." Her weapon was as steady as Simone Biles on the balance beam.

What felt like ten years but in reality was more likely three seconds ticked by.

Finally, Thackeray opened his hand, and the gun hit the ground.

Ekstrom rushed him from behind. "Kneel down. Hands behind your head, fingers laced." She yanked cuffs from her belt.

MC cleared what turned out to be a shotgun and walked over to investigate the heap on the ground. She pressed on her phone's flashlight and discovered Tyler Kempffer on his back, a pistol not far from his outstretched right hand. She kicked it further away. His entire torso was a mess of dark red blood.

She squatted next to him and felt his neck. No pulse. She held a hand beneath his nose. No breaths. His eyes were fixed on the starry night sky.

"Lights out for Tyler Kempffer," she said to Ekstrom. "I guess the phrase 'no rest for the wicked' has been disproved. He's in a very permanent state of rest. I can't say I'm all that busted up about it. Radio for a bus."

About a foot from his head a round slab of metal lay on the spongy earth next to a hole. MC wondered why there was something resembling a manhole cover in Thackeray's yard. She shone the light down into the opening. Metal rungs led downward, but her cell phone flashlight wasn't bright enough to penetrate very far into the black depths.

"What have we here, Pastor?" MC flicked her light toward Ekstrom and the now cuffed Thackeray. "An old well? Tunnel built by a drug cartel?"

He remained mute.

A breeze picked up and the aspen trees whispered, sending a shiver down MC's spine.

Chapter Twenty-One

Chief Deputy Johnson rolled up to Thackeray's house, lights and siren going. He thankfully cut the siren and charged out of the car. Within seconds another LCSO squad car parked alongside Johnson's. The headlights along with all the flashing lights cast eerie shadows across the yard.

"Everyone good?" Johnson asked.

"Not everyone," MC said. "I'm sorry to inform you Deputy Kempffer has been wounded and killed."

"No less than he deserved," Thackeray mumbled.

Johnson said to Thackeray, "You responsible for this?"

Thackeray kept his mouth shut.

Ekstrom said, "He is. When we got back here, he was standing over Kempffer holding the shotgun. There wasn't anyone else around."

"Get him out of here. Put him in Munson's squad car. He can bring him to Two Harbors and process him."

"You got it, chief." Ekstrom grabbed Thackeray's arm. "Let's go."

MC said, "Kempffer and Thackeray are involved something nefarious." She showed him the hole in the ground.

"What the hell am I looking at?" Johnson asked.

"We're not one hundred percent sure yet, but my guess is it leads to some kind of tunnel. A tunnel to the pastor's house or somewhere on the grounds. Ekstrom and I were waiting for backup to take Thackeray before we investigated."

"Okay. I'll get you a flashlight from my car. Then I'll coordinate the crime scene."

Ekstrom returned holding a tactical flashlight. "Johnson said to give this to you." She pulled her own light from her duty belt. "You want to go first, or should I?"

They pulled on gloves and stood at the opening.

MC played her flashlight over the hole. "I'll go first. Keep me lit up, okay?"

"Afraid of the dark?"

"In this situation? Hell, yes." She descended into the bowels of hell. Twenty metal rungs landed her in a small space about the size of a phone booth. The only option other than going up the way she'd come was a tunnel she'd have to crawl through. She shined her light into the gap.

"Ekstrom, we've got a tunnel here. Come on down. I'm going in so you'll have room."

"I'll be right behind you."

MC crept into the tunnel, feeling grit and pebbles under her knees. *This pair of pants is toast*, she thought. She felt like a giant toddler on all fours, moving through the cylindrical concrete tunnel. The further she went, the less she felt like she could breathe. She stopped, took a couple slow deep breaths.

"You okay up there?" Ekstrom's voice echoed weirdly.

"A touch of claustrophobia. I'm good." She forged ahead. The light hopped and bobbed along the rounded walls as she shuffled forward.

Finally, about fifteen feet ahead, she could see light leaking into the tunnel. "Getting close to the end."

"Good because I'm so ready to be out of this tube."

Five feet, three feet, one foot. MC grabbed on to the open hatch attached to a wall and lowered herself to the floor.

Ekstrom scrambled out of the tunnel behind her.

The nightmare laid out before them made MC sick to her stomach. They'd entered what had to be an old bomb shelter. She'd heard about people in the 1950s who had these built in case the Soviet Union decided to bomb the US. But she'd never seen one or known anyone who had.

"Well, that was not fun," Ekstrom said. "Are we in Thackeray's basement?"

The room was lit by a couple of hex-shaped, metal-caged lights hanging from the ceiling. A full-size mattress lay on the floor. Three standing lights were aimed at the mattress.

A black cloth or drape was duct-taped to the concrete wall at the head of the mattress. A jumble of blankets and stuffed animals were strewn across the makeshift bed.

Two camera tripods were wedged between the standing lights. No cameras attached to them.

"What the actual fuck?" Ekstrom's words came out in a horrified whisper.

"I second that. I'm not sure if this is part of the basement or what."

They walked around the mattress and past a four-foot-high concrete wall. On the other side, an ancient air exchanger sat on a built-in shelf, above it a wall safe. Ekstrom yanked on the safe's handle. "Locked."

A hallway about ten feet long brought them to a black metal door. A black phone hung on the wall next to the door. MC tried to open the door, but it refused to budge. "Guess we're going back the way we came," MC said. "Then we'll hit the basement."

Outside the crypt-like tunnel, MC paused and sucked lungfuls of the cool, fresh air. She'd rather be dead from radiation poisoning than be stuck down in that tomb.

They trekked across the yard and entered the house through the back door. MC flipped on the light in the mudroom and led Ekstrom down the stairs to the basement. When she reached the bottom of the stairs, she hit all the switches on the panel.

The room lit up, bright as the antiseptic hall in her dream. She shoved the memory aside.

Now the kids play corner Thackeray had shown them earlier gave MC goosebumps. "I have an idea. Remember the switch plate I saw when we were in the storage closet yesterday?"

"Yeah."

"I think it might have something to do with the mystery room." She skirted all the gym paraphernalia, pushed open the door to the storage closet, and flipped on the light. She yanked a pack of towels and a box of sponges from a shelf and revealed a red button to the devil's den.

MC pushed the button, and a door opened a couple of inches. Silently. She met Ekstrom's gaze. "Couldn't even tell there was a door there. Here we go." MC opened the door wide, revealing a set of concrete steps. She clicked another switch at the top of the stairs, lighting the way for them.

At the bottom of the steps a hallway ran to the left about fifteen feet and ended at a black metal door. The lock was more contemporary than the rest of the set up. MC wondered if Thackeray had changed it so he had the capability of locking someone in. A fire burned deep in her belly at the thought.

On the wall to the right of the door was another black phone.

The whole scene defied believability. MC shuddered to imagine the horrendous acts committed within the space. "Bet crime scene techs find a wealth of evidence down here."

"I don't wish that task on my worst enemy," Ekstrom said.

MC thought of all the victims who'd suffered at the hands of a person in a position of trust. Someone who was meant to protect children, a mandated reporter. Instead, he was a monster hiding behind a gold cross and a musclebound body.

At this point she was positive Thackeray was running a CSE ring and probably physically abusing children. A wretched deviant shattering childhoods with impunity.

Chapter Twenty-Two

MC got about three hours of sleep. The alarm woke her, and she stumbled to the shower.

She'd made it to the cabin after a grueling night at Whispering Aspen Ministries.

Exhausted.

Disgusted.

Furious.

Ready to reap justice for the small, innocent, defenseless victims.

She chugged a pot of coffee before leaving for the Law Enforcement Center. A meeting with Ekstrom and Chief Deputy Johnson was set for nine a.m. Afterward she'd interview Caleb Lewis again and Pastor Curtis Thackeray, although she much preferred the thought of stringing the guy up in the woods and leaving him to a pack of wolves.

On second thought, subjecting the wolves to a poisonous piece of shit like Thackeray was inhumane. They deserved better.

Once she arrived, Chief Deputy Johnson, Deputy Ekstrom, and MC gathered around the table in the conference room. They were about to begin when Sheriff Tollefsen joined them.

MC assembled her files and notebook. She stifled a yawn and grabbed a small bottle of eye drops from her pocket.

"I feel ya," Ekstrom said. She covered her mouth as she yawned. "A caffeine IV might help."

Tollefsen said, "Who wants to start? It sounds like there are several situations that tie together. Mostly up in Castle Cove."

Johnson rearranged a stack of papers in front of him. "This first case is actually separate from the others that Ekstrom and Inspector McCall have been chasing down, although Inspector McCall was present for the discovery."

MC opened her notebook ready to take notes. Another incident?

"Yesterday," Johnson said, "Munson and I arrested Pete and Alicia Norberg for operating an illegal distillery out in the state forest."

The moonshine shack. But that was the least of the problems in Castle Cove. MC clicked her pen. Snick. Snick. Snick. She half-tuned Johnson out as she reviewed her scribblings about the— in her opinion—more important investigation.

Johnson continued. "Hauled them out of the Dirty Minnow, both drunk by noon. Had to call Child Protective Services to send someone to their house to pick up Gracie and Cole. They'll go into foster care until we can find a family who might take them."

At the mention of CPS, MC dialed in. Some people simply should not be parents. "How old are the kids?"

"Gracie is twelve. Cole is nine, almost ten. There's a connection to the Caleb Lewis kidnapping. Gracie asked the CPS person if her parents were in trouble because of the phone call she'd made after church on Sunday to report the man tied up in one of the cabins on the Whispering Aspen property."

"What?" MC leaned forward.

"Gracie told me she'd followed Kempffer out to the cabin. She hid while he was inside. Heard him threatening to shoot someone. When he finally left, she waited a bit and then went in and found Caleb Lewis handcuffed to a bunk. Blindfolded, tape over his mouth." He took a breath. "Lewis told her he'd been kidnapped and begged her to call the police. Gracie, bless her heart, didn't have a cell phone, so she used a landline at the front desk in the Meeting Hall. She got scared when she saw Kempffer and made up a story about a lost book and skedaddled over to the church to pick up Cole."

"Wow, the kid has guts," Ekstrom said. "Don't know I could've done what she did when I was twelve."

Johnson nodded. "At the church she said Pastor Thackeray was acting weird. 'Like he gets around the younger boys, especially Cole.' were her exact words. Had his hand on Cole's shoulder, squeezing real hard, like he wasn't going to let him go. But Gracie grabbed her brother's hand and pulled him away so they could get their donuts and juice before their parents picked them up." He spread his hands wide. "The mystery of the 911 caller is solved."

MC felt bad for Gracie and Cole. She hoped they'd land in a safe place together while their parents dealt with the repercussions of their crime.

Johnson held up another document. "That's not all. Gracie's assessment of Thackeray was spot-on."

MC held her breath. *Here we go.*

He sighed. "Cole spoke with a licensed child therapist while a CPS person was present, and revealed he'd been a victim of sexual abuse by Thackeray, Kempffer, and," he glanced at Tollefsen, "believe it or not, Town Supervisor Bradford Symons."

A collective gasp sucked the air from the room.

"Well, hold on," Tollefsen said. "Where you going with this, Johnson?"

"Sheriff," Johnson said, "I know you and Symons are good buddies. I wouldn't point fingers, but we have some pretty damning proof."

"Nothing substantial. It's circumstantial, at best," Tollefsen said. "Stories from a nine-year-old."

"Sir, with all due respect..."

"Enough, Johnson. I don't want to hear it. I've had more encounters with Symons than all of you put together, and he's never exhibited aberrant behavior...or talk. I want all other avenues exhausted before you start pointing fingers at a well-respected businessman. He's Castle Cove Town Supervisor for Christ's sake. Understood?"

Tollefsen didn't wait for a response. He was up and out, slamming the door closed behind him.

No one moved or spoke for a solid minute.

MC gazed evenly at Johnson. "I need to ask. Could Tollefsen be involved?"

Chief Deputy Johnson scratched his head. "I find it hard to believe Gunnar Tollefsen would be involved in sexually exploiting children. But his response to Symons as a person of interest is out of bounds, even if they've been friends for a couple of decades. Tollefsen doesn't brush off evidence."

"I'm very troubled by his lack of concern over the allegation Cole was abused," MC said.

Johnson set the document he'd been holding on his stack of paperwork. "Symons is coming in for an interview in a little while. Should be interesting to see how that plays out." He stared at the door and shook his head. "I guess we continue without the sheriff. Cole explained to the therapist how Thackeray came to youth group and pulled him from the class and took him over to the house. An area in the basement had been set up with a TV and video games and such. Also snacks, soda, candy, all the stuff to lure a kid in."

"Yeah," MC said, "we saw that setup when we were there on Sunday."

Johnson checked his notes. "Cole said a really tall man with short brown hair came out of a room and he always wore a black mask over his eyes."

"The room was the closet where the secret door's located," Ekstrom said.

"Right." Johnson paused. "The masked man, who we believe to be Symons, Pastor Thackeray, and most times Kempffer, blindfolded Cole and took him down some steps into the 'icky' room. His exact word, icky. He said the room smelled old. No windows. A big mattress on the floor along with stuffed animals and blankets. Cameras and lights on stands. Cole said they'd make him take off his clothes, and things get uglier from there."

Ekstrom said, "How do we know the third man was Symons? How could Cole identify him if he was wearing a mask?"

"We did a six-pack photo array," Johnson said. "Cole's description fit Symons, so I included his pic. I used his official headshot. Cole pointed to Symons as the one he thought was the masked man. Then I called Symons, on speaker phone, and asked if he'd be in his office because I had something to discuss with him. At the sound of his voice the kid clammed up, shutdown. We took a break until he was able to talk again."

MC wondered if Johnson's stomach was doing somersaults like hers. She took a long slow drink of water, hoping it would stay down. "Ekstrom and I saw a couple tripods when we were down in that dungeon. But there weren't any cameras."

Johnson paged through his stack of documents and pulled one free. "A black nylon duffel bag was found near Kempffer's body. Inside it we found clothes, toiletries, his wallet and phone, and two digital cameras. Maybe he took them before he attempted his great escape."

Made sense.

MC said, "Did anyone check if there are SD cards in the cameras? I'll want to get them to our Digital Evidence tech in the Cities."

He made a note on the sheet. "I'll find out."

"And his phone," MC said, "I'd like to send it to our tech as well. He'll be able to excise every crumb of information Kempffer may have left behind."

"I'll have the sergeant chase down these items and work with you to get them dispatched today. Do you have anything to share?"

MC opened the file in front of her. "Caleb Lewis. He admitted to robbing the post office. Though, in my entire career I've never had a robbery quite as bizarre." She explained about the DVD mix up and his nephew and how Caleb had only grabbed the cash to make it a more legit robbery. "He'd planned on mailing the cash back anonymously."

That got a chuckle from the group.

"He was roped into the CSE scheme by Kempffer." MC and Ekstrom did a back-and-forth recap of how the speeding ticket led to Kempffer's coercion.

"Kempffer was rotten to his core." Johnson shook his head. "How did I miss those flags? Someone should've picked up on his proclivities during his background check."

MC said, "Don't beat yourself up. We can't always know

someone's true self until they show us."

Johnson said, "True. Anyway, I'll get with Tollefsen later and see if I can drill down on his reaction."

After the powers-that-be meeting broke up, MC stayed in the conference room to prep for her interviews. First on the docket was Curtis Thackeray. She bet anything the interview would be short. If the previous evening were any indication, Thackeray would be very closemouthed.

The next interview would be another round with Caleb Lewis. MC wanted to tie up some loose ends with him and move the process along.

Can of Diet Coke in hand, MC entered the interview room she'd become so familiar with lately. Inside Curtis Thackeray sat handcuffed, with a chain attached to the metal loop in the center of the table. His nearly shoulder-length brown hair hung limp and oily. Though he'd been bulky and well-toned a couple of days ago, his posture was now warped and caved in. The gold cross necklace was missing from around his neck. Probably confiscated during the booking process.

The recording equipment was rolling.

"Good morning, Curtis. May I call you Curtis?"

He lifted his head and squinted his slate-colored snake-eyes. "Pastor Thackeray."

Like hell. She'd not acknowledge his title as pastor. He never deserved the designation in the first place.

"I'll go with Mister Thackeray." She didn't ask him. "I need to get some housekeeping items out of the way. Today is Tuesday, June 2. Time is ten-twenty. Present for the interview at the Lake County Law Enforcement Center are myself, US Postal Inspector MC McCall and Mr. Curtis Thackeray." She took a drink of soda. "Mr. Thackeray, I have a few questions for you. Before we begin, I'm going to read you the Miranda Warning." She recited it from her laminated card. "Do you understand these rights as I've read them to you, Mr. Thackeray?"

Seconds ticked by. MC calmly examined Thackeray. A fiery hue slowly infused the greasy-gray pallor. Was he going to blow a gasket?

"Mr. Thackeray, do you understand the rights as I've read them to you? I need a verbal response."

"Fuck you. How's that for a verbal response."

"Very eloquent. However, I need a yes or no. For the record."

"I want a Coke."

The pastorly shawl had completely fallen away.

"I'd be more than happy to oblige as soon as you provide me with a response as to whether or not you understand your rights."

"Fine. Yes. Happy now?" He tried to pull away from the table and was brought up short by the length of chain hooked to his cuffs.

MC nodded at the one-way mirror to indicate someone should get Thackeray his soda.

"Do you wish to have an attorney present? I'll preface by saying we have collected plenty of evidence from your den of deviance. I'd like to talk to you about what's been happening at your church. With minor children." It was all she could do to keep a level head when every fiber of her being wanted to throttle the hell out of the soulless predator across from her. This supposed man of God who'd utilized his calling in life to take advantage of the most defenseless in his congregation.

A knock at the door and Ekstrom entered holding a can of Coke. "Deputy Ekstrom has entered the room at ten-twenty-six a.m. to deliver the soda Mr. Thackeray requested. Thank you, Deputy." MC accepted the can and slid it across the table to Thackeray. "Deputy Ekstrom has exited the room."

Thackeray popped the metal tab and, holding the can awkwardly between his cuffed hands, took a long swallow. He smacked his lips together and set the can on the table.

"Mr. Thackeray, what can you tell me about sexually explicit images of minor children saved to a cloud storage account?"

"I don't know anything about any images on a cloud." He dragged a finger down the side of the can.

"The images were sent through the IP address associated with Whispering Aspen Ministries."

"I have no knowledge of those images." He held up a pointer finger. "But if you want to show me the pictures, maybe I can figure out who took them." He leered at her.

Thackeray was the whisper in a locked room, the cold hand behind a child's vacant eyes.

"Let's talk about the setup in your basement and the fallout shelter."

"I'm not going to answer any more questions. I want a lawyer. Shouldn't talk without one. Every cop show I've seen, people end up saying whatever the cops tell them to because they ignore their rights and don't request a lawyer. I'm not going to fall for any bullshit. I want a lawyer."

"You committed a series of very deliberate acts against defenseless children. You didn't just break the law, Thackeray—

you broke lives."

He slammed back against his chair. "You should've heeded the warnings and minded your own business. None of this would've happened."

Probably if he could cross his arms to emphasize his point he would, but the cuffs prohibited that move.

"Tell me more about these warnings." Then it clicked. "You're my unknown caller? You called me numerous times and told me to mind my own business and leave town. Pathetic attempts at threatening me, but threats, nonetheless. Might add some charges to the pile the prosecutor is already building. Sure you don't want to answer a few general questions? You had a lot to say for someone who didn't want to talk."

"Lawyer."

"As you wish. Mr. Thackeray has requested an attorney. Interview terminated at ten-forty-five."

MC gathered her papers, phone, and notepad. Grabbed her Diet Coke and left.

Inside the observation room she took a breather with Ekstrom. As soon as a jailer came to whisk Thackeray out, another could bring Lewis in.

Ekstrom said, "He's a piece of work, eh?"

"More like ten pounds of shit shoved into a five-pound sack. Honestly, I didn't think he'd talk, so I wasn't surprised when he said he wanted an attorney. The dick move of refusing to acknowledge his rights was probably a ploy to waste time."

She stood at the one-way mirror. Thackeray nonchalantly swigged the Coke until the door opened and a bearded jailer entered.

Thackeray held up the can. "Can I finish my Coke?"

"Nope." The jailer confiscated the can and set it out of Thackeray's reach. Then he unlocked the chain. "Up you go." He hoisted Thackeray by the armpit and hauled him out.

"One down. One to go." MC joined Ekstrom at the round table and waited for Caleb Lewis to be brought in.

An hour slipped by and finally Caleb Lewis was escorted into the room and placed in the chair vacated by Curtis Thackeray. His left arm was a lump of plaster from knuckles to elbow. MC had requested the soft restraints be removed. He'd been cooperative, and she doubted he'd break that streak now.

Before she joined Caleb, she grabbed a soda for him and a bottle of water for herself.

Recording devices engaged, MC settled across from Caleb. She set the beverages to her left and laid out her files and notepad in front of her.

"How's jail treating you, Caleb?"

"Not great." Dark circles ringed his eyes.

"I'm sure. Not the easiest place to try to sleep. I won't take up too much of your time. But I do have a few more questions for you."

Like he had anything better to do.

MC went through the spiel of housekeeping items. Read the Miranda Warning again.

Caleb agreed to talk without representation, same as last time.

"You may have heard by now Kempffer was shot and killed Sunday night."

"Yeah. Word gets around inside a jail. Is it true Thackeray killed him?"

"He is a person of interest." MC folded her hands over her stack of documents. "Caleb, in a previous interview, you admitted to receiving images from Kempffer for the distribution business you were running. We executed a search warrant while you were in the hospital unconscious, so prior to your admission, our digital evidence tech accessed your files."

"Let me guess. They found my logon taped to the bottom of my keyboard."

"Yes. I thought I was the only one who did that," MC said, half-joking. "We have copies of all the files, images, videos, everything. But I'd like to know more from you about how you operated the distribution."

Caleb said, "The website thing is a bit complicated."

"Complicated how? Oh, I almost forgot, this is for you if you get thirsty." She handed him the can of Coke.

"Thanks."

"Tell me about the complicated process."

"Basically, I create a website that's front-facing and appears legit. Let's say Save Green Hippos in Tanzania might be the name of the site. The page would have a bunch of text about hippos and then the hook might be if a customer donated a hundred dollars or more, they'd receive a free DVD. A link would show a preview with about ten seconds of sickly hippos. A full-length video would show how funds would be used to help the hippos. The customer clicks the donate button, and a box would pop up for username and password. If the person was a legit customer, they'd have a secret code from Kempffer. They'd enter the code in the password box. The next screen would be name, address, and payment information. Every couple of weeks I changed out the front-facing website. Clearly Seeing Specs—donate old eyeglasses. You get the picture. False front sites to disguise the real deal behind the scenes."

MC took notes and did her best to follow the thread. "How did Kempffer give out the secret code?"

"I don't know how he handled his end of the process. Honest. I created the website and the code, which I would change every two weeks. When he came with the SD cards for me to download new images, I'd give him the new website and code information."

"You did all the distribution on your own? What about the payment?"

"Yes. I'd burn the DVDs, however many had been ordered, and mailed them out to the addresses provided. As for the payment, the funds went to an encrypted account Kempffer had access to. I got twenty percent of the proceeds, and I don't know who else besides Kempffer got the rest."

Jesus. MC's head pinwheeled. Kids' faces flicked by: Cindy, little Emmy, an accidental OD case she'd worked months ago, Cole, Gracie and MC's own ten-year-old visage. What the hell was wrong with these people that they committed horrible atrocities on children?

"Did you purchase the mailing materials and blank DVDs?"

"I bought the mailing materials, but Kempffer bought the DVDs, in bulk usually. Not sure where. I never asked."

"Have you ever supplied these customers," she could barely keep the sarcasm in check, "with photographs? What I'm asking is, were the DVDs the only commodity?"

"All I did for Kempffer was DVDs. I can't speak for what other stuff he might have been into." Caleb took a slug of soda.

"Why'd you do it, Caleb?"

He spun the can between his hands. The silence was deafening. After what felt like hours but was only a minute, he cleared his throat. "At first because I was freaked out by Kempffer. Homie was seriously messed up. But then the money coming in...well, it was good. I got these grand ideas, maybe buying a server and top-of-the-line desktop and monitors. When I worked with those pictures I'd zone out and power through. Pretended like it wasn't real."

"Here's the problem, Caleb. It was all very real. Every click, every file, every action left a scar on a child's life. There is no justification, no excuse, no misunderstanding, only abuse. Did you not ever consider all the victims you exploited? What if someone had done something like that to your nephew?"

"I'm sorry. I was dumb. I should've taken the ticket and lived with the consequences. If I could go back..."

MC bowed her head. The weight of all the children who suffered at the hands of these grown men was an albatross

around her neck. But she'd carry the weight of their pain so no
child had to carry it alone.

What kind of sick human defiles kids?

"We're finished. I'm finished. I'll let them know to return you to
your cell."

"Wait. What happens to me now?"

"My advice is to hire a criminal defense attorney. The county
prosecutor and the US Attorney's office will determine which
charges to file against you."

"But you're going to help me, right? I mean, I cooperated."

"Caleb, it is not my job to help you. My job is to investigate and
get to the truth. I explained earlier that sharing honest discourse
might work in your favor down the line. I don't have the power to
enact any deals. Get a good lawyer, Caleb." And godspeed.
"Interview ended fourteen-thirty."

MC stepped outside. She stretched her arms over her head and
sucked in a lungful of fresh air. The exercise reinvigorated her,
releasing tension from her body and mind. For the first time in
more than a day she thought about a drink.

Her phone pinged and the thought was gone. Email from Felix,
with attachments. MC squeezed her eyes shut tight and let the
sunlight warm her for a moment before she dove into the cold
depravity of the attachments.

Then she opened the email. Felix apologized for taking so long
but he'd been pulled away to work on something urgent for the
past week. He was still going through files, but had sent her
several images, the most recent batch. He informed her the files
probably contained thousands of images and videos depicting
prepubescent children in sexually suggestive and erotic positions.
Some of the material included adults, men, their faces hidden
from the lens, engaged in explicit abuse of those children.

One photo ripped a hole the size of Lake Superior through MC.
A waif of a boy, maybe eight or nine, blond-haired, holding a toy
lightsaber. The bright green of the lighted sword a sharp contrast
to the dull vacant shadows in the child's eyes. In the shot he was
fully clothed, but a haunted air clung to him, as if he'd gone off
somewhere until what was about to happen was finished and he
could return to his body. A soul marked by betrayal before trust
was fully learned. He looked like Cole Norberg, the brave boy who
told CPS what had been happening at Whispering Aspen
Ministries for God knew how long.

MC forced herself to view every disturbing image Felix had attached. Each one was worse than its predecessor. Enough to make her eyes bleed.

Her problems dulled in comparison to what these kids had endured.

She closed the email. The screen went black, as black as the souls of those demons in human form.

Ekstrom joined MC. "You look like you've swallowed a lemon."

"Worse than swallowing a thousand lemons. Far worse. Got a snippet of the vileness those degenerates produced. Felix sent me some pics."

Take a breath.

She did as Barb suggested. Several deep breaths, in fact.

Ekstrom said, "I can't even imagine."

MC lifted her phone and accessed her email. "Trust me, you don't want to. But I'd like to know the identity of one of the victims. Maybe you'll recognize him. Brace yourself." She swiped through the photos, Ekstrom next to her.

"That's Cole Norberg," Ekstrom's voice cracked. She cleared her throat.

"I thought it might be him." MC pocketed her phone.

Ekstrom said, "What a fucking twisted mess."

"You got that right. And there's still one loose end. The images sent from the Whispering Aspen IP address. Felix hasn't found anything so far linking Caleb to those images. so I think he told us the truth about that. We'll have to wait until Felix digs through Thackeray and Kempffer's computers and phones."

"My god. I suppose that could take a while. In the meantime, I thought you'd want to know Johnson interviewed Symons."

"Did you sit in?"

"Yeah. Well, first Tollefsen demanded a one-on-one with Symons, off-the-record. Not sure what was said during that meeting. But when Johnson went in to do his interview, I went into the observation room. I tell you Symons looked like he'd gone twelve rounds with Floyd Mayweather. Johnson asked him what happened, and he claimed he slipped and smashed his face on a toilet. Then he admitted to everything. Maybe the worst thing that came out his mouth was when he claimed the kids consented to their game."

MC said, "*Consented?* Their *game*? That's rich. They enticed the kid with video games, candy, and toys. You saw the photo with Cole holding a lightsaber. His vacant eyes. How Symons equates that with a game is beyond comprehension. And don't even get me started on kids and consent." If she hadn't heard that Tollefsen had engaged in a special discourse with Symons already, she'd be all over him herself.

"The whole situation is mind-blowing. Symons also owned up to making anonymous phone calls to you. Apparently, he and Thackeray decided calling and threatening you would scare you off before you could uncover their crimes. Thackeray gave Symons your business card and Symons placed the calls. Burner phones. Voice modulator. Whole nine yards. Came clean as winter's first snowfall."

"Interesting. I thought Thackeray had made the calls. He said something when I tried to interview him, something about how I should've listened and left town when I had the chance. I can't remember his exact words. But it reeked of the same language the caller used. Did Symons implicate Thackeray in the CSE? Because he's erected a dam on the information flow."

"Symons blabbed about Thackeray and Kempffer. Barely batted an eyelash telling what all they did to those kids. Sounded like for the past several months it had been solely Cole Norberg. Freaks. All of them. Enough to make me want to puke my guts out."

"Cole, and probably his sister too, will require a lifetime of therapy. Jesus. All the trauma those kids suffered and who knows how many more. They're all bearers of scars our eyes can't see. All I want is to prevent that from happening to anyone else. Or in absence of being able to prevent it, I want to go after those monsters in human skin. Be the loud voice of justice for the powerless." She'd walk into darkness armed only with truth, rage, and compassion.

Ekstrom said, "I hope you get a chance to do it. To be a fierce protector."

MC offered a silent prayer, not to God but to the universe, that Cole and Gracie and all the victims of these horrifying crimes would get help and be able to lead healthy and productive lives.

Chapter Twenty-Three

MC arrived at the Senior Center ten minutes early for the 6:30 p.m. Thursday AA meeting.

As if by preordination Ellen Bensen stood next to the iconic harvest gold coffeepot holding two steaming cups. "I hoped you'd be here." She passed a cup to MC.

"Thanks. This week's been about ten-years-long. I need this," she lifted the cup, "and one of those to-die-for donuts."

"Chocolate frosted or jelly-filled?" Ellen asked.

"Jelly-filled is the only answer to that question." Competing emotions warred inside her. She was flattered Ellen remembered how she took her coffee, but she didn't want to send the wrong signal.

Friends.

Ellen used a napkin to pluck a jelly donut from the box and handed it to MC. "Are you okay? Your eyes glazed over for a second. I thought you might faint or something. We should sit." She guided MC to a couple chairs away from a foursome gabbing with the leader.

"I'm fine. Exhausted really." Unsure how to communicate I'm not in the market for anything but friendship. But had Ellen even made moves to indicate she was after anything but friendship? So many questions she was ill-equipped to answer.

"You finish your investigation?" Ellen took a bite from a plain-glazed donut.

MC set her donut on an empty chair on her other side. "Yes. Both investigations. By the way, the people responsible for the moonshine still have been arrested."

"Were you responsible for their capture?" The corners of Ellen's mouth twitched upward.

"No. But bafflingly enough their story intertwined with one of my investigations."

"I don't suppose you can elaborate?"

"I can say a post office was robbed, and the suspect is in custody. A group of people involved in child exploitation crimes has been investigated and apprehended." She voiced the facts and the flames that had been ignited deep roared to an inferno. She wanted to gather that fire into a blowtorch and use it to burn down more offenders of the same ilk. They were evil incarnate and deserved the fires of hell.

"I saw on the local news a deputy had been shot and killed. Let me clarify. I saw the chyron at the bottom of the screen announcing his death. I didn't catch the story."

"Sadly, yes. He was shot and killed. Not in the line of duty. He was involved in some criminal activities, which culminated in his demise."

"You really hold information close to the vest."

MC gave her a ghost of a smile. "Part of the job."

Trusted Servant Max clapped his hands. "Okay folks, let's find a seat, please, so we can get started." He was dressed in his typical pressed khakis and white and blue striped button-down shirt with bright white New Balance sneakers on his feet. He radiated church deacon, but MC liked him anyway. She especially enjoyed the treats he provided from his bakery.

There were about a dozen people in attendance. MC thought she recognized one or two people other than Ellen and Max.

"Good evening," Max said. "Welcome to this open meeting of Alcoholics Anonymous. We're glad to have you. My name is Max, and I am an alcoholic."

The group recited the Serenity Prayer then settled in chairs.

There were no newcomers when Max asked. "Moving on," he said, "we'll begin with a reading from *The Big Book*."

MC avoided eye contact with anyone. Her copy was still buried under a pile of detritus in the back seat of her car.

"Would someone like to read 'How it Works' from Chapter Five?" Max asked.

A woman around MC's age, maybe a bit older, volunteered. MC felt the urge to bolt. But then something about alcohol being cunning and powerful penetrated her shell. The words resonated as her lizard-brain snapped at her about leaving and getting a drink.

Then Max declared it was time for round-robin sharing. Anyone who wished to speak about their journey could do so. Members shared about what they were like, what happened, and what they were like now.

MC tuned out as the attendees droned on.

"Choosing to change wasn't something I did one time."

Ellen's tone hummed and MC dialed into her frequency.

"I wake up and swear to do it every day. I do it again and again and again, ad nauseam. With the addictive element, alcohol for me, removed, I'm finally able to interact with people and be present for others. I'm internally centered, mostly, and able to be emotionally available for people in my life. To me that's a crucial aspect to sobriety. That's where I am now." Ellen concluded her share.

Choosing to change must be done every day. Exhausting.

But worth it in the end, no?

Damn Barb with her quiet logic.

After the final prayer, MC and Ellen helped stack the folding chairs on the wheeled cart.

Ellen said, "You've been quieter than usual."

"Have I?" She hadn't spoken one word until now.

"Something on your mind?"

"I'm leaving tomorrow morning. Time to return to the office. I may have to come back here to wrap up some stuff down the road. But my day-to-day will be in the Cities."

"I see." Ellen leaned against the wall next to the chair cart. "I guess you'll be back to the dreary church basement meeting with the skunky brew and cardboard cookies. Sucks for you." She smiled.

"Yeah. No. This was my sixth meeting. I've completed my pledge." She'd fulfilled her promise to Dara. No more meetings. No more Trusted Servant. Praise Jesus.

"Seriously? You don't think you need to continue? MC, listen, I joke about the coffee and cookies, but meetings are supremely important for those of us in recovery. Without a support network it's a matter of time before you lapse."

"I already almost did." MC stared at the Exit sign above the door. Every fiber of her being screamed at her to run. To escape. But she didn't want to see the disapproval in Ellen's face.

"Do you want to go somewhere and talk?"

Did she?

"Yeah."

They reconvened at a corner table in the rear of Harbor Java.

"Tell me what happened." Ellen said, a look of honest concern in her eyes.

MC whirled her coffee with the slim wooden stir stick. "I had a waking dream, or a repressed memory, however you want to classify it." She shared what happened to her at age ten. "I freaked. Grabbed my car keys and drove to the Wheelhouse Pub. Asked Bill for a vodka tonic, with lime. Gotta have a bit of color in all that clarity." Her voice cracked. "I held that glass. Watched the bubbles fizz. Felt the ice bump against the glass. Smelled the tang of the lime hooked over the rim. All the while a voice inside egged me on, 'you know you want it. Drink, drink, drink.' I brought the glass to my face. Leaned in and breathed the clean scent. Felt the bubbles tickle my nose." MC relived the moment. "Then I asked Bill if he thought anything could stop the past from haunting the present."

"Did you drink it?" Ellen asked.

"No. I did not. I set the glass on the coaster. Left twenty dollars for Bill and drove to the Cities. Did a session with my therapist the following afternoon."

"I'm proud of you, MC. That's huge. But might I also point out you made my case for me about why you should continue with AA?"

"I have weekly therapy appointments."

"Two is better than one. More is better." Ellen dunked her teabag a couple times and set it on a napkin. It resembled a slug with a tiny string attached.

"I don't know." A flint of anger lit low in her belly. Why did Dara and now Ellen think they knew what she needed? She had a mind of her own, for chrissake.

Because they're friends and they care. You are stubborn and don't always know what's best for you.

Barb's critique hit hard.

I do know what's best for me, she argued. Great. Now she was arguing with the ghost of her dead partner inside her head.

"MC?" Ellen's brows knit together. "What's going on?"

"Thinking about things I have to deal with at home." Avoidance tactic engaged.

"You have my number if you ever need…or want…to talk. Anytime you want to get away from your everyday life and clear your head, we can arrange to meet for a hike. Perfect head-clearing activity, if I do say so myself. Lots of trails around here."

"Thanks. I might take you up on that. I enjoyed hiking. Felt good to be out in nature. As long as we can avoid snakes. I cannot do snakes."

"Good to know. I'll keep that in mind. I should get back. Lots to do at the lighthouse. Tourist season is ramping up." Ellen stood.

MC followed suit. "Thanks for listening."

"You're welcome. I'm serious about calling me if you want to talk. Or text if you don't want to talk."

They stood awkwardly for a moment, next to the table, facing each other.

MC scooped up her cup. "Are you finished with your tea? Or?"

"Yeah, I'm done." Ellen stuffed the napkin and teabag into the paper cup.

"I'll take it with mine to the trash," MC said.

"Thanks."

They stood outside the café. The night sky was a dark blanket with pinpricks of light sewn into it.

Ellen said, "Safe travels."

"Thank you. For everything. Take care." MC got behind the wheel and brought up a podcast on her phone for the drive to the cabin. She needed to engage her mind in something other than her life for a few minutes.

Chapter Twenty-Four

Friday morning's drive from Two Harbors flew by. MC listened to some episodes from the podcast she'd listened to the previous night, interspersed with a replay of her and Ellen's conversation at Harbor Java.

She formed an agenda for the remainder of the day. First, the office. Then Flannel, where she'd happily share her accomplishment with Dara. She'd completed the six AA meetings. Six and done.

She arrived at the office a bit after noon. Chelsea smiled when she saw her. "Hi, MC, good to see you. How are you?"

"Thanks, Chelsea. Good to be back. I'm doing well. You?"

"Me too. Let me know if you need anything."

"Will do. By the way, thanks for taking care of Pearl these past couple weeks."

"Pearl?"

"The succulent you gave me. I named her Pearl."

Chelsea smiled wide. "I love that. And you're welcome."

"Now, is Jim Bob in or is he in the field?"

"Far as I can tell he's in the office. He may have gone out for lunch, but I didn't see him leave."

"Okay. Thanks."

MC booted up her desktop computer. An email from Felix sat in her inbox. She clicked on the message. Felix had received Kempffer's phone and the two SD cards from Lake County. He cracked the phone and discovered images saved that matched the ones that were sent through the Whispering Aspen IP address. He went on to say that he hadn't even begun on Kempffer's computer, but he thought she'd want to know right away about these.

She fired off a reply thanking him and asking that he please keep her updated. Then she sent Ekstrom an email letting her know the latest. Finally she plugged her notes into DigiCase.

Then she hit up the breakroom for a bottle of water from the vending machine. Next stop was Jim Bob's office. She wanted to check on the newbie.

She knocked on the door.

"Come in."

MC stuck her head in. "Hey, Red. How goes the battle?"

"McCall, you're back. Have I got news for you." He popped up and sent his chair backward into the wall. "Come in. Sit."

"Good news?" She twisted the cap from the bottle of water and took a long drink.

"We got him. Nailed his ass. The surveillance paid off. Ran him down and hauled him in. Not like the first time when I chased that poor high school kid. You already know about that snafu. I'm so bummed I messed up. But, hey, I stuck with it and got the bad guy."

"Good work, Red. Does the bad guy have a name? I'm willing to hear a few more details if you want to share."

"You bet. Kyle Justiss. Can you believe it? What a name for a criminal. Sorry, alleged criminal. Anyway, I played it cool on the last surveillance. I spotted a guy dressed in a dark-colored hoodie, black jeans, and black New Balance sneakers. The N on the sides of those shoes is ginormous. Oops. I digress. Anyway, he had a duffel bag which had a bunch of paper spilling out of it." He paced and waved his hands around. "I got out of the car and followed him to the same building as in a video that a woman walking her French bulldog sent in. Bulldog's name was Frank. Love it."

"Red, stay on track," MC said.

"Sorry. But the dog was cute. Anyway, I nonchalantly followed him close enough," he held up a hand, "but not too close, and I could see the bag was chock full of mail. He went up to the door of the complex and somehow got it open. I jogged toward him and said, 'Hey, bud, can you do a bro a solid and hold the door?' And he did. Can you believe it?" This time he was so excited he didn't even pause for whatever snarky remark MC might have. "But the clincher was...drumroll, please." He paused in front of her, hands on his hips.

"I'm *not* about to do a drumroll."

"I hoped." He shrugged. "Anyway, he had one of those carabiner things hooked on his belt loop, bunch of keys hanging from it. Know what I'm talking about?"

"Yes. Yes, I do know what a carabiner is. Can we get to the point sometime this year?"

"Guess what stuck out like a sore thumb on that ring of keys. Come on. Guess."

"Nope. Not going to guess." But now that song, "Ring of Keys," from the musical *Fun Home*, played in her head. "Not going to do drumrolls. Listening. That's what I'm doing. Listening. And hoping you'll get through this story before I retire."

"You're no fun. Wait. What? You're going to retire?" He waved a hand to stop her protest. "I know, get to the point. An Arrow Key. That's what I saw nestled in the fifty bazillion keys on the carabiner. Then calm and cool, I shoved him against the bank of mailboxes and told him he was under arrest for mail theft. I slapped the cuffs on and hauled him to the Ramsey County Jail and booked him in. Guy had stolen checks stowed in the bag too. Another Arrow Key, and a bunch of cash. All logged into an evidence locker here."

"Wow, Red. That's some badassery on your part. Good job."

"Thanks."

"I can hardly wait to hear what's on the docket next week. Anyway, I've got to check in with Jamie and then I'm going home. I need a weekend to recover. Sounds like you do too. See you on Monday."

"Hey, McCall. Just one more thing..."

She stopped at the door. "What?"

"Got you again."

"Jesus. You and that Columbo crap. Put a sock in it, Red." Her tone was serious, but she smiled.

His laughter echoed behind her down the hallway.

Jamie's door was open, and he sat behind his desk, a sheaf of papers in one hand.

MC said, "Knock knock. Got a minute?"

Jamie waved her in. "Yeah, come on."

She closed the door and sat in one of the chairs in front of his desk. "I've updated DigiCase with everything I have so far on the Castle Cove investigations. All the wheels are in motion. We'll see what charges come down for Lewis, Symons, and Thackeray."

"What a shitshow. Good job, by the way."

"Thanks. I wanted to talk to you about the job. My job."

"Oh?" He nudged his glasses up the bridge of his nose. "Something wrong?"

"No. Not at all. In fact, you might say I've experienced a sense of clarity through all the crap."

He set the papers down. "I'm all ears."

"Listen, I know I've been less than present in a lot of ways the past several months."

"You've had a lot happen in your life over those months. We've got your back, MC. We're family here."

"I appreciate you. Here's the deal...hear me out before you say anything. Okay?"

Jamie raised an eyebrow. "Intriguing. Sure. Go ahead."

"Investigating crimes against children is excruciating. But it's something I found fulfilling. Maybe that's not the right word. What I did, it felt like it was something I was made to do. I'd like to dedicate the remainder of my career to taking on those challenging crimes-against-children cases. I want to go for the belly of the beast. I want to make a difference in a child's life.

Every day."

A choice, like Ellen had said.

Jamie leaned forward. "MC CSE work is some of the toughest stuff we deal with. Are you sure? That kind of work is disturbing and will take a hell of a toll on you. It's emotionally draining."

"I understand your hesitancy. All the turmoil I've existed in since Barb's murder, the drinking, rehab, all the mishaps along the way…I get you might not have faith in me. But I promise, I'm not requesting this on a whim. I feel like this is what I was destined to do, to be a guardian who stands between innocence and the jaws of evil. A justice seeker for the powerless victims. Why not me?"

Jamie remained silent. MC swore she heard the ticking of a clock, though he didn't have one on his office walls.

He drew in a deep breath and let it out slowly. "I can see you're determined, and you've thought this through. I'll approve, with stipulations."

"Great. What're the conditions?"

"First, we'll get you into the FBI's Child Exploitation training class since the Inspection Service's training was just held in conjunction with NCMEC, and we won't have another class for eighteen months. We don't want to wait that long. If we're doing this, I want you up to speed now. Second, you continue with your therapy and AA. Debriefing with the therapist will be especially vital if you're going to work on CSE crimes. Does that sound fair? Can you commit?"

"Absolutely it's fair and I definitely can make those commitments."

"One more time, MC, are you sure that's the work you want to do?"

"I've honestly never been more sure of anything in my life. I can't stand by and let these atrocities happen again and again."

"All right. You realize there are limitless incidents of these crimes, so there won't be a shortage of work to keep you busy— probably into the next decade." He shook his head. "You're taking on a load, MC. Other inspectors will assist as needed, and you'll be working closely with other agencies and NCMEC. I'm proud of you. You've always been one of the best inspectors in this domicile."

"Thanks for trusting in me."

He stood. "I'll get the wheels in motion for the training, and we'll take it from there. Now why don't you take off? You deserve a weekend to unwind. We'll touch base on Monday and develop more of an action plan."

"Thanks, Jamie."

At home MC unpacked. Number one chore during the weekend would be laundry. Second would be grocery shopping. In the past, the third chore would be picking up a bottle of Grey Goose, but not today.

Old habits died hard. But, dammit, they were going to die.

MC changed into jeans and a T-shirt and was out the door.

Five minutes later she walked through Flannel's front door.

"Well, lookit what the cat dragged in." Dara's cheery voice hit her like a Mack truck.

Meg said, "Dara. Inside voice." She hustled from behind the counter and made a beeline for MC.

MC hugged her, then held her at arms' length. "How's it going?"

"Great. Rang the bell last Friday at the clinic. Final radiation. They gave me a certificate and everything."

"And they gave her a Toblerone candy bar," Dara said. "I call that a win-win."

"Yeah, because you ate most of it before I even got a bite." Meg took MC's hand and drew her toward a table.

"My god. I'm..." MC lost her words.

"What's wrong?" Meg asked.

"Meg. I'm so sorry. I was so wrapped up in work I didn't realize you'd completed your treatments." Here she was following the same path she'd traveled before. Not being present for her friends.

"You were up north. We were fine."

"Please tell me you forgive me for not being here. For not even calling to check on you. I made a promise to you both and I've let you down. Again." The sting behind her eyes built up. She swallowed. Hard. Then she leaned over and hugged Meg tight.

"It's fine." Meg patted MC's back. "If we'd needed you, I promise we would've called you. You know Dara. She'd have been hollering through the phone night and day."

"Truth." Dara plunked a mug on the table. "Come sit. Drink. Well, coffee."

"Thanks." She swirled the brew around and blew on it before taking a sip. "Speaking of drink." MC eyed Dara. "Last night I attended my sixth meeting. Check that box. Done."

"Excellent, pal. I'm proud of you."

Nice to hear a few people say they were proud of her these days.

"But maybe done isn't what you need to be. You're truly only at the beginning of a lifelong journey. I've been sober decades. I still go to meetings. I know you promised you'd go to six meetings, but

I thought you'd realize how helpful they are and keep going. They will help you."

A tinge of resentment tweaked her. "Dara, don't pontificate. Please. I know you mean well."

She's right. No need to be churlish. Dara only wants what's best for you. We all do.

I don't need to keep going. For chrissake, MC, stop arguing.

Dara said, "Will you at least think about it? I'd be willing to go with you every week."

Meg laid her hand on top of MC's. "We're here for you."

MC waged an inner battle with herself. Ellen had said pretty much the same thing. But they could all be wrong, and she could be right.

Or not.

The echo of Jamie's conditions for her transitioning to CSE work included attending AA meetings.

MC swallowed her irritation. "You two are the best friends I could ever ask for." She could make the choice to change. But like Ellen said, that choice would have to be made every day. Could she do it? Did she want to? The siren call of the Goose sounded, but off in the distance. Jesus, could nothing in life be easy? Miles to go. She chose to move forward, one conscious step at a time.

"Geez," Dara said, "Now you're getting all sentimental. Does that mean—"

Meg let go of MC's hand and grabbed Dara's. "Let's table the discussion."

"I say it's time to order pizza." MC was impressed that for once Dara took the high road. "Celebrate Meg being done with radiation and MC being home."

Meg said, "I'll call in an order for delivery. Pepperoni okay with you both?"

"Yes," MC said.

Dara said, "Abso-tively, posi-lutely."

Two minutes later the ordered was placed. "So everything else is good?" MC scanned the café. "Looks like business is booming."

"Business is excellent. Zane is a godsend. We have you back home. I think it's safe to say we're living the dream," Meg said.

"Meg, you are a wise woman." MC kissed her cheek.

"Hey, hands off my woman, McCall," Dara said. A marshmallow masquerading as a blowhard.

They chatted until a pimple-faced kid who barely looked old enough to drive walked in with a red DoorDash hot case. "Pizza for Meg."

"Right here." Meg stood. She exchanged a fistful of cash for the pizza.

"Thanks. Have a good one." The kid tripped over his feet but caught himself before taking a header. Face beet red, he rushed out the door.

"Poor guy," Meg said.

"Let's dig in." Dara flipped the box open and warm waves of melted cheese, tomato sauce, and spices floated through the air.

MC sat back and watched as Meg batted Dara's hand away. "You wait. For one second. I'll get plates and silverware. Keep your mitts off."

For the first time in months, MC felt complete. She'd found a missing piece from her life at work.

Dara said, "Aw, come on. We're all family. Can't we just use our fingers?"

Suddenly the last puzzle piece clicked into place. They really were family. Dara. Meg. MC.

Put a stamp on it.

She was home.

THE END

Acknowledgments

To my editor, Terri Bischoff, so much gratitude for your honest insights and guidance with the 'big picture.' You were right in recommending I 'kill off' two of the storylines in this book, hard as it was to do.

To my writing group, The Minions (Jessie Chandler, MB Panichi, and Lori L. Lake), undying gratitude for your multiple reads of this story. And for the line-editing and brainstorming and for just being you. Thank you, thank you, thank you! Love you all!

Special thanks to Lorelei for the awesome cover design. I love this cover so much.

Thank you to my publisher, Launch Point Press for believing in me enough to put my books out into the world.

Research about the US Postal Inspection Service (USPIS) is challenging. I'm lucky to have found a few resources to answer my questions—most of my questions anyway. I am grateful for the time and consideration I've been afforded by contacts at the USPIS Public Information Office. Thank you so much! And thanks also to a retired inspector who has been so gracious in sharing his background and basic investigatory information with me for all three books. I'm so lucky to have these resources so I am able to provide my readers with a plausible story. Keep in mind that this is a work of fiction. All credibility in details is thanks to the aforementioned resources, and any mistakes are strictly my own.

This book was especially difficult to finish. I was at about the midpoint of the book when my mom was diagnosed with cancer. Sadly, we lost her at the end of June 2024. But I'll always remember the day of her final radiation session, which was only two weeks before she passed: I was talking with one of the oncology nurses about being an author and that I was working on my third book. Mom walked up at that point in the conversation and said, "I keep telling her she better finish that book before I croak." Mom, I'm sorry I didn't finish before we lost you, but I hope you'll be proud that I eventually did it! This book is for you. I miss you every day.

I'd like to thank my family for their continued love and support. Especially my daughter Erin for being my rock this past year. I love you and Ryan so much. To my partner JJ, my undying love and gratitude for supporting me and this crazy writing journey. Writing is a time-consuming and sometimes lonely endeavor, and JJ accepts and understands when I spend endless hours in front of the computer, sometimes revising the same sentence a million times. Thanks to my son Jeremy for at least responding to me when I ask his opinion on my book cover! Love you, son. To my stepsons Javi and Rickey, you guys bring lots of excitement to this family of ours, love you.

Thank you to my dear friends Judith and Paula for your constant support. You were invaluable resources as well as beta readers for early chapters, but mostly the best friends a gal could hope for. Love and appreciate you both so much.

And to my readers, thanks for choosing my books. I hope you enjoy reading them as much as I enjoyed writing them!

About the Author

Judy M. Kerr lives and writes in Minnesota. *Black Friday* and *Silent Service* are the first two books in her MC McCall series featuring a US Postal Inspector protagonist. *Postmarked Castle* Cove is the third installment in the series, published by Launch Point Press. A number of Judy's short stories have been published in various anthologies, including "Ruby Red Heist" in the *Dark Side of the Loon: Where History Meets* Mystery anthology published in 2018 by the Twin Cities Chapter of Sisters in Crime. She has an avid interest in crime—true and fiction—and is always working on ideas for her next story. Judy's website: **www.judymkerr.com**.

Other Books by Judy M. Kerr

Black Friday is the first in the MC McCall series. When US Postal Inspector MC McCall is assigned to an FBI joint task force, she's excited to investigate a tricky Ponzi scheme—that is, until a critically important whistleblower goes missing. Two murders follow, and MC's professional and personal worlds start to implode. Will she survive? Or will she be destroyed by the corruption and dark deeds surrounding her?

Silent Service is book two in the MC McCall series. Postal Inspector MC McCall is struggling in her personal life. She sneaks around investigating outside her jurisdiction fruitlessly while drinking too much and shutting out all offers of help. Will a new case revitalize her? Or will she spiral into darkness?

Note to Readers

Thank you for reading a book from Launch Point Press. We have made every effort to edit this book. However, typos do slip in. If you find an error in the text, please email publisher@launchpointpress.com so the issue can be corrected.

We appreciate you as a reader and want to ensure you enjoy the reading process. We would like you to consider posting a review on your preferred media sites and/or your blog or website.

For more information on upcoming releases, author interviews, contests, giveaways and more, please sign up for our newsletter and visit us as at Launch Point Press: www.launchpointpress.com and "Like" us on Facebook: Launch Point Press.

Bright Blessings

www.ingramcontent.com/pod-product-compliance
Lightning Source LLC
Chambersburg PA
CBHW020619110726
47899CB00002B/569